I am CRIMSON

Baptiste
Ordo Sicariorum

I am CRIMSON

B.D. VALLE

UR
PROSPECTIVE

an imprint of

P ROSPECTIVE P RESS LLC

1959 Peace Haven Rd, #246, Winston-Salem, NC 27106 U.S.A.
www.prospectivepress.com

Published in the United States of America by P ROSPECTIVE P RESS LLC

I A M C RIMSON

Cover and interior design by ARTE RAVE

ISBN 978-1-943419-41-8

First P ROSPECTIVE P RESS trade paperback edition

Printed in the United States of America
First printing May 2017

1 3 5 7 9 10 8 6 4 2

The text of this book is typeset in Minion Pro
Accent text is typeset in Hitman

P UBLISHER'S N OTE

Acknowledgements

Through thick and thin, I cannot take credit for the creation of this novel without first putting the spotlight on my close friends and family members who have stood by me through the worst of it all. You know who you are.

A giant tip of the hat must also go to Prospective Press forthright. It is you guys who have pulled my crummy manuscript out of a pile of slush, brushed it off, and reformed it into the incredible story that it is today.

And a bit of thanks to my editor Chip Putnam. Despite your sarcastic remarks and critiques, I still have faith in you as a human being. Thanks, Chip.

For Brendan Lackman and Calvin Heyward.
This one's for you, guys.

PROLOGUE

Rain spattered the dark blue car as it continued to roll up alongside me. Its wheels trotted slowly over the black asphalt. My chest thumped, overtaking the thunder. The car stopped, and I rubbed a thumb over the fleshy scar that streaked across the palm of my right hand.

Sometimes I wonder if I was meant for this life. And then other times, I wonder if this life was meant for me. I guess it was just luck of the draw. But in the end, isn't everything?

The car's headlights pierced through the darkness like a set of bright swords. As I walked up to the car, my hands began to tremble and I lost interest in the scar. In the distance, I heard the crack of thunder. But even that was not as scary as this. *Nothing* was as scary as this. A door opened.

My mother used to tell me everything happened for a reason. That every piece to the puzzle fit, that *no* piece was like any other, and the world—like a giant puzzle—was made up of these pieces. I just wondered if my piece fit in somewhere.

Glancing over my shoulder one last time, I crawled into the dark blue car, closing the door to the outside. Closing it to my freedom. A large man wearing a black suit and tie was seated next to me.

"Are you good to go, son?"

Feeling the bulge hidden away in my jacket confirmed I was. Silently, I nodded.

I wish I could say that I was ready. That I was prepared for this moment—and physically I was. There was no doubt about that. But mentally? Psychologically? That was a double no. To this day, I'm still never quite as prepared as I'd like to be. But then again, I don't think anybody ever is.

The car sped off and the rain kept pushing back against the windows, telling me to stop. Everything in my body was telling me to stop. But I couldn't. Something else, in my blood, was telling me different. I was, after all, bred for this. The man in the backseat remained quiet. Only his wheezing broke through the dense air.

An hour later, we were parked outside an old apartment building. It looked abandoned, and someone walking by would probably assume the same. But if you squinted just right you could see flashes of light breaking though dirty windows, even the ones that were boarded up. The large man opened his door and got out.

"Are you sure you're ready?" he asked again, dipping his head back into the car. His brown hair was combed to the side, making him look like a plump twelve year old.

"Yes," I said. My stomach churned.

Getting out, I followed the man toward the building, leaving the car to idle by the sidewalk. It wasn't too late to turn back. But at the same time, it really was. The rain had subsided, but low rumbles from the distant clouds threatened another storm.

Someone once said that you can pick your poison, but you cannot pick your destiny, and that destiny should not be confused with fate. But to me, this is only provocative musing. To me, this is irrelevant. My whole life is irrelevant, and I have no purpose. I have neither fate nor destiny to contend with. Only outcomes that control every waking of my being. Every step. Every measure. I am just a feather floating in the wind.

Stealing away to the back of the building I watched as the man found a fire escape and started climbing, ascending into the unknown. Despite his heavy-set appearance he moved with speed and agility, climbing even farther up, seemingly ignoring the rattling of the frail, rusty ladder. The way he moved was without error. It was, in layman's term, flawless.

Readjusting the bulge in my jacket, I quickly followed the path he had taken. The ladder shook only slightly as I rejoined my accomplice at the top of the building. Looking down, the ground seemed far away. And not just in the physical sense. Looking down, *everything* seemed far away. I was in another world—a euphoric state; I was on the edge.

The sound of glass shattering brought me back to my senses and I turned. A broken window stood before us, our entrance into the murky apartment complex. With a subtle wave of his large hand the man beckoned for me to go in.

The moon had come out to play, peeking its pale face through the wall of torrent gray clouds. It must have felt generous for it threw streaks of moonlight in our direction, illuminating the otherwise black building. The man crept inside the room after me.

Pity is for the man who runs a fool's errand, but honor is given to he who accepts a noble task. The difference between the two is vague, but the rewards are unmistakable. The hardest part though, is recognizing which is folly and which bears fruit.

With the moon at our backs, we moved through the apartment. There was no light, only puddled darkness, and it was difficult to tell where we were. Finally, I saw the frame of a door that was lit up from the other side. I started to walk toward it, but the man yanked me back.

"Mind your surroundings, boy," he whispered.

Sure enough, at the bottom of the door I could see shadows moving back and forth from within the room and heard disembodied voices to accompany them. Taking the lead once more, the man doubled back and headed in a different direction. Quietly, I followed, recoiling from my act of ignorance.

The voices in the other room grew louder. The people probably having been stirred by the sound of the window breaking. As I heard a door being opened behind, my companion pulled open another door and pushed me through. This time it was the right one.

The thing I remember most about my first job wasn't the building itself or the hit. It wasn't even having to carry my partner as he bled all over me. No, as strange as it sounds, it was the smell. A putrid stench of fresh paint mixed with burning coal. It lingered like a bad infection, and I could taste it just as much as smell it. As we walked forward, I held the crook of my arm over my mouth and nose. And even then, the smell was still there.

The second door led us into a hallway. Its vintage wall-to-wall carpeting revealed ageless stains that the lazy landlord never bothered to shampoo out, while the beige paint was peeling from the top, exposing mold stains underneath. To say this building was grungy would be an understatement; it was just one health-inspection away from being closed down for good.

But there was no time for sightseeing. By the time we reached the end of the empty hallway my ears perked to the sound of a door opening behind us. A quick glance over my shoulder revealed that it was the door to the apartment we had just left. Letting my partner know, we rushed off to an intersecting hallway. After being sure that we weren't followed, we resumed our route, back on course with the objective.

"Hurry, boy." My partner pushed me down the new hallway, and within moments we were on the move again. The man went first, stopping at the building's only elevator. He motioned me into the cubicle, which looked as if it had not seen an inspector in many years. My partner showed me how to lock the machine in place to ensure a speedy escape. Taping the door open just far enough so that a boy and a heavyset man could get through, we exited the elevator.

Like the previous hallway, this one was just as shabby, if not more so, and the lights flickered restlessly as we made our way to our destination, apartment 313.

I could see lights on under the doors, and I wondered what type of people lived there. What type of people called this home? I didn't feel sorry for them though, as shameful as this place was. Pity was something the better off kids felt when they saw me walking down the street. When they stopped me and kicked my face over twenty-five cents. It was a lifetime ago. When I, too, could still call something home.

The man's deep voice startled and annoyed me. "Pay attention."

Despite my youthfulness and my lack of experience, I was still formidable. And if The Chancellor said I was ready, I was. After all, the only way to make an eagle fly was to send it into the air.

On the right side of the hall I could see the bronze digits identifying each apartment—309, 311, and then finally 313. I drew myself up against the left side while my partner took up the other.

The series of events that followed are still, to this day, seared into my memory. Even as I look back, reflecting on what course my life has taken, I often wonder what direction it would have gone in had this not happened. In a way, it paved the path I now walk. Placing the first layers of concrete of what would become the foundation of who I am today. Had it not? Well, this is one question I have spent many listless nights dwelling over.

"Are you ready, boy?"

He pulled out a black handgun with a silencer and checked the magazine. Nodding my head, I reached into my jacket and drew forth a chromed .45 revolver I had been carrying concealed ever since it showed up in a package at the safe house three days ago. I held the gun out left-handed and pointed it at the door. It took every ounce of effort within me to keep my hand from shaking.

The large man moved in front of the door. "Let's do this."

Taking a giant step back, he moved with lightning speed and kicked the door in. Its metal frame, once a strong and robust gate protecting the innards of the apartment, was unable to put up a fight against such force.

My partner had made a fatal mistake, however, and just as soon as the door came to, he was met by an even stronger force. From deep within the apartment two loud booming sounds echoed, followed by heavy shot tearing through my partner's wide chest. The damage was great.

Time seemed to freeze and my head began revolving. The hallway, the ugly carpet, even the lights started to spin. The blasts from the shotgun had been loud, and it took some time before the ringing left my head.

Disoriented, I knelt down to the ground, watching as my partner lay in the hallway. He was helpless. I was helpless. Crouched there, I wrestled with what was real.

There comes a point, while the young fledging is falling through the air, when he must decide to act. It is simple. It is binary. Sink or swim. Fly or die. And when that decision to fly is made, the eagle's instinct takes over. There are some things you can learn. Some things you can experience and adapt to. But there are other things, no amount of books or training can teach you. Some things are just instinctive.

A force deep inside took hold of me, and a calm wave rushed over my body. The spinning stopped and my head ceased to ring. I felt natural, organic, like I had been in this situation before.

Grabbing the gun, I picked myself up and waited, coiled like a venomous snake, waiting for the right time to strike. My partner, who was now gasping for air, had made a mistake. But so, too, had the assailant. It wasn't long before I could see the rustic double-barreled shotgun protruding from the doorway.

Letting instinct possess me, I shoved my gun back into its holster and grasped the assailant's weapon. I yanked it forward, exposing a bewildered man who tried regaining control of his gun. With the element of surprise still on my side, I twice shoved my knee hard into his belly, causing him to release his grip. He watched helplessly as the old relic, and his sole salvation, fell to the floor. He turned his attention back to me, and without warning I surprised even myself and rammed my skull into his face. When he looked back up at me, his nose was bleeding profusely and I could feel his warm blood in my hair. Shouting like a wild banshee, I stepped back and kicked him in the chest. He fell into the room and landed hard onto his back.

I entered the dark room, moving with caution to avoid making the same mistake of either man. Like a wolf, I stalked him, watching as he tried to slither across the carpeted floor. At length, I kicked him back over so that I could see his face—his tired, worn face.

I knew nothing about this man. But that wasn't important—his past, his family, whatever it was—I didn't care. It was irrelevant. *Us* being here in the room as I was about to kill him was also irrelevant. It all was. It was simply nature being nature.

Moonlight from a distant window joined us, illuminating the horrific scene. As I looked down at the man, I could see that his fortitude had been shattered just as much as his face. He began stammering, groveling, pleading for me to stop. But it was inevitable. I had no control over what was going to happen. I was just a machine and my actions were merely gears wound up by some supernatural force.

The revolver had since fallen to the ground during the brief scuffle. Picking it up, I cocked back its hammer and crept even closer, so that I was hovering over his trembling body. His dull brown jacket was worn beyond recognition and his black hair was in complete disarray. He was, without a doubt, expecting somebody to come for him. But the dark shadows under his eyes revealed that he had been unsure of *when* they would come.

I drew the gun up closer to the man. He flinched and reached into his jacket. I squeezed the trigger. The bullet ripped through his coat and bore into his collarbone, rendering his arm useless. The poor man let out the most horrible sound, howling loud enough to wake the dead. But as I cocked the hammer back again and pressed the short barrel up against his temple, all noise ceased. He shut his mouth and closed his eyes. Embracing the inevitable.

"Open them," I said, booting him in the ribs.

The man forced his eyes back open and glanced up at me. Kneeling down beside him, I stared back. The gun pressing even harder against his head.

I've been told that staring into a man's eyes is like staring into his soul—that making eye contact with your enemy just before killing him will render you incapable of doing so. For me though, this has never been a problem. For me, this is the best part. Like finding a prize at the bottom of a cereal box. For me, watching his eyes as the life left him was the prize.

The rain started to pick up again and the moon began its retreat behind the clouds. Inching closer, I could hear him breathing. For a second, I swore I could even hear his heartbeat. The man continued to stare back, exposing his blood-shot corneas.

He kept silent, but I knew what was going through his head. Wondering when I would make that final blow and cast him out of this abject life. Having that power over a man made me feel invincible. It made me feel like a god.

It never bothered me. Nothing bothered me anymore. Hovering over him was like standing over the edge of a cliff. I felt an adrenaline rush, and it made me high. I pushed the barrel hard against his skull. Staring deep into his sad eyes, I pulled the trigger.

So light and delicate was the touch that I barely had to put any pressure it. It stunned me how relaxed it felt—how *effortless* it was to kill somebody. Once you stopped thinking about it. The hard part isn't pulling the trigger—that is easy. No, the difficult part is blocking any thoughts from entering your head. And that part you *do* have to train yourself on. But after you master that—after you conquer withdrawing human psychology from the equation—you become an animal. You become nature's reaper.

The bullet pierced his cranium and mushroomed inside, causing blood and brain-matter to spew out the backside of his head and onto the much worn carpeting, forever staining the already undesirable flooring.

Having four more rounds left in the revolver, I shot him two more times: once in the chest, and a second time in the leg. I fired the last two bullets into the wall behind him.

Putting the gun in my jacket, I proceeded to walk around the apartment, knocking down anything I could get my hands on. In the kitchen, I broke glasses and plates, and threw the contents of shelves and cabinets onto the floor. I then made my way through the apartment's hallway and found the bedroom. It was already cluttered, but it needed to look worse. Under the bed I uncovered a suitcase partially filled with clothing. Snatching it up, I emptied the case over the bed and floor. Before long, the apartment was in shambles. Exactly what I intended, making it look like a random break-in—a robbery gone wrong. I took his wallet and headed back into the hall.

My partner was still lying on the floor. Although I could no longer hear him breathing, I felt a faint pulse in his neck. His eyes were glazed over and the blood had since soaked up the front of his clothing.

"Hell!"

But there was no response. The hallway was just as empty as when we got here. It surprised me that none of the building's tenants had stirred during the height of the conflict, when guns were blazing. No cops. No ambulances. It were as if nobody cared, and it's times like these that make me think I'm living *in* an empty planet. In the hollow shell of what used to be a world. Inside, I felt alone.

The wave of familiarity that had run through me during the encounter was gone. I felt human again. The wind whistled through cracks in the walls, telling me that it wasn't my fault.

Focusing on my partner, I struggled to gain the right hold as I tried to drag him over to the elevator. He was big, and I was just shy of my seventeenth birthday. But at long last I found the sweet spot and hoisted him with all the strength I could muster.

Everything seemed to happen so fast. Although I knew what had happened, and could see it as it happened, it were as if I was somebody else. My lungs knotted and I gasped for air, struggling to breathe in the tiny elevator.

When we hit the bottom floor, I grabbed onto his coat and started pulling again. He had lost more blood and it began spilling onto me, saturating my clothing as well. I made it as far as the lobby before I realized that the front doors were locked.

"Hell," I yelled again. Still, no reply.

Taking out the empty revolver, and holding an arm over my face, I smashed the gun against the glass door until I'd shattered a hole large enough for us to crawl through.

Feeling satisfied, I put the gun away and resumed dragging the man across the lobby and out the pseudo doorway, leaving in our wake smudges of blood streaked across the gray-tiled floor.

To my great relief, the car was still parked along the road. Although it was only fifty feet away, the distance felt greater. By the time I reached it, and the driver came out to help, I was out of energy. I slumped to the ground, watching the driver trying to resuscitate my partner. But by then, it was useless. We had killed a man, but we had also lost a man. There was no net-gain. Nature was in balance again.

CHAPTER ONE

I never knew my father. I had but one item that I knew came from him: a small pendant, golden in color, inscribed with the word *Crimson*, that I wore around my neck. My mother never told me what it meant or why he'd gotten it for me—in fact, my mother never wanted to talk about him at all. But by the time I had turned ten, I was forced to find out why that was. Although I had always berated her, asking about his past and why he wasn't around, finding out the truth wasn't all sugar and spice. After all, there's a reason why the saying goes "Be careful for what you wish for."

My birthday was January fifth, and on the eve of that night we got an unexpected visitor at the house. That cold, wintry night, and the next five days that followed, I will always remember, as if they had just happened yesterday. Very often in my sleep, to this day, I still vividly recall the events that unfolded next, before waking up sweaty and gasping for air.

We were both in the living room that night, my mother and I. She was on the couch watching some program on the TV—about nature I think—and I was lying on the floor next to her, playing with a new toy I had received from a distant relative. The smell of her favorite pumpkin spice candle scented the small living room, and I was battling some evil villain with my action figure toy. All seemed well until a subtle knock came from the front door.

It was eight o'clock, and I remember the exact instance because her favorite show always aired at the same time each night. My mother, blowing out the candle, got up to receive whoever was outside, and I returned to my childhood mischief, saving the world from a galactic sorcerer. It wasn't until I heard my mother start to cry that I turned my attention toward the dining room, where stood two adults. My mother was standing in the way of a tall man, as if trying to keep him from advancing further into the house. She was trying to hold back more sniffles in between shouts of protest.

He was a tall man, wearing a dark blue suit and a matching blue tie. His shoes were so refined and polished that I swear I could see my mother's reflection in them. Judging by his balding head and the slight wrinkles nestled beside his brown eyes, I put the man to be in his early fifties.

After letting my mother speak her mind, the unknown man began to talk, and as he did so, the rest of his tight face remained still and expressionless. He must have said something that unsettled my mother again because she responded by slapping him across the face and shouting in between sobs, "Leave! You need to leave this house now, before I call the police."

By then, I had put my toy down, deciding that the galaxy could wait to be saved, and was hiding behind the piano bench, listening in. The man glanced over at me and I met his cold eyes. "I understand your frustration," he said, turning back to my mother. "But the decision is beyond your control. He is of age now, and it's time for him to come with us." My mother reacted by pushing him back toward the door and grabbing the phone, exclaiming, "You must leave now. I'm calling the police."

The tall man did not put up a struggle. Instead, he smiled graciously as his tight face became even tighter. Acknowledging my mother's heated request, he nodded and retreated out the door. "As you wish," he said. "But this isn't over." He disappeared back into the darkness. The ordeal was finished, and the dust settled back down to normalcy—or so I thought. I can recall having asked her who the tall man was, and her response, after lighting a cigarette—out on the porch of course— was, "Nobody." We never talked about that night's incident again, for it was decided that *nobody* was at the door.

However, the following afternoon, I remember my mother being on the phone and talking to somebody. She was standing in the hallway of the dining room and was propped up against the wall. She was carrying most of the conversation as she twirled the phone cord around with a shaky finger. Although I did not listen, that phone call had lasted for just under two hours.

Aside from that peculiarly long conversation, nothing out of the ordinary occurred for the next three days, until once again, something interesting surfaced. It was an early afternoon, and I had been lying on my bed reading a book from the library. My mother was in the kitchen sitting at the table with a man she claimed was a work associate. I paid little attention at first because no reason was given to suggest the necessity for my engagement. Every now and again, I would hear the volume of her voice intensifying, loud enough for me to hear, but then it would fall back down to a faint clamor, and I would return to the depths of my book.

It wasn't until about an hour later that I could overhear the excitement resonating from the kitchen. Becoming all the more intrigued, I decided to put the book down and peep my head outside the bedroom.

Doing the best I could to eaves-drop on the adult conversation, I was able to discern the majority of the final dialogue that was still in play. My mother had been smoking a cigarette at the table, which was extremely unusual for her. The man sitting across from her at the table, the *coworker*, looked worn out and haggard. It looked as though he had been deprived of sleep for quite some time, judging by his sullen eyes and the long face. His blond hair was long and unkempt, and as it grew down past his ears, it screamed of some serious attention.

My mother had been pleading for the gentleman to help her. Help her with what, I was unsure of. All the man could respond with was shaking his tired head, which sent his frazzled hair swaying in all directions. He then reached out across the table and took my mother's hands into his. I watched as their eyes met. "If there was something I could do to stop it, I would, and I wish there was," he said. "You know that. I want to protect Crim—"

"Brendan!" my mother almost yelled.

"Of course, *Brendan*."

Being just ten years old, I became bored with the scene in the kitchen soon after, and once again, I reverted back to my bed, where sat my lonely book, longing for attention.

After the epoch in the kitchen was over and the blond-haired gentleman had left, I heard my mother go outside to finish smoking on the porch. She never told me who that man was and I never had the chance to ask. The following morning, I accompanied my mother to the grocery store and to run some of her weekend errands. She seemed particularly uneasy about something, but I wasn't quite sure of what, and knowing my mom, I wasn't going to press the issue. Instead, I just sat in the seat and kept listening to the radio—it was oldies rock music—blasting Credence Clearwater Revival.

In order to keep the food from going bad, we hit the few miscellaneous stops she had to make first before completing our long voyage to the grocery store. When we finally *did* arrive, with it being Saturday and all, the store was packed. Obviously, this took up the bulk of our allotted time and after two more hours of food finding, our Saturday morning mission was complete and it was time to return home.

The series of events that followed happened so fast, it felt like a blur to me. To this day, I wince at the thought of what happened to us—what happened to me, and what happened to her.

With it being close to noon, the weekend dwellers were beginning to stir, and we found ourselves stuck amidst the Saturday rush. We were at a traffic light for what seemed like forever. By now, the car smelled like fresh produce and Credence Clearwater had made way for urban dance jams. Looking over to my left, I watched as my mother made a rhythmic cadence with her fingers, tapping against the steering wheel. Her lips were quivering and she murmured something to herself. Although I could not hear what she was saying, I could tell that something was amiss. Even for a small adolescent, I caught on to things pretty quickly. She stopped her drum beat momentarily and reached for her pack of cigarettes. At that moment the light turned green.

By now, the ice cream in the backseat was surely beginning to melt from such long neglect, and so when the light morphed colors, my mother wasted no time in slamming her right foot down onto the gas pedal. The car made a quick sputtering sound as the wheels spun to life. We got as far as halfway across the intersection before a large vehicle crashed into us. The black suburban came out of nowhere, blindsiding us, and its heavy frame cut into our little sedan.

From the passenger's side I remember spotting the black giant out of the corner of my eye. It was just in time to feel the shock as the vehicle smashed into the side of ours. The window to the driver's seat exploded inward, sending shrapnel in all directions. The driver's door inverted and caved in almost instantly, it was like watching paper being folded. The metal door pushed into my mother so as to wedge her in between it and the steering wheel. She let out a scream as this happened. There was a loud *popping* sound that followed, scaring me. But I didn't have time to react. Neither one of us did.

The force of the impact caused my head to slam up against the passenger door and the world began to spin. The urban jams soon faded away and were replaced with static as the radio lost reception. The last thing I could hear of the horrific event was the obnoxious blaring of the car horn. My head was stuck in a fixed position, forcing me to watch my mother while her face rested up against the steering wheel. A film of blood was smeared across her forehead and small dribbles of it were trailing from her mouth. Her green eyes were open, staring back at me. I feel that the sight will haunt me forever. The loud horn soon dissipated, and my eyes closed, plunging me into complete blackness.

This part of my life I have trouble understanding, and I often wonder why it happened—*why* it was my mother who had to go, and *why* I was left behind to suffer. Call it a freak accident. A tiny *burp* on the radar screen that always seems to hit us when we least expect it; upending the balance-beam we so graciously attempt to teeter upon each day as we try to make sense of our own lives. To this day I try to make sense of it all. To this day I still suffer, wondering *why*.

Coming back into consciousness, I opened my eyes and let the world back in again. At first I had difficulty understanding where I was. My head was whirling at a hundred miles per hour. My mind was a blank sheet. I could not even think back to the last thing I remembered doing. It was as if my memory had been cleaned out.

After taking a deep breath I glanced around the room. The ugly steel-colored walls and the white floors gave a little indication of where

I was, but my memory refused to give up the goods. I was on some bed, in some room. To my left was a big window with its blue curtains drawn shut. To my right was a glass door with people fluttering by on the other side. At the foot of the bed there was a vase of yellow flowers; and then it came to me.

Hospital...I was in a hospital.

This part my memory could not hold out any longer. I propped myself up on my elbows and tried digging deeper, trying to find what else my mind was hiding from me. The ceiling burst to life with a woman's voice announcing that visitor hours would be over in ten minutes.

It was hard to think with my head still swirling, and I moved a hand over to scratch it. But as I did so, I found that there was something odd covering my head. Bringing my other hand into play, I began investigating. That's when it hit me like a foul ball, and my memory started to patch in again. I was in a car accident.

After patting down the rest of my body for any injuries, I was happy to come up empty. It seemed as though the only injury sustained from the accident was a bump on the side of my head, which was now covered up by layers of tightly wrapped gauze. I had come out unscathed.

Where was my mother? Where was the person who had sustained the most injuries? All at once I became sad and my eyes began to well up.

Frantically, I scanned the room again, desperate for any indication that she was near. The last thing I remembered seeing was her face, her green eyes, the *blood*. Being forced to recall the tragic event made my eyes well up even more and I started to cry. I cried at the thought of losing her, but I refused to think such a horrible thing. She was just in another room; she had to be.

As I hopped off the bed to get a nurse, I wiped the tears away. But before I could reach the glass door a dark figure appeared on the other side of it. It grabbed the door handle and pushed it down. The door opened, revealing a tall, stately man dressed in a blue suit. He looked familiar, although I could not put a finger on why.

My curiosity for the sudden intrusion overcame my panic. Who was this person? Why was he here? The man motioned with a finger for me to keep quiet as he closed the door behind him. He then drew down the blinds over the door. There was a bead of sweat glistening on his balding head. He never told me who he was, only that my mother was gone and that I had to go with him now. Still confused and disoriented, I didn't know what to make of the situation, or of the news of my mother's passing, I nodded my head.

He smiled back at me, baring a set of yellowed teeth, and opened the door. Before opening it, the man told me to keep quiet and not talk to anyone. He then held out his hand and I grabbed it. Grasping his hand tightly, I could feel his tough, callused skin as it pressed against mine, which was soft and clammy. Together, we left the hospital.

Outside, we were greeted by another gentleman wearing a similar suit, standing next to a black vehicle. No words were exchanged between the three of us, and I remember looking back at the hospital as we drove off, wiping the drying tears from my face. Although I was very young at the time, I somehow realized that the life I knew had come to an abrupt end and was over. And that a new one was about to begin.

CHAPTER TWO

I've always known that I was different. And I've resigned myself to believe that I was different from everybody else in this world. Even before The Program, it felt as though I had been living in some form of marginalized life. Aside from acknowledging the occasional passerby on the sidewalk as I walked home from school each day, I rarely found myself conversing with another person outside of necessity. It just wasn't my thing.

Growing up on just the edge of poverty didn't help to alleviate my situation either. I constantly found myself at odds with everyone else, wondering why I wasn't like them—further exacerbating the belief that I was different. However, through the early years of my desolate childhood I had come to terms with where I stood in the social hierarchy and come to accept it. This, I believe, is what afforded me great solace when I was introduced into The Program.

In my head, I was already living in the underworld as a social outcast. Being in The Program only made it three-dimensional. For the past ten years, I had existed within society, and it would be for the next ten years that I would exist without it.

And so it was that for the next decade, my sole source of human contact would come from within The Program; surviving on the fringes of an already marginal society. From the hospital, I was taken to a small airstrip where a private plane smuggled me out of the country and into Europe. It was here that I would spend the majority of the decade, just outside of Beivrus, a small village 70 miles south of Belgrade, Serbia.

If you were to look on a map you'd see that this place doesn't exist. Not officially, anyway. Plagued by so many years of political turmoil and civil strife, by the late 1990s nothing but a scant population of Eastern dissidents remained. It is here in Beivrus that I would become fully immersed into an entirely new way of life and receive an education, not just in the books and arts, but in ultimate survival as well.

Knowledge is power, and power is dangerous. I learned a lot throughout the course of my extensive training in Beivrus. Thriving in complete secrecy and isolation I was forced to embrace a life of solitude and self-reliance. The Program trained me in combat, and having adopted the five main styles of martial arts, I was an Archangel of Death. But it wasn't all brawn for me. The Chancellor believed that for every hour spent in the field, killing, an assassin should spend three more in the classroom, learning. He said it's how the great powers of the world came to be so great; that you may have deadly execution, but what's the point if there is no careful strategy to go along with it?
Conventional and occupational focus was ironed into my brain so that not only could I drive a vehicle, but I could also take it apart and put it back together. I learned how to manipulate a whole warehouse full of weapons, as well as how to disarm anyone holding them. I learned to be quick, and nimble; getting anywhere in the world I needed to be without getting noticed. In the end, I had become the perfect soldier.

The things they made me do in The Program were horrific, but necessary. In the depths of the underground world there are no rules—only outcomes—and anything goes. Like financial investors, professional hitmen have private portfolios, what I call murder folders. By the time I had completed my training, I had forty-eight confirmed kills, all of which had occurred within the last four years of my training.

After the bitter-sweet success of completing my first hit that night in the old, three-story apartment building, The Chancellor was convinced by someone in The Vice to promote me to an operator.

Within the fraternal organization exists a rank-and-file system, similar to what you'd expect with an army. While there are some military personnel who get picked up along the way, most of us start out as children of patriarchs—me being one of them. We kids all start off as recruits; lowly grunts with little more than an inkling of what was coming. After a couple of years of training, depending on merit, we'd rise to an operator level. In addition to our training, an operator is also required to take on hit jobs.

Upon completion of training, if we were still alive that is, we'd then become a freelancer. Still very much underneath the umbrella of The Program, Freelancers are able to accept independent hits.

As seldom as it is, after years of proving our worth to The Program, we might be asked by The Chancellor himself to further advance into the small, but very privileged order of The Vice. Every army has their own special weapons and tactics administrators, and we are no exception to that. This tiny outcrop of The Program is responsible for most of the killings that happen around the world, but it comes at a price. To put things into perspective, the average fee for a Freelancer's services is about a hundred thousand American dollars. The lowest fee for the services of The Vice is nothing short of one million. Only on a rare occasion will he be commissioned to complete a special job, and I have yet to run into them.

Ordering a hit on somebody is a lot like buying something online. Someone places a request and, after the funds have been wired, the hit goes out. Once the funds have been wired—to one of The Program's many accounts—The Chancellor then approves it and passes it down.

The majority of approved jobs trickle down the chain of command to the Freelancers and even to the operators, with only a very small share of the hits being appointed to The Vice—on the rare occasion at a high cost. Unless a Freelancer is approached by an independent party outside of The Program to take on a hit, members cannot be specifically requested, so as to preserve as much anonymity among both parties as possible. Only by this way can we neutralize the potential for a murder to be traced back to us.

While paying people to kill others has not changed over the years, the weapons and the ways of ordering hits have. What has changed in particular is the adoption and use of the Internet. As much slander as the black-market gets, it remains one of the most elusive and amorphous economies in the world.

Whenever white hat or legitimate businesses change, so to do the black hats. The economy of the underground market is estimated to be about three times that of the world markets, and it's of no great surprise that the practices of the underworld change just as fast, if not faster.

The new millennium marked a milestone in the underground black-market. It was during this time that an entirely new subculture of the Internet arose. Labeled the *Deepweb*, its usefulness exploded after a special routing program called *TOR* knocked down the walls to it. For the first time in cyber history, this program bridged a gap and opened up a cyber-portal into the underworld. Containing many petabytes of unregistered domains that are unable to be accessed by traditional browser software, the *Deepweb* creates a labyrinth of unfiltered layers, perfect for hiding what the black-market does.

Going through these many layers and exploring even deeper through the *Deepweb*, eventually you will find a much more sinister region of domains, which for good reason, are nearly impossible to find on accident. Coined the *Darknet*, it is a special subdivision of the *Deepweb* wherein lies the heart of the underworld's online operations and its obscure market community.

Ranging from hard drugs, like cocaine and heroin, to RPGs and assault rifles, just about anything you can imagine is bought and sold through the *Darknet*. Top dollar transactions from all over the world go through the black-market each and every day.

But the most expensive item isn't something you can touch. It is here that one can purchase the services of a hitman for the right price. No longer are the traditional days when you need to know somebody or make a slew of phone calls to order a hit on someone. Just as you would buy your wife a Christmas gift online, with the right routing program, it's just as easy to hire a professional to kill somebody. As long as the funds get transferred the hit goes through, and both parties never have to meet.

CHAPTER THREE

For me, killing has become a drug. It is euphoric. Nothing in the world makes you feel more alive than to take another man's life. But like any other drug, I have become dependent upon it. Being alone for so many years with the smallest of contact with other people has made me dead inside, and it's the thrill of the chase that keeps the rest of me from dying as well. It's what keeps me going each day. Without it, my skin would crawl as my body rejected itself, craving for another taste. There is no cure for what I suffer from. To go cold-turkey would be my absolute death.

During moments of extreme desperation, people will experience what is called an adrenaline rush. It's the fight or flight scenario when a mother will lift her car off the ground so that her child may roll out from underneath it. We all have this hormone and the capability to use it, but rarely ever have to.

What's referred to as an adrenaline *surge*, The Program teaches us how to harness and control the feral hormone. Serving many applications for combat and self-preservation, it heightens the body's senses and even blocks pain receptors. By manipulating adrenaline we can extend the longevity of its surge, wielding its untapped potential. A typical adrenaline junky will jump off a cliff or parachute out of a plane; I like to hunt people—after all, it's in my blood.

I became good at killing, and I became good at it fast. I was on fire, completing my hits with a perfect success rate. With the eventual attainment of my twentieth birthday, my ten years of training and re-education would come to a close, but not before my Final Challenge.

All operatives within The Program cannot become full members of the organization until they have completed their last challenge—and it is only then would they become baptized into a life of death.

And so it was that on the night of my twentieth birthday I accepted my Final Challenge from The Chancellor. This challenge would be unlike any other, and would never be replicated again. Not just a simple hit job, but much more than that. For it to be worthy of a Final Challenge it needed to be nothing short of extraordinary, and above all else, of high risk. The Final Challenge sets to push an operator to his absolute limits, and only then, does it push even harder. I had only one shot. It was all or nothing. To fail would mean my death.

Taking nothing but the clothes on my back, I was flown from Beivrus to a private airfield in Amsterdam the next day. It was early that January morning and I remember watching the sun rise through a window of the private plane. Three hours later we had hit the tarmac.

From the private airfield I was driven to a large hotel where I rendezvoused with three others. I was in disbelief when I realized that they were all part of The Vice. I had never met anyone from The Vice before, and now I was standing in a room filled with three of them, creating a strategy for that night's operation. You wouldn't ever pick them out of a hat, dressed as casual as they were in common street clothes, but it's the language they spoke that gave them away. Although considered an official dead language, Latin was still very much alive within The Program, and it's used most often by The Vice; call it a code of sorts.

Across from the grand hotel was ground zero—Paradiso, Amsterdam's largest casino—and it was here that the Final Challenge would go down. This truly was a challenge unlike any other and I soon found out why three members of The Vice had been integrated into it. Not one, but four hits would be orchestrated that night, and an undertaking that difficult would require nothing short of prodigious precision and flawless execution. I was ready.

As we waited in the hotel room for the hours to pass, nothing outside of necessity for the night's operation was said. Being isolated for so long, you learn how to speed up time in your own way. You develop your own method for dealing with boredom. Some people read to pass the time, and some people are forced to stop certain memories from coming back as they replay their life over and over again inside their heads. For me, as was often with having to wait for the job to play out, I would find myself thinking about the job itself. How it would go down. How it would succeed. And how it would fail. Although the end result is always the same, the methods are usually different.

When the sun finally went down it was time for us to begin. We placed our books down and put our personal thoughts on hold, knowing deep down that we would be forced to confront them again. The four of us walked across the street and entered the casino separately in different intervals. Relying on our watches, we set distance between each other, using only visual eye contact to keep us together.

I was the last person to enter the casino, and as I walked across the busy intersection I remember how the building seemed to come to life.

Its glass face stood two-stories tall, and its radiating interior pierced through the many windows, casting different colors of light onto the street before me. The sounds were vibrant with many different jingles of gambling nuances coming from all corners of the casino. A giant water-fountain depicting a massive red shield and three white X's, Amsterdam's Coat of Arms, stood in the center of the entrance. It greeted me with a shower of water that disappeared into a deep clear pool as I walked past it.

Inside, the casino floor was like a living organism. Thousands of bustling people swelled around the gambling section. Loud sounds and flashy lights announced the *big payout*. Everyone was here for the same reason, even I...to win.

Blending in for over an hour, the four of us waited patiently for our targets to enter the casino. We each took up separate areas of the floor, melting into the packed crowds of tourists and gamblers while being cautious of keeping visual contact with one another. While the rest of my team was spread out, I had taken up residence between an old man and a French couple at the slot machines. My left leg bounced up and down as I sat there waiting. I kept glancing at my watch. I was tired, but the smell of coffee colliding with cigar smoke kept me alert.

Mentally I kept going over the plan, imagining seeing the piece of paper with instructions written on it. I kept flipping it over in my head, reading the backside, and then returning to the first page, only to read it and then flip it over again. The hits were put out on four wealthy European barons and it was our job to take them out, no questions asked. I glanced down at my watch again.

After what seemed like forever, the barons trickled in. One by one, the targets entered the casino, accompanied by flashy escorts and usually two or three bodyguards. Each of us had a designated baron to take out, and as our hits entered the floor we moved in to tail them. Being careful not to be seen.

Like clockwork, the first three barons came into the casino in half hour lapses apart, and I watched as each member of The Vice moved in to follow them. Their clothing blended in and eventually I lost visual on all of them. They had been swallowed by the sea of gamblers, disappearing completely into the throngs.

Another hour or so had gone by and the French couple had moved on, leaving me at the slots next to the old man who refused to leave without winning some coin. The cigar smoke became overpowering and it started to nauseate me. A female voice with a Dutch accent announced over the floor that it was couples night and to buy your significant other a drink at the bar. Checking my watch for the thousandth time, I saw that it was getting late, and I started to think that something had gone wrong.

The already-dense casino was becoming more packed by the minute as people kept flooding in through the set of double sliding doors at the entrance, but still no sign of a baron followed by his royal court. At one point. after a rowdy crowd of Americans had come storming it, the floor had become so filled that I thought the whole building was going to burst at the seams. It made me nervous being around so many people. I liked being alone.

Having done my best to blend in with the local crowd of gamblers and miscreants, I was sporting a dull-gray parka and a pair of brown slacks. On my head rested a brown fedora that seemed to be the icing on the cake. It was holding back the layer of sweat that had culminated over my short brown hair.

I noticed that inside the casino existed a whole sub-culture; an entire population bent on striking it rich, waiting to cash in their chips and turn from rags to riches. So many people were congregated into such a small place with the same thing in mind—winning. But so too was the casino. In the balance existed a constant struggle between the thousands of gamblers and the casino itself, both trying to make money off of each other. It surprised me how much this reminded me of nature. How two polar opposites had somehow met in the middle as they tried to take everything from each other.

The word *survival* can take on many meanings and principles, and what was going on in this casino in Amsterdam was no different—a common situation of two animals just fighting to survive. But in the end, the house always wins, and the apex predator comes up on top. The casino and I had something in common that night, and we shared a common goal. We both intended to take the lives of others in one way or another.

There was a break on the floor as the seas momentarily parted, and I caught a glimpse of two of my partners. Their faces looked blank and I watched as they followed their barons from a distance to the back of the casino. Their targets disappeared through a set of black double-doors that were zoned off by two security guards, leaving The Vice cut off from them. I watched as they doubled back and were swallowed up again as the sea of people flooded the floor once more.

Still waiting at the slot machines, I sat there dormant, uncertain of how the night's events were going to unravel. The old man had finally given up and I watched him creak through the crowds and out of sight. Minding my watch for the millionth time now, I continued to scan the entrance area with some degree of desperation. The layer of sweat had boiled over and started streaking down my forehead.

It was close to ten PM, and I had lost complete visual on all three of my accomplices. Fearing that something else had gone awry, I made a judgment call and stood up. Just as I was about to move away from my position I saw the gold. I had finally located baron number four.

After walking in through the clear doors of the lobby, my target stopped and glanced around. He was fashioned from head to toe in a lavish cashmere suit. The neon lights of the casino lobby glowed from his shiny black shoes.

What had shocked me the most though wasn't his candid appearance…it was that he was alone. My heart jumped out of my chest at the sight of this and I forgot how sick I was from the heavy smoke. Seeing the enormous opportunity standing just fifty feet in front of me, I wasted no time in acting upon it. During our briefing, intel had said the barons would be accompanied by guards, as was standard European customs. However, given the obvious but advantageous flaw from this intel, and the simple fact that I could no longer account for where the rest of my team was, I knew that I had to make another call and act swiftly if we were to have any chance at all of salvaging the mission and completing my Final Challenge.

The images of The Vice and any thought of the consequences that would undoubtedly follow for my insubordination quickly evaporated as I began to stir. In layman's terms I called an audible and changed my whole strategy for the hit. Instead of letting the target lead while I followed from a safe distance, I readjusted my course and came right for him; to me, he was a wounded animal waiting to get picked off.

I left the safety of the slot machines and headed straight for the lobby. Gaining more momentum with each stride, I quickly closed the distance between the two of us. My heart kept racing and my skin tingled as I got closer. I blocked out the sounds and the noises of the casino floor. The only thing I could hear was a distant voice inside my head telling me, *this is it. This is your chance. Don't fuck it up.*

The distractions of the casino melted into a blur as I continued to push through the dense mass of gamblers. What had become thirty feet was soon twenty, and then ten, and then five. As the final distance was closed I was soon able to make out the baron's wispy face. His skin was tight and oddly pale. He looked in desperate need of some Vitamin

D, no doubt the acute side-effect of some hard drug. His lips were thin like his face, and pursed, giving the impression that he was upset or confused.

"Good evening, Mr. Reece," I said in my best Dutch accent, tapping him on the shoulder.

Seemingly bewildered, the man spun around and met me with large brown eyes. His skin was indeed pale and so tight that it appeared as though his eyebrows were receding up toward his forehead.

He did not answer me though. Instead, his eyes kept rolling back and forth as he continued to scan the floor. He had a poor poker face and I was about to go all in.

I took a step toward him, removing the fedora and placing it gently against my chest as I did so. "I am terribly sorry for your long wait." I said. "Casino management extends their deepest apologies."

Things seemed to cool down after that. His eyes stopped darting around the room and he finally acknowledged me.

"Why that's very kind of you, sport," he replied, smiling. He was British, and I had a certain disdain for Brits. Out of all the people, the English were the most annoying.

I placed a hand inside my pocket and felt my knife, momentarily considering killing him right there. It would have been so easy too; a quick strike right through the jugular. He would have bled out in under fifteen seconds. The crowd was thick and too busy throwing away their mortgages to notice. But that wasn't the plan, and I let go.

"Mr. Reece," I said bowing, "We are terribly sorry for the inconvenience and head of casino services wanted me to see to it personally that you be escorted to the Estates Room."

At first he was slightly taken aback by my sudden gesture of blatant flattery, but then his smile widened and his face became tighter. He extended a hand and I shook it, feeling his warm flesh as it met mine.

It's sometimes hard to keep a straight face and maintain your composure—especially when under pressure. Life is a lot like a game of poker. The world is the green-felt table and all the players seated around it are us. Each hand dealt to us is but a stroke of luck. Sometimes we get lucky and hit pocket aces. But then other times our luck falls short and we get a 2, 8, off-suit. Not all of us start out with the same pile of chips, either, and it's up to us to make it bigger. But not every pair of aces is enough, and sometimes the 2, 8, off-suit comes up on top. Sometimes, the trick is to keep a straight face, and maintain your composure. Only then, will your pile of chips become bigger.

Waving my hand out toward the casino floor, I ushered the baron to follow me. "Right this way, Mr. Reece. The other players have been expecting you for quite some time now."

Nodding his head, the man followed.

As I made my way through the crowd, carving out a tiny sliver for the both of us to get through, I did my best to mimic the buoyancy and airiness of someone important and of special privilege. I liked to role-play and it seemed to make Mr. Reece more comfortable as his face lit up around all the glamor of the casino floor. He looked like a kid in a candy store.

The casino floor itself was laid out exactly like a rectangle. The front entrance was on one of the shorter ends, and the black double-doors, guarded by the security guards was at the other. In between both ends was all the hoopla and bedlam of a thriving casino district.

After requesting that he keep up with me lest we get separated, I took a hard left after passing the blackjack tables and led Mr. Reece through a different set of doors. Having memorized the building's layout on the blueprint back in the hotel, I knew exactly where I wanted to do it.

Still leading the way, I waved my hat toward the hall. "The private room is just beyond those second set of doors," I said.

When we made it through the first set of black doors I stopped. "Mr. Reece," I said, still holding the fedora in front of me, "if you will, please lead the way." He let out an anxious laugh and, as he passed by me, he put money into my hat.

He started to thank me for all the help I've been and when his back was to me I acted. Like a machine, I sprang to life and did what I was programmed to do. The gears inside me ground as I came up behind him. Reaching my right hand over in front of him I covered his mouth and used the other hand to lock his arms behind his back.

At first he didn't struggle, as I acted quickly. But soon his fatal mistake became apparent to him. He began to squirm and I locked my arm tighter around his. His mouth was full of air as he tried to scream, and my right hand got warm.

Taking control of the situation, I jerked him into the bathroom to our right. I then removed my power over his mouth just long enough so that I could lock the door behind us. He started shrieking, but my hand was back over his mouth in no time, and my palm became wet.

I forced him into a bathroom stall and threw him onto the toilet seat so that he faced the wall. He kept struggling, making the toilet lid rattle against the porcelain seat. Releasing my death-lock from his arms, I reached my left hand inside my parka and pulled out a black pistol. Unlike the chrome .45 from my first hit, this one had a silencer attached to its barrel. There would be no mistakes. This one would be flawless.

By now my right hand had become caked in the man's saliva as he continued to scream. I knew that he was fully aware of his miscalculation and that he now regretted it. We all regret the mistakes we make, but sooner or later, we have to face the consequences.

Drawing in a deep breath, I sighed. When I was ready, I ran the gun up the inside of his cashmere jacket and squeezed the trigger three times. Having shot him from behind the blood sprayed across the wall, staining the bathroom tiling a dark red. Mr. Reece's body slumped forward and I no longer had to hold my hand over his mouth.

It had been four years since I first saw another man's blood and watched as the life left his eyes, and nothing phased me now. I was a well-oiled machine, geared for war.

Putting on a pair of latex gloves, I rummaged through the dead man's pockets. When I had his wallet and identification and was certain that I had everything I needed, I left the stall and closed the door, leaving behind Mr. Reece and his elegant cashmere suit.

Before vacating the bathroom, I took a moment to brainstorm my next move. Pacing back and forth in the small room, it took another minute until I knew what to do next. Unlocking the door, I turned around for the last time and shot out the bathroom's lights, sending shards of glass showering down onto the floor. Outside, I peeled the cheap bathroom sign off the door and tossed it back into the dark room. I put in a fresh magazine and threw the discarded one into the room as well.

With the hallway still empty, I turned my attention back to the casino floor. This night was not over yet, and I was still in control of my own fate.

Things were changing now and I could see it. No longer was I a helpless child, the product of a broken family and victimized by an impoverished upbringing. I had just killed another man in cold blood, and felt no remorse for it. If someone were to come up to me a year before my tenth birthday and tell me that in a year my whole world, the life in which I had grown accustomed to, would come crashing to an end like a violent, out of control train, I would have laughed in their face.

However, I also feel that deep within I would have actually embraced it. Knowing—perhaps even *hoping*—that what they said would come true. Nothing up until then pained me more than having to go through the same bland motions, living the same transparent life day after day; wondering why I wasn't good enough for the world. But things were changing now and I could see it, and I have now come to the conclusion that it is the world who was not good enough for me.

I headed back through the first set of double doors and then stopped. Before returning to the sea of gamblers and tourists, I reached into my pants and pulled out a silver lighter. I had taken it from the old man before he left the slots. Fully extending my arm up, I lit a flame just under the hallway's fire sensor. The wail of a siren filled the air, followed by a thumping noise from the ceiling. Moments later, a rush of water came pouring down from above as the sprinklers came to life.

I put the lighter back into my pocket and pushed through the second set of doors. The casino floor had turned into a frenzied panic as the sea of people ran in all directions, every one of them trying to flee the water. It made me slightly amused seeing all the chaos; seeing everybody's plans go to hell as their hair and their clothes became drenched in water. It was only water, yet it meant much more than that. It meant the addict could not keep gambling away the last dollars he had, and the casino could not keep siphoning money off of everybody. It disrupted survival.

The entrance to the casino was jammed by a mob of people struggling to push their way out of the lobby doors. The red carpeting was saturated and the abandoned tables were left to suffer the same fate. Chairs were overturned and drinks were smashed to the ground. The only things that kept going were the music and flashy lights drilling away, claiming that every hour there was another winner. But then the electricity was soon cut off, and there was darkness. Only the hurried shouts and screams of frantic people broke the silence.

After a while the floodlights came on as I made my way through the emptying casino. My body was soaked. My fedora, my parka, my shoes—all of me was drenched in water, but I did not care. *I* was not like the rest of these people. Occasionally, crap falls from the sky, and the only thing you can do is keep walking through it.

Making my way through the diminishing crowd I headed toward the back of the casino, firmly gripping the black handgun in my left hand. With a wet thumb I caressed the scar on my right palm. It felt fresh and never seemed to heal. But I guess some scars never do.

As I approached the back end of the giant rectangle, I noticed that the two security guards had not left their posts, standing just as still as ever despite the obvious chaos ensuing before them. Their wet jackets were matted down against their bodies. I knew that it was only a matter of seconds before the private card game would stop, and my chance at completing my Final Challenge shut down with it.

A crowd of straggling gamblers crossed my path. Emerging through them, I surprised the guards and cut through the floor like a sharp dagger. Their heads turned to greet me and our eyes met. They were not expecting me.

Without giving them a chance to react I drew up the pistol and fired off two rounds each into both of their skulls. Their bodies dropped to the floor as I sprinted past them. Pushing through the black double-doors, I kept my gun aimed up, not knowing what to expect on the other side. I held my breath.

Unlike the other hallway, this one was much wider and tiled on either side with black glass. The floodlights pulsated a red light that reflected off the glass and created an eerie glow as I made my way toward the next set of double-doors. The red walls matched the red carpeting. It was all crimson.

After coming out the other side of the doors, I found myself in another hall. This one ran perpendicular to the hall I had just vacated, with doors on either end. As I turned to go down the left side, I suddenly found myself face-to-face with another guard standing in front of the door to the private card game. Standing in the way of my future.

He gave me a sinister grin as he reached into his jacket. But before he could pull anything out I sprinted toward him. Throwing my body into his, I knocked us both into the door. It broke instantly from our weight and we fell into the next room, colliding on top of a giant red-felt table.

The sudden entrance as we came crashing into the room startled everyone seated around the table. I felt the door below me shake; there was somebody underneath it. The guard directly below me reached for his gun again, but I was quick to pin his arm down with my knee. He then looked up at me with a helpless gaze as I raised my gun to his throat and squeezed the trigger. Blood spurted back into my face. Wiping it off, I put two more bullets into the guard stuck under the door. It stopped shaking.

The people around the table stirred at the sight of this. In a panicky frenzy, they jumped from their seats and rushed to leave the room. But after seeing me wave my gun at them, they stopped, they obeyed. It just dawned on me that there were more guards in the room. As they came at me, I braced for impact.

There were five more guards in all, and they all moved at once. The first guard tried to kick me in the face, but I blocked his advance. Pulling him onto the floor, I put a bullet through his face. The next two guards came at me with more resolve, and only with extreme swiftness was I able to stop them from shooting me. Pushing the closest of the two away, I used my gun as a blunt instrument and knocked the other man's gun out of his hands. I hit him over the head with it and when the first guard came back in, I shot him twice in the chest; the other guard suffered the same fate.

I heard the familiar clicking of two automatic weapons coming to life. This was one of those things I had been thinking about over in the hotel room as we waited for the job: what weapons would they use? I moved fast. Speed like this was ingrained in me for such matters. Whirling around, while reloading my weapon at the same time, I ducked low enough to avoid getting sprayed by the guards' weapons. The room was lit up for a few seconds. My ears rang. I waited for the right moment to strike and fire back. The last two men didn't stand a chance.

What shocked me most was not that I had survived, but rather, how calm and serene I felt. I hadn't had time to react, but I didn't need to. It was during moments like these that something else in my body took over. I was just along for the ride, watching on the sidelines as some other entity within me played the game. It didn't feel like an out-of-body experience though, and I could still feel everything as it happened. I could smell the odors and hear the sounds. Yet, I was not in control.

Before me lay a pile of corpses with more blood than a donor clinic. The people had since sought refuge underneath the table and a few of the flashy escorts were crying amongst themselves. Using my sleeve, I wiped as much blood off my face as I could, although it was useless. My whole body was covered in *red*. I was *red*…I was *crimson*.

Getting back up I took out the empty magazine and let it fall to the floor. The room smelled of cigar smoke and expensive perfumes. The floodlight in the room bounced off the terrified faces of the three barons and their posh call-girls. As I was putting in a fresh magazine one of the barons made a break for it and scrambled toward the door.

I pulled back the slide of the gun and, just as I was ready to pick him off, I watched as he fell back from the doorway and landed on top of the poker table, breaking it in half. When I turned back toward the door, I was staring down the hollow barrel of another gun.

"I was wondering what happened to you guys," I said, lowering the gun to my hip.

The Vice came pouring into the room, one after another. Their faces looked tired and their clothes were soaked.

"Do we have you to thank for this?" the one man asked as he tugged at his jacket.

"It's only water," another man replied. He smiled at me and shook my hand. "Well done, boy."

"It's not over yet," the third man said. "We still have to get out of this bloody shit hole."

From here, my job was done. I had successfully saved the entire operation and secured the fate of my Final Challenge. My baron was lying dead in a bathroom stall and it was their turn to kill the other three. Leaving them to do their job, I left the private room and stepped out into the empty hallway. Taking a deep breath, I exhaled and smiled.

After a moment of internal joy, hiding my smile, I peered back into the poker room. I stood in the hallway and watched as The Vice cleaned house. They flipped over the large table and gathered the remaining barons into the center of the room, forcing them to kneel on the floor. The three men gathered the escorts' phones, smashed them on the floor, and let them leave. After the girls were gone the hitmen stood behind their targets, put a gun to each baron's head, and fired execution-style. I was mesmerized.

Later on, The Vice would inform me that after losing visual on their targets, they had gotten lost trying to race around the back of the building to find another way into the private room. They told me that they had almost given up, when my resourcefulness and artistic distraction had taken care of the security guards, allowing them to retrace their steps back into the casino floor. They followed the trail of bodies into the back, which is when we joined up once again. I almost blushed, having heard this.

Stripping away what identification the barons had on their bodies, The Vice moved quickly. Interpol would be on our asses soon enough, and it was all we could do to keep our trail cold long enough to get out of this country and back to the safety of Beivrus. When we were ready, we moved out.

Leaving behind a room filled with ten bodies, we started back toward the casino floor. With our guns drawn, not knowing what other surprises might lie just around the corner, we made our way through the empty hallway, took a right, went back through the first set of double doors, and stopped to catch our breaths. Beyond the next set of doors was the casino floor, now entirely empty. Nothing but knocked over remnants of a good time remained. The floodlights continued to blast red, pulsating like a heartbeat.

As we broke through the last set of doors, the sound of sirens cut into the silent room. Through the glass lobby I could see firetrucks sitting idle. Their red and white lights penetrated through the glass and pushed up against the casino walls, joining the already-red floodlights.

With a hand, I motioned for The Vice to follow me as I led them back toward the small hallway I had so easily lured Mr. Reece into. We moved swiftly, hopping over fallen chairs and other gambling obstacles knocked over by the stampede of desperate animals as they evacuated the casino. We made it into the hallway just in time, for behind us, I could hear the sound of fire personnel pouring in through the lobby doors behind us.

We then raced down the short hallway. At the end we were met by another set of black doors. The four of us pushed through cautiously, emerging into the casino's kitchen pantry. The sweet aroma of half-finished cuisines and abandoned appetizers still lingered in the dark air. We spread out, in search of the door that would lead us out the side of the building, and ultimately, completing our mission.

A clock on the wall revealed that it was well-past eleven PM.

"Over here," one of the men said. "Come on quick."

Standing under an EXIT sign whose light had gone out, one of The Vice was ushering for us to go through. The red glow from the floodlights illuminated the dark pantry, and without exchanging words, we converged once more and followed him out the metal door.

Not knowing what was behind it, we blindly left the building, but to our relief, nothing was stirring. We had been brought out to a parking lot, occupied by a few cars and an empty firetruck. One of the men made a phone call, requesting for a plane to pick us up at the airfield, and under the cloak of darkness we cautiously cut across the street back to our hotel. A crowd of bystanders stood huddled around the front of the casino, too busy staring at the scene to notice our dastardly retreat.

Doubling back to the hotel room, we gathered our belongings and all evidence of our mission. The Vice made sure to wipe down everything and destroy traces of our fingerprints to keep the trail cold. Outside, we were met by a black vehicle and our escort who took us back to the private airstrip.

I remember sitting in the backseat of the vehicle and staring out the window as we sped through the dark countryside of Amsterdam. I also remember thinking that by the time the sun would rise over these hills the following morning, the whole world would learn of the horrific murders of four of Europe's wealthiest moguls.

The reality was that we were murderers who had traveled thirteen hundred miles up through Europe with the sole intent of killing four men we had never met before. But that didn't matter. Our reality—the only reality that existed as far as I was concerned—was that we were paid to take out four targets. No questions asked. No looking back. And we didn't. I couldn't help myself from smiling, knowing that I had saved my fate and completed my Final Challenge. I had been flawless.

CHAPTER FOUR

Returning back to Beivrus the next morning felt different. Although I had done it a thousand times over, this time was not the same. The cool morning air that greeted us as we touched down and left the plane even felt different. It all did. Leaving Beivrus, I was just another operator, nothing more than a glorified trainee who had yet to prove his worth, not just to The Program, but also to the world. Coming back to Beivrus unscathed, I held my chin up high. I was now a man.

Growing up as a young child, I had the greatest difficulty in grasping who I was to become. Knowing that I was different from all the other children was a hardship, and I sometimes struggled to find myself. Not having my father around to guide me through those difficult struggles didn't lend me any comfort either, and I would often catch myself questioning my purpose in life.

The four of us left the plane and walked across the tarmac. Under the growing sun, the dark surface gleamed. We were greeted by two men wearing matching black suits. Their ties flapped in the airy distance as we came toward them. Standing between the two men was none other than The Chancellor himself. My heart began pounding against my chest and I wasn't sure whether or not I should make eye contact. Save for the one other time when I had actually seen this elusive man in person at the commencement of my training, as far as I could remember, I had never met the phantom man face to face. He was as enigmatic and secretive as The Program, evading even the world itself. My palms began to sweat.

Standing a resounding six feet tall, The Chancellor was dwarfed in the middle of the two men, who were yet even taller than he. As I came closer, I began to notice the intricate features about him. Like the black tie around his neck, the way his receding brown hair was picked up by the wind that blew across the airstrip. The part of his head that was exposed shimmered against the morning sun, but no sweat seemed capable of beading from his skin. While he looked a little aged, having distinct crows-feet on the outer edges of his dark brown eyes, I knew better than to mistake him for an old man. He was as sharp and dangerous as he was mysterious. And to mistake him for anything else would be fatal.

Drawing nearer to the three men, I was surprised to see The Chancellor hold out his hand and greet us. When he smiled, his face creased, and his crows-feet became even more distinguished.

The four of us, with the addition of The Chancellor and the other two men, were taken back to the training facility in a limousine. With the exception of The Chancellor making a phone call, announcing our arrival, not a single word was said during the entire car ride. It was nerve-wracking to be in such close proximity to people I knew were much more important than I. Men who had killed scores—possibly hundreds—of people without hesitation. It felt a little surreal and I didn't feel worthy to be in their presence.

At this point, I was filled with all sorts of mixed emotions that seemed to coalesce into one giant feeling. My mind was speeding faster than my heart rate as I tried to piece together what would come next. I knew I had completed the Final Challenge and I knew that my training was complete—at least I hoped so—but I was unsure of what would follow. The last ten years of my life were sacrificed and given up to prepare me for this one moment; all the learning, the combat, the blood-shed. Ten years of it, and it was finally over. I took a deep breath as the limousine rolled into the training compound.

After the vehicle parked, and I was let out, I watched as it took off again. Its shiny black hood glistened in the morning sun, and it kicked up dirt as it sped off and out of sight. Before getting out of the limousine, I had been asked to accompany The Chancellor in his private lounge later that evening. Holding back the thousand questions I had for him, I simply nodded my head and shook his hand again, doing my best not to fuck up anything as I exited the vehicle. Shocked, and slightly agitated that I had to wait yet another few hours before learning what would come next, I walked back to my barracks, holding a stupid grin.

CHAPTER FIVE

Although we can't see it, chaos is always around us. Circling our bodies like hungry crocodiles, chaos waits for the right move to strike; waiting with precision to make that decisive deathblow. All there is to do—all we *can* do—is hope that we're not the youngest wildebeest who's too small and weak to fight it off as chaos moves in for the kill. In the end, that's all one can hope for. Nature is chaos.

Back in my room, I was forced to endure yet another evening of wondering in complete uncertainty what secrets would unfold later that night. As I lay there in the same bed I had slept in for the past ten years, my arms folded behind my head, I couldn't help but feel sentimental. For an entire decade, this place had been my home, and this room had been my castle. Yet, I was neither a king, nor a prince. And I knew that my time here was fleeting.

My advocate and personal advisor to The Program had refused to divulge any information concerning what to expect after the Final Challenge. Only that it was inevitable, and that my time would come soon enough. I guess it only made sense. What's undoubtedly the most clandestine organization in the world must leave all facets of its internal ops cloaked in secrecy. I rolled to the side of my bed, deciding that those secrets would reveal themselves when they were ready.

Out of everything I had learned about myself since being in the Program, what has perhaps surprised me the most is how easily it was to sleep at night. As a young child, I had tremendous difficulty in falling asleep. My mother often got frustrated and even had me tested for a sleeping disorder once. Before my tenth birthday, I would get four, maybe five hours of solid sleep, if I was lucky. Some nights I would get no rest at all. Instead, I would just lie there, tossing and turning as a layer of sweat caked the flesh of my neck. Something always haunted me as a child, but I never could quite put a finger on it.

Since being enveloped into The Program though, that all seemed to stop. It surprised me how all the fighting, the bloodshed, all the murders—it seemed to calm me, and I no longer fell victim to restless nights only to rise drenched in perspiration. In some odd way, it did what my mother could not. It let me feel at peace.

Having spent the past twenty-six hours awake, and feeling physically drained from the Final Challenge, I soon found myself in a state of lethargic stupor. Staring up at the same ceiling I had seen for the last ten years, my eyelids slowly shut, and I was asleep.

No sooner had I drifted away, than an abrupt knocking at the door woke me. Three times I heard a hand banging at my door, and each knock brought me farther out of my sleep. It was time for the secrets to be revealed.

From the corridor of my barracks, I was led outside to another building. The air was warm that night, and I could see many stars glistening against the black sky. The man escorting me was a bit taller than I was, and his hair was jet black. He said very little on our way over, yet when he did speak, his voice was heavy with a thick French accent like The Chancellor's.

When we reached the other building, I found myself in a hallway I had never seen before. At odd intervals I kept wiping my sweaty palms against my pants. My escort remained silent as he led us farther. It wasn't long before we approached a plain metal door and the man stopped. After smiling at me queerly, he opened the door and ushered me through it.

The plain appearance of the door I walked past had thrown me off completely. My mouth dropped at the sight of the large room I was in, and the sudden realization that I was inside the Chancellor's private lounge. The metal door lurched shut behind me, and I had difficulty maintaining my composure as I proceeded down a set of oak stairs. At their base was The Chancellor himself, greeting me with a warm smile and an outstretched hand.

"Sit down, my boy," he said as I took his hand and shook it.

Taking him up on his offer, I slumped down on a black leather chair. It was comfortable and squeaked as I resisted the urge to fall back into it. I watched as he joined me in another black chair. It too made squeaking noises.

While I had planned on asking him questions, I was temporarily stunned by the magnificence of his stately quarters. The room was large, far larger than any quarters I had seen, and covered on one end with a giant bookshelf that went ceiling to floor. It was stuffed with all sorts of books; big ones, small ones—red, blue, and black. There were even some books on the bottom shelf that were bound together with what appeared to be aged wood.

Looking very baroque, the room resembled a miniature war museum with all of its peculiar trophies and displays of weaponry showcased on the remaining three walls. Standing on bronze podiums were big guns, as well as small guns and all sizes in between. In the middle of the room rested a large oval-shaped table made of some dark wood, with eight equally dark wooden chairs placed around it. Positioned in the center of the table was a long fixture made of clear glass. Laid horizontally across the glass box was a bastard sword with a Latin inscription brandished across the sharp blade in red ink.

The Chancellor disrupted my hypnotized gaze. "So I take it you are wondering why I asked you here this evening." He was wearing a different suit than earlier, and he had a pack of cigars sticking out of the pocket of his gray blazer.

My gaze went from the table to The Chancellor's face. Although I had heard his voice before, hearing him speaking to me directly made my spine tingle. It felt as though a bucket of ice had been poured down my back.

I opened my mouth with the intent of responding to him. But no words could be found from the depths of my throat. Instead, I simply nodded. Very few people in this world, even in The Program, receive the opportunity of speaking to this man. I felt humbled and nervous. My stomach gurgled.

The chair made more squeaking sounds when I tried to straighten. I watched The Chancellor as he rose from his chair and made his way over to a mini bar positioned against the distant wall. He got out two glasses from a cabinet and began pouring what looked like scotch into them.

"The Vice tell me you performed very well yesterday."

Trying to hold back a grin, I nodded my head again. "Y—yes, sir," I said, finding my voice.

"In fact," The Chancellor said, "they told me that if it wasn't for you, the whole operation would have failed." He came back over and handed me one of the glasses.

Waiting for him to sit back down, I took a healthy sip. It *was* scotch.

The chair made a few more sounds as The Chancellor pulled something out of his jacket pocket. It was a CD, and he proceeded to place it onto the glass table between us.

"We were able to acquire the casino's security footage before those Interpol fucks could get their hands on it," he said, taking a sip of his scotch.

The Chancellor stared back at me, as if expecting a response. I didn't have any, and instead, I took another healthy gulp. It burned my throat as the dark liquid splashed down into my stomach.

"Having observed the entire recording," he continued, "I was impressed by your deft handling of an unfortunate situation. Truly a red-letter day...even *crimson*, if I may say so." A wispy smile appeared at the edge of his mouth. "You should be proud of yourself...boy."

"I was only doing what needed to be done," I replied. "For the greater good of the mission."

The Chancellor laughed and his brown eyes sparkled. "For the greater good of the mission," he repeated. "I like that." His dark eyes flashed with the flames in the fireplace beside us. "I will see you when you wake from your slumber."

I felt a look of confusion run across my face at his closing words. Nonetheless, I took another sip of the scotch. I wanted to thank him for the opportunity in meeting him. But as I began to speak, I found that my words were slurred. I looked to The Chancellor for an explanation. He only smiled back. My mouth went numb and the words stopped altogether. At length, I started to lose feeling in the rest of my body. I sank back into the depths of the chair and could hear the squeaking of the black leather as it swallowed me up.

From head to toe I had lost feeling completely and was unable to move. For a split second there was a flashback, remembering the utter helplessness I had felt in the car accident; paralyzed with fear as I watched my mother die in front of me. Her green eyes staring back. And then all at once I was losing consciousness. My mind drifted away and my eyes closed.

The last thing I remember seeing was The Chancellor as he got back up. "Don't worry, son," he said. "You have nothing to fear here."

The last words The Chancellor had said to me were still resonating in my head by the time I finally woke. Looking around me, I realized that I was somewhere different. I struggled to grasp what had happened, remembering that I was in a room with The Chancellor, but nothing more. It was as if my brain had erased that part of my memory, leaving only a blank gap for me to try and fill the missing pieces.

The room smelled like iron, and I felt cold. As I tried to move, I found that I was tied down to a table. At first I thought I was paralyzed, but then I realized my hands and feet were bound together and I was lying face-down. To make matters worse, I found that my clothes had been removed and I was naked. The cold metallic surface of the table kissed my flesh as I continued to squirm helplessly. Trying to scream for help was useless as well for I had also been gagged. A piece of cloth was clenched in between my teeth, preventing me from forming words.

And then slowly, like water creeping back to a dried up lake bed, my memory came back to me, and I remembered at once what happened. The last thing I had ingested was that scotch. The Chancellor had drugged me. But why? What was going on? Was this it? Was this the end for me? Why did he say I had nothing to fear?

The room was bright. Its four walls were as white as my face and a light fixture above me kept flashing. With limited mobility, I could move my head left and right just far enough to make out a metal chair positioned in the middle of the room. What were they going to do to me?

As I attempted to roll myself back and forth, in hopes of being freed from my restraints, I found that a dull sensation crept up my back. From my tail bone all the way up to my shoulder blades I felt an acute pain that would eventually go away when I stopped moving. The pain was not overpowering, but it felt obnoxious enough to make me stop momentarily; and when the pain subsided I would start thrashing again; stopping again when the pain came back.

About twenty or so minutes into fighting my pain receptors as much as I was fighting the leather straps, I was startled by the sound of a knock at the door. It was a steel, one-sided door, with no way of exiting from within. From the other side, I heard a latch clicking as the door sprang to life and slowly opened—revealing the last face I ever expected to see again.

"I trust you're feeling better now."

Rolling myself as much as possible, ignoring the dull pain that ensued, I stared back at him. Closing the door, the aging man proceeded to sit down on the metal chair. His black suit creased as he folded his legs over.

"By now, I imagine you've figured out how you got here," he said. When he smiled, his face creased as much as his pants. "And you're probably wondering why."

I stopped squirming and my nostrils flared. The fabric stuck in my mouth was soaked in moisture and the sensation running up and down my back refused to go away.

"Remember, my young friend," he said. "I told you that you have nothing to fear here." And with that, The Chancellor got up from the chair and made his way over to me. He scanned my body with his dark eyes. Then, bending forward, he removed the hard cloth from my mouth.

"Relax, my child. This was necessary to prevent you from biting down on your tongue while we finished your baptism."

The last part of his sentence sounded distantly familiar, like I had heard it before. He retraced his steps and fell back onto the chair. Although I was free to speak again, I chose not to.

"You see," The Chancellor said. "You were drugged, so that we could complete the process. You now bear the Crest of The Order on your back."

Finally I did speak, but out of all things possible, all I could muster was "*Oh.*"

The dull throbbing sensation that had crept up my backside was from the mark of The Order. A series of Old-World-style tattoos that would spread across my shoulders and run down my back. A traditional and intensive process dating back to the very first days of The Program. Inscribed in black ink across my shoulder blades were the Latin words *Baptizsatus est in Sanguine.* Underneath this was an incredibly large depiction of a Reaper spanning from either side of my back down to my lumbar. Held in its left skeletal hand was the Latin word *Vitae,* and held in the other hand was a large scythe with the word *Mortem* inscribed on its sharp blade. Below even this graphic display was yet another phrase just above my tailbone. Written in Latin were the words *Non modo in minibus habebat messorem decernere vitae aut mortem: Held in his hands, only the Reaper can decide life or death.* During the Dark Ages, in early European folklore, the Reaper was believed to be the only one who held final judgment over a man's life, even more so than God Himself. And I was now the Reaper.

The Chancellor left his chair again and made his way back to me. He reached into his jacket and pulled out a knife. Its steel blade glistened under the room's intense light. With a few short strokes he had cut me loose from the leather bindings. I sat up on the cold table and massaged my sore wrists and ankles, watching intently as The Chancellor walked over toward the door. He knocked once on its metal frame. Shortly after, the door creaked open. Before leaving, he turned back to me and put a finger up in the air as if he had just remembered a fleeting thought.

"Oh, and if you're wondering where your clothes got to," he said. "Just knock on the door and they will be returned. I trust you will like your graduation gift."

And with that, The Chancellor had disappeared, leaving me alone in the small room to make sense of everything. On the table, I couldn't help but to reach my hand around and touch my sore back. Scar tissue had already begun to heal over and I could feel the fleshy indentations from the artist's renderings. It reminded me of my own scar just inside my right hand. I was the artist for that doing.

After spending another five minutes licking my wounds and in deep contemplation, laughing at myself over fearing I was to be killed, I hopped off the table. The ground felt cold beneath my naked feet as I made my way over to the door, ready to receive my clothes and return back to my quarters—ready to forget this bewildering event.

My knuckles bounced off the metal door three times, and after a few seconds, I heard the clicking of a latch and the door slowly crept open.

As I went to accept my clothes, I was blindsided by a man of similar height as me. Rushing through the door, he threw his body into mine and knocked me down against the hard concrete floor. Still disoriented from being drugged, it took me a moment to realize what else had happened.

Towering over me was a man wearing a stunning black and white suit—*my suit.* The unknown assailant had on my clothing, and I knew this because of the gold pendant displayed over the left breast-pocket of the suit. My mother had given it to me one day after I came home crying. My face was bruised, having been beat up by neighborhood kids. She told me that the pendant was from my father and it would keep me safe, but that was all she would say.

The man pulled out a long knife and licked it. His teeth were discolored and his eyes flashed wildly. Backing up a few feet, the man motioned with his other hand for me to get up. Doing so, I had just barely enough time to gain my footing before he spun around and kicked me square in the face. I was thrown back onto the floor, harder than the first time, and my head slammed against the wall.

As I got up again, he nearly sent me back to the floor, but this time I was quicker. Catching his foot with both hands, I yanked him toward me. He lost his footing and fell backwards.

By the time the man recovered and was back on his feet, I had already taken up a defensive stance. With my feet shoulder-width apart, one arm in front of my stomach and the other extended outward with fingers curled out like a claw, I was ready to take him on.

Pointing the sharp knife at me and then pulling it up to his neck as if slitting his own throat, he tried taunting me. I had never seen this man before in The Program, although I only knew of a small number of others, mainly contacts and teachers, but I did not believe in coincidences; especially when those coincidences were wearing *my* clothing.

Making the first move, the man lunged forward with the knife, thrusting it toward my side. But I was quicker, and instead, as his arm came forward I pinned it between my own and my body, and slammed the top of my skull into his face. Again, I let the man fall back a few feet and recover as I waited vigilantly for him to make another pass at me.

From the precise blow I had given him, I knew that his nose was broken. With both thumbs he took a moment to set the bone back into place. It made a slight crunching sound as he did so.

Turning his attention back to me, the man glared. There I was, standing alone. Cold and naked, I had never felt so safe before in my life. The result of years of training was flowing through my veins like an infectious disease and I was ready to take him on—I was ready to take *everyone* on.

This time, I made the first move. For the next minute we exchanged a series of blows as both of us blocked and parried each other's advances. When we were done, we both found ourselves facing each other in silence again. Small traces of blood dripping from either of us as we stood there patiently waiting for someone to make the next move. Both our eyes were transfixed on each other. It was like staring into a mirror.

Finally, he moved first and lunged toward me. Ducking his superman punch as he jumped at me, I rolled forward on the floor, dodging him completely. Grabbing the metal chair that had since been thrown against the wall, I swung it against the man's back. He went face-first into the wall and I heard his nose crack again.

Without giving him a chance to recover this time, I thrust the chair's four legs into the drywall, pinning the man into it. As he tried to free himself, I kicked the chair even deeper into the wall. He started gasping for air, his sternum no doubt having collapsed into his lungs. Taking the knife from the man's hand I threw it to the ground. Extending one hand across his chin and the other behind his ear I snapped his neck, severing the spinal cord at the base of his skull.

With all the strength I could muster I dislodged the metal chair from the wall and watched as the man's lifeless body slopped onto the floor. Who was this man? Some hapless, half-witted strong man from a poor village nearby? His muscles built up from long years of day labor, and his knuckles scarred from nights of drunken brawls? I'd probably never know, but as I rolled his body over, something shiny fell out of the jacket. It was a silver key fob. An idea popped into my head and I began to search the rest of the jacket. Beneath the pocket, lining the inside of the black jacket, was a white envelope.

It was blank. Sitting down on the chair, I proceeded to open the envelope. Doing so revealed a carefully written letter—and reading it—I found that it was addressed to me.

> *Congratulations on successfully completing your Final Challenge,*
>
> *Inside this jacket you will find the contents of items that will aid you greatly toward your first mission as a Freelancer.*
>
> *Included is a credit card with enough transferable funds for you to find temporary housing, cash, and a key to an Aston Martin that will take you anywhere in Europe you wish to travel to.*
>
> *Please take a week to situate yourself and keep the cell phone that we've provided close to you as we will contact you.*
>
> *Again, Congratulations & Best of Luck*

When I was done reading the letter, I re-read it again. Tilting the paper left to right, watching as the gold-platted words shimmered under the room's bright light, I couldn't help but feel overjoyed. I was finally done with my training and would join ranks among the other Freelancers. I was free to move about the world again.

Returning to the dead body, I resumed my probing of the black suit, searching for the *items* mentioned by the letter. In the left outer-pocket I uncovered a nondescript black cell-phone. There were no labels on it, save for the tiny white numbers written on its buttons. On the other outer pocket, on the right side, I found what appeared to be an authentic passport. Turning over its blue cover, I found a picture of myself taking up the left side; and information about me on the right; the information was fake.

Searching the inner pocket opposite to the one containing the envelope, I recovered a black leather wallet and a glossy credit card just as the letter said I would. The only thing written on it were the words *Personal use* in the center. It too shone in the light as I tried bending it. In the field, during training ops, I would sometimes come across such black cards. Exclusive to The Program alone, these cards contained enough funds to be transferred from anywhere in the world in a matter of seconds. I threw it to the side with the other items.

Sure enough, nearly every pocket of my jacket contained something mentioned in the letter. In total, I had found the key fob, the letter, a fake passport, the phone, the wallet, credit card, and a wad of Euros. To keep it safe, I slipped my pendant inside the wallet. I even took the knife that the man had tried to kill me with. It was a stiletto knife and I liked it.

After I was certain that I had gone through all the pockets, I began undressing the body. Stripping off the clothes, I proceeded to dress myself. In a way, I was wearing the clothes of a dead man; but in another way, I already was one. Buttoning up my dress-shirt, I took one last look back into the room, scanning its small interior in case I had missed anything. Since the door had been left ajar, I slipped through it, wary of another surprise waiting for me on the other side.

With haste, sort of knowing where I was going, I made my way up a flight of stairs, through a hallway, and soon I was back outside again. The coolness of the night was there to greet me, brushing up against my sweaty forehead. The stars were sprinkled above, and I had changed my own stars.

I knew I had nothing to fear, trusting the words of The Chancellor, but something in the pit of my stomach was telling me otherwise, fearing that, having completed my training, I was no longer welcome here in the isolated compound outside of Beivrus.

Stealing through the vacant compound under the cloak of darkness, I made my way back to the barracks. The shear clearness of the sky made it look glossy, yet transparent, generating an illusion of an awesome aura; one of complete solitude and remoteness from everyone and everything.

Back inside, I quickly retrieved what little remnant of personal belongings I had, knowing full-well that this was no longer my home. Knowing that, after ten long years of living here, this would be the last time I would ever see this room again.

However, in entering the sleepy building, I was dismayed to find that my room was locked tight. I had already been forgotten. Searching for my door key, I instead found the key to the vehicle. Taking this as a sign, I doubled back outside for the garage.

I had no trouble in gaining entry into the concrete building. Sitting adjacent to the training facility, I slipped in through an unlocked door. Clicking the key fob, it led me to a nearby Aston Martin already parked facing the garage door. While sporty, it was not overly flashy. It should blend in nicely as the car of an up-and-coming European elite.

Sparing no time, for fear of something else going awry, I yanked down the chains, opening up the wide garage door, and getting into the stylish convertible, I quickly sped off. Just as I had done that day in the hospital after the car accident, I couldn't help myself from glancing back at the compound one last time. This had been my fraternal sheltering for the past ten years, where I had learned to survive and adapt to a world that had long since forgotten about me.

I looked ahead as the car picked up more speed—its engine roaring as the gears moved up—knowing full-well that not only was I leaving the past, but that I was also heading toward the future. *My* Future.

CHAPTER SIX

D riving past the quiet countryside as I left the battered region of Beivrus, and then Serbia itself, seemed like a blur to me. It wasn't long before the sun began to rise from the darkness and revealed its glowing presence as I left Eastern Europe. With a slew of fake passports and documents in as many different colors as a small box of crayons, driving through countries in Europe was like driving from state to state in the US.

The sun to my back, and the unknown, laying just beyond the horizon before me took my breath away.

The letter had said that I could go anywhere I wished in Europe. I decided that my destination was to be Italy. I had always been fond of the *old country*. It had a rich culture and even richer foods. A few years back I was assigned to a job in this country. The target was living along the southern coast next to the Mediterranean in a small city named Reggio di Calabria—ever since, I dreamed of returning. Its beautiful and charming atmosphere called out to me instantly. One day, if I ever get out of this life, I wish to go back there permanently.

By the time I had crossed over into Northern Italy, it was high noon and the sun was starting to creep up over the silver car as it continued to speed through the streets. My eyelids were heavy and it took an occasional slap to keep myself awake. Giving into my sleep-deprived state, I stopped at the next town I came across. It was the historic city of Udine, which had played its part in World War I with its rustic-walled palisades of when it had once been the central theatre of the Italian High Command.

It wasn't long until I found a hotel and pulled off into its parking lot. Having paid the old gentleman at the front, I grabbed the key and dragged myself over to my room. Inside, I bolted down both of the door locks and tossed about a thousand Euros taken out of my pockets along with the credit card onto the nightstand by the bed. Throwing myself onto the white sheets, I quickly drifted off and everything went black.

It's unbecoming of you, Brendan, my mother had once said after she caught me stealing gum from a store. She would say this anytime I did something wrong and wag a shaky finger over my face. Although she never hit me or took me over her leg, those words hurt—and seeing the look in her eyes hurt worse. We had an unspoken agreement never to hurt each other, and I would often break that agreement. Even to this day those words still ring through my ears just before I pull the trigger or sometimes in sporadic, odd intervals when I'm in a deep sleep. *It's unbecoming of you, Brendan.*

The distant chiming of church bells woke me the following morning. While just a faint clamor in the background, it woke me all the same. I was a light-sleeper. The rising sun pierced an open window and blind-ed me. Rolling to the other side, I was once again brought to the re-alization that I was wearing clothes taken from a corpse. Who that man was, or where he was now, did not matter to me. It was irrelevant. What *was* relevant was my next move.

Grabbing the crumpled up pile of Euros and unbolting the locks, I proceeded to leave the room. At the entrance of the hotel I was greeted by the same old gentleman with a wispy smile strewn across his dry face. Giving him a healthy tip and thanking him for his hospitality I walked out to the parking lot.

Being too lethargic to do so last night, I was curious to see what was inside the trunk of the Aston Martin. Checking over both my shoulders I popped the trunk and swung it open just far enough for me to get a good look at what was inside. I opened my mouth and let out a laugh.

To my astonishment, I was greatly relieved to find a duffel bag filled with my clothes from the barracks. It had my suits and undergar-ments folded up neatly. Lying next to the duffel bag in the trunk was a black suitcase. Its exterior was metallic feeling and the hinges made a popping sound as I unlatched it. Opening up the briefcase I was very pleased to find a set of semi-automatic pistols with extra magazines. Nestled into dark fabric beside the pair of guns were two silencers. My body full of elation, I closed the trunk door and hopped back into the car. Heading south, I continued toward my destination, doubling my speed and smiling from ear to ear.

With how fast the Aston Martin was, it was only a matter of hours until I found myself in the peripheries of the coastal city. My eyes flashed and my heartbeat picked up. I was back in Reggio.

Almost twice the size of Udine, I would have no difficulty in laying low for the next five days.

By the time I reached the heart of Reggio, it was well into the after-noon, and with it being the winter season in Southern Europe, I knew that the sunlight would be fast receding. After driving around for an-other ten minutes or so, I spotted a hotel that stood nestled in between a couple of boutique stores and what appeared to be a post-office on the opposite side of the street. It was extremely close to the promenade, a small garden section famous in the city, comprised of vibrant rare magnolias and exotic palm trees.

The hotel itself was white and stood a solid five stories high, shad-owing all the other buildings around it. Each floor had a giant railed deck that extended over the cobblestone street below. A set of enormous, matching white pillars stood at the grand entrance and gold-plated vines were coiled around them like giant serpents. The stately hotel was but a few blocks from the coastline and the street upon which it was situated ran parallel to it. This hotel was special, not because I had been here before or that it was opulent, but because it possessed the largest indoor parking garage in the entire city. Heavily guarded by twenty-four hour surveillance, I needn't worry about my car and its devious items going missing. I was a calculating man who made calculated decisions and would not screw anything up during my stay here.

"Come posso aiutarla?" called out a young guy inside the lobby. He was standing behind a wide marble counter and smiled as I approached him. Behind him was a security camera, and behind me were two more pointed toward the lobby doors and the entrance into the parking garage which was connected to the hotel. Glancing around, I took note of all the exits.

"*Quanto a notte, per favore?*" I asked, wondering what the cost was per night.

After I got past the lobby doors and the man could size me up, his smile receded to the edge of his mouth and he squinted his dark eyes. It just dawned on me how I looked; I hadn't bathed for several days and was still wearing the same pair of clothing. Still, I flashed the thick wad of Euros out in front and grinned back.

As I approached the counter though, I was momentarily cut off by a group of rowdy girls who sprinted across the lobby to exit the building and meet a taxi that had been parked along the street.

After the sudden intrusion had passed I made my way to the lavish counter. My stomach was making loud noises. The last thing I had consumed was that bitter glass of scotch.

Throwing a stack of Euros onto the marble top I watched as the man straightened up.

"250 *Euro a notte*," he said apologetically, lowering his eyes and avoiding contact.

After handing the young man enough cash for the next five days his beaming smile returned and he offered to show me the suite himself. Taking him up on his offer I held the duffel bag and the brief case close to me and followed him.

It began to drizzle outside as we made our way through the spiraling hotel stairs and halls. Each floor had a fire-escape connecting to a faux window, and there were security cameras on either ends of the lengthy halls. Before too much time had passed, we had arrived at my suite. Back in the lobby, I had requested for a room on the third-floor close to the southwest forecastle; not because it faced the beautiful promenade outside, but because it was situated next to one of those fire-escapes. As I said, I'm a calculating guy.

Having tipped the man, I closed the door and locked it. After I was certain that he had left, I proceeded to place my baggage onto the bed. I took out the cell-phone and flipped it open.

Nothing.

After being on the move for the past couple days, I finally had the time to slow down and thoroughly examine everything. It was time to make sense of it all, but not before ordering room service. It felt like a lifetime ago since I had sipped the Chancellor's drugged Scotch.

With the remnants of my meal sitting on the room's small table, I emptied my pockets and placed everything onto the bed. I spent the rest of the evening sorting through it all, especially the passport and learning and memorizing my new alias. I was Johnathon Goodwell from San Francisco, California; age 26.

Unlatching the hinges for the second time, I opened up the black briefcase and examined my new arsenal of weapons. Having ripped off a few sheets of toilet paper from the bathroom, I cleaned the already clean guns. You can never be *too clean* with guns, or anything else in life, I have learned.

Before turning in for the night, I couldn't help but re-read the letter with its gold-platted inscription. Written by The Chancellor himself, I tried to decipher its semi-cryptic meaning.

After a while though, I put the letter to the side and reached over to turn out the light.

CHAPTER SEVEN

Having done so much the past four days, pushing my body beyond its physical limits, I had temporarily *checked out*. My stamina was depleted and the out-of-gas light was flashing. I spent the following days holed up inside my luxurious suite, hibernating like the monstrous bear that was inside me. For the remainder of my sojourn, two things occupied my time—sleeping and waiting. I was a volatile volcano, lying dormant until it was time to erupt and destroy once more.

It rained for the majority of my stay in Reggio. Tucked inside the room, I was safely locked away from the outside world. Blissfully enjoying the solitude at hand, before it was time to depart from this long-sought vacation.

I liked it here, and even though I spent most of my time behind a closed door, away from the world, this was different—it was of my own free-will. At least that's how it seemed. By now I had grown used to living behind closed doors, in one form or another, always hiding behind the black shrouds and the fringes of society. In all honesty, it comforted me.

Growing up, I was never fond of others, as they were never fond of me, and so during the early years of my limited childhood I had made a pact with humanity—an unspoken, mutual agreement—to keep away from each other as much as possible and at all costs.

The rain had grown relentless, and on the fourth day, lying there in the warmth of my over-sized bed, I gave up trying to fall back asleep. A coastal storm had picked up, throwing heavy rain against the room's stained-glass windows, pounding them with excessive force. Each flash of lightning lit up the entire suite, revealing an unkempt room full of illegal contraband scattered about the floor.

Relinquishing the idea of any immediate sleep, I turned my undivided attention toward the growling sounds made from within my stomach. I was famished, having eaten little since the meal on the first night. Directly below, two floors down, was the hotel's restaurant.

Before leaving the safety of the suite, however, there was something I had to do. Walking over to the distant wooden desk, I fumbled for the latches and opened the suitcase. The metal pistols shone through the dark as I stretched for the nearest light-switch.

I reached in and took one of the guns, screwing on a silencer to the end of the barrel and pushing in a full magazine. Shoving it deep down inside my new suit, I took the black suitcase over to the cabinet. Inside was a stainless steel safe. I placed the briefcase, along with the passport, inside the safe and closed the cabinet door.

Leaving my suite for the first time since arriving at the hotel, I took the long way down. Letting my muscles stretch and unkink themselves, I took the longest, most indirect route to the restaurant on the first floor, glancing through every window I passed and noticing that the storm outside was increasing in intensity.

I was relieved to find the small restaurant mostly empty. There were but a few tables of dining couples and a lonely, old man sitting at the distant bar. He looked over at me when I entered through the wooden doors, but we never acknowledged each other.

The storm must have forced everyone else to recede back into their rooms, leaving me to a quiet atmosphere of delicious smells and intense tranquility.

In no great time after finding a suitable booth, a waitress emerged from the kitchen doors. In a soft-spoken Italian accent, she took my order and vanished back into the kitchen. Left alone again, I slung my arm over the booth rail and took a sip of wine. It was pinot noir, my mother's favorite.

After downing two whole glasses of the thick wine, the waitress had reappeared from the set of kitchen doors, bringing with her my meal between her arms. The aroma from it was almost more than I could bear.

I had just begun cutting into my chicken penne when, from the corner of my eye, I noticed somebody watching me, and it wasn't the old man. Looking up from my plate, I glanced across the room toward another booth directly ahead of me on the other end of the room.

Living in the shadows for so long, it was easy for me to spot a pair of eyes staring at me. The booth was occupied by the same group of people who had so brazenly cut me off a few day ago back in the lobby. There was a young woman staring at me with fixed eyes. Unlike her other friends, she appeared to be the youngest, probably early twenties. She had dark brown, almost black, hair that was braided down over her right shoulder.

Stealing a look at her, I quickly flicked my eyes back toward the table. I was not expecting this. Tilting my head to the side, I considered the options. Was she from another organization? Was she fucking Interpol? I slowly reached into my suit and clutched the gun, pushing down on the safety button until I heard it click.

These days, I did not know what to expect. In my line of work, you *never* know what to expect. And after nearly being killed in that small room by my doppelgänger, one can never be too cautious.

I glanced at the kitchen doors. No movement. I looked back at the wooden doors I had come in through. Nothing. The old man was still draining his sorrows away at the bar. My hand began to shake and I could feel the barrel of the gun tapping against my chest.

Soon my heart was pounding, and just as I was about to flip the table over, the unexpected happened. The young woman smiled at me. I momentarily stared back. My face was blank. Her smile grew wider and it made her eyes glisten; they were warm and green.

I jerked my head back and released the gun. Wiping my sweaty hand on a table napkin, I took up the silverware and resumed my cutting—not daring to look back across the room for the remainder of the evening.

After the meal was done and my stomach had ceased to make any more noises, I finished my fourth glass of wine. By then the green-eyed girl and her small party had left, along with the rest of the other restaurant diners. The only souls who remained in the room were me and the old man, who still appeared able to withstand a couple more rounds of whatever he was drinking.

Having returned to the safety of my hotel suite, I was once again left to my own accord. Looking up at the dark ceiling, I tried to fall asleep. The heavy storm from earlier had since calmed down to a mere drizzle and I could hear the beads of rain as they bounced off the windows.

Folding my arms behind my head, I lay there looking up; staring pensively into the darkness. The room was a black sea and I was lost in it. Neither the captain, nor his first-mate—I was a simple stowaway, left to endure the unending ravishes of the infinite black sea. Each wave took me further and further away from land. And further from salvation.

Thumbing the fleshy scar hewn across my right palm, I listened to the gentle rain. Doing what I've done all these years has made me impassive as a person. At a young age I succeeded in building up a concrete wall around myself, making me impervious to any emotion. For The Program—for me—emotions seed vulnerability, and vulnerability produces weakness. Back in the restaurant, I was not just turning my back on a silly girl. I was turning my back on a life I knew was not possible, one I did not have the luxury of experiencing.

Even in the car accident, watching as my mother was dying, I felt indifferent. Not indifferent to her dying, but indifferent to the pain I experienced seeing her die. These days wearing such a brutal scar on my hand is the only thing that still makes me feel human in such an inhuman world.

Taking a deep breath, I resigned myself. There really was no rest for the weary. My eyes finally closed as I continued to drift farther out to sea.

CHAPTER EIGHT

The sound of laughter coming from the hallway woke me up the following day. Sitting up on the bed, I noticed that the room was unusually warm. Living in the mountainous region of Beivrus for so long, I've grown accustomed to cold temperatures and adjusted the room's central air to fifteen degrees Celsius.

Looking around, I noticed that the room was still dark, and it did not take me long to realize that the power had gone out; probably during the night too. While sleeping, the storm must have intensified enough to kill the power. And glancing outside the window, it appeared that our hotel was not the only building without electricity.

The street below was empty, with the exception of an occasional passerby zipping by on a compact motorcycle. Even the sky seemed to be barren of any trafficking birds. It was like a ghost-town.

This was the sixth day since I departed from Beivrus. Knowing that it was my last, and that tomorrow I would be awaiting the inevitable phone call, I wanted to go out and explore. I wanted to see something enjoyable during my stay here—not just handguns and fake passports—I wanted to experience something *real*.

The storm was blown away, leaving behind a high-pressure atmosphere of warm weather—even for January—and cloudless, blue skies. Because the outside world seemed empty of other people, I decided it was time to venture outside and see the world through my own eyes.

Before leaving the suite, I swung the cabinet door open, but something in my chest was telling me I didn't need protection. Wearing only the clothes on my back, I left the safety of the dark hotel, venturing out just far enough to still be able to keep visual on the hotel's giant white cap.

Outside, the sun was high and there were no puffy, gray clouds to block its radiating heat. Beads of sweat began to form over my head as I made my way past the Patagonia store next to the hotel. The storm left behind a cloud of misting air that created a watery layer over the broad green leaves of the exotic palms and vibrant pinks and whites of the magnolia flowers. Staring into the tiny droplets, I could see my reflection and my tired face.

It felt nice being on the other side of a concrete structure for once, and not because I had to end somebody's life either. The absence of people and vehicles out on the cobblestone street created an artificial atmosphere that still seemed as real as touching my own skin. It was quiet and blissful as I walked past the Patagonia. The only sound was that of a distant church bell announcing the hour. It was moments like these that made me cherish life; a sort of paradox when you get down to it.

Making my way down the hill, I passed more shops and buildings, which all seemed equally as vacant and hollow. I did not pass a single soul as I wandered down further, mindful of the giant white cap still within eyesight behind me.

After another minute or so, I could begin to see the parallel line of the blue horizon. It amazed me how beautiful and serene the sandy shoreline was. The sea was a colorful mixture of green and blue and its glossy surface shimmered under the bright January sun. If I tilted my head to the side just right it was a tremendous spectacle of bright white spanning the entire width of the Italian beach. A few tiny boats broke through the glass like black dots.

With the exception of an occasional tourist, the boardwalk stretching across the entire beach was just as empty as the streets. Farther away, it tapered off into a narrow pier, which stood like a toothpick against the enormous bay.

At long last my black, polished shoes made contact with the gritty sand. Between the shore and I were but a few sparse patches of vacationers and locals sprawled out along the beach, accepting the sun's heat with the Italian January's abnormally warm temperature reinforcing it as they tanned their bodies thoroughly. And although we did not speak to one another as I continued closer to the water's edge, it was as if we had made an unspoken pact with one another. We were all here to get away from something and to enjoy the harmony that was at hand. Nothing needed to be said, for no words could be found to describe it. This was our blissful getaway from reality.

As I made my way to a plump mound of white sand, I sat down, letting the sand further creep up against my suit. I looked out ahead, staring idly beyond the shoreline, transfixed by its awesome stillness. If beauty had a visual description, this would be it.

An hour easily lapsed by as I continued in my stupor, marveling at the calmness and tranquility of the vast blue-green sea. My skin tingled and my eyes started to swell—something I had not felt for a very long time.

Apparently, I was not the only one who stole away from the hotel to seek the shore's quietude. In the far distance, I watched as a tiny shape ran alongside the beach and became larger as the shape got closer to me. It wasn't long until I could make out the shape to be someone I recognized.

There was no crowd of rowdy friends with her though. She was alone, jogging along the white beach, her hair done in a tight pony tail. With each stride she took, her hair moved as elegantly as her body. It looked effortless.

She too must have noticed me there. As she got closer, kicking up tiny clumps of sand in her wake, the young woman turned and smiled at me. As was done that night in the restaurant, our eyes connected. I had no gun this time, and was completely defenseless. Her deep green eyes stared right through me and I felt vulnerable. Coming even closer as she jogged by, the girl smiled and waved at me. Her lips parted and, in an Italian accent, she said *hi*. But also like the previous night, I could not endure the alien moment for long, and instead, I forced my head away. It was a life I was not familiar with any longer and could never know again.

Before long, the moment was gone—*she* was gone—and I was once again left to my own, with nothing but an empty sea in front of me. My heart sank. Soaking up what remained of the peaceful day, I tried to enjoy it, knowing full well that moments like these were not meant to last forever, and that, like all good things in life, they would eventually come to an end. Nature is infinite, but happiness is not.

The following morning, the sound of ringing woke me up. As I sat up on the bed, I realized that my head was throbbing. It pounded profusely and seemed to pulsate in cadence with the strange ringing sound. Rubbing my temples didn't seem to alleviate any of the pain either.

The ringing sound kept going, and I slowly came to my senses, yawning as I looked around. The room was no longer dark and it felt cool again. To my side, the cell-phone was vibrating as it continued to ring. Reaching a tired hand over the nightstand, I grabbed the phone and opened it. *Unknown Caller*, the screen read. Pulling it up to my ear, I gulped. This was it.

"I'm terribly sorry to disturb you a day early, mate," a man's voice said.

He had an English accent. "*Things* got moved ahead of schedule by thirty-six hours and we need you to get here as soon as you can. I'm going to text you the address on this phone."

I began to speak, but the voice cut me off.

"If you can, catch a ride from the nearest airport. No time to explain. Good luck, mate."

The voice on the other end disappeared and I heard a *click*.

I must have been sleeping heavily and it took me a minute or two to fully comprehend what was just said. But when I did, it hit me like a bullet and the air left my lungs.

The man had said, *I'm terribly sorry to disturb you a day early*. How was this possible? Today was the seventh day...at least I thought it was.

But the taste of pinot noir was still fresh in my mouth and I soon realized what the throbbing in my head was coming from. I then came to the stark realization that yesterday hadn't happened. The empty streets. The Beach. The *girl*. It was all just a dream.

Nonetheless, the call had been made, and my time had come. It was time for me to leave Reggio.

A perk of traveling light is that it did not take long for me to pack up and vacate the suite. Within seconds the text message came, announcing my next location. I made haste to collect my things and book it. With the suitcase in one hand, and the duffel bag in the other, I left the room and made my way downstairs. I was relieved to find the lobby empty.

After checking out at the marble counter—with a different young gentleman—I started for the garage door, but was called back to the desk. The man handed me a white slip of paper. Assuming it was the receipt, I tucked it into my wallet and darted for the door.

It did not take me long to find the Aston Martin, parked idly close to the garage's entrance. Throwing my stuff in the trunk, I left Reggio.

Being just a stone's throw away from the island of Sicily, I used the Catania International Airport. Leaving my luxurious car to the whims and ravishes of airport security, I took the 10:15 for Berlin, Germany, not knowing what lay ahead of me and if I'd ever return to this place again.

Given my small cache of weapons, it was not difficult for me to gain access past airport security. It wouldn't even matter if I had a grenade, which I *have* done before. All it took was a simple diversion; a quick distraction so that I could pass unnoticed. Sometimes it was as small as a bathroom fire. Sometimes it was a phony bomb threat. Either way, I knew how to get through an airport terminal unscathed.

The flight itself took less than four hours, and if it wasn't for the turbulence over the Alps, it would have been closer to three. Touching down in the Tegal International Airport was a big contrast to the mild Mediterranean weather of Italy and Sicily. Traveling just a mere four hours north the climate of northern Europe changed dramatically and the temperature dropped. The weather in Berlin was nothing short of dismal and the plane was greeted by cold rain pelting its windows.

It was high noon when I left the airport, but it felt like night. A row of taxis was outside and, taking the closest one, I read the driver the address supplied on the phone and we hurried off. The rain continued to slap the sides of the car as we made our way through the industrious city. It took us about twenty minutes, passing by modern skyscrapers that stood adjacent to aging buildings that had survived the bombing raids of another life ago.

The address took the taxi to an old, two-story *Menden Hausen*, which served as an intermediate safe house, one of many scattered throughout the world. The Program had many like these that provided sanctuary for its many internal operations and other affiliate services.

I told the driver to go past it and park the car up a block. Although I was sure that nobody had followed me here, I was not going to take my chances. Handing the driver the cab fare, I pulled my jacket over my neck and trudged the rest of the way.

From the outside, the meetinghouse looked quaint. Its gray paint blended in with the other drab buildings alongside it. A film of dust had a great start on its many windowsills, giving it the appearance of a long-forgotten building. The windows themselves were caked in a layer of black paint, hiding whatever stirred behind the walls.

Before getting out of the taxi, I had called back to whomever I spoke with on the phone earlier, announcing my imminent arrival. After walking around to the back of the house I pulled open the screen door and knocked three times. The rain kept nailing my exposed hair as I waited.

Within moments, I was met by a middle-aged man. He asked me who I was, and after pulling up my right sleeve and showing him a tattoo, he smiled. On my forearm bore a small black inscription written in Latin. *Ordo Sicariorum*—Order of Assassins. Moving aside, the man glanced over my shoulder and allowed me entry.

I entered the safe house and was glad I was spared from the onslaught of rain. Inside was what I expected it to be. Looking just as plain and unchanged as the outside, it still showed the scars of its former glory. The man led me through the kitchen and past a short hallway to the left. He opened the first door we came across and beckoned with a hand for me to go first. A set of shaky stairs led the two of us down into the basement.

Acting as a forward operating base, the basement was uncharacteristically large; much larger than the actual house itself. Contrasting greatly with the upstairs's ancient vanity, the downstairs was packed with the interworking of a clandestine organization.

The first room I entered—the main room—was filled with steel tables, and all sizes of hardwired computers that sat on top of them. Retrofitted with communication receivers, a table stood to the side of the room. A couple of dispatch boxes were flashing, and voices in different languages were going off on either box. There was but a single person sitting at the table, speaking to each of the receivers. I watched as he rolled his chair to each station like clockwork.

I knew instantly where I was, having been told long ago of this elusive place. Interestingly enough, this safe house served as the entire underground Berlin network, and I was in the heart of it.

I felt a hand on my shoulder. "Welcome to our humble abode," the middle-aged man said.

He was British and I soon connected him as the voice over the phone. Pointing a thick finger to another table, he led me to the center of the room. A wide circular table occupied most of the floor. On top rested a large blueprint sheet of some enormous building. The top of the layout had a title written in German. *Abteilung fur Internationale Wahrungsfonds.*

Smiling at me, the Englishman tossed two photographs onto the table next to the blueprint.

"This cheeky fellow is Howard Fronz," he said, pointing to the picture on the left. It depicted a brown-haired man wearing wide-rimmed glasses.

"And blondie over here," he said, tapping on the other, "is Francine Bernstein. She's Mr. Fronz's assistant and *mistress*." His face gleamed having said the last part.

I took both the pictures and scanned over them, squinting.

"These blokes work at the IMF building here in good ol' Berlin." This time the Englishman pointed down at the blueprint. It was Germany's Department for International Monetary Fund.

When I had their faces burned into my head, I handed the pictures back to him. I then nodded my head toward the other man in the room, who was typing so fast I could barely see his fingers move.

The Englishman looked at me and pulled out a pack of cigarettes from his coat. Rejecting his offer of one, I waited for an answer.

"Who do you think runs the Silk Road, mate?" he asked, lighting one of the pale cigarettes. He used a Zippo lighter that had a Union Jack flag spread across it.

"Is this a double-target operation?" I asked, changing the conversation back to the photographs.

The Englishman paused and took a really long drag of his cigarette. Turning away, he puffed toward the wall.

"I hope that won't be a problem."

I shook my head. Double-targets weren't hard. The difficult part was coordinating both hits at the same time. Reaching out, I grabbed the man's hand and we both shook on it. The deal was made. In The Program it was taught that if you accept a deal, there was no backing out. You either followed through with the hit at all costs, or found yourself to be a target. This was one of the few laws of the underworld.

The rest of the night was spent going over briefing for the operation. If the hits were to be flawless, I was going to need a thorough game plan.

The two targets, I learned, were corrupt IMF employees. But there was no surprise there. A lot of my hits were on other crooked people. I was simply the apex predator thinning out the rest of the food chain. Both Mr. Fronz and Miss Bernstein were laundering funds from one of the Silk Road's many bank accounts. This too was not uncommon. Money gets stolen, and it's skimmed at the top.

Like all other nefarious underground black-markets, the Silk Road is not able to set up legal bank accounts. Lucky for them though, the IMF doesn't care; to them, money is money, and money is power. The downside, however, is that from time to time these bank accounts get skimmed. Everyone knows this and it usually is not a problem. The problem is when people get greedy, and too much is skimmed off from the top. That's when people like me get a phone call.

Entities such as the Silk Road do not have a government body to turn to for justice. Instead, they have organizations such as The Program. We are the governing body. We are justice. In all likelihood, the stolen money would never be recovered, but it was my job to stop the bleeding.

The downside of shaking the Englishman's hand is that I was not going to get paid. Although I was now a Freelancer, able to do my own work for money, this job was going to be done *pro bono*, on behalf of the Program. Because of how extensive the Silk Road was to the under-world, a collapse of it would have a domino effect, reverberating back to us. It is so deep-rooted in all corners of the underworld, that stealing from them is essentially the same as stealing from us.

Nature has a way of maintaining equilibrium. Sometimes things get dirty so that they can become clean again.

As a newcomer to the world of freelancing, The Chancellor must have thought this a great first job for me. To teach an eagle to fly, you have to push it into the air. Looking around, I realized that this building was more than just a safe house. It was the entire underground infrastructure for the Silk Road. Tomorrow I would be gearing up for an assault on the IMF building. Unlike past hits, gaining access to the building would prove very difficult, but still it was not impossible. Nothing, I have since learned, is impossible.

What I did not understand though, is why it was deemed necessary to break into the high-risk building. Doing it this way ran the risk of getting caught or even killed. We didn't have just the building's heavily armed guards to look out for. It was a governing IMF building, and this was one dog to be wary of pulling its chain. It would have been much easier to follow the targets home and take them out quietly from there.

Something didn't seem right about the operation, and I didn't trust the Englishman. But I was not there to ask questions—I was there to kill people—and kill people I would. I was not afraid of dying for I have since learned that there are far worse things to fear than death. I am haunted by the things I have done and witnessed and there will come a day when somebody faster and better will kill me. I have long since accepted my fate in this lonesome world, and truth be told, I embrace with open arms the day I finally leave it.

Sleep was a luxury few of us got to experience, and I was glad to have a taste of it back in Reggio. Having spent the entire night pouring over the giant blueprint, combing over each floor of the building, we finally came to a plan that we both could agree upon. But by then it was dawn. Things move quickly in my world and can pass by at the blink of an eye.

We started to gear up for our assault. A distant window of the basement that had not been completely sealed off revealed the sun's rays as it crept into the underbelly of our covert safe house. Helping the Englishman, we pushed aside a bookshelf that hid a secret room inside the basement's walls. A hollowed out concave, it was a contemporary addition to the old house, and served as an armory.

Inside the small room was a cache of weapons and other contraband. Hung up on metal racks were assault rifles of all sizes, and laid out on tables were various handguns of different calibers. Displayed above the assault rifles were NATO gas masks.

Opening up cabinet doors revealed automatic shotguns fixed with ammunition drums. Underneath the tables were two green boxes of different grenades; the one on the left read *BOOM*, while the one on the right read *FLASH*.

The sheer number of guns in this otherwise invisible room surprised even me. A flickering incandescent bulb lit the room, and I watched as the Englishman dove in first. His bulky frame moved about the room as he grabbed anything he could tuck away under his coat. Given the nature of our operation, only pistols and small arms would be required.

Although I already had my own pair of guns, I picked up a few more just to be safe. These were chrome and had snub-nosed silencers on them. I filled my jacket with as many magazines as my pockets would allow.

"Here," the Englishman said, throwing a black vest at me. "You might need this." It was an armor vest made of some polyester fabric. The Velcro cringed as I fit the vest underneath my jacket. It made me look husky, but this would have to do.

The Englishman then pulled out the boxes of grenades. He handed me two grenades from the box labeled *Flash* and took a few from the other one for himself.

"You never know," he said with a twisted smile. Before we left, he gave me a watch. "You *definitely* will need this."

Armed to the teeth, for what could easily be mistaken as total war readiness, the Englishman and I set out. It was a cold Sunday morning, and we had a jump on the rest of the city. Leaving behind the sanctuary of the safe house, I followed the Englishman out front to a beige car parked along the street. As we got to the doors, he stopped.

"Wait a sec," he said. "Are you sure you're ready?"

The morning air kissed the nape of my neck, and although I was padded in many dense layers, I was still cold. Hearing his words reminded me of my first job. Not only could I see that fat man's face asking me the very same question, but I could also see the blood. THE BLOOD. It made me shiver to think about his plump body and the blood that trailed behind as I dragged him outside the apartment.

I nodded. "Yes."

It was a perfect morning for doing the job. With it being Sunday in an old-world Catholic city, most of the population was either sleeping or getting ready to kneel and pray to their God. My mother had tried to drag me to church before, but the whole kneeling thing never appealed to me. Now, people got on their knees and prayed to me. Now, people clasped their hands together and asked me for forgiveness. I was their god.

Although the sun was peeking through the clouds, it was still lightly raining when we set out through the streets. Neither one of us said much on our way to the IMF building. The Englishman had his arm out the window, switching between puffs of smoke and taking partial drags of his cigarette. The car reeked of it, but even the dense smoke could not mask the smell of apprehension. No job was certain and we lived in an uncertain world.

Large pockets of water lay sprawled out across the streets, causing dirty water to spray the sides of the car each time we went over a pothole.

Having passed through to the other end of the city, we finally reached the sleeping IMF building. Stacked between two other structures, it stood of equal height to either one. In front, on a manicured lawn, stood a row of flagpoles. The tallest, Germany's, dwarfed all the other flags and flapped hard against the wind.

As we drove past the trio of gray buildings, our car reflected off the many mirror-like windows covering the ground floor. Although the building was closed, we knew that it was not empty.

"Sunday fun-day, mate," the Englishman said, pointing to the front. "No security."

Circling around back, we parked about three buildings over in an empty lot. The rain slowed down to a drizzle, hitting our car like tiny needles, and the sun tried making another appearance through the gray sky. We waited in silence inside the car.

A minute went by before the Englishman checked his watch and made a phone call.

"Yeah, I'm here,. Killer's here, too." He turned and winked at me. "The building looks empty from both sides. We're ready when you are."

"Who's that?" I asked.

The Englishman held his hand over the phone, "The distraction."

It was not just the two of us. An operation of this magnitude could not be done by just two people. The Englishman had another operative, waiting on standby, whose job was to create a distraction that would give us enough of a window to complete our task without police intervention.

Something else was said between the two of them and the Englishman chuckled over the phone. Although I wasn't sure what the distraction was going to be, I overheard fragments of the conversation. They were two parts: *car bomb* and *town-square*.

Ending the phone call, the Englishman took out what appeared to be an old police scanner. He proceeded to place it on top of the car's dashboard and fiddled with one of its knobs. After a few tries, the beat-up scanner came to life and chattered away on the analog receiver. A red light kept flashing on the box as a female voice spoke in German.

She was requesting for all available *Landespolizei* to respond to a car bomb explosion outside the Brandenburg Gate. Miraculously enough, nobody was killed. But then again, it was Sunday, and miracles tend to happen on the Sabbath.

The Englishman took a few more drags of his cigarette before flicking it out onto the street. When the female voice was done sputtering commands across the dispatch, the Englishman turned the knob and the machine went silent again. "Lucky them, eh?"

He rolled up his window and I checked my watch. We had just fifteen minutes. Our window had come and it was time to take advantage of it.

The car was left to idle as we hurried over to the back of the IMF building. Stopping just short of its iron doors, we turned our attention to a long metal pipe, which extended from the base up the entire height of the three-story building. As odd as it looked, this metal piping actually contained wiring for the building's electrical grid. Taking my knife I made a large gash in the side of it and with one of the guns I shot out the power-charge meter and all seven of the connector cables. The bank's power was out, along with any hard-wired security measures inside.

At the same time I was doing this, the Englishman had climbed up the fire escape. Shattering the closest window, he climbed inside.

One of the agreements we had made last night was on the time it would take for police to catch wind of our actions and show up in full force. I was meticulous about the time, and got antsy having to wait another minute until the steel doors finally swung open.

"Fourteen minutes," I said as he waved me in.

Although it was dark inside, I was immediately drawn to the three bodies sprawled across the marble floor. Pools of blood were staining their hair and I shot the Englishman a wary eye. They were two office workers and a janitor.

Nonetheless, I helped him drag their bodies over to the side. They were necessary casualties.

"We got less than fourteen minutes," I said.

"Aye."

The Englishman opened a set of wooden doors that led us to a dark hallway. With one of the chrome pistols drawn, I took the safety off and motioned for my partner to lead.

The wide hall was darker than the lobby and the scant light that was able to penetrate through the tinted windows did little to guide us. With one hand on the gun, and the other on the wall, we both fumbled for the right door that would take us to the stairs.

Having found it, we ascended the spiraling flight of stairs, leaping multiple steps to save time. With all the gear on me, I was beginning to sweat, but my heart wasn't racing from running—it was from the adrenaline that was coursing through my veins. At long last, we arrived on the third floor. Twelve and a half minutes left.

Before going through the doors, we took a moment to collect ourselves. Wiping a coat of sweat off my face, I gave the Englishman the go-ahead.

He held up three thick fingers and began to count down. "Three... two...one."

On the third mark, we launched ourselves through the door with guns drawn. The Englishman took up position on the left side of the hallway, while I took up the other. Seeing no sign of movement, we started down the dark corridor, checking each room that we passed.

Given our finite time, we split up to cover more ground; he took the rooms on the left side while I took the offices on the right. All the rooms we checked were empty. Nothing but unused computer desks and bulky file cabinets took up the rooms.

Glancing at my watch I cringed. We were already down to eight minutes left. For some reason the Englishman took longer than anticipated, and after reaching the other end of the hall, I waited for him to finish his side. When he finally did show up, he had a sly grin cocked to the side of his face and was wiping on a handkerchief what looked like blood from a large bowie knife.

"We're all clear, mate," he said, seeing me eyeing his knife.

There was one last door at the end of the hall and as I turned to open it, the door swung open. I had just enough time to avoid getting hit and a young woman's face popped out into the hallway. It didn't take her long to see us, but before she could retreat back inside I shoved my gun into her mouth and yanked her out.

"*Halten sie ruhig*," I whispered into her ear, placing a finger over my lips.

Her body was light and she bounced when I threw her against the wall. Making a shushing noise, I removed the gun from her mouth and pushed it into her sternum. I asked her where Mr. Fronz was. The young woman had brown hair pinned up into a crown braid and she trembled when I asked the question again, this time louder.

"*Wo ist Mr. Fronz?*"

She looked at me and then over at the Englishman who had pressed the barrel of his pistol into her neck. Her brown eyes began to well up instantly, and tears were starting down her youthful face. Staring back at me, the girl moved her arm up and pointed back toward the room she had been forced out of. I let her go and she sighed.

"Danke," the Englishman said.

He put the gun to her stomach and squeezed off three rounds. Letting her go, I watched as the she slumped to the floor. It happened so fast. She sputtered blood out of her mouth and, gasping for air, she grabbed onto my pants. As I pulled her hands off me, I realized that they were covered in blood.

Allowing a couple of precious seconds to melt away, I knelt down before the woman. With two fingers I felt her pulse, but finding none, I motioned with my gun for the Englishman to advance into the room.

After closing her eyes with my hand, I stood. The image of my mother's face came into view and I shut my own eyes. Killing another person was second nature to me—an instinct—but it was with great reluctance that I found myself killing a woman. Letting the image of her pass, I opened my eyes again and proceeded into the dark room.

Stepping inside, I checked my watch. The Englishman was standing in the middle of the room and had just put a fresh magazine into his gun.

"Seven minutes exactly," I said.

"Aye."

The Englishman then took out the two photographs and scanned over them, scratching his head with the gun in the process. He then handed me the pictures and nodded over to three people who were huddled against a filing cabinet by the back wall. Amidst our interrogation outside in the hall, they must have heard us.

As we walked up to bankers, they trembled. The Englishman brought out a flashlight and shone it in their eyes.

"Where did you get that?" I asked.

"I've had it, mate."

My eyes grew. "This whole time?"

"Yep."

Laughing at me, the Englishman took the photographs back out and held them up to the bankers' faces. When he was done, he stood back and turned off the flashlight.

"That bastard in the middle is Mr. Fronz," he said, pointing his gun toward the frightened man. He was wearing wide-rimmed glasses and looked like a comic-book nerd.

Moving his gun to the right, the Englishman pointed at a blonde-haired woman. "The cheeky blonde is Francine the mistress." He winked at her.

The Englishman then waved his gun at the last person. "And I don't know who the fuck this is." He squeezed the trigger and shot the man in the head, killing him instantly. The man's lifeless body fell over onto Mr. Fronz.

"Bitte nicht!" he said, pleading for us to stop. Oddly enough, Francine was the calm one and glared up at us. Leaving Mr. Fronz for the Englishman, I turned my attention back to the watch.

"Five and a half minutes," I said, retracing my steps back over to the doorway to guard our flank. Peering back into the office, I overheard the Englishman. "Where are the files?"

When the banker shook his head, he got a gun pushed into his mouth. The man made a whimpering sound and the Englishman took the gun out.

"Please don't kill us," said Mr. Fronz in broken English.

My partner sighed. "I'm not going to ask you again. Where are the files?" This time he pressed the gun against Francine's head, hard enough that she whined.

"Okay, okay," Mr. Fronz said. "I'll show you. Just please don't hurt her."

The Englishman yanked him off the ground and shoved him over to his desk. "Quickly," he said, placing the gun to the back of his head.

Sobbing, Mr. Fronz cleared off the desk. His hands were trembling uncontrollably as he rummaged through it. At length he came across a key.

"It's behind me," Mr. Fronz said. "The box is behind me."

I kept peering in and out in shifts, watching the hall, and also keeping tabs on the Englishman. He took the gun off Mr. Fronz's head and allowed him to walk back to the distant wall. Pulling down a large canvas painting of a ship titled, *KMS BISMARCK*, revealed a false wall behind it. Mr. Fronz took out the wall and recovered a glass box. Returning to the desk, he laid the box on top of it. Inside appeared to be floppy disks; something rare and unusual to find in such a technologically diverse age as the twenty-first century, and in an international bank building, to say the least.

The Englishman picked up the box with one arm and shot Mr. Fronz in the throat. The banker fell backwards onto his chair and bled out. Seeing the bloody execution of her lover, Francine began to wail.

She got up and tried to run off, but as she made for the door I stabbed her in the stomach with the stiletto knife. As she fell forward, I caught her and leaned her against the wall. Gesturing for her to keep quiet, I put my gun to her temple and pulled the trigger.

Before I could collect her identification, I heard a door being opened out in the hallway. Glancing outside, I saw four men emerging from the stairwell. Although it was dark, I could see the unmistakable shine of handguns as the men headed down the hall toward me.

"We got company," I called back to the Englishman.

He nodded, and setting the glass box down, he flipped the desk over and pulled out another gun. "Let's make this quick, mate."

As I took up position alongside the Englishman, I glanced down at the watch again.

"Three minutes and...seventeen seconds." My stomach churned and my skin startled to crawl.

Lying between us was the glass box, but no sooner had I started for it, that the Englishman opened up in a barrage of hellfire. A discarded magazine fell to the ground as he loaded up a new one and his gun made a clicking sound.

"Feel free to jump in," he said.

Joining the gunfight, I peered over the desk to see the bodies of two dead guards lying in the doorway. The arm of another guard extended into the room as he fired back. His bullets went in all directions and a few splintered into the thick desk in front of us.

I shot back and put a bullet into the man's arm. When the guard stopped shooting and the arm disappeared, I advanced forward to take up a better spot while the Englishman laid down suppressive fire. The guards only had handguns. They didn't stand a chance.

When another arm reached in from the hallway I grabbed onto it, and pulling in a guard. The Englishman ripped three bullets into his chest.

Another standoff ensued, costing us more skin as a minute we did not have passed by. Silence befell the room until the Englishman broke it, yelling out that one of the guards was running away.

It was the fourth one, and throwing my gun to the floor I ran after him. Hurdling over obstacles of fallen furniture, I sprinted out of the room and down the hall. The guard was already near the door to the stairs, but I was faster.

He was just starting to push open the door when I caught up to him. Throwing my arm around his neck, I used the other to lock his arm behind him, which forced his gun to drop. Placing a leg in front of his, I pushed him forward. The guard fell flat on his face, and when he struggled, I forced him harder onto the concrete, pinning him down with my body.

With one hand over his head, I pulled out the knife and stabbed him in the side. The more I jabbed into his body, the more blood spilled out onto my arm. He stopped squirming in seconds, but just to be sure, I pulled out another gun and put a bullet into the back of his head.

I was cleaning the knife off with the guard's shirt when a sound from the other end of the hall grabbed my attention. It was the Englishman. He was jogging toward me with the glass box held at his side.

"Time to go, killer."

He ran past me and started for the door. Tucking away my knife I got up and followed in his footsteps. The Englishman creaked open the door, and with a finger he ushered for me to look down.

"The bloody cops are here," he whispered.

My stomach flipped at the thought of getting caught. Time was no longer on our side as the window quickly closed in on us.

But just as I began to panic and lose my shit, the Englishman brought to my attention an emergency ladder in the ceiling at the top of the stairwell. There was hope for us yet.

Going first, I ascended the ladder where at length I found a hatch that gave way after the second push. Swinging open the door revealed a gray sky; we were on the rooftop. The smell of rain could not be any sweeter.

Having climbed out, I watched as the Englishman came up after me. Smiling, he took out one of the grenades, and pulling the pin, he let it drop down the hatch.

There was just barely enough time to close the door and dive to the side before the grenade exploded down below. It shook the roof and the blast ripped the hatch door clean off, sending it flying into the air and back down into a heap of scrap.

The explosion also ripped into the ceiling below, causing panels close to the epicenter to fall back down through fissures in the roof. There was no doubt that the Englishman had succeeded in maiming any police below, as well as dismantling part of the building. When I looked up at him, he grinned back.

A cloud of black smoke began to billow up through the roof and the air fanned it out beyond the building. Holding an arm over my mouth, I followed the Englishman over to the ledge. He had spotted a maintenance ladder, and after peering down below to make sure the coast was clear, we climbed down.

The ladder creaked and groaned as we made our way down, but it held up. In no time we were back on the ground again, standing in the alleyway. But as we sprinted around to the back of the building, the sound of a police vehicle ringing in the near distance made my heart pound again.

The Englishman and I were the first to reach the back, but as the squad car came into view, it stopped in front and cut us off. The doors of the car started to open, but we still had a few tricks up our sleeves.

My partner took out his last grenade. Pulling the pin he rolled it under the police car. Seeing him do that, I pitched one of the flash-bangs under as well. Learning from our near-death experience from the rooftop, we bolted for a Dumpster in the alley and hid.

Taking up positions behind it, we laid down gunfire to prevent the German police from getting out. In no time the squad car blew up and was engulfed in a vortex of fire. The blast from combined grenades sent the car about five feet into the air before falling back to the ground in a ball of flames.

The Englishman turned and beamed at me. "Well-done, mate. Well-done." He patted me on the back and we both stood back up. "Now let's get the bloody hell out of here."

Without wasting another second, we made for the getaway car stashed in the lot a few buildings down. Although my heart was still pounding, I barely noticed. Adrenaline was surging through my body and I felt light. I had never been through such a close-call experience before, and it felt bittersweet.

When we reached the car I stopped and turned to the Englishman. All at once, fear crept back over me, and I began to panic.

"What's wrong?" the Englishman asked, seeing my white face.

"*Dammit*! I think I left one of my guns back in the building. My prints were all over it."

I searched my jacket again, but still counted only three guns. Taking a deep breath, I exhaled and looked back.

The Englishman unlocked the car and laughed.

"Oh I don't think that will matter soon."

He reached into his coat, and for a split second I thought he was going to pull out a gun. Watching him, I reached into my own jacket, but to my great relief, he brought out something else. It was an explosive detonator.

"What's that for?"

The Englishman got into the car. "Just get in."

I obeyed and hopped into the car. Once inside, I began to fumble about the seat.

He showed me the device in his hands and winked. "This is to cover our bloody tracks."

Raising an eyebrow at him, I watched as he laughed and proceeded to squeeze the metal trigger to the detonator. Within about two seconds my head was filled with a deafening ring.

The concussion of an extremely large explosion rushed over our car and rattled its small frame. The windows of nearby buildings shattered and glass was sprayed out all over the street and sidewalks. It was as if a great big bomb had been dropped, something Berlin was all too familiar with just a half-century ago.

With the heels of my hands pressed into my ears, I stared at the Englishman. While doing the same as me, he smiled back. His lips moved, and although I could not hear anything, I made his words out to be *holy shit, that was loud.*

After taking another moment to gather ourselves—our ears still very much ringing—the Englishman started the car and we high-tailed out of there.

Mindful of the piles of fragmented glass sprinkled about the street, we drove back past the IMF building...or what remained of it. My jaw dropped at what lay before me, and I had to blink. Past the manicured lawn and flagpoles was utter destruction.

The entire third floor and parts of the second were completely engulfed by giant red flames. As the fire grew, the walls and support beams were being chewed up by flaming teeth. Even the windows gave way to fire that seemed to curl out like deadly fingers.

I could no longer see the roof where we had stood not too long ago. It was completely absorbed by the hellish inferno, and blackened ash fell to the ground like snow. I felt bad for the people inside.

Through a mirror, I watched as the smoke began to rise high above the building in thick, black pillars. The wind carried it and the pillars converged into even larger columns of smoke. Surely, Berlin was now awake.

The Englishman, playing with the knob, brought the scanner back to life. It was flashing like crazy and the female voice was sputtering out orders in German faster than I could understand her. Two words I could hear though, were *terroristischen bombenanschlag.* We were now terrorists.

We made our way back through the city, passing by police cars and ambulances going the other way. About three blocks from the safe house, we parked inside a vacant warehouse. Leaving the weapons, and all other traces of our dubious operation inside the vehicle, we got out. The Englishman drenched the car with gasoline stored in the trunk. When he was done he stepped back.

"Almost home-free," he said.

I nodded and took a few steps back as well.

The Englishman lit a match, took a long drag on his cigarette, and flicked the burning stick at the car. As the gas combusted, the vehicle went up in flames—and any evidence along with it. The ground shook as the sound of rotors announced a helicopter flying over. But the sound soon faded off into the distance.

Crowds of people were gathering outside on the streets as we walked back to the safe house. More police vehicles with blaring lights sped by and I watched as another helicopter flew over in the same direction.

CHAPTER NINE

The Englishman and I agreed that it was in both of our interests to lay low the next few days. It was unknown how much calamity would ensue in the aftermath and this next phase would prove life or death for us.

There were now four of us in the safe house, having acquired an additional associate of the Englishman's. The man showed up later the same night as the IMF heist. He seemed cultured and well-behaved, bearing little resemblance to The Englishman who seemed more savage than man. But then again, there's a savage in all of us.

We had added more black paint to the house's windows and secured an additional padlock on either door. Soon after the Englishman's friend showed up, the three of us gathered around the kitchen table. Placed in the center was the glass box.

"This box here is worth more than all three of us bastards combined," he said, turning to me.

The three of us scooted our seats closer up to the table and gazed through the box. I watched the man's eyes flash as he pressed closer.

There was an eerie pause and I waited for someone to say something. As I waited, I glanced around the room. The kitchen had a unique feel to it. Although the house was old, it was like being inside a time capsule from the early '50s. The quintessential model of a post-World War II home.

The cabinets and even the counter top of the kitchen were layered with matching veneer made of yellow tiles. Painted inside the yellow were tiny flowers alternating between roses and lilacs. Coated across the entire kitchen was clear lacquer, which had since began peeling away. A sign of humid air.

The more I stared, the more I became lost. It was moments like these that allowed me to melt away and hide from the world. And the realities of it.

The sound of fists slamming against a wooden table brought me back.

"Damn this rubbish poppycock!" the Englishman said. He banged his fists against the poor table once more and the legs shook.

The thick glass of the case was getting the best of him as he tried prying at it from all angles. I couldn't help but picture a small child, frustrated over a box of candy he couldn't open. I chuckled, and hearing me do this, The Englishman gave me a hairy finger.

"Here, allow me," I said. With the butt of my gun I slammed it against the box.

The first strike seemed to do no more than merely crack its shell. But after a succession of four more rounds, hitting it precisely in the same spot each time, the box finally gave to and shattered in large shards of glass.

The Englishman picked up one of the pieces and stared at it. "Well I'll be damned," he said. "It's Plexiglas."

The glass shard was close to a quarter-inch thick and when he threw it against the wall, it did no more than create a dent.

"Would you look at that?" The Englishman rubbed a finger over the dented wall.

Laughing, the other man patted him on the shoulder. "I can see why you were having such difficulty, my friend."

This was the first time hearing him speak once inside the safe house. He reached over and picked up one of the floppy disks. They were gray and had streaks of black lines running across the face.

Unlike the Englishman, whose hair was thinning, the man's head was covered by a patch of thick brown hair, completely intact. He looked to be around forty and was without crows-feet or aging blemishes on his face. If anything, the man looked a little like me.

When the man stood up, holding one of the disks close to the kitchen's chandelier, his gray trench-coat straightened. Underneath the coat was a white dress shirt and a pair of black pants. His shoes were as black as the pants and when he saw me staring he smiled, baring a row of white teeth.

After flipping the disk around a few times, the man sat back down. He handed the disk over to The Englishman, and took another one out of the box for me. When I said *thank you*, he grinned.

"What are these?" I asked, tossing the disk back into the box.

The Englishman frowned. "Don't do that," he said. He shuffled the disk in with the others and moved the box closer to his body. "These are *very* fucking valuable."

I reached my arm across the table, and The Englishman begrudgingly let me pick up another disk. This one had a band of red masking tape around it. There were black letters written inside the tape. I read them aloud.

"Executive Account #12. What does that mean?"

The Englishman pointed a hairy finger at my hand. "That there disk you're eyeballin', boy, is worth about fifty million large."

My eyes became saucers, and I saw the other man jerk his head toward the Englishman.

I turned the disk over in my hand and felt its smooth surface. It was light and delicate—almost flimsy. People were killed and a building blown up for this disk. All of Berlin was in a state of panic over this. Lives were taken for this flimsy piece of plastic. I thought of the girl in the hallway. She was innocent. Wrong place at the wrong time. She died at my feet over this.

My head got light and my stomach began to churn. The Englishman started talking again, and although I could see his mouth move and hear his words, they sounded distant. I was a mile away and no matter how many times I blinked, that girl's face kept showing up. Her braided hair and her hands covered in blood as she looked up at me. She looked up at me for help—for *forgiveness*. What God lets the innocent die like that? I threw up in my mouth and felt the burning effects against my throat as I swallowed.

When the image of her dying face finally faded away, I was back in the room and I could hear the Englishman as he droned on.

"Every single one of these disks has anywhere from ten to fifty bank accounts on them," he said, "each worth millions of untaxed dollars from off-shore accounts."

The other man was rooting through the glass box. He picked up each disk and stared at them. A fiendish smile was spread across his handsome face.

"Our good ol' friends from the IMF have funneled all these accounts into security funds," the Englishman continued.

He took another disk out of the box and flipped it over, then back again. "Each of these has its own set of encryptions. But I know just the chap who can crack them all." The Englishman pointed downstairs and grinned.

It did not take me very long to figure out that my services had been exploited; that, in a way, I was duped and deceived into believing this was going to be a simple hit job. But it was too late for playing the blame game. We were past the tipping point and there was no undoing the damage. As sad as it was, there was no bringing that girl back. She was after all, a necessary casualty. And some casualties hit closer to home than others.

When I got the chance, I stole away from the kitchen and went upstairs. Finding the quietude I had been seeking the whole night, I made a quick call back to Beivrus.

A dispatcher on the other end received my message to The Chancellor. I said there was a crisis on hand, and that I was going to need help with getting out of the city.

Although very short, the message was direct and concise. Before hanging up, the dispatcher assured me the message would be sent right away and that I was to remain in the safe house for the time being. Someone would be sent out to me. But when?

Putting the phone away, I closed my eyes and sighed. I have since learned that *nothing* is black and white in this world.

The following two days passed by with the smoothness of sandpaper. Inside the safe house, it was so quiet that not even the sound of a penny dropping would break the eerie spell. But outside…outside was different. I never saw Berlin so quiet and alive at the same time. It was a ruthless paradox that kept my gut pushing up into my lungs.

It was too dangerous in the daytime to venture upstairs, so we all found ourselves taking up quarters in the basement. The Englishman spent most of his time with the computer guy, relentlessly hacking away at the many executive accounts on those flimsy disks. This left the man in the gray trench coat and I to fend for ourselves.

I kept to myself like a hermit, finding my own ways of making the time go faster. Having found an old tube television upstairs, I brought it down and secured it in one of the rooms. Turning it on revealed the ever-constant patrols out on the streets day-in and day-out. We would use this television as our eyes and ears to the outside world. Although old, it still had its uses, and I was very thankful for that. I was thankful for it all. I did not want to die here.

After the first twenty-four hours, a curfew had spilled over the city. Although many of the Berliners were returning to their normal lives, the police were not. To make matters worse, they joined up with the German National Guard. Together they took to the streets in force and even began searching houses as well, going door-to-door to every business and residence. What started out as a mile radius around the epicenter of the explosion soon fanned out to encompass the rest of the city. Peace was hard to come by in the safe house, and I shuddered to think of the day when a knock would come at our door.

Watching the news drone on made me smirk as well, though. They had their own special way of inflating propaganda, morphing Berlin into some chaotic war-zone. Local authorities claimed the explosion was an attack by Al Qaeda; that the IMF was just the first of many buildings to be hit.

The news is nothing more than smoke and mirrors created to twist and distort people's minds into believing anything. Behind beautiful faces lie false pretenses and deep fabrications spread by forked tongues of malevolence. Like herds of sheep, people will believe anything.

You cannot trust this world as much as you can trust mine. Nothing is binary and there is no good or bad. There are only good people doing bad things, and bad people pretending to do good.

Nonetheless, propaganda or not, my gut still wrenched at the jarring reality laid out before me. I was trained to get out of situations, not to put myself in them. If it wasn't for the reassurance of that phone call made back to Beivrus, there wouldn't even be a light at the end of the tunnel, as faint as it was.

But don't call this hope. Do not confuse this with a lie. Hope is as much a deception as the words spewed out of the mouths of those news reporters on the tube. To believe in hope is to believe in what is not there. Nature does not act on impulse or sway from irregularities. Whatever is to happen will happen. Nature is just being nature.

Sleep was quickly becoming more and more of an issue again as I found myself spending fleeting nights in hollow isolation. There was a lot to think about and even more to make sense of. It's funny how during that certain time of the day, when you're trying to drift off to sleep, that everything seems to come at you all at once, rushing in like a vortex of water.

With the disappearance of the sun, it was safe to climb out of the basement and up to the floors above. This I could do as I pleased, and so could gray trench coat. The Englishman, however, chose to give up such lavishes, and instead would swap out shifts with the computer guy. Flipping a coin, some nights he would get heads and find the comfort of a soft pillow. But other nights he struck tails, and would be staring at a computer screen till kingdom come. Life itself, I've learned, is a lot like the flip of a coin.

As dense as he seemed, the brute was a pretty authentic and commendable man. He always saw to it that everyone's comforts were met before his, especially mine. The Englishman sort of took me under his wing and taught me some things he had picked up through the years. He became funnier the more I got to know him. Underneath his thick outer layer was a beautiful person and I admired him. He was like a mentor to me, perhaps even more than that.

After a very long and tedious day of code-breaking down in the basement, The Englishman came upstairs, where the two of us were gathered around the kitchen table, and announced that *it was time to fuckin' drink*. His eyes were deep and his face was hung like a tired cloth rag left out on the clothes-line for too long.

He walked over to one of the cabinets, patting my head as we went by, and opened one of them. Its wooden door creaked open, revealing a bottle of whiskey.

"You're drinking it straight…and no glass?" I asked, watching as he sat down at the table.

The Englishman smiled as he unscrewed the cap. "Do you see a pussy between my legs, mate?"

The other man laughed. He scooched closer to his friend.

I shook my head and the Englishman laughed heartily. His belly shook and he patted it. In some messed up way, he looked like Santa Claus. Only this one was more apt to steal your presents and slit your throat in the night.

The two men shared the whiskey. Each one taking a healthy swig from the bottle before passing it on. The more they drank, the more their faces lit up, becoming as red as the painting of flowers hung on the wall behind me.

Not being one to drink—besides the occasional bottle of pinot noir—I sat back in my chair. With fingers interlaced on the table, I watched the merry spectacle unfold before me. As sober as I was, I had just as much fun seeing them make fools of themselves.

It wasn't long until their eyes got that certain glossy sheen that only people who drink would know about. Their faces became more flushed as the redness overtook them, and their laughs got more childlike. By the time the bottle of whiskey was half-empty, the two men were absolutely drunk.

The Englishman was amusing on his own, but when intoxicated, he became hysterically entertaining. His unique idiosyncrasies were getting the best of me for quite a while now as he came to resemble more of a child and less of a man...hell, he no longer seemed like an adult at all. At one point, as he leaned back on his chair, he went too far, and he began to fumble helplessly as his chair teetered back and forth. His friend, too drunk to help, watched as he flailed his arms desperately before the chair finally settled forward, and the Englishman wiped beads of sweat off his face.

"That was a close un," he said, taking another big swig from the bottle.

But eventually, I started to fidget around in my own chair. Sobriety getting the best of me, I became bored after a while, and a clock on the kitchen wall announced that it was already one in the morning. We all had a busy day ahead of us and I wanted to salvage what was left of any possible sleep, assuming any would be found at all.

Amazed that the two men were still conscious, I bid them a good night and dragged my weary body up to the second floor—to a windowless bedroom.

Through tiny cracks in the old wall, shards of moonlight stole into the space and settled onto the floor. Peering through one of the larger holes, I stared up at the full moon. The sky was oddly clear, and the moon was bright. I got a chill just looking at it.

Resting myself onto the bed, which consisted of nothing more than a frame and an ancient spring mattress—its springs having long since lost their effectiveness—I folded my hands behind my head and stared off into the dark room. This was a way of living that I was used to...and felt more comfortable with. Even the jacket my head rested on as a pillow felt comfortable.

With just enough visibility from the reflective dance of the moonlight, I could see a distant bookcase at the other end of the otherwise black room. I could make out the bindings of books still housed between each shelf of the case. On the top shelf rested ancient artifacts that once served the hobbies of the room's previous occupant—perhaps a young boy. The bed I lay on belonged to someone else. It was a place of solace for a tired body after a long day. From another lifetime ago.

I spent a long time, perhaps longer than I anticipated, scanning the room. It seemed foreign, but at the same time, familiar, like I had done this dance before. It's amazing how everything looks the same after a while. Eventually, all things taste like chicken in my world.

I wanted to see more of it—to see what else lay behind the shrouds in the old bedroom. I wanted to *feel* it. To *feel* what it was like for this person...this young boy. But there were no lights in the room. There were no lamps. There was only the flickering light of the moon doing a jig on the floor. This room, too, was a time capsule, and I was stuck in it. I wondered what happened to the boy and where he was now.

The more I thought, the more restless I became, my body tossing back and forth on the old spring mattress; its tired springs coiled and shuddered under my weight. The moonlight was receding and I could no longer see the shelf with its old books and even older toys nestled on top of it. The sound of commotion from downstairs broke the silence. It sounded like glass being shattered.

It was faint, but listening more closely, I heard the sound again. It was coming from the kitchen. Those drunks. An image of the Englishman sloshing wildly at the kitchen table as his friend watched projected in my mind. I laughed thinking about it.

Having been kept in closed isolation for so long, I've learned to adapt and thrive by retreating into the depths of my own mind. In times of solitude, I find this happening the most. Like the tide going back out to sea, I shut down and let my mind...my thoughts...recede back to the deep abyss.

It's been two days since last forming a line of communication with The Program—and anyone from the outside world for that matter— and each additional day that passed made me all the more nervous and apprehensive. But putting all doubts aside, things weren't so bad in here. In this safe house. The men downstairs seemed all right in my book and I've grown to trust the Englishman, as much as one can trust anybody in this world, that is. Being cut off from the outside for so long, I've put up a wall around myself. But while dense, it is not impenetrable, and I've since taken down a few bricks the past couple days here.

After a while, my eyelids got heavier and I could no longer keep them open. Turning over on the bed, away from the light, I gave in and closed my eyes.

This dream, I could account for. It was wildly vivid and I was viewing it from the third-person, watching as I again left the hotel and ventured out onto the quiet street of Reggio. I knew that I was dreaming, but I could not stop. Besides, I did not want to. As I continued down the hilly street, glimpses of the pristine, blue-green sea popped out from behind the many buildings and homes of the hollow city. Nothing but the distant ringing of a church bell pierced the eerie silence.

When I reached the city's edge, stepping onto the sand with my polished, black shoes just as I did before, I stared out toward the pier. There was that same absence of people stretching from the pier and boardwalk, and onto the beach itself. I heard the waves as they slapped up against the pier's wooden legs.

Staring down from above, like an omniscient bird, I watched as I pushed forward and sat down on the sand, amongst the other scattered few. The sun was high, floating above the horizon like a giant yellow ball. Its light flashed on the sea's surface, lighting it up like a bright white field.

I saw a few ships dotted along the white sheet. But something else got my attention. I watched as I turned my head, but I don't remember doing that the last time. The black shape got bigger as it continued up along the beach's edge.

It was the girl from the hotel. Her tanned skin was a beautiful bronze that seemed to put even the sun to shame. Her blackish hair, tied up into a ponytail, bobbed up and down elegantly with her athletic stride.

But this dream was different.

Instead of jogging past me and waving, the girl stopped, and I watched as she walked up to me. Smiling, she handed me something white. And no sooner had the dream appeared, than it tore away like an old black-and-white movie feature.

In its stead was a different scene.

Watching again from the omniscient view, I saw myself somewhere dark with heavy rain pouring down on me. My body was shivering. I was standing over something...it was a person. I was standing over someone who was kneeling on the ground with their back to me. I could not see their face. It was blurred out. But I did see that I was holding a gun to their head.

This scene too tore away as quickly as it manifested. The blurred out person and I evaporated into wisps of air, leaving me to an empty darkness.

Rarely—almost *never*—can I account for such lucid dreams. Even through my early years of training in The Program—when I would waken in the middle of the night to fits of rage, my skin caked in a layer of sweat—I never experienced anything like this. A loud thud from downstairs ripped me from my sleep and I was glad, almost happy to hear it. It was like hearing a magical tune.

I opened my eyes again, but it was to a pitch-black room. The moon was completely gone, leaving behind a façade of darkness in its wake. As I left the bed, its coils shuddered some more in a way that sounded glad I was leaving it. Fumbling around, I searched for the door. After a brief struggle, I felt the metal knob and turned it.

To my astonishment, however, it would not twist, and the door would not budge. After jolting the knob in all directions a few more times and pulling on it unsuccessfully with both hands, I stopped.

"What the hell?" I scratched my head, feeling the scar as it rubbed against hair.

I didn't remember locking the door. And besides, it could only be locked from the *outside*.

With more tenacity, I threw myself against the door. But it only swayed. Strike two. I then tried kicking it in with bare feet. For some reason, this seemed to work better. On the second kick, I found the sweet spot right next to the door knob and the door burst open. I heard a heavy padlock fall and hit the ground on the other side. I *definitely* didn't remember doing that. This must have been a prank...it had to be.

Free of the locked door, I left the room. I left *the familiar*. The hallway was equally as dark and I shuffled my hands against the walls to find a bearing. The floor creaked under me as I meandered down it. I wondered who was still awake downstairs. I gripped the broken padlock in one of my hands, and I couldn't wait to chuck it at whoever had done this.

I found the staircase, all sixteen of its flimsy steps, and descended. With the comfort of a wooden railing, I had little difficulty making my way down. As I reached the middle step, I heard the front door come to life with a loud knock. I stopped, one foot still clinging to the air.

Straining my head closer, an ear tilted toward the source of the noise, I heard the resolute sound of someone knocking at the door again. What is going on?

Putting my foot back into motion, I ventured toward the base of the stairs. Another knock, and I could see flashes of blue and white lights bouncing off the walls of the living room. My heart pounded and my mouth dried up.

With more caution, I slipped down the remaining steps and through the living room. Behind me I heard the door shake as a much heartier knock came pounding down on it. I brushed past the living room chairs and sofa. They were being lit up by the flashes of blue and white light and so was the kitchen where I found the dark body of the passed out Englishman still seated at the table. His head rested on the wooden surface, and the bottle lay smashed on the floor beside him.

I heard another, even *louder* knock. One of the living room windows was not blacked out enough and I could see glimpses of a squad car parked outside. Someone outside was yelling, but it was in German, and I was too stunned to comprehend the situation.

Instead, I hid behind a brown sofa chair and panicked. Comfort is a fool's best friend, and I have been exposed to it for far too long in this place, letting my *hopes* get the best of me. I deserved this. I deserved *all* of this. My hands began to shake violently.

"Hey, *you*," I whispered back to the Englishman. "Wake the hell up!"

No response. I picked up a piece of trash and threw it at his sleeping body. It bounced off the side of his face and landed gently back on the ground.

This time, I didn't even bother whispering. "Wake the FUCK UP!"

The men standing outside pounded on the door again and sputtered some more German rhetoric. I thought about the phone call I had made back to Beivrus. "Any day now," I said to myself.

My hands continued to spasm and it took clenching them into tight, white fists to stop the shakes. I felt blood swelling up under the fleshy scar of my right palm and stopped. Closing my eyes, I took three deep breaths. This wasn't something I was taught in The Program. No, my mother showed me this.

When I was sure that the hands were good to go, I opened my eyes and made a break for the kitchen. The blue and white lights continued to flicker deep into the room, lighting up the central table and the Englishman.

"Hey, wake up, you drunk bastard," I said. His head was still turned to the side.

I took a step closer and went to slap the back of his head. But what I felt made me grimace. It was matted down and moist, and my hand was covered in dark blood. It was still warm.

The pulsating effect of the lights revealed fragmented brain matter spilled out onto the table. I almost fell backwards, clutching onto an empty chair to break my fall. The Englishman's skull had been bashed in. A pool of dribble from his mouth and blood from his head was forming on the table. His eyes were still open. The Englishman had been murdered.

My jaw dropped and I stood there for a moment in disbelief, ignoring the knocking at the door as the police continued bang on from outside. I don't know why, but I still went to check his pulse anyway. It was then that I heard the distinct and jarring sound of a .45 going off downstairs.

The men outside must have heard it too, because the knocking ceased. Hell, the whole neighborhood must have heard it. The Englishman's jacket was folded over his chair. I reached into it and found his gun. Ignoring the lesser of the two threats, I headed for the basement.

Passing through the short hallway, I left the kitchen and found the door to the basement. Before descending, I stopped and checked the magazine. It was full.

I proceeded to open the door. Thankfully, this one was not stuck and I had no trouble in opening it. I made my way down the stairs, careful not to announce my presence. But it didn't matter, the sound of a quarrel ensuing down below was deafening and it drowned out the sounds of the police battering on the door.

Another round from the .45 popped off. Being in such a confined space, the noise slammed against my eardrums like painful splinters. I stopped for a second to massage my ears. When I was ready, I continued down the remaining flight of stairs.

The main room—the one I had spent most of my time in—was in shambles. The fluorescent light fixture hovering above the room was swaying back and forth haphazardly, casting black shadows of all shapes and sizes around the floor.

What the light was able to show in chaotic waves of illumination was the aftermath of a violent struggle. It appeared as though a tornado had run through the basement.

Most, if not all, of the tables were overturned and lay there like virgin girls with their legs sticking up. The largest of them, the one the Englishman and I had consulted over for the IMF operation, was amongst those flipped on their backs. Wads of paper and other miscellaneous items were scattered about the floor and some of the computer monitors lay there with the screens punched in.

I heard somebody screaming and darted my eyes over to the far end of the room.

The man who I had seen typing away at all those computers, who, according to the Englishman, was a *fucking computer wizard*, was lying face down on the concrete and groveling. His white tee shirt was ripped and stretched at the sides and a large splash of red tarnished his shoulder blade. Positioned on top of the man's back was the last man I expected to see doing this.

My heart, if I still had one, sank a little deeper, and I almost dropped the gun. His gray trench coat swayed, and then straightened, and then swayed again as he pulled the computer man's head up. In one of his hands was a knife, and I watched as he slit the guy's throat. The computer man stopped struggling and the screaming ceased.

The temperature seemed to drop hard and I froze. My muscles, my face—they all tensed and tightened up. I could barely manage to inhale and then exhale. I lost feeling in my left hand and watched in helpless horror as the Englishman's gun slid out of my pale fingers and hit the floor.

The noise was not loud, but it was loud enough to attract unwanted attention, and my eyes flashed from the dead computer guy, to the man staring up at me. He no longer looked friendly, having replaced his warm smile with an expressionless face. He moved to get back up.

Sensation crept back into my body and jolted me to action. My hand bolted down for the gun that was lying on the floor. My fingers were no longer pale and my reflexes were on point. I rose back up with beaming tenacity and the gun out. But so was his.

Our eyes clicked and there was silence.

For a couple seconds neither of us said a word. The silence alone was deafening as each of us waited for the other to make the first move. We were sizing each other up; we had been doing so ever since I first saw him come into the house. I could feel my index finger shaking slightly across the trigger guard. It was metallic, like *blood*.

"Not what either of us expected," he said, going first. "I thought you'd be green, first time out, but you're bloody red, aren't you?" He smirked. "Blood red. *Crimson*, even." The fluorescent fixture slowed down, producing slow black shapes that seemed to creep across the floor between us. His face was barely visible, then it was visible, then it disappeared behind the shadows again.

The man took a step closer, coming into the light that waxed and waned. He had a malevolent grin.

"Please put the gun down," he said, hearing me take the safety off the Englishman's gun. It was a good gun, owned by a good man. My blood began to boil thinking about him.

Using up a few more seconds I stood there like a statue. The gun was drawn, ready to do what it was made to do, waiting for me to do what *I* was made to do.

In The Program I was taught that a gun, like any other weapon, was just another inanimate object, and nothing more. By itself, the gun was no more lethal than a pen or a coffee cup. By itself, a weapon was harmless. What made it do harm was the person controlling it. It wasn't the weapon that made the man. It was the man who made the weapon.

He took another step forward and the tails of his trench coat flapped under him. The man moved his feet and stepped closer for a third time. I could see his chest pushing in and out. His dark eyes seemed to stare into mine, like he was trying to reach through my skin and into my soul. This too felt familiar and I could not break the trance.

This time I spoke, tasting a subtle tone of uncertainty laced beneath my words. "Who are you?" I asked.

"Put the gun dow—"

"Put yours down," I yelled back. I could feel my finger inching closer to the trigger.

The man's smile extended into the grin I had seen many times the past couple days.

"Please, put it down, boy. My fight's not with you." His words sounded warm and wholesome, like he had switched personalities at the snap of a finger.

I wanted to shoot him. I wanted to pull the fucking trigger and put a bullet through this man's skull. But as much as I tried to move my finger, it wouldn't budge any farther. A wave of some weird feeling raced over me and I couldn't do it. Instead, I caught myself lowering the gun to my side. And then dropping it again.

His smile continued to grow until his cheek muscles couldn't flex any further, exposing a set of off-white teeth. The gun was still drawn up on his end and I was staring down the thick barrel of a revolver. To his left, in the back, was the body of the computer guy. A pool of blood expanded under his neck. My blood began to curdle again.

The tails of his trench coat flapped back to life as the man took a few more steps toward me, gun still pointed at my face. But the light was no longer his friend, and as he neared closer, I saw a gash on one of his legs as he limped out of the shadows. It was like seeing an Achilles Heel. It broke the strange power the man held over me.

Still having a good fifteen or so feet distance in between us, I watched as his weight shifted over onto his bad leg. When it did, I sprang to life. Kicking the overturned table close to me, I was able to take his eyes off me. Being free of the trance, I lunged forward and grabbed his gun with both hands. He got a shot off, but the bullet ricocheted off the ground and nestled into the concrete behind me.

"This is not your fight, boy," he said in between grunts. A bead of sweat raced down his forehead.

I was finally able to overpower the man just long enough to slam his hand into the adjacent wall. After two successive hits, he dropped the gun.

With a look of astonishment, the man countered almost instantly by wedging his foot in between us. He pushed against my stomach and freed himself. Stumbling back a good foot or so because of his injured leg, the man regained his balance. We again found ourselves in a face-off and our eyes reconnected a second time.

His face was completely barren of any traces of a smile, as his other personality resumed control. Shaking his head at me, he reached for the large knife tucked inside his belt. But before he could pull it out, I threw my body into his and grabbed onto his arm.

Instead of resisting though, the man let out a sigh, and I felt the muscles in his arm loosen up as he let go of the knife.

"I wish you wouldn't have done that," he said.

I opened my mouth to respond. But before I could, I watched as the giant palm of his free hand came at me. He grabbed onto my face, forcing my head away. In another quick motion, he rammed his head into the side of mine. For a very brief moment, my mind went numb and I blacked out.

At the last second I regained consciousness. I could feel the man holding my arms back as he forced me toward the concrete wall. My body felt limp, but I was able to muster enough strength to shake off the sensation.

Throwing both my feet up at the right time, I pushed against the wall with all my strength and forced the both of us onto the ground.

Another struggle ensued and momentarily it looked as though I had the upper-hand.

It was then that I caught out of the corner of my eye a peculiar gray backpack laying on the floor next to an oval table. It was laying sideways with a stack of floppy disks spilling out from the edges.

"You mother fu—"

All at once, I felt myself drifting off again. My head started to spin and blackness overcame my sense of direction.

When I came to again, it was to a scene beyond my recollection.

Recovering as quickly as I could, I found that I had a death grip on the man's head. I had gone from seeing red to unconscious savagery. As if watching from a third-person's perspective, I saw myself slamming his head against the hard concrete floor beneath us. A gash of blood was smeared on the side of his face and his face was contorted into a painful expression as I went to jar his head in again.

But as he opened his eyes and looked up at me, I felt that supernatural sense wash over my tensed up body like a wave. I stopped. One hand was gripping the back of his head, and the other was wrapped around his trachea.

I had never known such a feeling before. It was paralyzing. I let go of him and rolled over onto the ground beside him. He jostled around and gasped for breath as his lungs slowly recovered from the traumatizing act.

But I had made a careless mistake. My compassion was my weakness and in moments he had rolled himself on top of me. The tides had turned as he proceeded to unsheathe his knife and pushed it up against my exposed throat.

The sharp metal of the blade kissed my skin with dangerous animosity, and I was soon staring death in the face. But instead of resisting, I let go. My muscles loosened up and I felt a calming sensation overcome me. It was at this moment that I found myself welcoming death—anticipating the fatal slash to my jugular that would finish me off. I spread my arms out, embracing the kiss of death that would send me from this lonesome world just as I had initiated the journey for countless others.

The man, looking down at me with a dark, unrelenting gaze, held the knife with unquivering tension. Closing my eyes, I could feel his heart beat as his chest expanded and contracted. This was it. This was my fate.

But fate never came.

What seemed like a feverish eternity went by as I waited for death to claim me. But it never did.

I then felt the cold steel blade being removed from my throat. And I slowly opened my eyes again.

Looking up, I was met by the end of a gun barrel staring back at me. The man holding the gun was slowly picking himself back up and I felt the pressure of his weight on top of me going away. I could breathe again, but only in short, sporadic bursts.

"Do not move," the man said in a hushed tone. "Do not speak. Do not come after me. If you do, I will not hesitate to pull this trigger."

The man sighed as he recovered himself. His eyes let up, but the gun in my face told a different story.

"Do you understand me, boy?"

I took a moment to consider his demands. They were heavy and difficult. It's not that I was delirious. Far from it. My mind was as clear as glass, and my senses were on overdrive as I struggled to control the surge of adrenaline racing through my veins and capillaries. My body wanted to fight. But my mind knew better.

Like a young child acknowledging when he had done wrong, I obediently nodded my head. I could still feel the phantom presence of the knife pressed firmly against my throat.

"Good," the man said, pulling the gun back. "You're much smarter than I imagined you to be."

He grinned that cunning smile of his. The Trojan Horse he so flatteringly brandished the past few days inside the safe house. The one that disarmed us all...including the Englishman whose deposed body now lay lifeless upstairs.

My blood began to boil.

I watched as the man in the trench coat stepped away from me. His hand flinched ever so slightly that caused his gun to jerk. He dipped over, shuffled the floppy disks back into the gray backpack, and then slung it over his shoulder.

His footsteps became less and less apparent as I saw him make his way up the basement stairs and then out of sight completely. Left to my own accord, I looked up at the darkened ceiling. Then, turning my head to the side, I stared at the body of the computer man. His blood gurgled out onto the cold floor. It was a fate, I should have endured.

My blood was hot. The strange spell had been lifted.

All at once, I picked myself up. Finding the gun I had dropped earlier, I picked it up and proceeded to race up the stairs after him; after what belonged to me.

The wooden steps groaned under my weight as I flew up to the next floor. Desperately, I wanted to hunt down the man. I wanted to do it for the disks. I wanted to do it for my comrades who had died tonight. And I wanted to do it for myself.

Pride befalls us all at some point in our lives. Sometimes for the greater good, but sometimes for lesser evils. I had graduated from training with a perfect track record. Even though this man was not my target, *per se,* I was not about to let him slip away that easily. Not without a fight at least.

By the time I reached the next floor and started down the hall toward the kitchen, the assailant was already through the kitchen and making his way to the back door. The flashing lights outside indicated that the police were still there.

Slamming the basement door closed loud enough for him to hear me, I chased after him, gun drawn. The lights were out, but I could still make out the distant bulging shape of the Englishman's body slouched forward on the kitchen table. It was a heated memory that made my stomach churn and my trigger finger become restless.

The man spun around just before opening the screen door, and I dove behind a large chair in the dining room as he pulled out two guns and proceeded to unload gunfire in my direction. It was all I could do to throw myself behind the fraying piece of furniture, ducking just in time to feel only the fiery-hot air of trailing bullets whizzing over me and splintering into the wall behind. Wood fragmented and sprayed me as more bullets came. It was a death-match of which I was ill-prepared. Clutching myself as tight as possible, I waited for the madness to stop.

And when it did, I reached over and fired back. The booming ring of my revolver as I returned fire ripped through the silent room. The muzzle-flash was great and it temporarily lit the bottom floor in a spectacle of bright white as I fired haphazardly in all directions of the kitchen, hoping the bullets would somehow find their mark.

When the cylinder was spent, I slouched back down. The air was thick with gun smoke and I heard a distant door being flung open. But it wasn't the back door.

Peering over the chair, I was not surprised to find that the cops from earlier were barging into the scene. The sound of our fight must have motivated them to renew their efforts with the door. Two dark silhouettes announced their entrance, and they made their way over to my position on the other side of the room. Reloading my gun, I braced for impact. My knuckles were pallid as I clenched the gun.

Their booming voices soon followed as they demanded that we put our weapons down. But it was like stepping over tripwire and what happened next was lightning fast.

As the two officers came closer, the man in the trench coat shot at them from the kitchen. With both guns drawn at eye-level he pushed forward and fired off numerous rounds. Each step he took was colossal, and his guns were like hellfire.

The officers didn't stand a chance as I too joined in the tumult. Their chest cavities were ripped open by bullet after bullet as the man strode closer to them. There was little they could do, and I was too stunned to intervene. Who was I to shoot at first, anyway? I felt no remorse for the poor fools. I watched their bodies collapse onto the ground. They were necessary casualties. Wrong place wrong time.

But, perhaps I should not have intervened after all.

Turning his attention back to me, the man continued his barrage of gunfire, pelting the rapidly deteriorating chair that served as the sole barrier between me and the lethal bullets being sprayed in my direction.

I fired back, but it was to no avail. I had six shots in the revolver, and all six missed their mark. Tossing the gun to the side, I lay there and listened for my chance.

And my chance finally came. Hearing the distinct sound of magazines hitting the floor announced its arrival. As the man reloaded his guns, I made a dash for the other side of the room, throwing myself over a couch.

I would like to have said that my thoughts were clear and that my heart wasn't racing. But that would be a lie. Everything up until now seemed like a distant lie. I had been as unnerved as I was then and I lost all control. My hands were shaking as I reached for the semi-auto tucked behind my back. There was but one magazine left. Twelve rounds.

I reached over the puffy couch and unloaded my entire arsenal of hollow-point rounds. The trigger, much lighter than that of the .45 caliber revolver, drilled back and forth as my finger moved like a deadly pianist.

At long last, I heard the infamous *click* of dry-fire. My arsenal was depleted and I was out of cartridges. I patted the entire length of my body, but came up with nothing. No more ammo, no more guns.

Pressing my head up against the couch, I listened for the man to fire back. He had two guns, and God only knew how much ammunition. I wondered how much it would take to bring me down.

My ears, attuned to the sound of gunfire, waited for it.

I was surprised, however, by what I was hearing, or rather, by what I was *not* hearing.

There was no return gunfire. No blasts. No *boom*. Just silence.

Peering over the touch, I scanned the musty outline of the kitchen. Looking for any hint of my assailant moving about in the dark.

But my eyes only came across the Englishman and his drained, lifeless corpse. When I squinted my eyes, I could see that he had absorbed a few bullets from the gunfight, and I frowned.

In a last ditch effort to regain control of the evening, I hurdled over the couch and sprinted over to the back door. There was no rhyme or reason behind my motives. Seeing the Englishman—whom I had grown fond of since arriving—invoked a fit of blind rage to come over me. My body was no longer shaking as I ran past his body to the door. I was enraged more than ever and it was time to make my move.

The screen door sat there in darkness. I thrust it open and hopped outside. But much to my dismay, there was nothing. No man in the trench coat. No more cops. Nothing. Only the lights from the lone patrol car driven by the two dead officers indicated that anything had happened here. Turning my head either way, both ends of the alleyway were barren of activity. I wanted to run. But to where? Which direction?

My throat knotted up. I wanted to hunt him down. How could I let this happen? The cold air gave no reply and like a dog with his tail tucked between his legs, I reluctantly walked back into the empty safe house.

A hush enveloped the dark room as I walked over to the kitchen table, still wondering why there had been only two officers with as much gunfire as there had been. Pulling out my phone I went into the living room with the intent of letting Beivrus know what happened. That I had failed.

As I did so however, I saw the split flash of a dark shadow moving in toward me. I was not alone. A hard kick to the side of my back, followed by a dull pain, sent me flying forward onto the floor.

I got up just in time to see the man wearing the trench coat greet me. He pressed a gun up to my stomach. I watched in helpless horror as his finger slowly twitched against the trigger.

"I warned you, child."

His words were distant, like a muffled voice.

It took some time before I realized what had happened. At first I thought everything was still okay, but in those desperate seconds it soon became apparent that I had been shot.

I looked down, but it was from ten feet above. The man's face was stolid and expressionless. He gave no hint of remorse, only condescension.

I watched my body drop to its knees before him—before the reaper who had now come to claim his prize. When the pain receptors finally kicked to life I reached forward to grab my abdomen. The pain I now felt was surreal and beyond anything I had ever imagined. It was as though a searing hot spear had been thrust into me, burning me.

I looked up at him, as he looked down upon me, and I for a split second I felt the urge to laugh. It was like a paradox. I could sense him looking through my eyes and into my soul, watching with pleasure as my life slowly drifted out. It was nature being nature.

Before turning away, the man gave me a good push, which sent my stiffening body backwards up against the wall.

"Put pressure on the wound," he said as he vanished into the kitchen, out of sight, and out of my life.

Doing as I was told, I pressed my hands hard against my skin. But it was futile. Although it was dark, with only the flashing lights of the empty police car parked outside to illuminate the tragic scene, I could feel my warm blood spilling out onto my hands.

Giving up on trying to subdue the bleeding, I leaned back against the wall. Once again, I found myself to be all alone. Not just in the safe house, but alone in the world. I was born into this world alone, and it only seemed fitting that I should die in it alone.

Not knowing when exactly I would die, I spent what I felt were the last moments of my life replaying the final scene over and over in my head. It was all I could contend with at that moment.

Lying there on the floor, I could not tell what angered me more; being betrayed, or the simple fact that I had fucked up so bad as to get myself killed. In some respects this felt like a much larger betrayal to myself. I knew I could do better, and *should* have done better. Spending the past ten years of my wretched life training for this very moment, and *this* was the putrid end result.

As the time slowly crept on, the excruciating pain emanating from my belly began to fade. This is how it starts. My body was going into shock.

When the searing sensation finally abated, it was replaced by the sudden rush of coldness that swept over me. I felt my lips begin to quiver as the coldness seeped into every orifice of my body. My veins, my lungs, my heart, all felt like wintery death.

It wasn't long until I had lost feeling completely. Wriggling my toes and fingers was useless and I had to look down to reassure myself that they were still there.

Sitting in chilled silence, while my body rapidly declined, my ears and mind became acute to my surroundings. For the first time since entering the safe house, I was now aware of its intrinsic sounds. I could hear the gasps and sways of the failing house as if it were alive, like a giant aging beast refusing to surrender to death as it took its final deep breaths, causing it agonizing pain.

Every minute creak and noise made by its decaying wooden beams and the cool whispers of cold air stealing in through the many cracks and crevices were loud and audible. Every sound it made came to life in an organic orchestra of heterogeneous noises.

The last of my body I still had control over was my left arm. With great force I was able to move my hand to the ground, gingerly caressing the frail, wooden beast—soothing the old giant as we both patiently waited to die.

Then, pulling my arm up over my lap, I struggled to loosen my belt. At last, I heard a *click* as the buckle loosened around my waist, allowing better blood flow for death to circulate through my body faster.

Both hands were stained in deep red. But it was like I was covered in not just my own blood, but in the blood of all those I had killed before. My death was their penance.

The chilling effects of shock began creeping up the rest of my body. But I gave no further struggle. Soon, I was delirious. I was in a partial state of euphoria. And everything felt warm now.

The last thing I could hear was the distant ringing of the police sirens outside. Through my drunken-like stupor, I failed to realize that more police had showed up. As they entered the safe house, my heart began to pick up. Or at least I imagined it to. It was another set of cops, and they saw me almost immediately.

As they walked toward me, I braced for the worst. But then again, the worst was already about to begin, and they had front row seats. My gun rested at my feet, but I could not move my arms, nor did I desire to put up any degree of struggle. I was already checked out. My mind was all but gone and I closed my eyes to accept what fate had in store for me. I was ready for nature to reclaim what was hers.

I heard the clunking of boots against the floor as the cops drew nearer. The harsh trill of a radio voice from a dispatcher filled the air and drowned out the house's faint whimpers.

Soon, I could smell the pungent odor of a cigarette, as they got even closer. It was strong and acrid, and I could all but taste it in my numbed mouth. Was this what death smelled like?

My hands curled up, or at least I imagined them to. I could hear my finger nails clawing at the hard wood. At this point, it was a race of lesser evils. Who was going to kill me first?

I heard a third voice in the background. This one was slightly different from the Germans, who I feared were standing over me, deciding amongst themselves how to finish me off.

But this sound became stranger and I became curious. Forcing my eyes open again, I found myself in a world of vagueness. My vision was all but gone and I could barely see in front of me. Everything was blurry, and the two cops were blackened shapes against the silhouette of the dark room.

And then all at once the black shapes stopped moving forward. They began to spin like pillared columns and the third voice I had heard came to life again behind them.

What followed next was a state of utter chaos as the final play of the night unraveled. I heard the police yelling something, although I was unable to make out what. At this point, my eyelids became heavy and I grappled with consciousness.

The cops said something else, but the third voice refused to respond. Instead, I heard the familiar *wush* of a silenced pistol going off not once, but twice. And then I saw the two blackened shapes collapse in front of me.

A third blurry object came into view and progressively became enlarged. My energy was all but gone and I felt my lips become cold. It all felt cold, like I was stuck in winter's death. Before losing consciousness for good, I saw the shape kneel before me. It became the outline of a lengthy person. Of a long-haired man.

Reality is merely a perceived state of mind. It's subjective and changes with the tide. As of late, I found great difficulty in figuring out which was real and which was an impartial truth fabricated from my lackluster imagination as a teetering between life and death.

The last thing I could remember before slipping away indefinitely was being hoisted up onto somebody's shoulders and getting carried outside. From there, I heard a door close and an engine kick to life as the ground under me started moving.

CHAPTER TEN

At length, I woke up again. I was in a white room, decorated with white, white, and a little bit more white, spanning across all I could see. Like being plucked from a vacuum of time, I woke up confused, wondering what had happened and where I was now.

Propping myself up on the bed, I looked around. My vision, vague, revealed just enough evidence to show that I had all but recovered. A quick test revealed that my sense of feeling was back, and I once again had total mobility.

I blinked a few more times and rubbed my eyes.

As the vision slowly crept back in, I could see farther. I scanned the room, in hopes of finding some sort of clue or indication of where I was. But doing so brought little relief, if any at all.

In a corner of the room was what appeared to be an oval-shaped table—also white. On top of the table was something dark, but my vision was not strong enough to tell for sure what it was.

Turning my head over more to the left, I could see a wooden door, and much to my relief, a doorknob facing *inside* the room. Opposite the door, and next to the bed, was a wall with a small glass window near me. It was framed by wood, similar to the door, and to my even greater relief, I found that the window could slide up and down. However, upon twisting my torso toward it, I felt a sharp pain. Cringing, I bit down on my tongue, which hurt just as badly.

The pain was coming from my belly, and all at once I could remember what had happened to me. The pain was like pulsating daggers and it took a couple minutes before dulling down enough for me to breathe normally again. Any thoughts of moving again however, were put on hold indefinitely.

I was heavily confused. Even with the pain, I could not tell if I was still alive or in some quasi after-death state of being, waiting for the gates to open up. Or perhaps for the brimstone fire to come up from underneath and pull me under.

Shaking off either theory, I pulled off the blanket covering my body and looked down. I was naked from head to toe, with the exception of my lower torso, which was completely wrapped by thick medical dressings.

Curiosity getting the best of the cat, I started to unwrap the dressings. I was surprised with how much was on me and in no time I had accrued a large pile beside me on the bed.

Under the dense layer of dressings was another layer of stained gauze pads. Peeling off those revealed a small, star-shaped wound just to the left of my navel, looking down. The blood on the inside of the gauze was mostly brown and dried, but there were a few splashes of fresh blood painted on as well.

So this was it. This was how it happened. I'm still alive.

In comparison to the copious swabs of blood, I was surprised with how small the bullet wound actually was. It was like staring down at an Achilles Heel—so much from so little.

For some reason, I decided to touch the wound. I rubbed a finger across the fleshy scab. Nothing. I decided to go even further and apply pressure.

Wrong move.

This spurred an unbelievable amount of pain, almost as harsh as the night it happened. The pain was acute, but it also felt like forever. Alone in the room, I made a ball with my other hand, punching the air as I bit my tongue again.

When the pain finally went away, I lay back down.

It wouldn't be for another five or so minutes until the pain was bearable enough that I could move. When it was, I started the process of re-bandaging my waist with the dressings piled next to me. When I was certain that all the gauze and all the dressings were firmly snug around my waist, I resumed my efforts of exploring the room.

I suppose it would be fair to say that I was just as curious of knowing where I was as much as when. The pallid walls were absent of any clocks and I had no way of telling how long I'd been here.

Perhaps a *week*? A *month*?

The only things that gave me any indication were the medical dressings. Most of the blood on them had already browned. It had to have been at least a day or so. But remembering the firmness of that scar pushes my guess up to at least a week, maybe more.

These two clues, however, would stand alone.

As I flicked my eyes across the room, hoping to find something—*anything*—that would answer my question, my heart began to sink.

The only furniture in the room, aside from the bed, was that oval table lying at the far corner of the room. Remembering the stuff on top of it, I strained my eyes to see what it was.

However, doing so made me nauseated again, and within seconds my head started to ache as well. Lying back down, I shut my eyes for the next few minutes.

Surprisingly this helped a lot and it wasn't long before my head stopped spinning. I propped myself up, ready to resume my detective work.

While my vision was still pretty shoddy, I could at least look out the window and discern that I was on the second floor of whatever building this was.

Beyond the building, I noticed a chain-link fence with razor wire extending around the confines. Past that, there was a sea of gray stones and rocks fanned out a great distance before what looked like hills blocked out any further landscape. The sun, tinged a dark yellow, was halfway behind those hills. It cast golden splashes of light onto the walls of the room.

Despite the barrenness of the outside view, I spent the next half hour or so marveling over it. Seeing the sun descend behind a range of hills was a sharp contrast to the dismal setting of the safe house back in Berlin. Just about every day there it had rained, and each time it had, I had felt myself slipping further and further away from reality.

But thinking about the latter made my heart sink even further. My memory was still intact and I would never forget what happened there.

A few minutes later—at least what I imagine to be a few minutes—the final splashes of sunlight trailed up the walls and began creeping across the ceiling toward the window. A sliver of light was still stretched across my bed and I grimaced at the thought of it leaving me.

Although I had not been up for very long, it felt as though I had put in a full day's work. It was the first time I was conscious since that fateful night.

Eventually, that sliver of light *did* leave me. In its stead was the black void of night, spreading its shrouded wings across the sky like Death's Roc.

Having done so much today, I slipped back and rested my head once more onto the pillow. A wave of drowsiness crept over me and it was on their own accord that my eyes shut themselves.

If my questions were to be answered at all, they would have to wait until tomorrow. At least one thing was for sure. I was not dead yet.

That night I slept well. Like a wintered bear deep in hibernation I slept with a purpose. Through the night I woke up intermittently, but then shortly after would fall back to sleep again. This went on a few times, and each time I would experience a different dream.

Although each dream was more lifelike than the former, the last one, stuck out in particular. Like the taste of coffee still lingering in your mouth hours after you drained the last cup, this dream was with me even after I woke up the next morning.

It was very similar to the one I had before, and again I found myself back in Reggio; only this time I was back to seeing everything from my own set of eyes.

The dream was so vivid, that waking up I could still smell, hear, and taste it all as if I were still there. Everything had come alive again. The sound of a distant church bell greeted me once more as I ventured down the cobble-stone street toward the same destination I always found myself drawn to in each dream.

There was nobody around me, and with the exception of the bell chiming off somewhere, no sounds were heard.

Eventually I could see the shore thinning out over the jutting buildings and as I made my way toward it I suddenly stopped and closed my eyes. Holding out my arms I took in a deep breath.

A breeze of the most pure and heavenly kind brushed over me. The tails of my suit flapped out and it seemed as though I was being lifted off the ground. I tried to open my eyes again but couldn't. Or maybe I didn't want to.

What followed the breeze was a rush of warm air that swallowed me whole. It carried with it a sweet scent no words can describe. The feeling was euphoric, and as I drew in another, deeper breath, I felt something I had never known before. It gave me goosebumps.

At last the warm gust of air and all its divine attributes dissipated and I could again open my eyes. But when I did, it was like seeing the world through a different lens. What I now saw too, was indescribable, and as I recall the fond memory it pains me to know that it was not real.

I resumed walking toward the beach front, and as in my previous dreams, it was just as empty as the sleeping city behind me. Only sparse patches of the occasional vacationer or sunbather occupied the beach.

Another feeling—this one of intense serenity—washed over me when I joined them on the beach. As I continued farther a gust of wind picked up and threw my tie over my shoulder. Finding the spot I always seemed to venture over to, I sat down on the sand.

Looking around, I couldn't help but smirk. The few people who were out here, myself included, shared something special. Something unique. While we never made contact with one another, we all seemed to possess a deep understanding for one another. It was as if each one of us had carved out our own little niche on the beach.

It was as if nature was harmonized and I felt at peace. For the next hour I sat back with my hands buried in the sand and watched the waves come in. Everything around me melted away and I continued to stare deeper and deeper into those teal-blue waves.

More than once, I could sense a tear falling down my face. Through the intrinsic lens I now saw the world, I watched as each tear dropped down onto the sand where it then disappeared amongst the many microscopic particles of silica.

Staring into the ocean with a transfixed gaze I marveled at the vastness of it. The sun was once more positioned over the water creating a shimmering spectacle of bright white reflecting off of the blue field of water. My vision had returned to me, and I felt no pain coming from my abdomen as I watched distant boats sailing smoothly parallel to the horizon.

This magical spectacle could be seen for as far as the eye could resolve and the blue sea was just as infinite in its vastness as it was in its awesome beauty. This marvelous exhibition went on for quite some time before a distant dark object caught my attention out of the corner of my eye. Becoming increasingly larger by the second as it came toward me it wasn't long until I could make out the distant shape to be that of the brown-haired girl from the hotel restaurant.

Similar to my previous dreams about her she was jogging effortlessly across the white beach. Almost as natural as the fluent tides coming in and out of the shoreline, her dark brown hair swayed flawlessly up and down, almost synchronously with her athletic stride. Just as the sun had been reflecting sparkling white against the unwavering Mediterranean Sea, small beads of sweat visibly seen on her face and bare shoulders glistened poetically under the intense and radiant heat. It wasn't long before she was but thirty feet away from my relaxed figure and, as she closed in, our eyes once again made intense eye contact that only broke when she smiled at me and I looked away.

But then something else made me look back at her, smiling. Much to my surprise she broke her usual route and stopped in front of me. Her relaxed smile had since widened to a broad, attractive gleam. One I was familiar with, having seen it back at the hotel restaurant. And as she opened her mouth to speak, I saw a brilliant set of white teeth surrounded by beautiful lips. That nostalgic feeling of deep warmth I felt earlier had suddenly come back, and my smile grew as well.

"Hello," she said. The girl then walked up and handed me a white envelope, which I accepted, as if I already knew what was in it. Her eyes, a deep green, flashed when I took the envelope, and her smile expanded even more. For a minute, we just looked at each other. I was transfixed. It was as if she were staring directly into me, but instead of taking my soul, she was returning it. For that moment we stood in a vacuum of time, unaffected by the tribulations and decay of reality. For that moment, everything was all right.

It was then that I awoke, gasping for air like a fish out of water. My lungs were tight, as if someone were strangling me. And as I looked around, I soon realized that I was back in the room with the white walls, but it was dark now. When my breathing evened out, I put my head back on the pillow, and in moments I was back to sleep.

In this next dream, I was somewhere dark. Visibility was so bad that I could barely see my hands in front of me. What I could hear though was a torrential downpour all around me. At first I was dry, but then all at once, like turning on a light switch, I was drenched from head to toe with water. My body then began shivering, as if the temperature in the room dropped instantaneously. When I held out my hands again, I found that a gun was now in my left hand.

It was then that, out of the darkness, I heard a man whimpering somewhere in front of me. His voice was near and as I moved forward, I discovered that someone was kneeling on the ground in front of me. He then started to mumble something, but his back was to me, and out of the loudness of the rain, it was impossible to tell what he was saying.

Unbeknownst to me, my left arm had since moved up, so that the gun I was holding, was pressed up against the back of his head. I then watched as my finger squeezed the trigger. I had shot the man.

But as I did so, the man's head quickly changed into that of a man with long blond hair. At the same time this was happening, the rain intensified and a rush of water came crashing down over me.

When I woke up, I was drenched from head to foot in sweat. For a second, I thought I was still there. I thought the layer of sweat caked around my neck was the rain from that dream, constricting me like some liquid, amorphous hand, reaching out to take me under. It took me a moment or two to realize that I was no longer in that dream. And what more, that I was not alone in the room.

Seated at the foot of my bed was the last man I ever expected to see. It was The Chancellor. He was dressed in a sleek suit of black and white and the sun piercing in through the now open window did little to alleviate the aging of his face. He had been staring out the window, and when he saw me sit up in the bed, he drew his attention to me. His gaze was like a sword, thrusting into me. I felt my throat close up once again.

What baffled me even further is that The Chancellor was not the only guest in the room. Standing next to the door, was a man of equal height to The Chancellor. His erect posture was as solid as his slicked back hair that seemed to reflect the sun's warmth with tenacity. This man was the personal assistant to The Chancellor. A Frenchman, like

The Chancellor, he was the one who had escorted me into The Chancellor's personal chambers that night after I had completed my Final Challenge.

The Chancellor looked away, staring back through the window. Part of me was relieved, but part of me was scared shitless. A silent minute passed by and I soon found my hands clenching the bed sheets.

The craziest ideas rushed into my head. Why was he here? Was this *it*? I had failed at retrieving the disks from the safe house, and now The Chancellor was going to finish the job himself. Perhaps he may even think that I had something to do with what had happened. Either way, whatever was to come next, would not wait. I looked around the room for something—*anything*—that might be used as a weapon. But the room was empty, and I was still in no shape to move, let alone fend off two men.

Sinking back into the bed, I closed my fists even tighter around the bed sheet. And took a deep breath.

The Chancellor was the first one to make a move. Still looking out the window, he began to speak, and as he did so, he pointed a large finger down toward the floor. "Ten long years ago you came here as an orphan." His voice was deep and raspy and I could feel my veins turning to ice. My knuckles were as white as the room.

"We took you in and provided you with warm food," he continued, still looking outside, "a roof over your head," to this, he looked up, "safety from the wolves outside, and a particularly *unique* education. Am I wrong?"

With the last part being said, The Chancellor finally directed his attention back toward me. Stabbing through my soul once again with those piercing eyes of his. I opened my mouth with the intentions of confessing an apology, perhaps even confessing to what I had not done, in hopes that he might yet spare me. But before I could get a word out, he cut me off again. Raising a hand up, he stopped me dead in my tracks, as if he already knew what I was about to say.

Another unnerving minute trailed off. A breeze from the open window rolled in, sending a chill down my spine and into the soles of my feet. Although the sun was out and it was bright that morning, an eerie façade of dark silence had been cast over the room. So thick, that a knife could cut through it.

The Chancellor shifted his attention back to the window once more, and for a second, I thought that things would be okay. The man standing with his hands coupled in front of him remained silent. At his hip I could see the familiar dull sheen of a Glock 22.

It was then, with the simple wave of his hand, that The Chancellor ushered his assistant to leave the room. I watched in silent horror as the man disappeared and closed the wooden door behind him. All at once, my fears and concerns had returned in full force.

"I know you did not choose this life," The Chancellor said. "And I am deeply sorry for what happened to your mother."

This time, he spoke in a hushed tone. Before I could respond, it took me a moment to let his words soak into my head and resonate, leaving me to wonder why it was that my mother had been brought up.

"Sir, with all due respect, this is the only life I have ever known." Not knowing how The Chancellor would react to this, I took a long pause and waited before continuing. "And if I had the choice, I would still pick this one."

It was true. This really was the only life I had ever known. And the only one I would want. Despite my youth, it was too late, and I had already become too adulterated in the underground way of life that it would be impossible for me to survive in a normal one. When I spoke to The Chancellor, I was pulling the words out from the innermost depths of my heart. For I wasn't just being honest with him, I was being honest to myself.

Nodding in a way that exposed the top of his balding head, The Chancellor began to speak. "If you can recall, not too long ago I had promised that you would be safe here." Then, turning his head back to me, and making his voice more stern, he added: "When I had sent you off on your first freelance I did not anticipate things going astray like this," he said, waving an outstretched hand across the bed.

"I failed to stop him, sir, I should have performed better."

The room fell silent.

"Sir, I know I can do better."

"Perhaps you'll get another chance."

"What do you mean?" I asked, pondering his five words deeply. I then tilted my head, as if seeing from a different angle would somehow provide an answer.

The Chancellor got up. "I want you to meet somebody, Brendan." He started for the door.

Then, a thought occurred to me, and I spoke, surprising myself. "I saw the markings on his wrist, sir."

The Chancellor, who had been in the midst of turning the door-knob to leave, stopped.

"What did they mean?"

Taking his hand off the doorknob, The Chancellor turned back around. He proceeded to walk across the room, back toward the window. He then grabbed onto its frame as if it were about to fall apart.

I saw those piercing eyes of his look out into the courtyard below. He muttered something under his breath, but I could not hear what. His aging face seemed to tense up.

"The man who tried to kill you last week and succeeded in stealing those executive account files used to be a part of The Program."

"A Rogue?" I asked this without hesitation. The Chancellor then turned to respond, but before he could say anything, someone knocked at the door. Shortly after, the assistant walked back into the room.

Closing the sliding glass window, The Chancellor spun around to address him.

"*Je viens de recevoir mot sur une avance possible.*"

The Chancellor's face went cold. "*Quoi, ou au?*"

Lying there quietly on the bed, I listened in as The Chancellor and his assistant exchanged words with each other. My French was good, although not at the speed in which the two men in front of me were speaking, but I was able to make out the majority of the conversation. The man with the slicked back hair said he had just received word on a possible lead. The Chancellor was asking where. I assumed this all had to do with the executive account files on those floppy disks.

The Chancellor then said something, and his assistant glanced over at me, cocking his head to the side as if he just now noticed me. "Please excuse us," The Chancellor said, also looking over in my direction. Both men then vacated the room.

With them gone, I sat back up in the bed. Momentarily, it seemed as though the air had shifted back to normalcy, and I could once again breathe without that phantom noose around my throat. Perhaps my fate wasn't yet entirely sealed. Perhaps there was still a shiny glimmer of hope for me after all. In the absence of The Chancellor and his assistant, I was left to my own accord once more. In quietude. In absolution. Left to wonder what the stars would reveal for me.

Ten minutes passed by in earnest silence. I was just starting to surrender to sleep when I heard another knock at the door. Watching the knob turn, I sat up even straighter, ignoring the sharp pain that followed, expecting The Chancellor to come through again. Hopefully with some good news.

Much to my surprise however, it was not The Chancellor. Nor was it The Chancellor's personal assistant. Closing the door gently behind him, it was a tall fellow of slender, but sleek features. He had long blond hair that extended past his shoulders in an equally sleek fashion.

With the door closed, he quietly made his way to the foot of my bed, where he stopped and then smiled.

"I have been waiting a very long time to meet you," he said, bowing in a way that made the bangs of his long hair rush forward and dip.

While he spoke proper English, there was a mild presence of some Scandinavian tongue in his words, possibly of Swedish origin. Either way, I did not know how to respond. Who was this man?

Seeing no response from me, the blue irises of his eyes bounced back and forth, as if hoping for one. The Swede's face lit up again. "How are you feeling, my friend?"

"It hurts when I move too much," I finally said. "But I'm alive."

To this, the man's smile grew wider, almost from ear to ear. "So it appears, good boy!"

His voice was warmer than the rays of sun stealing in. The way he looked and his tone of voice seemed to scare out all traces of coldness that lingered from the previous conversation. It was as if he were radiating the warmth himself.

Still hearing no response from me, he went over to the window. "Ah," he said, sliding it back open. "That's much better." Then, turning his head toward me in a way that made his hair sway he said, "A boy in your condition requires all the fresh air he can afford."

"You were the one who saved me in Berlin," I said. There was something familiar about him, and ever since he walked into the room, I kept flipping through pages of my memory bank. Finally I had found the right page and pulled it out. Although I had been slipping in and out of consciousness that night when I was shot, I could still see enough of his face. And remember it. "Why did you do that?"

His eyes scanned over me, but instead of stabbing through my soul like The Chancellor's, they seemed understanding, as if he knew.

"My good boy," he said, sitting down at the foot of the bed, "I once promised someone special that I would do my best to look after you."

Having said this, the glow of warmth had seemingly flushed itself out of the room. It was as if the air particles themselves had been sucked out through that window, flowing out onto the courtyard below. It dawned on me that I hadn't just recognized this man from the safe house. I had seen him in *my* house before as well, sitting with my mother in the kitchen. Holding her hands. Then, his hair—his entire demeanor resembled that of a broken man. But now, he looked anew, like a phoenix rising from the ashes. Sizing him up, time stopped, leaving me and the man before me in a vacuum.

"I saw you with my mother that day," I said, finally being able to unravel my vocal chords.

He opened his mouth to speak, but after a brief pause, pursed his lips. He then squinted his eyes, as if trying to read my mind. When it hit him, he spoke. "Oh no, dear boy," he said. "I'm terribly sorry to say this, but I am not your father."

Hearing those heavy words, if there was ever a heart left inside my chest, it would have shrank now. I had merely played around with the idea. But hearing the words actually come out—*physically*—made it all surreal. And I felt the world's gravity crushing down on me.

"Look…*Brendan*," he continued, "I knew your mother well, and she cared very much for you. This I promise you."

Now his words were beginning to confuse me. Why did he feel it necessary to tell me all this? The death of my mother and of my childhood was a long-since closed chapter in my life. A section of a book I wished to never again open—for fear of what emotional monsters might become unleashed again.

In The Program, I was taught that emotions are the Achilles Heel of any man. And that it was better to bury them, before they buried you. During times of war, emotions serve only to falter the cause, not aid it. And I lived by this code.

Desperate to change the subject, I broke the silence. "Who are you?"

"Oh forgive me," the man said, picking himself up off the bed. He stood up and straightened himself out, displaying the entirety of his lengthy body. "How could I forget my manners? You may call me Theo." To this last part, he bowed. His hair dipping forward once again.

He then held out a hand to me, which I took cautiously.

I grabbed his hand more so as a means of leveraging myself up into a sitting position. Perhaps his name really was Theo. And perhaps it was not. Anonymity was a key to survival in my world. Some people chose to hide their names out of necessity. Others, out of fear. For whatever reason, the man standing in front of me wished to keep his from me, and to address him only as *Theo*.

After propping a pillow behind my back, I continued with my barrage of questions. "How did you know where to find me?"

Theo looked toward the window again, as if the answer lay some-where just beyond the compound. The sun was making its daily ascent past the hills, and the rays from earlier had splashed over Theo's pale face. "The man who stole those disks from the safe house," he said in a stern voice. "I have been tracking him for quite some time now."

"What do you mean," I asked, propping myself up even higher, the way a young child does after suddenly being intrigued by a bedtime story.

To this question, Theo took a pause. "He goes by Rafael. And he used to part of The Vice." Saying the last bit made his blue eyes dart toward the floor, as if he were ashamed of it.

But while Theo felt ashamed, I felt suddenly jubilant. I couldn't believe that I had gotten myself into a fight with someone from The Vice...and lived. Confronting one of these high-caliber, lethal hitmen is like poking a stick at a two-thousand pound Grizzly bear. And I had nearly succeeded in taking one down.

"I almost had him." The sudden confidence surprised myself as much as it did Theo, who directed his attention back to me.

"What do you mean?"

I thought back to that night. How I had him by the throat. "I mean we were fighting each other down in the basement. I reached him just after he had killed the other two men, and I tried to stop him from stealing those disk things." It took me a second or two to catch my breath. Even talking seemed to hurt, and I felt a pain coming up from my diaphragm. "At one point I finally had the upper-hand. I had a death-grip around his throat. And then…."

I ended my sentence abruptly, realizing that having said all that, I had my hands held out in a murderous fashion, as if Rafael were in front of me right now. But I had let him go. My open hands quickly turned into clenched fists.

Recalling the past event frustrated me and I sank back into the bed. It was not like me at all to have let something like that happen. Be it fighting against The Vice or not. And I still couldn't comprehend what had come over me, causing me to let him go like that. Maybe it was just brain trauma suffered from the fight, and under normal cir-cumstances, I would have succeeded in stopping him. Perhaps even *killing* him.

"I saw your portfolio," Theo said consolingly, as if he had seen the shame hidden in my eyes. "You're very skilled at what you do, and far greater ahead than when I started as a Freelancer."

Although he tried to smile, it did little to comfort me. The pain coming from my belly was bad, but failing to do my duty hurt far greater. It seemed there was little that would comfort me. But then again, nothing ever really did.

"Why were you with him?" I asked, changing the subject again. "And what do you mean he *used* to be part of The Vice?"

Theo started for the door. "That's enough for today. You need your rest. I will answer your questions another time."

"Thank you, Theo."

Stopping just short of the hallway, he turned around and smiled. "You're most welcome, Brendan." He then vanished down the hall and out of sight, letting the door close gently from behind.

When I was sure that he was gone, I sat back and closed my eyes. Listening as the wind blowing in through the window gave a sweet melodic whistle against the fibers of the wooden frame, I took a mental step back and brought myself back to the age of ten when I had eaves-dropped on the conversation my mother was having with the then haggard looking, long-haired man—*Theo*.

Why did my mother know him? And more specifically, *how* did she know him?

However, like all uncertain things in life, I knew that these answers would come in due time. If they were to come at all. The more I thought about how the different conversations played out today, the drowsier I became, and soon I found myself drifting off again. Perhaps to a world in which my mother would still be alive. And I hadn't killed all those people.

CHAPTER ELEVEN

The sound of a door being clanked shut woke me up. Blinking lazily, it took me a few seconds to realize again where I was.

I tried moving, but was immediately drawn to the dull pain emulating from my midsection. Glancing down, I saw that my bandages had been changed. While sleeping, someone must have come in and tended to my wound. What more, I was no longer seeing through glazed lens. My vision was back in full swing. And no headaches or dizziness either. Tearing off the bed covers, I ventured around the room.

As careful as I could, minding the dull sensation still gnawing at my abdomen, I made my way over to the corner of the room. Remembering the blurred pile of stuff that had been sitting on the small table, I was surprised to find that it had vanished. I was even more surprised to find that in its stead was a black suitcase with a note on top.

There was nothing else in the room, and I had no desire to inch back to that medical bed. Turning back to the letter, I picked it up. It was of the same variety as the one I had received after completing my Final Challenge. The paper was egg-shell white. The letters were gold.

> *Brendan,*
>
> *Please excuse my premature departure on Wednesday. By the time you are reading this, Saturday has already come. It is with the greatest hope that you are well enough to continue, for your services are required to retrieve what has been taken from us. An escort will come for you and you will then rendezvous for a briefing. There is no room for error once you leave this building, and only with the utmost deftness can we succeed.*

I let the last sentence roll off the tip of my tongue like a pill of ecstasy. What was going to happen next? Setting the note aside, I engaged the suitcase with my attention, letting my fingers slide against its leathery surface.

Carefully, I unlatched its silver buckles, mindful of whatever contents might be hidden inside. Much to my relief, but still creating more questions, there were only neatly placed items of clothing inside. From left to right, there was a black and white suit with a pair of dress shoes next to them. On top of the suit was a cell-phone, similar to the previous one, and a gun tucked inside a leather holster.

Taking it out of its holster, I examined the gun. Two magazines of sixteen rounds came with it—hollow-point bullets, which were standard-issue for my line of work. The serial numbers had been scratched off, and juggling the gun between both hands, I estimated its weight to be between four and five pounds—pretty heavy for a handgun. I took the gun back to the bed and sat down. Admiring the craftsmanship. Admiring the weapon. With this gun I would kill people. And not think twice about it. I was Nature's Reaper once again.

I then aimed the gun at the window and dry-fired a few times. Squeezing the hair-trigger made me smile. In a way, it always did. Walking back over to the table, I slid the gun back into the holster. But before I did, I screwed on the suppressor that had come with it. Putting the now-holstered weapon to the side, I began dressing myself with the newly found clothing.

I had just began slipping the black tie around my neck when a knock came from the door. Quickly I fitted the tie. Another knock came and I glanced down at the gun on the table, which I had since loaded. But before I could think about picking it up, the door swung open. A man of comparable size to me walked in.

"*Monsieur,*" the man said, giving me a wispy smile, "I am to take you to Nikola Tesla Airport."

His voice was soft, almost as soft and innocent as his pale skin. He was wearing a blue suit with a dark red tie, which contrasted greatly in my opinion. Coming down from his bald head was a scar that lined the left side of his cheekbone.

Nodding his balding head toward the door he added, "Please gather your things at once."

With that his smile quickly faded, leaving behind a cold, expressionless face that made the scar become more menacing. Without protest I nodded in confirmation to his request.

The man stepped aside, lapping his hands in front of him, as I tucked the gun into a pocket inside my suit. The cell-phone and extra magazines went into my pants, and when I was sure the suitcase was empty, I closed it.

Smiling once more, the man ushered me through the door. But as I made my way to it, I noticed something laying on the floor by the bed. Walking over to it, I discovered that it was the large jacket I had on during the IMF heist. I must have pushed it off the bed at some point. I put it on and proceeded back through the doorway, the man closing the door behind us.

For the first time in weeks I was finally leaving the room, seeing what lay beyond that solid, wooden door. But what shocked me most was that walking through the rest of the building was like traveling back in time.

The failing wallpaper, the aging green doors—it all screamed of the 1950s—as if we had been snipped from a fragment of history and lay stuck in a jar like a firefly while the rest of the world looked in on us with boyish eyes. The ceiling, low and bow-shaped, extended for what had to be a half mile in either direction of the hall we were pacing down. Antique carbide lamps hung scattered about the ceiling every five feet or so, dimly lighting up the white paneling and green paint which lined the bottom of the walls. There were rooms on either side of the hall, but unlike my room, these were cut off from the world by bulky doors with little rectangular holes carved out and tiny metal bars crisscrossing over them. Peering through them only added to the mystery of the building. Each room I passed lay empty and barren inside, with cold stone walls lining the interiors, and a single carbide lamp suspended from the top of each room.

At last we found the exit. Even though the rocky landscape beyond the building told me that I was back in Beivrus, it was obvious that this place was different than the others.

"It was used during the Cold War," the man said as we got into his vehicle. "For torturing captured NATO spies."

The car took off and I looked back at the building, grimacing. It was a haunting relic that had served an ancient clandestine purpose. At one point in time, it had been full of destructive power. But like most things in history, it has since been forgotten. Like all things in life, the world simply forgot and moved on.

But then something worse sent a shiver down my back. I wondered how many spies had been tortured and killed in the very same room I was in. How many of them had looked out that very same window and saw freedom lying just beyond the compound. So close was I to a similar fate as them. Yet I had been spared and given a second chance. Why?

Even though it was mid-day, the clouds above threatened of an impending storm. Or at least that's how it felt inside my mind. It felt as if Heaven was about to open up and send forth rain, creating the next Great Flood that would rid the world of all my sins. And prevent the new ones I was about to commit.

The ride to the airport was a silent one, as neither I nor the French escort said so much as a word to each other. This silence, however, afforded me time to fumble through my jacket once more, seeing if perhaps something new had been stashed inside. After a thorough search, I discovered nothing out of the ordinary. Just the first note from The Chancellor, and my wallet with my pendant and the enveloped receipt from the hotel in Reggio.

When we finally reached the airport, the escort stopped the car in front of one of the gates. Its engine hummed silently. Outside, drops of rain began hitting the car. The Great Flood was about to begin.

I reached for the car door, but found that it was locked. When I turned back to the driver, I saw that he had a little red book in his hand.

"What's that?"

The man formed a tight smile that made the scar on his face stretch. "Make sure to go through Line B," he said, handing the red book to me. "Good luck, *monsieur*." A second later I heard the door unlock.

Taking the book, I climbed out of the car. Before shutting the door, I turned back. "Thank you, sir."

The engine kicked to life, and I watched as the car left the entrance. But the rain had picked up and I could not stay out for long. The dry spot where the vehicle had just been was already being eroded by the rain. Turning my attention back to the terminal, I pulled the collar of my jacket close to my neck, pursed my lips, and headed inside.

You could tell it was the weekend because tourists and travelers of all kinds were fluttering through the busy halls. Large screens with ticker times announcing departures around the world stood atop the giant walls of the lobby. Looking down, I opened the red book. It was a passport and inside was a one-way ticket to Taoyuan International Airport.

I was heading to Taiwan.

The ticket was first-class and the plane was set to leave Gate C7 at 4:30pm.

Straining to see past a sea of passersby, a distant clock revealed that it was already 4:12.

Before heading for Gate C7, I found a bench and sat down, taking a few minutes to study my new alias. As I flipped open the red book again, I heard a scream. Expecting conflict, I jerked my head up. Another trill scream followed and I soon found the source of the noise. By the entrance was a small boy yelling in protest as what appeared to be his mother tried coaxing him over to the lobby. I thought of my scar and began caressing it.

Becoming so caught up in what I must do each day, I sometimes forget where I am. Not just here in the world, but also in my head. Being forced to live a life of constant and vigilant distrust, having to always keep my guard up and looking over my shoulders, I've developed a hard-strung paranoia. But I guess it just comes with the territory. Subsequently, I find myself becoming distracted. Forgetting the world I still live in, and the people I still share it with.

Turning my attention back to the passport, I resumed my memorization of the alias. In most instances, it's easy to slip past a busy Customs agent using a fake or even a camouflage passport. And for added protection, the best results occur when I obtain a passport from an obscure country that the part-time Customs agent knows very little about and will have difficulty in contacting the consulate for authenticity. In this case, I was Aabraham Otto Gregori. Born March 11, 1984 in Thallinn, Estonia. Although my Uralic tongue was lacking, my ability to speak fluent Russian would serve me just as well.

When I was sure that I was ready, and after scanning over the passport one last time, I got up and made the daunting task of sweeping through the sea of travelers toward C7. But as I proceeded through the hall, getting in line at the security checkpoint, it just dawned on me what I was carrying. I forgot about the gun tucked inside my jacket.

What made matters worse is that the line I was in was for Line A. The French escort had told me to find Line B. Immediately realizing my errors, I tried shifting my body through the pelage of people. After a series of pushing and shoving I had succeeded in getting in the right line. However, to further worsen the situation, the distant clock revealed that I had wasted yet more valuable time. I had just four minutes to reach Gate C7.

But there was still another problem. The gun. Ahead I saw a row of security guards lining the three check-points, with weapons drawn. Looking back, I saw the lobby now empty of the young boy and his mother. I still had a cell-phone and would call back to Beivrus. There had to be another way.

Clutching the passport as tightly as possible, I made for the lobby. But doing so, I soon discovered, was futile. Since stepping into Line B, more people had congregated around the checkpoint area. With the crowd closing in on all sides I felt like I was drowning. I was stuck in a sea of people. Flesh and blood. And the more I tried pushing my way through, the tougher it got. Doing so reminded me of a time long ago, when I was five and my mother was still alive. She had taken me to the beach for the first time. Being so young, I still had difficulty swimming. While my mother had her nose in a book, I made a break for the water. It wasn't long before I realized that I was in trouble. The water wrapped around my body and the tide rolled me around like it was nothing. Between gasps for air, I managed to scream loud enough to get the attention of my mother. Within seconds I felt her warm arms grab me out of the water. She had saved my life.

The crowd had since began inching me back toward the front of the line. Toward the row of security guards. Their faces were as smug and absolute as the guns they were holding out. I felt my heart beating against my chest. If only my mother were still here, I thought. If only she could reach out and save me yet again.

In a matter of seconds, I was next in line. In front of me, a middle-aged man was placing his briefcase onto a conveyor belt for inspection. He then walked through the security door. No lights or sirens went off.

He appeared to be a businessman, wearing a matching suit of blue and white. As he spun around for the guards to check him, I saw that his face was weary. Perhaps he was traveling to, or *from*, a weekend convention somewhere. In a way, we were both the same, traveling off to some place to conduct business.

Before I knew it, I was up next. I had made it through security countless times with no fear but for some reason this time was different. My throat dried up and I thought my heart would surely rip out of my chest, dropping onto the floor like a bloody sponge. In front of everybody. The sea of people. Flesh and blood.

Bracing for the worst, I handed over the little red book. The guard accepted it without saying anything. Every now and then he would glance up at me, and then his eyes would go back to the passport. I am Aabraham Otto Gregori, born March 11, 1984.

After another series of glances, the man beckoned another guard over. My palms began to sweat as I watched him proceed to whisper something into the other guard's ear.

This was it.

Upon entering the airport, I had scoped out all nearest exits. But the closest one to me now was fifty or so feet away. Too far. Too late.

In the event of a stand-off, there would be far too many witnesses. Too many cameras. Again, too late. Seeing no other means, I quietly slipped my hand into the jacket, feeling my fingers touch the deadly weapon inside. Clenching my teeth, I waited. I waited for the bloody inevitable to start.

With a sharp eye still on me, the first guard waved the other guard away. Inexplicably, he then muted the microphone that was clipped to the collar of his uniform.

"Please excuse me, sir," he said in a hushed voice that only I could hear. "We've been expecting you."

Even more surprising, he then looked over both shoulders and proceeded to flick a switch on the side of the security door. Handing me back the passport, he motioned with a hand for me to go through.

Seeing this, I froze. It took me a moment to realize what had just happened. When I had regained enough composure, I took my hand out of the jacket and slowly crept through the security door. To my great surprise, nothing happened. No flashing lights. No alarm announcing a security breach. And most importantly, no shootout.

When I was through the door, I continued walking, not daring to look back. Still in disbelief at what had happened, I quickly picked up my pace and headed for Gate C7. I had just three minutes to get there.

Fortunately for me, the line to enter Gate C7 was significantly shorter than the former lines, and it would be just moments before I would finally be boarding my flight, and as I merged myself into the line I noticed that I was among a pretty even mixture of Europeans and Asians.

Onboard, I found my seat and quietly sat down. Having a window seat, I stared out beyond the tarmac, looking at the many blank faces of those inside the airport waiting for their plane. Waiting, for their time to come.

Ten minutes later a strong jolt announced that the plane would soon be taking off, and I could feel the engines kicking to life. This was it. No turning back now. But the reality was, there was nowhere to turn back to—there never was—even before my unsavory admittance into The Program as a child. They say, 'home is where the heart is,' but I have never known either one. I had been taken from my home, and my heart was taken from me.

A minute later the captain spat his usual announcement over the intercom. But in my absence of focus, I could only hear garbled up words, like some distant voice echoing softly a mile away.

As I sat there, surrounded by all these people and their blank faces, I couldn't help but admire them. For so long I had existed, living a transparent life, that I've become transparent myself. In essence, I am a glass man. A hollow man.

There are times when I close my eyes and imagine myself in another life. One that's not transparent. And I see myself with these people. I lick my lips, imagining what a life like that tastes like. And it's almost too real. Even now, I find myself craving what these people have. Their homes. Their hearts.

The plane started moving and soon, the airport and all its lights and staring faces was behind us. Rain kept slopping up against the window, but for some reason I kept the blind up. Putting the cell-phone on vibrate, I closed my eyes and let my mind wander. Imagining *that* life.

Another announcement through the intercom woke me. I had been drifting off intermittently during the thirteen hour flight; it's hard to stay asleep long with a healing bullet wound in your belly, even when flying in first class.

According to the pilot we were within fifteen minutes of touching down. Glancing out the window, I saw the storm had ceased. The dark clouds had dissipated, and although it was now nighttime, I could still see the blue waters of the South China Sea as we neared the industrious island of Taiwan.

I must have been out cold though, because when I reached for my phone, I realized that it had slipped out of my pocket and onto the floor. When I reached for it, I saw that the screen was flashing.

MISSED CALL

Picking it up, I flipped open the cell-phone. Another, dimmer light was flashing.

NEW MESSAGE.

It was an address for the next rendezvous location. The missed call was from an unknown number, but I assumed it was for the same thing. Closing the phone, I dipped it back into my pants. I also patted down my jacket, making sure that nothing else had fallen out.

Minutes later, the plane's landing gear touched tarmac again. And unlike Nikola Tesla Airport, Taoyuan was large. It was an engineering marvel of its own, with gigantic windowed walls showcasing the many people moving about inside. There was even a metro system interconnected with the enormous airport. As I exited the plane, I noticed the vibrant lights of the nearby terminal cascading in all directions onto the black tarmac. Somewhere behind me, another plane was taking off.

Inside the airport, I struggled to find a kiosk for directions that were written in a language I could understand. My Mandarin was very limited. But finding a lit up map that was in English, I swooped toward it, fighting my way through a horde of travelers who were headed to the nearest gate.

I started scouring over the map, but a voice from behind stopped me.

"Glad to see you made it safely, good boy."

The voice was familiar, and I recognized it without having to turn around. Instead, I kept my eyes glued to the illuminated screen of the map. Here, in such an exposed location, I did not know what to expect, or who was watching us.

"I wasn't expecting to see anyone here," I said, still looking forward. "The message said to meet you at the safe house."

I felt the man move forward so that we were shoulder-to-shoulder with one another. Likewise, he too was staring at the map. Pausing, he waited a long time before responding.

When he did, I detected a subtle shift in the pitch of his voice. "Yes, I know. I just thought I'd see to it that you got here safely is all."

Curiosity trying to get the best of me, I considered following up with another question. What were we doing in Taiwan?

But knowing better, I kept the words stuffed down my throat. It was not wise to discuss such information in a place like this. My question, along with any others, would have to wait and play out in due time. Patience, I've since discovered, is a hard virtue to learn, but one that must be learned nonetheless.

We started for the nearest exit. No more words were exchanged. The silence was loud enough. From Taoyuan, we took a cab to the northeast of the island, into what is referred to as the Old Taipei County. I had been all over Europe, across the Americas, and even into parts of Western Asia, but never have I ventured as far abroad as the Far East. I knew little about the geography, and even less about the culture. Although I was not in any way afraid of what dangers might lie ahead, having Theo by my side comforted me greatly. And although I would never say it, part of me wanted him here.

After reaching the outskirts of our destination, Theo requested that the cab stop and we be dropped off. I began to protest but quickly stopped myself. The Taipei Metro would take us to the heart of the city, in Banqiao, within a few blocks of our target location. Had the driver taken us right up to the safe house, we would have risked compromising the entire operation.

With the exception of an occasional motorcycle zooming by or an intoxicated couple walking haphazardly home from some bar, the streets of Banqiao were barren of nocturnal activity. Somewhere distant, crickets were playing a tune. It was February, just a month or so after my twentieth birthday—when all the shit in the world seemed to hit the fan for me—and although it was no longer raining, you could feel the strength of the wet season in Taiwan. The humid air was fierce and my clothes stuck to my skin the way a piece of gum sticks to the bottom of your shoe.

Walking through the hollow streets of Banqiao was an experience like no other. Although New Taipei City itself was incredibly modernized, its historic roots could still be seen, assimilated amongst the updated counterparts. Here and there a building, fraying from the inside out, was squeezed in between a new apartment or a flashy business store. Seeing the vibrant splashes of blood-red bamboo rooftops suggested a revival in a culture that has all but disappeared. Refusing to die like the archaic and inflexible part of me that still believes there's hope.

By the time we finally reached the safe house, it was so late into the night that even the crickets had abandoned their musical efforts, leaving behind a blissfully eerie silence.

"Isn't anybody inside to let us in?" I asked, watching Theo pull out a set of keys. Finding the right one, he plugged it into the door and smiled sheepishly at me.

Opening the door he said, "Not for the next couple of days, good boy. We had the place emptied out to make room for...more *pressing issues*."

Before going inside, I glanced up at the tall, three-story building. It had once been some telecom center. Now, but a vacant building, as empty as the rest of the block. Only it wasn't really vacant.

"You mean for us?" I said at last.

Theo waved me into the safe house with a lengthy hand. I followed.

But as Theo came in, locking the door behind us, it soon became apparent why. "What's with the extreme hardware," I asked, watching as Theo plugged a dead bolt into the doorknob.

Theo tossed a sad glance at me. "What happened to us—to *you*—back in Berlin carried heavy weight throughout the entire organization." Taking a deep breath, he nodded into the dark room. "Certain *precautionary* additives were set in place for the remaining safe houses."

He nodded once more toward the living room we were now standing in, and the words *precautionary additives* soon became apparent. Plastic explosives of all sizes had been hardwired to the inside of the building, on all floors. It amazed me how Theo could throw around those words so lightly. In essence we were inside a giant, three-story bomb. Inside the belly of the beast. And I couldn't tell what I was now more afraid of, the deadly decorations of C4 or that my failure in Berlin had carried such blowback. Either way, I was determined to right my wrong, one way or another. And one thing was for sure, there was *nothing* that would stop me from completing this mission.

Putting my incessant anxiety, and the thought of all those high-end explosives, to the back of my mind, I followed Theo downstairs, where we spent the remainder of the night in the basement, discussing tomorrow's covert operation.

"The man we are after goes by the name *Mr. Blanco*," Theo said as we delved into the files and uprooted intel that had been cascaded across a wooden table. "But he is also referred to as *The White Dragon*."

Theo tossed me a black-and-white photograph across the table. I picked it up, scanning over the picture. It was obvious why our target had earned such a powerful name. Standing an astounding seven feet, Mr. Blanco was a towering man—easily the tallest man I had ever seen before. And his frame was built just as large. A formidable opponent, to say the least.

Something peculiar about the photograph—aside from the obvious—stood out. "What happened to his hand?" I asked, tossing the photograph back to Theo.

Theo took it, and squinted. "Our giant friend here does business with the Triads." He moved a finger over the photograph and tapped down on it. "A few years back he was caught stealing from them. So to teach Mr. Blanco a lesson, they cut off the index finger of his right hand."

"Why not just kill him?"

Theo mused the question. Smiling, he said, "Well, I guess the leaders saw some use out of the American after all. But they should have killed him. Not long after his *mutilation*, Mr. Blanco came back and personally decapitated one of the Triad's leaders," Theo used a thumb to mimic his head being sliced off. "And now, they fear him, which is why he has been given the heartfelt name of *The White Dragon*."

Theo smiled again as he fully extended his arms to emphasize the name, which in turn caused me to even chuckle a little bit at the sight of the spectacle. Seeing a broad smile produced from my face in return caused Theo to respond harshly.

"Do not get me wrong, Brendan, this man is not to be taken lightly. He is very dangerous."

There was a distinct sharpness in his voice that I had never heard before. It surprised me, and for a second, he did not seem at all to be the Swede I had come to know.

Finding my own set of crude words, I spoke. It felt as though I were now on the witness stand, defending myself. "Nothing's more dangerous than sincere ignorance and conscientious stupidity." Having said this, I took a step back from the table. A look of mild confusion ran across Theo's pale face. I watched as Theo's face became taut, and it were as though I could hear the cracks in his face move. Somewhere outside, a motorcycle was zipping by the safe house. When the noise was gone, I continued. "I am not the naïve fool you take me to be, sir."

To this, Theo lightened up, taking up the familiar jubilant expression that I had come to associate with him. He walked over to me saying, "My dear boy, I know you're not. And you do not have to address me as *sir*." He placed a hand on my shoulder. "I would not have brought you here if I thought otherwise."

I wanted to smile, but something else inside kept the muscles of my face from twisting up. Instead, I moved away, letting Theo's hand fall to his side.

"Back at the airport, why did you really show up?" It had been one of those questions that kept gnawing at me ever since we left. "And please don't lie to me. I could sense something was wrong by the tone of your voice then."

It was true. Like a dog smelling the subtle change in the air, I knew something was amiss back at the airport. It wasn't what he had said. It was *how* he had said it.

Theo grabbed a nearby chair and melted into it. He looked away, letting a long pause ensue before either one of us responded.

"You're all that's left of her," he finally said. His voice, now but a faint whisper.

"My mother you mean?"

Another series of motor vehicles went by outside. For the first time, I noticed the stale odor of the musty basement we were in. It was dank.

"Yes, good boy, your mother. Adeline."

When Theo spoke again, I couldn't help but feel sorry for him. But it wasn't in the way one feels sorry for another's loss. It was the sorry you felt, watching as a wounded animal died slowly, and painfully.

It was weird hearing her being called that. Adeline. My entire life, even up to now, I've just naturally referred to her as *mother* or simply *mom*. But hearing her being called by her actual, *real* name, gave confirmation that Adeline had once been a real person. With a real story to tell. Sadly though, my mother could not tell that story. It was up to others like Theo to speak for her. To tell her story in hopes that Adeline, my mother, might yet live on.

The death of my mother was a closed chapter that I wished to keep closed forever. But perhaps the *life* of her was far too important to be kept shut. Although I could not choose the life I was born into, or the unforeseen fate that has brought me here today, I was still at liberty to make a choice on how I chose to accept it all. I could either keep burying everything deeper and deeper, in hopes that nothing ever surfaced again, or I could accept the things I could not change and learn how to live with them.

After all, it is not the ghosts of our past that haunt us the most at night, but rather, it is the fear of failure that keeps us from sleeping.

I looked across the room, staring at the man slumped down into a wooden chair, his blue eyes glassed over. The last thing I ever expected to see here in Taiwan was a professional killer—a grown man to say the least, who had probably murdered countless people in cold blood—confiding in me his innermost emotions. Groveling to himself.

And it made me sad. Not just for him, but for me as well. Is this what would also become of me one day? A lonely man, in a lonely world that knew nothing of his existence—and didn't care. Was this too my fate?

A lonely tear streaked down Theo's face. Watching it move down and disappear onto the cold basement floor, I felt my own eyes well up.

Taking a deep breath, I put down the piece of intel I had since been looking at, and walking over to Theo, I touched his shoulder consolingly.

"You loved her, didn't you?" I asked, feeling for the first time my own set of emotions.

He looked up at me with red eyes that flickered under the basement's light. His face alone told a story of a depressing past.

"Yes," he said in between coughs. "Yes I did."

There was another chair next to the table with intel, pulling it out, I joined ranks with the saddened man.

"If you don't mind, Theo," I said, scooting close to him, "may I ask how it was that you and my mother met?"

Another pause. Straightening himself up, he pulled out a handkerchief and proceeded to rid his face of any remaining tears. Putting it back in his pocket he said, "Why yes, of course, dear boy, that's quite all right."

Grunting a few times, he cleared his voice. The room became silent.

"As you already know, Brendan, your father is the reason that you are here in The Program. Many years ago, he and I were great friends." Theo smirked to himself. "We both entered into The Program at the age of ten, like you, and spent a lot of time together during our training and education."

Having said all this, Theo smiled boyishly, and under the scantiness of the dimly lit basement, his pale face looked even younger. Whatever it was he was thinking, it made him laugh softly.

"Your father was six months ahead of me, and so naturally, when he had turned twenty, he completed his Final Challenge." Theo tilted his head up at me. "And might I add, if I can recall correctly, both you and your father had performed very well with your Final Challenges. Almost *flawlessly*."

I felt my face become flushed. But unlike Theo, I could not spare a smile. Sitting in that chair across from him, I continued listening, the way a young child does to an old relative as he recalled old war stories.

Somewhere outside, it started to rain again, and the watery bullets pelted the basement windows. Leaning over my chair, I listened intently as Theo continued with his story.

"Anyway, after his Final Challenge, your father graduated from TP and was immediately swooped up with a job. That was the last time I saw him in Beivrus, and, for the longest time, I hadn't heard from him."

I opened my mouth to speak, but Theo cut me off.

"It wasn't until about a year later when I myself had completed my Final Challenge and was four months into being a Freelancer that I received a letter from your father."

"What was it about?" I asked, seeing my chance to finally speak.

"It was about *you*, good boy," Theo said lightly, taking a moment for himself as the words seeped into my brain. When he saw me tilt my head, he pressed on. "The letter was announcing that he was having a child, and that he wished for me to be the godfather."

But how was this possible?

Theo gleamed, as if he knew what I had been thinking.

"Your father was living back in the United States with a woman he had met during leave-time and—"

"With my mother?"

"Yes, Brendan," Theo said. "With your mother, Adeline."

The storm outside had picked up intensity, and lightning was shooting down somewhere off in the distance, momentarily lighting up the basement in two great flashes. Both Theo and I glanced at the nearest window before he continued, trying to remember where he had left off.

Finding the spot, he said, "And he wanted me to meet her after you were born."

I felt my mouth dry up. "Why would he do such a thing?"

At first Theo pursed his lips, but then, realizing what I had meant he said, "Brendan, you are free to do as you please outside of TP. And don't forget, if it wasn't for your father, you wouldn't be here today."

He saw me look away. "Don't be discouraged. Your father was a very smart man and would never do anything that could potentially compromise anybody or the organization."

If only this were true. How could I thank such a man though? It wasn't *him*—my father—that had given me everything. It was him who had taken everything away from me. My childhood. My mother. It was him who made me wish I had never been brought into such a cruel and indifferent world.

Theo's blue eyes danced up to the wooden ceiling of the basement. "When I was finally able to visit his new family, I had just completed a job in Russia." Telling the next part of the story made Theo's eyes drop back down to the floor. "The very first time I laid eyes upon Adeline, my heart stopped. She was the most beautiful woman I had ever seen, and knowing your father, I knew that your parents were a good fit."

"But you were wrong," I said without thinking.

Theo frowned. Looking up at me he said, "He used to be a very good man at one time."

"What do you mean by that?" I asked. "How can you make such a bold claim on a man who had killed so many people? In what we do, there is no good or bad. Only outcomes."

I could feel my knuckles becoming white as I slowly dug into the sides of the chair. "You speak of my father as though he were a saint. But there is no Heaven for people like *him*, or *us*. Only Hell. We are the devil's abandoned children, and one day He is going to claim all of us."

I didn't realize how loud my voice had become by the time I was finished talking. In the absence of the lightning, it was now *my voice* that was doing the booming. Lighting up the room with my heated words by my heated tongue.

Across from me, Theo continued to stare at my face, as if examining me. And for a split second, I wondered whether all I had just said had simply been inside my head.

"You have her eyes and ears you know," Theo said at last, as if trying to change the subject.

"But my mother's dead now," I said, shaking my head as if to throw off the words.

"Only if you allow her to be," Theo said. Placing a finger on his left breast he continued, "Inside that bold chest of yours, Brendan, there is still a heart. And if you allow your mother to be, she is still alive inside it."

As the wind outside shifted, the rain continued to slap against the windows with more tenacity. Above us, the aging building creaked and moaned like an old man.

Theo looked away for a moment. But under the faintness of the light I could see that his eyes were still glossy. Staring at him, I continued to dig my nails into the wooden chair.

"How did he die?"

Theo sighed, wafting a burst of breath into the room. I watched as it slowly crept up and dissipated into the floorboards above us.

Still looking away he said, "He took a solo op in Algeria about six months after you were born. But the intel was false. He walked into a trap by a competing organization."

The building above continued to sway, and I began to worry about the explosives. Theo didn't seem to notice though. It was obvious he was worried about something else.

"I had remained in distant contact with Adeline," he said, turning to me. "And what were words of sorrow and mourning, in time flourished into words of fondness and affection. It wasn't long before we fell in love with each other. But hear me out, I never meant for that to happen, it was never my intention to replace your…."

Theo's words trailed off, the way a sled does in a snowstorm.

"My father," I said, completing the sentence for him.

I felt my hands let up, retracting two sets of nails from the depths of the wooden chair. Theo stared back at me, his eyes going right through my body, across to the brick wall behind me.

The conversation we had about Theo's past, which had somehow become intertwined with mine, lasted for the greater part of the evening, until we finally parted ways for the night.

Living as a loner for as long as I had, the conversation with Theo was undoubtedly the longest I had ever had with another person—inside, or outside of The Program—and it unraveled a tier of emotions I had never known existed within me.

Before parting for the night, I knew I had to say something to my partner—for the sake of lifting his spirit back up. For the sake of the mission. After all, I could not afford, nor would I be responsible for a man so emotionally vulnerable. But somehow, deep inside a part of me that rarely saw the light, I truly *did* want to lament with the man.

"Theo," I called out from behind.

He had since gotten up and was making his way to a bedroom at the other end of the basement. It was too dangerous to go upstairs.

Theo halted. His blond hair trailed down past his shoulders. "Yes?" he whispered.

"Perhaps some time you can tell me about my mother."

My voice echoed against the walls of the basement. Although his back was to me, I knew that he was smiling.

"Yes, of course, good boy," he said.

And with that, I watched as his tall figure slowly disappeared into the darkness. Day one had come to a turbulent close.

CHAPTER TWELVE

Inside my own room, I found a military cot stacked up against the wall. Putting it on the floor, I brushed off the dust and sat down. The room was musty and smelled of moisture that had undoubtedly seeped in from the rain outside. Nonetheless, it was a room. It was shelter.

Despite having slept a little during the flight into Taoyuan, I still felt lethargic. But although my eyes became heavy, screaming for more sleep, my brain was racing. Sleep was the last thing on my mind. I took a deep breath, ignoring the pungent odor of the dank room.

As much as I wanted to think that there was a hard outer layer shielding me from years of loneliness, what Theo had said unsettled me greatly. Coupled with the thoughts of tomorrow's impending actions, wondering what events would unfold, I couldn't bring myself to lie down and close my eyes. No, there would be no room for sleep that night.

A single oil lantern sat on the floor alongside the cot. For what seemed like an hour, I watched as the flame swayed back and forth on the tapered wick, casting silhouettes of dancing shadows on the walls.

Somewhere beyond what the lantern could illuminate was a clock. *Tick tock. Tick tock.* The indifference of the noise produced by the clock as the hands of time moved forward seemed to coalesce with the flickering of the flame. It was as if light and time were partners. I wondered what my own partner, Theo, was up to. Was he sleeping? Or was he too kept awake by the ghosts of his past? I shuddered to think that what I was to become when I got older was a man like Theo. Alone. Sad.

There was a painting strewn on the wall adjacent to my cot. After gingerly swinging my legs up on the bed, being careful not to agitate the still-healing wound, I rested my head on my jacket and stared up at the painting. It was an oil canvas of a small wooden boat being thrust around by a violent sea. I took another deep breath, this time, welcoming the musty smell.

For the rest of the night I kept thinking about my mother. My mind was working on overtime. Part of me wanted to remember what she looked like, particularly her face. But then another part of me was trying to block it out, as if trying to get me to forget everything from my childhood for fear of what it could do to me lest the truth be unraveling.

After another series of painstakingly long hours the clock finally struck six. A minute later, the sound of a door being closed from outside my room announced that it was finally time and I was free from my imprisonment. Quietly, I crept out of the room, leaving the wooden ship in that painting at the mercy of the violent sea. Behind me, the clock kept chipping away at time. *Tick tock. Tick tock.*

The kitchenette in the basement was surprisingly well stocked with canned foods. Although I was not in the least bit hungry, I knew that we had a long day ahead of us. Theo and I ate with avid ferocity. For all we knew, this could be our least meal.

After breakfast, we prepared for war. Like the many other safe houses scattered across the globe, this one had a stockpile of weapons for our disposal. However, given the nature of our task, neither one of us found it necessary to bring more than what was needed.

Based on what had happened last night, I expected the worst out of Theo, and to be honest, I was not sure if we would still be able to complete the mission. Much to my surprise, it seemed as though Theo had recovered full tilt. Perhaps he had found solace in the night and was able to sleep. The familiar airiness had returned in him, allowing me to regain my own confidence. As Theo and I moved about the table in the basement, grabbing the necessary supplies, scouring over the intel one last time, I couldn't help but admire my partner once more. It was not that he could feel emotion, or even that he seemed able to resume his responsi-bilities as a professional killer, but rather that he could balance both ends of the spectrum. This, I envied most about the tall man standing before me. And for this, I knew that Theo was a better man than I.

When we were ready, we exited the building from the side. Walk-ing down the narrow side alley we were met by a taxi cab idling on the street out front. Unlike last night, the bustling streets of New Taipei City were now in full swing. Even before leaving the basement, I could hear the unmistakable clamor of a busy city. Through the night, it had come to life again. Like a phoenix rising from the ash.

The driver didn't say much as we made our way across the city, or perhaps I just wasn't paying attention. Although I was there, my head was someplace else. In light of everything that had happened the past twenty-four hours I suppose I was just anxious to get the job done.

After what felt like an hour, watching as the tiny cab wove in and out of traffic, we finally parked. Getting out of the cab and paying the driver, Theo and I walked the remaining block to our true destination.

Theo's hair was tied back into a tight ponytail and his blue eyes glis-tened indulgently under the intense Asian sun. Letting him lead the way, I followed close behind, still trying to wrap my head around everything.

It was getting warmer as we continued toward our destination, and I was glad that I had left my jacket back at the safe house. I had made a good call doing so, and I hoped that it would not be the only good call made that day.

About five minute later, Theo stopped. He was staring across the street at a four-floor building nestled in between tiers of smaller apart-ments. On the ground floor was a restaurant. Our destination.

But before crossing the street, Theo motioned toward two Asian men standing on either side of the restaurant's front entrance. They both had on black suits and matching red ties. Although it was too far to see, I knew what was buried underneath their suits. Digging a hand into my own suit, I felt for the grip of one of my pistols.

Theo and I circled around the block once more, and in time, the men standing in front of the restaurant had disappeared inside. Nudg-ing Theo in the side, I advanced across the street, still gripping the gun.

Stepping inside the restaurant, we waited to be seated. Ahead of us was a group of tourists, and while waiting, I took the opportunity to scan the layout.

There were no security cameras in sight, but then again, I didn't expect a place like this to have any. In the underworld, justice was administered by other means. Instead, the ceiling was decorated with red and white silk tapestries, lining the interior from wall to wall. Where the tapestries ended, gigantic mirrors fanned out across the walls, with the exception of the glass windows facing the street.

When it was our turn to be seated, we quietly followed the hostess. I had since taken out my hand, seeing no further threat inside the restaurant. For the time being anyway.

Despite it being so early in the day, there were a good number of people seated at the various tables and booths. As the hostess led us around the heart of the restaurant, I noticed that Theo refused to look at himself in the walled mirrors, making me wonder what he was afraid to see in them.

At length, Theo nodded toward at an empty table toward the back. "This'll do," he said to the waitress.

Theo sat down with his back to the mirrored wall, while I sat across from him, allowing both of us plenty of visual throughout the restaurant. Somewhere in the large room lavender and vanilla candles were wafting away—something an Asian would not typically do, but rather, an *American*. I thought back to the black and white photograph of Mr. Blanco and all of his gigantic figure.

Within minutes the kitchen doors had swung open from the other side of the room, and a middle-aged man wearing a black apron was trotting over to our table.

Stopping in front of us, the man smiled. 'What can I get you?" he asked in broken English, pulling out a pencil and tablet from his apron.

"Just two coffees please," Theo said politely.

The waiter raised an eyebrow. "No food for you?"

"We just ate," Theo said.

The waiter gave us a puzzled look, and Theo smiled back at him. Putting his writing utensils back into his apron, the waiter thanked us and disappeared back through the kitchen doors. When he was gone, Theo and I looked at each other and chuckled. His blue eyes twinkled and for some reason it made us laugh even harder.

After a few minutes the waiter had returned with our coffees. It seemed we both liked ours black, no sugar or spice. Nothing nice. We began discussing the day's Op.

Something near the front of the restaurant caught my eye in the mirror and I broke from what I had been saying. Coming in through the front were the two men in red ties from earlier. They began conversing with the hostess.

Theo was quick to pick up on what I was staring at and casually glanced over my shoulder toward the front as well.

Their blood-red ties seemed to glow under the restaurant's overhead fluorescents. Although they were different men, they were of similar features and similar build. From the other side of the room I could see the subtle bulge jutting out their backsides. My guess?

Pistols.

The waiter had reappeared at our table, replenishing our coffee. He smiled at us as he did so, and for the first time I realized there was a slight scar just above the man's right eyebrow. Seeing it made me think of my own scar. I guess everyone has scars that don't seem to ever heal. Under the table, I ran a finger across my right hand, just inside the palm.

When the man was gone, Theo took a sip of the fresh joe. The men at the front were still conversing with one of the hostesses. Although my attention was turned to Theo, I kept a watchful eye on them.

"How is it?" I asked, taking a healthy gulp of my own coffee. It was hot and, coupled with the heat of the day, despite a wooden fan circling above our table, I began to sweat. Taking off my blazer, I rolled my sleeves up. One of the pistols was just under the table, within arm's length.

"Not bad," Theo said, taking another sip. "Tastes a little *Asian* if I say so myself."

At first Theo's face was taut, but then a slight twinge in the corner of his mouth revealed that he was making a joke. Putting my coffee back on the table, I stared down into the dark liquid, looking at a distorted image of myself. I stabbed a spoon into the coffee and began stirring the face away. I guess I too didn't like what I saw.

"You know, I've done over a hundred hits, and been on twice as many jobs," Theo said. His voice was soft. I looked up at him, still stirring my cup. "But to this day, I still find myself getting the jitters before the mission."

To this I smirked, wanting to feel the same way. There was a time once, when I too could feel the same sentiment. But sadly, that was a long time ago—another *life* ago. My apathy is what set me apart from this world. Keeping to myself was a familiarity in a world so unnatural and foreign.

But it came with a price and was a heavy burden to bear, and at times I wanted out. Sitting there in the restaurant, I wanted to tell Theo everything. I too wanted to let my innermost sacramental thoughts out. I wanted to feel sentiments again.

"Theo I—"

"May I get you gentlemen anything else?" the waiter asked, having returned to our table.

Theo's focus went from me, to the waiter. Quietly, I resumed stirring my coffee.

"There is one thing, my friend," Theo said.

The waiter got closer to Theo and pulled out his notepad again. As he took out a pencil to write though, Theo placed a hand on the waiter's arm. The man looked up, startled for a second.

"No, no," Theo said, smiling. "My friend and I were actually meaning to talk to Mr. Blanco. Is he here?"

The waiter took a step back so that Theo's hand fell to edge of his seat. "No, Mr. Blanco is no here."

Theo tried again, this time his voice getting softer. "Please, we wish to see him. We have some business to discuss with the man. Can you help us?"

The man's face twisted, causing his scar to vanish under his black hair. "What kind business do you have with Mr. Blanco?"

His voice was sharp, and despite Theo's charming performance, foreplay was over. Theo's eyes went from the waiter, to me. Straightening himself up he said, "My friend and I have *private* business to attend to. So if you will, please go fetch him now?" A stream of agitation was tapered to the end of Theo's voice.

Listening, I crossed my arms on the table. The waiter glanced down. He then shot a strange look at both of us. To my surprise he threw down his notepad and bolted from our table.

Theo squinted as the man dashed for the other end of the room. Alarmed by what had just happened I stood up, carelessly knocking over my cup. The black liquid glided across the table.

"Your wrist," Theo said, still looking over my shoulder to the rest of the room.

"What do you mean?"

Theo grabbed my wrist and twisted it over. "He saw the tattoo on your wrist. He must know who we are."

"But how—"

As I began to speak though, nervous clamor from the surrounding tables of bewildered faces announced that we had an audience. Through the walled mirror I saw the waiter making his way to the front of the restaurant, knocking over a chair as he did so.

The restaurant became silent.

I looked at Theo for answers, but now was not the time. His lips were pursed and his pale face revealed tightened cheek bones. "*After him*," he said.

Grabbing my blazer from under the table, I joined Theo in pursuit of the waiter. By then he was feet from the front door, running past the two guards who appeared confused.

Theo and I were quick to catch up, running past tables of blank faces. Somewhere behind me I heard a plate crashing on the floor.

When we were at the front entrance the two men in red ties tried stopping us. They stood in front of the door and held their hands out in protest, but Theo and I simply threw ourselves into them, knocking them over. We crashed through the doors, almost falling onto the sidewalk outside.

It was a lot hotter outside and the sun beat down on our faces as we struggled to find the waiter. However, the sound of a cart being knocked over on the other end of the street grabbed our attention. And before long, we were on the waiter's trail again. He was running with tired speed and his black apron had since been torn off. It lay idly on the street as we went by. Theo drew his gun.

A loud burst of gunfire from behind announced that we too were being hunted down. The two men had since gotten back up and were chasing after us. Each man held a black pistol, just as I had suspected, shooting haphazardly as we weaved in and out of their line of sight.

The chase was on.

Theo and I had a good ten-second lead on the men behind us, but their bullets were getting dangerously close to hitting their mark. More than once I heard a bullet whizzing right past my head, sinking its metallic teeth into the pavement in front. Reminding us that distance meant nothing to a gun.

The waiter was slowing down and he turned a corner ahead. We were closing the gap on him and I could see beads of sweat rushing down the back of his head. Theo held his gun up to shoot, but by then the man had gone down the alley.

There was a stand displaying vegetables ahead of us. Passing by it, I flipped the stand over. Behind me I heard one of the men grunting as he stumbled over both display and vegetables. The other man stopped to help him up, buying us time.

We turned the corner in time to see the waiter cutting through a building. Picking up speed, we followed him through, leading us out the other side. More blank faces were staring as we continued our pursuit. It was a game of cat and mouse. But unlike the cartoons, the cat would not be bested.

My veins were coursing with adrenaline. In moments like this, I *lived* for the excitement. Unlike Theo, who continued to run ahead of me with a stern face, I couldn't help but allow a wicked grin to cross mine. If ever I were to enjoy something—it would be this. It was a challenge, and I liked a good challenge.

I could no longer see or hear the men in crimson ties. Behind us, the streets were still bustling. Business went on as usual. After all, the world did not care.

With each second that passed, Theo and I gained more and more ground on the waiter. I could hear his heavy gasps of desperation. He was a wounded animal.

And I was the wolf.

Theo was the first to catch up to him. The waiter had made the mistake of turning down a dead-end alley. Cornered on all sides by brick walls, the man began stammering.

There was a metal grating running up one of the walls, and in a last ditch effort the waiter started to climb it. Theo was too quick and he ripped the man off the grating, throwing him down onto the ground like it was nothing.

"What's the matter, my friend," Theo said, circling him like a hungry shark. "Why did you run?"

The waiter didn't say anything.

Theo kicked him in the side and he let out a cry. His hair was matted down by sweat and I could see the scar above his eye once more.

Leaving Theo to interrogate the man, I headed back to the alley's entrance to keep a lookout. Behind me, I heard the waiter whimpering in protest.

It wasn't long before I spotted our two friends from earlier. They were jogging up the sidewalk not too far away. I stepped out, making sure that they saw me. I headed back down the alley when I was confident they had taken the bait.

By then Theo was sprawled on top of the waiter. He had a gun shoved inside the man's mouth and was yelling something at him.

"We're about to have two guests at the dinner table," I said, lunging into a pile of wooden pallets stacked up alongside the one wall.

Sighing, Theo nodded at me. Taking the gun out of the waiter's mouth, he grabbed the man by his shirt and proceeded to drag him across the ground to the other wall, behind a Dumpster.

With my back against the brick wall, I crouched down as best as possible with the wound in my gut throbbing. Despite the pain, I managed to hide behind the stack of pallets thankful that my injury had healed enough to not break open.

Theo had the man propped up against the Dumpster with his back to him. He then positioned his arm over the man's shoulder, cocking back the gun held in his hand. "Don't move," he whispered into the man's ear. "You say anything, and I'll kill you." He pressed his gun into the back of the man's neck for emphasis. Silently, the waiter nodded his head.

I drew my gun. Peering through a fissure in the pallets, I waited. Coiled up like a trap. Although I was sweating from the heat, my heart was calm. I glanced over at Theo. His face was fixed on the alley's entrance. His hair was unnervingly taut against his right shoulder. I thought back to what he had said about getting the jitters before every mission. It was doubtful that he was nervous now. The way he looked, I envied it.

The sound of men panting brought my attention back to the other end of the alley. I heard footsteps as they slowed down. Two weary men with guns drawn soon came around the corner. The one was whispering something to the other as they walked toward us.

I scooted even closer to the edge of the pallets, bracing for impact. I saw Theo fitting a silencer to the end of his gun. The waiter in front of him had his eyes squeezed shut. I too screwed on a silencer.

Our ambush was set.

When the two guards were within five feet of the Dumpster, Theo struck. Reaching over the waiter, he fired two rounds into the closest man, dropping him instantly. The blowback from the two shots sprayed the other guard in the face and shoulder. But before he could react, I leaned over the pallet. I shot him square in the temple. His body fell sideways.

The waiter let out a scream that quickly turned into a garbled noise as Theo pressed his hand over the man's mouth.

"You'll end up like your friends here if you don't cooperate with us. Understand me?" Theo said. The waiter nodded again. Tears were streaming down his face.

While Theo was occupied with the waiter, I got up to hide the bodies. Compared to others I've had to dispose of in the past, these were light.

After searching their clothes and coming up empty, I went over to the Dumpster and flipped its lid open. I then tossed one of the bodies into it. As I made for other one though, I stopped.

Laying there on the ground, the guard that Theo had killed looked peaceful. Being spared of the bloody ending as his partner, this man's face was in complete bliss. Seeing it angered me. In some way, this man was better than me. I didn't like how happy he looked.

Before throwing him in with the other body, I put two more rounds into his face, abruptly ending any peace. Or happiness. Theo saw me, but did not say anything. To me, before one could experience such true peace, one must first go through true violence.

When I was done I turned around, catching a glimpse of Theo staring at me as he tied up the waiter.

"Find anything?" He picked the man up and pressed his face up against the brick wall.

Shrugging, I said, "Just wallets and a pocket knife."

I held up the two leather wallets and tossed my head over to the Dumpster.

Theo shook his head. "Take those. We'll need them."

After slipping the new items into the inside of my blazer I walked over to assist Theo. "What do we do with *him*?" I said plainly, not caring that the man was still in tears.

"Oh he'll have his use," Theo said, spinning him around so that his back was against the wall. Glaring down at the short man he said, "We'll take him with us for now."

The man resumed stammering, but Theo was quick to put a hand over his mouth again, leaving him to produce those garbled sounds once more. With his other hand, Theo grabbed the man's shoulder. As he pulled him away from the wall, something fell from the man's front pocket and hit the ground.

Theo shoved the man against the wall again, this time hard enough that he cried out in pain. He then bent down to pick up what had fallen.

It was a gray cell-phone. Theo flipped it open. Despite taking a nasty fall, it still appeared to function.

"And what is this, my friend?" Theo said, knocking the waiter against the wall again. This time even harder.

Theo's large hand was still over the man's face and he struggled to respond. "*P—please* no kill me!" he managed to say in between whimpers.

Theo tossed the phone over to me and I studied its contents. All the contacts were in Mandarin.

"Mr. Blanco," I said. "Is his number on here?"

At first the waiter refused to speak, but after seeing Theo flash his gun at him, he quickly changed his mind. His eyes danced back and forth from me to Theo.

When he nodded his head, Theo removed his hand so that he could speak. After a few deep breaths the man spoke, his voice quivering.

"Ye—Yes."

"Good. Call him," I said, pitching the phone back to him.

Looking up at me with swollen, red eyes, the waiter flipped open the phone. His hands shook as he scrolled through the list of contacts.

When he found the right number he smiled queerly. Then, after pressing a button on the phone, he held it up to his ear. Out of impulse I grabbed it from him and listened for a ring tone. Hearing one, I gave Theo the thumbs up.

Theo nodded in confirmation and I plugged the phone back into the waiter's ear. Theo then pressed his gun into the man's stomach. "Talk," he said.

The three of us pressed our heads together as the phone continued to ring. Each ring seemed long and tedious and it reminded me of the clock on the wall back in the basement. Its black hands chipping away at time without remorse. *Tick tock. Tick tock.*

At last the ringing stopped and someone on the other end picked up. Theo and I listened while a male voice spoke into the waiter's ear.

"Yes, yes, Mr. Blanco. Everything okay," the waiter said, staring up at us. His eyes were blood-shot.

The voice on the other end said something else. "No, no. Mr. Shao and Mr. Xing okay." He glanced over at the Dumpster. "They with me. Everything okay."

Theo pressed his gun further into the man's stomach. Grunting, the waiter said, "Mr. Blanco. I need see you about *personal business.*"

Theo grinned, having heard the last part.

There was a pause on the other end. At length, the voice spoke again.

The waiter nodded. "Yes, thank you, Mr. Blanco." When the conversation was over, he flipped the phone closed and held it out.

"No," Theo said, pushing the man's hand away. "What did he say, my friend?"

The waiter glanced down at the gun. Theo removed its presence from the man's gut. Packing the cell-phone back into his pants he said, "Mr. Blanco see me *now.*" He then raised his hand and pointed toward the restaurant.

After we were sure that the coast was clear, we doubled back to the restaurant. The waiter led the way with Theo close behind, concealing a gun that was pressed up against the man's back. Taking up the rear, I watched cautiously for any hint of trouble.

We were not naïve to the notion that someone back at the restaurant might have notified Mr. Blanco. Our impromptu exit had undoubtedly stirred the waters. For now though, it seemed we had things under control.

Walking back to the restaurant though seemed different. And not in the sense of *trouble* different. Something in the air made my skin crawl. While at first I could not put my finger on it, I soon realized what I was feeling. It was something I had felt my whole life. I was just too blind to notice it before. The atmosphere surrounding Taipei had shifted—in what direction, I was unsure of. But in the air was a familiar taste, and I knew it all the same.

It wasn't by chance or good fortunate that Theo and I did what we did without being noticed. After carrying the bodies over to the Dumpster, I had looked back toward the other end of the alley. I saw the shuffle of people going by. I saw their absent, pallid faces. Nobody bothering to look our way. Nobody *caring* to look our way. The feeling I now felt as my skin crawled and my tongue dried up was the realization of the world's apathy. My whole life I had known this sensation. But only now, for the first time, could I place a finger on the feeling. The world just simply did not care. It never did.

The two men we had slaughtered back in the alley—who I assumed to be *Mr. Shao* and *Mr. Xing*—had a history. They had a past. They had a present. And if it wasn't for us, they would have still had a future. They came from somewhere. Secreted inside my blazer were their wallets. I had seen the pictures of their families inside them. They had wives, children; people whom they loved and cared for. Unlike Theo or me, they had people to come home to each day. Unlike us, they *belonged* somewhere.

It was times like these when I struggled the most, trying to cope with who I was. With *what* I was. I was a monster—and like Theo—I hated seeing myself in the mirror. Like the man walking next to me, hiding a gun that would go off at the slightest movement from the waiter, I was afraid to see myself for who I truly was. I had but one purpose in this life, moving through a world whose naked apathy for the horrors that occurred in the darkness ate at me, chewing away every inch of my soul like rats. I was Death's soldier. But even the Reaper had no place in Hell.

It wasn't long before the three of us had returned to the place where our day had begun. To the epicenter. Stopping just shy of the entrance, I stared up at the tall building, towering over the lesser structures with its restaurant and three stories of slums, where somewhere above, Mr. Blanco sat in his office. Waiting for us.

Instead of going back into the restaurant, Theo and I followed the waiter through a door connected to the building from the side. A set of stairs spiraled up the remaining three floors and we wasted no time in going up them. The waiter still leading the way with a gun aimed at his back. Theo and I, close behind, nipping at his heels lest he change his mind.

Reaching the top floor, the waiter stopped. His heavy breathing hung in the air and echoed down the stairs below. I looked back down, making sure we were still alone.

Theo waved his gun at a door leading into the fourth level. "Lead us, please."

A wide hallway connected to the door, and walking through it reminded me of my first job. As we made our way toward Mr. Blanco's office, passing by closed doors to unknown apartments within, it brought me back to New York, and I could begin to smell that acrid stench of burning coal mixed in with drying paint.

They had made me go back to his apartment a month later to get rid of the body. Even now, I can still see his bloated carcass; his face chewed off by rodents. Even now, the smell of rotting flesh stung my nostrils. Although it was supposed to be done by someone else, The Chancellor had charged me with the daunting task. It felt like a punishment, but willingly I had said yes. It was my duty after all. Anything for The Chancellor.

Bony knuckles knocking on a door brought me back to the present. We had arrived. Taking up both sides of the door, Theo and I waited for it open. Guns drawn up at eye level.

The waiter took a step back. But Theo ushered him forward with his gun. Raising his hand, he knocked on the door again. His bony knuckles driving into the oak door with more tenacity.

I looked over at Theo, who simply smiled in return. But I knew his gesture was as empty and hollow as the hall we were standing in. In the back of my head I kept thinking the worst. This is a trap. The fucking waiter was leading us right into a trap.

But then again, I always had those thoughts. Just as Theo felt jittery before each job, I saw myself going to my own death. I went into each job wondering if it would be my last. In what I do, paranoia was my best friend...my *only* friend. But it was also my worst enemy, having two sides like a coin being flipped in the air. So far, that coin had always landed *heads*. But I knew it was only a matter of time before it came up *tails*.

Subduing my baser fears, I took a deep breath. The waiter knocked again. This time, a muffled voice on the other side of the door answered. It sounded Mandarin, and although neither Theo nor I could understand it, the waiter seemed to comprehend. He replied to the voice in his native tongue, but Theo nudged him with his gun. Whispering in the waiters ear he said, "In English, my friend."

There was pause. I could see this going south at any moment.

The man on the other side of the door spoke again. The waiter stepped even closer to the door. The pits of his white shirt were stained a light yellow and by now, he began to stink of sweat. Swallowing, he said, "It is Jin Lu. I have meeting with Mr. Blanco."

Another pause. Then, the disembodied voice mumbled something else, and the door cracked open.

At the sound of the door's mechanical latch being opened I had pulled back on my gun's hammer. I was ready to go.

The door swung open, revealing an Asian man who resumed speaking with the waiter. Before our hostage could respond though, I moved swiftly behind him. Extending my gun over his left shoulder I tapped the trigger and fired into the room, sending a single bullet tearing through the man's head.

The silencer created a distinct *puffing* noise, and although it was not loud, it could best be compared to Paul Revere's "Shot heard around the world." For shooting the Asian man unleashed a deadly chain of events to occur in the fourth floor apartment.

After shooting the man in the head, a barrage of gunfire from deep within the room immediately erupted. The doorway was quickly chewed away and wooden splinters exploded into the air.

There had been three other men standing toward the center of the room, in front of a large wooden desk. Two of the men, who were quickly getting into position behind some overturned furniture, had submachine guns. The third man remained standing amidst the chaos that ensued. His bearish physique and towering height led me to assume that this was none other than Mr. Blanco himself. He had a

Desert Eagle in each hand, aimed right at us.

Theo, who had since dropped down to his knees, returned fire almost immediately, unloading his entire fifteen-round magazine in a matter of seconds. While he stopped to reload, I provided cover fire, recoiling from the high-pitched bullets of the machine guns that sank into the doorway and hall behind me like deadly nails.

Caught in the midst of the crossfire was the only single man who deserved none of the carnage that followed. Still having a grip on the back of his shirt after offing the first man, I tried to yank the waiter back into the safety of the hallway. But by then it was too late. By the time I could safely get him out of the line of fire, he had sustained a line of bullet wounds running horizontally across his chest. Stains of dark red soaked into his white shirt. He was dead on impact.

As sorry as he looked though, the waiter had been a casualty of a necessary outcome. While Theo came back into the fight, having both guns drawn out this time, I too pulled out my other pistol. This one was a semi-automatic, and its heated bullets ripped through the air with more purpose.

The man on the right side of the room was hiding behind a beige loveseat that had been toppled over. Bullets had been splintered into its wooden belly and the ugly green fabric was ripped on all sides. As he reached over the loveseat to shoot, I nailed him in the arm. For some reason he stood up, howling from the pain. When he did, Theo finished him off, putting two rounds in his chest.

Although the gunfight only went on for a couple of minutes, it felt longer. Time had become lethargic. It was as if the clock of life had been momentarily slowed down. *Tick tock. Tick...tock.*

After putting in a fresh magazine, I glanced over to my partner. Theo was in the midst of exchanging gunfire with both men, Mr. Blanco having since hopped over the desk. Theo's blond hair was still tightly drawn into a ponytail. His face was enigmatic and his posture was mechanical as he shot both guns. Despite the hot weather, there were no beads of sweat running down his face.

Both men were now hiding behind the wooden desk. The four of us were no longer exchanging volleys. Now, we were in a war of attrition. Trying to beat each other down at all costs.

After reaching into my pants pocket, I realized that I was down to my last magazine. If things kept up as they were, this war would not last very long.

"Last magazine," I shouted over to Theo as I plugged it into my gun. The other pistol was already out of ammo and I had chucked it at the desk.

Theo, instead of saying anything, simply nodded toward the room. It was time to move in.

As Theo lay down more covering fire, I advanced into the room, ducking and shooting at the same time. On the left side of the room, a shelf of books connected to the wall. Lunging behind it, I dove into a pile of knocked over paperbacks, hoping that the bullets of the men's guns wouldn't chew through and find me.

It was then that both sides stopped shooting.

I could hear heavy breathing coming from the center of the room. Blood had been sprayed across the other wall. A morbid painting that any artist would cut his ear off over.

There was an open bay window at the far end of the room. Its gray curtains fluttered as a breeze rolled in and grabbed the noise of traffic and honking vehicles from outside. Above us, a giant bamboo fan swung around. One of its blades had been shot off.

But like all things in life, the impromptu ceasefire didn't last long. The shrieking sound of the submachine gun going off again announced the war was back on. Theo and I quickly returned fire.

It wasn't long before my gun was empty, making clicking sounds as I continued to squeeze the trigger. I motioned to Theo, who was still behind the doorway. He tossed one of his guns to me and it glided across the floor over to the bookshelf.

Theo was motioning with his hand that he would advance into the room. Picking up the gun, I shot off three rounds while he sprinted for the beige loveseat. Theo cautiously reached around it and grabbed the submachine gun from the man we had shot earlier.

Like wolves, we moved farther into the room, stalking our prey. With each inch forward, we gained more and more confidence, until eventually, I had no fear at all. It surprised me how calm I felt. Like Theo, I was not sweating. My pulse was steady.

After seeing us moving in, the guy with the machine gun made a break for an open door connecting into the next room. Seeing this, Theo quickly homed in and sprayed bullets from the automatic weapon into both the man's legs. Although he dropped to the ground, he started crawling immediately. Theo put another round into the back of his head. The man stopped crawling.

As Theo went to inspect the dead body, I walked over to the overturned desk in the center of the room. It was caved in at the middle from all the shooting, and the dark bullet holes riddling the thick oak exterior made it resemble Swiss cheese that had been left out in the sun.

Remembering the two Desert Eagles, I was cautious approaching the desk. Theo was kneeling down and searching the dead body, and it was just me. I leaned over the desk with the gun Theo had given me. Without notice, a giant shape jumped out from the other side. Mr. Blanco lunged over the table and threw himself into me.

Before hitting the floor, I had the image stuck in my head of a large grizzly bear pouncing on a human. At least Mr. Blanco lacked claws.

Nonetheless, the towering man had me pinned to the ground, slamming my left arm hard into the floor and causing me to drop the gun. With my other arm still free I began to reach for the stiletto blade tucked inside my pants, but before I could reach it, Theo had wrapped an arm around the man's massive neck.

The man snarled as Theo tried prying him off me and saliva from his mouth started dropping on my face. Again, the image of a giant grizzly bear came into view. Out of nowhere, an incredibly large fist swung over and popped me in the mouth.

For a splint second, I saw black. As he reeled in for another punch, I clenched my free hand into a ball and slammed my fist as hard as I could into his kidney. The man groaned and Theo was finally able to rip him off me long enough for me to get free and roll away.

However, no sooner had I gotten to my feet than the beast rammed into me again. This time, in knocking me over, his broad shoulder went straight into my stomach.

I almost wished I *had* seen black. Up until then, I had forgotten all about the bullet wound. The pain was so bad that it felt like I had been shot all over again, but this time, without the numbing effects of shock to dull the sensation. And then I did begin to slip away from consciousness. The last thing I heard before drifting away was a single gunshot.

CHAPTER THIRTEEN

The streets were hollow. No cars. No vehicles. No people. Every store and boutique I passed seemed just as empty. Not a single person could be seen as I made my way through the dormant city. The only sound I could hear was of the church bell in the distance. Only this time, it wasn't making the familiar *gong* sound that I was used to. It was a different sound this time. High-pitched. But I keep walking anyways.

The warm breeze of salty air brushed up against my face as I walked toward the beach. The sun had been just as bright as it always was and its rays bounced off the green-blue waves of the ocean, painting an orange-yellow mural across the horizon. The beach was empty again too, save for the same few people who had already claimed their stake on the shore. The gritty sand felt both cool and warm at the same time as it swallowed up my feet. Behind me, a ways off, I could still hear the faint, abnormal sound of the church bell.

Finding my usual spot, I sat down on the beach, not caring that my suit touched the sand. For the next few minutes I watched in awe as the gentle sea grew into small waves that eventually folded over, crashing into a million particles, and were once more absorbed back into the sea. *The cycle of the sea* I thought to myself.

The church bell kept ringing somewhere behind me. But I could also hear the water slapping up against the pier in front of me. The waves were competing against the sound of seagulls. They were cackling like banshees as they skimmed the ocean's surface.

In deep silence, I waited for the hotel girl to come whipping by. Her dark hair tied back into a bun that would flop up and down as she jogged. Her green eyes radiating in the bright sunlight. Her stunning smile that transcended all things beautiful to mankind.

But she never came.

The beach-goers around me had soon vanished in time, leaving me to my own accord once more. Leaving me isolated, in an already isolated world. I was alone as I had always been.

The church bell began shrieking louder and its volume kept increasing like on a television. The sound of waves hitting the pier had become much louder too. As well as the cackling of the seagulls. It wasn't long until these sounds drowned out all others. First, encapsulating me. Then, imprisoning me.

What were once melodic tunes eventually became sharpened noises. They were too much for me to bear. I raised my hands up to my ears, but in doing so, I felt a piercing pain coming from my gut. I looked down to see blood staining through my shirt. Something made me glance up and I saw that the sea had also turned a dark red. All around me was blood.

I startled myself awake, quickly realizing where I was. Back in the apartment. I was lying in the same position as when I had passed out. For a moment, I thought that I truly had been bleeding out, but after a hasty inspection of my torso, I found no blood in sight. The pain was real as ever though, that much *was* real, but I knew from my experience back in the hospital room that the pain would go away soon enough. At least I hoped so.

What I could still hear from that dream though was the shrieking sounds, now coming from the middle of the room. At least now I knew the source of the sounds.

Theo had since tied up Mr. Blanco to a desk chair and was interrogating him. After mustering all the strength I could find, biting my tongue at the pain, I got to my feet and dragged myself over to them.

"How are you feeling, good boy?" Theo asked. His back was turned to me and he hadn't even looked over. But he didn't have to. The pain coming from my belly spoke for me.

Finding a chair nearby, I plopped myself down. "Could be better. I should be fine in a few minutes." That was a lie. Then, thinking about my dream I added: "How long was I out?"

Still with his back to me, Theo said, "Not long. About twenty minutes. Give or take."

But twenty minutes *was* long. If Theo hadn't been able to subdue the beast that was Mr. Blanco, or if I had been by myself, I would not be here now, sitting in this chair. Thankfully, that was not the case, and Theo had been able to manage the situation for the both of us. Well, for the *three* of us, I guess.

Theo moved aside, and I could see Mr. Blanco better. The gunshot I heard just before slipping out of consciousness became apparent. On the man's right shoulder, just below his scapula, there was a gaping wound of dark red and fleshy skin. Theo must have put that dandy ouch on him to take him down.

The pain from my still-healing wound felt like small daggers coming in and out, and I could begin to taste blood in my mouth from biting down on my tongue so hard. Theo got in front of Mr. Blanco again and although I heard him say something, I couldn't make out what it was. I was quickly creeping back out of consciousness. The darkness had returned.

This time I was able to come back with more vigor, throwing off those drowsy chains and digging myself out of the deep dark hole that was the recess of my sub-conscious. Theo was still standing in front of Mr. Blanco. And Mr. Blanco was still tied down to the chair. All was still well...for Theo and me anyway. The man Theo was interrogating would not be well for too long.

I had slumped down in my chair, and without realizing it, I picked myself up. I winced, expecting the excruciating pain to follow, but was shocked to find that it was all but gone. Although not completely, it was enough that I could now tag back into the fight.

I slipped out of the chair, cautious of triggering more pain, and joined Theo by his side. He had been beating Mr. Blanco with the butt of his gun.

"Has he said anything yet?" I asked, whispering into Theo's ear.

"No, my friend," he said, still looking down at the hostage. Then, pointing his gun at him he said, "This one's got some balls on him."

"Why don't you put them in your mouth and choke on 'em," Mr. Blanco said to Theo. His voice was deep.

I was surprised to hear the man speak. I still had the image of a grizzly bear stuck in my mind. Hearing him talk sounded almost comical.

Theo momentarily stopped the pistol-whipping. "So," he said, lowering his gun. "Are you ready to tell me now who you bought the disk from?"

No answer.

"Mr. Blanco," he continued, "You can either die without any more pain being inflicted upon you. Or I can make your life a living hell before we kill you."

Mr. Blanco spat blood onto the wooden floor. I guess that was a *no*.

As if in answer to this, Theo started walking around the room. He opened drawers that had been overturned. Uncovered tables that had been flipped over. He picked things up here and there.

At length he returned, placing what he had found on a round table to the side of Mr. Blanco: four pencils—all sharpened, a very shiny pen with the words *Welcome to Taipei* inked across it in bright red letters, a few large shards of glass, the largest snow-globe I had ever seen—I found an item like this to be odd in a room full of criminals—and a Bic lighter.

After neatly placing them on the round table, he straightened out his ponytail and rolled up his sleeves. Then, looking around the room, he took a deep breath and smiled. It was time for pain.

Mr. Blanco, looking a bit nervous now, shuffled his feet. Theo had him tied down with some duct tape and pieces of cloth ripped off from the dead men. Mr. Blanco's head was both large and bold, glowing under the room's light fixture—above us, the bamboo fan, minus one woody blade, continued to spin around. Tattooed on either side of his head were a black and a red dragon, and it was as if they themselves were sweating from the impending doom, for beads of sweat raced down the sides of his face. The sweat coalesced with the blood smeared across him before dropping and making the ultimate descent on the floor where he had spat earlier. Maybe it was from the humidity. Maybe he was not just a wild beast after all and was afraid. Either way, he was going to be put down like an animal sooner or later.

Theo, without warning, picked up the pen and stabbed it into one of Mr. Blanco's hands. It went clean through to the chair's armrest, stopping so that only the letters W-E-L were still showing.

"Welcome to Taipei, fucker!" Theo shouted.

Mr. Blanco yelled, this time *a lot* louder, and for a second I was back in Reggio hearing those God-awful shrieks from the church bell. His massive frame squirmed in the chair. When he wriggled his fingers, blood streamed out from his wounded hand. He glanced down, seeing the forced impalement, and doing so made him pitch his body even harder in the chair. As much as he squirmed around though, trying to free himself, it was useless. Theo had done a crack job at tying him down with such improvised items. And in the end, we both knew what was going to happen.

Theo, ignoring the man's screams, continued with the interrogation. His voice was cool and collected, questioning Mr. Blanco the way a parent would ask where his child got the stolen candy from.

"Who did you get the disk from?"

"Stab me all you want, bitch," Mr. Blanco said, "I'm not telling you shit." He tried spitting at Theo's face this time, but missed. Theo didn't hesitate to pick up the large snow-globe and smash the blunt end of it against his face three times. When he put the globe back down onto the table its tiny flakes revealed that it was now snowing in New York with a chance of red blood seeping up from the ground.

Mr. Blanco began to pass out, his eyes slowly going shut. Theo slapped him across the face a few times. When he saw his eyes reopening he stopped. "Welcome back to hell," he said. Welcome back indeed.

Theo took a step back and tilted his head to the side, as if marveling over a masterpiece painting he had just created. It was sneaking toward the afternoon by now, and as the sun got higher its golden rays splashed into the room, exposing the darkness within. Overhead, the bamboo blades continued to swirl around with indifference.

"Please walk over and hold his head back," Theo said, turning to me. His pale face was illuminated up by the sun's light. His blue eyes glistened. I nodded my head silently.

Heeding to his request, I took off the outer layer of my garments and rolled up my sleeves. When I was behind Mr. Blanco, I reached over and wrapped my arm around his thick neck. The man gulped, and I could feel his Adam's apple rubbing against the inside of my arm. With the other arm, I held onto the back of his head so that my forearm was pressed up against his skull. It was warm and sweaty and for a second I thought the dragon tattoos were staring up at me. I then glanced over at Theo, who nodded his head. I pulled Mr. Blanco's head back so that he was staring up at the ceiling and the bamboo fan.

"Are you ready, Mr. Blanco?"

There was no answer again. The only sound made by the man was his wheezing as his massive chest heaved up and down. I knew that deep down, he was bracing for the inevitable.

Theo, I knew by now, was not one for theatrics. Although he was a patient man, I knew that his patience only went so far, like an indolent flame chewing at the wick of a candle. The sun flashed on his face again, and this time, a spark of something not natural was in his eyes. Even his pallid face seemed to now take on some color. This was not the man I had talked to last night in the safe house—the man who had spilled his heart out to me. No, it was as if the man standing before me had taken on an entirely new persona, as if the body of Theo struggled to contest with two polar opposites trying to possess it, each personality seeking victory over the other. The prize, Theo's body. The corners of his mouth curled up.

He wasted no time in picking up the largest of the shards of glass he had found earlier. Its fractured edges glistened in the light. Theo could just have easily unsheathed the knife he kept at his waist, but the knife would have been too easy. Too *clean*. And besides, I had an idea of what he was going to do with the piece of glass.

As Theo moved toward Mr. Blanco sounds of traffic drifting in through the open bay window announced that rush hour was fast approaching. A sweet smell of something home-baked wafted in as well, but it didn't last long as the smell of death overcame it.

"Keep his head steady," Theo said. He cut a piece of fabric off his sleeve with the glass. As he balled it up and shoved it down the man's mouth he said, "We don't want to harm him too much." Mr. Blanco tried to yell but his voice came out all garbled and inaudible. He tried jerking his head, but I tightened my grip on him. A wicked smile brimmed across Theo's face, matching the crazy stare in his cold, blue eyes.

He then pressed his hand onto Mr. Blanco's shoulder, the one with the bullet wound, leveraging himself up as he drew up the shard of glass at eye level. Mr. Blanco reacted in a muffled scream. This was going to hurt.

As the bamboo fan slowly ticked around, Theo inched closer and closer with the shard of glass, getting closer to Mr. Blanco's sweating face. This was *really* going to hurt. At length I had to look away, closing my eyes from the grotesqueness that was about to happen. As if looking away would somehow absolve me of the sin.

All at once I could feel the man's head pitching fiercely between my arms. His muzzled screams continued to get louder and it took every ounce of energy within me to restrain the giant. It soon became apparent that no amount of fabric jammed into his mouth could muffle his deathly cries, and I could feel the hairs on the back of my neck standing up like soldiers at attention.

Mr. Blanco was thrusting his head back and forth more violently. "Hold him steady," Theo said.

I was...or at least I thought I was. I was not ready to turn my face back and see the horrors before me. Even this was too much for me to take. The man's head was hot, and his sweat made it difficult to keep a firm grip. It was like trying to wrestle a greased up pig.

Squeezing my eyes tighter and gritting my teeth, I tried to ignore the man's cries. The screams. But I couldn't. It was as if the church bell, the seagulls, and the waves crashing against the pier were all around me again—their ear-splitting shrieks and shouts—spinning around me. Faster. Faster. The volume quickly growing louder. LOUDER. **LOUDER.**

STOP, I yelled.

Or at least I thought I did.

When I opened my eyes again, I found that the clashing noises were gone and Mr. Blanco had stopped screaming as well. The only sounds were his quiet whimpers, the traffic outside, which had since gotten worse, and the fan overhead.

"You may let him go now," I heard Theo say. But had he really? It was difficult separating what was real, and what was still a dream. But in the end, I saw no difference. I looked around, at the blood spattered across the beige walls, at Theo, who was grinning fiendishly as he stared at the hostage, at the bodies of men who had been brutally murdered, at the waiter who was just at the wrong place at the wrong time. No, in the end, I found no difference at all. It was all just a bad dream. It had to be. I just wondered when I would wake up, and be back at home, with my mother, Adeline.

Slowly, I let go of Mr. Blanco's seemingly lifeless head.

"Is he dead?"

"No," Theo said calmly, "At least not yet."

Mr. Blanco was in serious pain. And what was worse, we still had *zero* information from him. He was a tough cookie to crack, to say the least. A cookie that could take being pistol-whipped a few times. And then some.

Looking down at Mr. Blanco revealed a startling and gruesome discovery. Theo had gouged out his left eye. The ocular muscle continued to twitch as if the eye were still there. But it wasn't. The left eye was on the table next to the shard of glass, now bloody. It just dawned on me that pink blood had been sprinkled across my one arm in the midst of the grotesque procedure. I felt my stomach flip.

Theo looked over at me and his smile faded. "He'll come to, in another minute or so." Gesturing over to the empty chair he added: "Why don't you go rest yourself for a bit?"

Naturally, I would have said that I was fine. And the truth was that I was not in the least bit tired. But I caught a subtle pitch in the tone of his voice that sounded foreign, and his request seemed more like an order wrapped up in a big red bow. The flash of wild was still in his eyes and I did not like that.

Quietly, I sat back down on the chair, trying to wrap my head around what had just happened. I was used to all sorts of bloody spectacles. But not this. *This*, I hadn't signed up for. Then again, I hadn't signed up for *anything*. Like a young grunt being drafted into war, I was forced into this. What added to the confusion was that Theo had stopped addressing me as *good boy*. Something changed in him—from deep within—and I didn't like it. I didn't trust it, or even him.

As the day dragged on, the ruckus of noisy vehicles outside began thinning out. The sun started its daily descent back down toward the threshold of the horizon, leaving an orange hue mixed with a deep purple that splashed against the beige walls of the apartment. Almost coloring over the drying blood and erasing it from the pages of history.

Just as Theo had predicted, Mr. Blanco eventually regained consciousness. His eye—the one that was left—fluttered a few times and, along with the ocular muscle of the other, raced a solitary gaze around the room; first looking up at Theo, then at me, then to Theo again.

While I had been deep inside my own thoughts, Theo had been moving about the room, as if looking for something. When Mr. Blanco came to, he was over at the bay window with both arms perched on the sill. He was staring out down below. When he heard Mr. Blanco coming about, he walked back over to him.

"How are we feeling?" he asked, taking out the rolled up cloth from his mouth. It was full of spit and mucus, and he tossed it on the floor at Mr. Blanco's feet.

The only answer he seemed to give was a deep sigh that sounded painful. He narrowed his eye.

"We can remove the other one just as well, my friend," Theo said, pointing at his other eye. "But it would be a shame for you to have to walk around in Hell blind as a bat."

Again, there was no answer. Again, this was the *wrong* answer.

Theo moved fast, gripping a sharpened pencil in each hand. He was even swifter in thrusting them right into Mr. Blanco's legs. They sank through like knives in butter. "Fine by me," he said, forcing them down as far as they would go. When the pencils hit bone he broke them off and grinned.

The giant beast of a man, no longer being restrained by the fabric, tried yelling, but as he started to howl, Theo quickly moved and held a hand over his mouth. When Mr. Blanco was done, he let go of him.

We still had no information from the bloody fool and his resilience to Theo's tactics was almost superhuman. But it was obvious that his fortitude was quickly decaying. Theo knew it, I knew it, and most importantly, *he* knew it. The chips were all in and no more cards would be dealt out. It was only a matter of time before his poker face would break down. Mr. Blanco was all in.

Theo, picking up the shard of glass again, moved forward to replicate the surgery on Mr. Blanco's remaining eye. As he did so, I stood up, reluctant to offer my services again.

Theo held up his hand, which was washed over by the sun's dying light. "No, my friend," he said. "He doesn't have much left in him. I got this."

Hearing him say *my friend* to me made matters worse. Those two words had a certain connotation to it. They had been reserved for the waiter and Mr. Blanco. But I was not these men. I was his partner. And partners helped each other.

"Theo, it is my job to hel—"

"I said, I got this," he shouted.

His voice rang throughout the silent apartment and it made me jump back. Up until now, I didn't think he had such a voice in him. He flashed his eyes at me as he resumed the procedure. It was obvious that he was no longer talking to me as The Vice. He was talking to me as a wild fiend who had gone off the deep end. Theo had become a madman.

Taking a deep breath, I stood there. For a second—for a split second—I considered pulling out my gun and shooting him on the spot. Like a boy being forced to put down his dog after biting the neighbor, I thought about doing it. The man had lost his marbles and I feared that he would bite me next.

What stopped me though, as I reproached my fingers from the gun, was hearing Mr. Blanco's voice. He let out a hoarse laugh that seemed to surprise even Theo, who momentarily stopped in his tracks. The bloodied piece of glass glistening under the light.

"Who did you get the disks from?" Theo asked once more. He started for his eye again.

Again, Mr. Blanco laughed, a little deeper, and more resolute.

"What's so funny, mate?"

"He knows," Mr. Blanco said, for the first time in a long while.

"Knows what?" Theo asked, stopping again. He let the glass drop down to his side. "Who knows what?"

"The boy knows," he replied, looking past Theo's tall figure and directly at me. His one eye glaring so dark I thought it was going to pop out of its socket and flop onto the floor, sparing Theo of the gruesome task.

"Knows what?"

"Everything!" the giant man yelled. His loud, deep voice filled up the large room before being absorbed by the old wooden floor boards and rafters. Theo was quick to pick up the giant snow globe in his left hand and smash it across Mr. Blanco's already heavily bruised face. He spat more dark blood.

"What's he mean, Theo?" I asked after fighting the knot that had been lodged deep within my throat.

He looked back at me. "I don't know, good boy." He sounded normal again, and a streak of genuine concern blew over his face. Even his eyes had been dissolved of the craziness. I felt relieved, but at the same time shameful, that I considered killing him. When his eyes met mine, I looked away.

There was a pause in the room, broken up only by Mr. Blanco's heavy wheezing. Outside, a motorcycle zipped down the street.

Mr. Blanco continued to flick his gaze, as well as the phantom gaze, across the room, staring at both of us intermittently.

Finally breaking the barrier of eerie silence, he said, "You sound just like him." He had fallen back to a low drawl.

"Just like who?" both Theo and I asked at the same time.

Intrigued by the man's sudden dialogue and wanting to hear more, I crept back over to the two men. Theo moved aside, putting down the shard of glass on the round table.

"And you have his eyes," Mr. Blanco continued—his sunken face now staring directly into mine. A weak smile piercing through the colorful veil of purple bruises and red blood.

I took a step closer, so that we were but a foot from each other. "Whose eyes do I have?" I could again see the beads of sweat racing down his head. For the time being, the red and black dragons were dormant. "Whose eyes do I have," I repeated.

The muscle in his eye socket was twitching left to right as he continued staring at me, as if trying to read my face.

"The man who sold me the disk," he said. "Rafael."

The knot in my throat had suddenly returned, lodging itself even deeper so that I couldn't say anything. All at once the air felt thick and it became difficult to breathe.

Mr. Blanco smirked. "I knew it the first time you spoke."

As he continued to speak, his words were like daggers stabbing at my chest, as if my heart were trying to rip itself out of my chest cavity and run away from this God-forsaken room. Away from this God-forsaken world. And if it had, I would not have blamed it.

"But that's impossible," Theo said. Under the waning sunlight I could see the fiendish glisten returning in his blue eyes. "Rafael's dead."

Mr. Blanco shook his head. "I wouldn't lie about something like that, kid. It isn't in my nature." He smiled, revealing a set of bloodied teeth. A few were missing from his bottom jaw. It looked fresh.

Before I could find something to say, Theo stepped in between us, pushing me out of the way. "Don't talk to him." He then pulled out his own gun and flashed it wildly at Mr. Blanco. I didn't know who to be more afraid of, the man who had tried to kill me, or the man wielding the pistol—both seemed just as likely to do harm, and I again found my hand slipping over my gun.

"I'll ask you again," Theo said. "Who did you get the disk from?" This time Theo was hovering over Mr. Blanco, with the gun pointed directly at his temple.

"When I saw you enter the room, kid," Mr. Blanco said, nodding over to the door that had since been destroyed, "I could tell by your face. You look kinda like him. I wasn't certain, but after hearing you talk, that is how I knew for sure. That's how I knew you were Rafael's son."

Fighting the knot in my throat, I said, "Why are you telling me this?"

Theo glanced over at me. For the time being, he had paused.

"A dying horse can only run so far before it must lie down and accept its fate," he said.

He wasn't lying either. The truth was evident in the way he spoke. His voice was weakened, and it sounded as though he was struggling to say every word. With each passing minute his breathing got fainter as he sat there in the chair, in his throes of death. Although I could not feel for him, I could imagine what was going through Mr. Blanco's head. I was in his state of mind not too long ago, waiting for my time to come inside the safe house of Berlin. Waiting for the grim specter to claim my soul.

But it never did, and here we were now. Death is a funny thing to me. When we least expect it, death creeps up behind us, latching its blackened tentacles onto our lives, pulling us under. But when we want it the most—when we *beg* for it to come—it's nowhere to be seen. Leaving us empty and abandoned, like the orphaned children I had grown up with in The Program, suffering far greater agonies than death itself. I did not know if Mr. Blanco was waiting for death, or if death was waiting for him. Either way, it would not be long until they would both be finally acquainted. How I envied him.

"Where is he now?" Theo asked. He raised the gun back up to Mr. Blanco's head.

Mr. Blanco sighed. At this point, holding a gun to his head was no longer necessary. Spitting up blood he said, "He told me he'd be in Taipei the next couple of days, if I wanted to buy more from him...." The last part of his sentence dragged on a good ways with difficulty and pain. The dying horse was done running.

"How did you know I was *his* son?" I said quickly, before Theo could cut in again.

The man looked up with his remaining eye to Theo, as if for approval. Theo nodded, his gun still pressed firmly against his bald head.

"I do business with Rafael—your father—from time to time," he went on. "He's the only other American I know here, and the only one that I trust." If he had anything left in the tank, he was now running on fumes. Each word seemed to hurt more than the last. But I did not care. Now I *needed* to hear more.

Theo tried to interject, but I cut him off, beckoning Mr. Blanco to continue speaking. It was a risk on my part, but a risk that needed to be taken. Theo, more reluctant this time, nodded for the man to go on.

Continuing with the story he said, "When we met for the drop, I saw that he was limping. He said he got into a tussle with...." This time he fainted. The horse was lying down.

After yelling his name a few times and slapping him across the face, he woke up. "I seem to be checking out early," he laughed. In doing so, he spat up more blood. "He said he got into a fight with someone in Germany. I think he mentioned Berlin? He said it was with someone who looked strangely like himself, although at the time he could not put a finger on it. Said he hadn't recognized you till after he left. Mentioned that you might even be after him."

"Did you know him well—"

Theo's gun went off without warning. The bullet tore through his dense cranium and blood mixed with brain matter splattered from behind, some of it reaching the curtains of the bay window on the far wall.

Theo had shot him and the horse was dead. At that moment I was filled with rage. More rage than I ever felt before. I was seeing red.

"Why did you do that?" I yelled. Not realizing that I had subconsciously pulled out a gun and had the nose of the barrel pointed at the back of Theo's head as I moved behind him.

Another gap of silence pushed into the room. Overhead, the bamboo fan ticked away.

"Please," Theo said at last. "Put the gun down." Was this the plea of my partner, or the desperate words of a madman? I could not tell.

I felt the gun begin to quiver in my hand. My left hand. The other was curled up into a fist at my side. "I thought you said my father was dead?" This time I was shouting.

"I said put the gun down, now." Although his back was to me, I could imagine seeing his wild blue eyes glistening under the light. Against my better judgment, against all reasoning in my body, I reluctantly obeyed and put the gun down. Hopefully it was a plea from my partner. My friend.

Fearing the worst from Theo, I slowly backed away. "I thought you told me he was dead?" I said again, this time in a hushed voice. Although the gun was now at my side, I still had it tightly gripped. I waited…perhaps even *wanted* him to give me a reason to pull the trigger.

What happened next stunned me completely. Even more so than having Mr. Blanco lunging at me like a rabid animal, or Theo then killing him at point blank. When Theo turned around to me, he had taken on an entirely different persona.

The craziness in his eyes and flushed skin had vanished without a trace, leaving behind the empty vessel of a pale-skinned man who looked like he had just seen a ghost. Or likewise, looked like one himself. For a long time he looked down into my face, and I didn't know what to expect, until finally, he quietly brushed past me and sat down on the wooden chair behind us. There were no exchange of words. It was as if Theo was no longer there. Just going through the motions like a feather in the wind.

Somewhere in the room, more of those candles, like the ones in the restaurant below, were wafting away. The smell of that, mixed in with the drying blood around me began to make me sick. I wasn't sure if it was the morbid smell of death, the sight of Mr. Blanco's grotesque face—what was left of it anyway—or just the unexpected news of my father still being alive that nauseated me the most. My stomach was doing cartwheels, and I had to go over to the open window, taking in a deep breath of fresh air to escape it all. Today surely was an unusual day. Unusual seemed to be in my bones. In my DNA.

When I was sure my stomach was done flipping over, I went back to Theo. He was still in the chair with his arms slumped to the sides.

"I thought you said he was dead?" I asked for the third time. I felt like a parent berating his child about a question he already knew the answer to.

Finally the words escaped his mouth. "I know. And I thought he was." There was still life left in that empty vessel after all.

"Then what was he talking about?" I was fishing for more words to come out of his mouth. No longer sure if that was still possible.

I saw his eyes move as he watched me put the gun back into my blazer. It was a sign of truce. A desperate peace offering I hoped would not backfire.

He then looked up into my face. They were the same warm, blue eyes that belonged to the man confessing his love for my mother last night in the basement. Not the cold stare of a fiendish madman. That person appeared to have went away when Mr. Blanco did.

"Look, good boy," he said at last. "There's something I have to tell you." He thinned his lips together and gazed down at the wooden floorboards, as if contemplating his next choice of words.

Before he could find those words however, our attention was drawn to the distant sound of a door being slammed shut outside of the apartment, down the hall. Voices, probably in Mandarin, followed the sound. Whatever it was Theo had to say, it would have to wait. At least for now.

Like a Swedish Jack-in-the-box, Theo sprang to life, jumping out of his chair before I could say or do anything. "You know what to do, good boy." His voice was both strong and resolute. It was as if the sound of impending danger had spurred him back to life. Like the godly jolt of a defibrillator on some cadaver.

Theo started pacing around the room, looking for something. Probably looking for any clues that would help us find Rafael—my father. As crazy as it sounded, I believed Mr. Blanco. In a world full of cruel chaos, a guy like me needed something to believe in, after all. As depressing as the situation was, a belief was a belief—and it was what made me start to feel human again. Something I had long since almost forgotten.

When I finally stirred, after soaking in the situation, I moved around the room to help my partner. He was patting down Mr. Blanco's body and when he saw what I was doing he waved me down, telling me to instead guard the door. I listened. It seemed like the old Theo was back again.

Just as I had done in the IMF building, I stood watch in the doorway, while my accomplice *cleaned house*. For a good ten seconds or so my eyes danced back and forth from the hallway, to Theo. As he went about the room his braided, blond hair remained taut against his back. His dauntless face giving up nothing in the waning light of the evening sun. To know Theo had such a sadistic and dark side to him, coming out in periodic cycles, was unnerving. And in the steaming humidity of the day, as hot as it was, thinking about what had just happened minutes ago sent a deathly cold shiver down my spine. My partner was a real-life Dr. Jekyll and Mr. Hyde.

More noise from the hallway took my attention from Theo. The sound of shoes beating against the wooden floor of the hallway were getting louder, in a crescendo of nervous ruckus. More people were going to die today, this I knew. It was the cycle of the sea.

It wasn't long until I could see the black shadows of people moving against the walls of the lengthy corridor. They were getting closer. Closer. "Theo," I called back into the apartment, "get ready."

Theo, checking his gun, acknowledged me. I dipped back into the room, remembering that low ammunition was still the biggest threat to me. I was not afraid of the men racing down the hallway toward us. I just did not want to die without a good fight.

I still had my pistol and a submachine gun dug up from one of Mr. Blanco's men. Together, we raced back to the doorway. The footsteps became loud clops and the shadows against the walls were like dark monsters coming right for us.

Looking down, I noticed that Theo had only one weapon on him. The gun he had used to execute Mr. Blanco with. We'll be fine," he said, seeing me frowning. "Let's live to die another day."

He had barely enough time to reload his gun when the first wave of men came at us. They were three to be exact, each one dressed in a black suit and red tie like the men from earlier. Two of them were a bit chubby, and the third was like a toothpick. This last guy towered over the other two, his thick black hair that swayed as he ran ahead, shouting something in his native tongue that neither I nor Theo could understand. Their crimson ties, flapping in all directions as they ran toward us, were like foreboding omens. Death was soon to be had.

At the very last second Theo and I ducked back into the room, just as a surge of bullets came ripping through the hall and digging into the doorway frame. Behind me, I heard Theo pulling back the slide of his gun, getting it primed to kill.

Theo, for some reason, poked his head back into the hall. Stealing back into the room he said, "Bloody hell, my friend. There's about seven or eight more behind those three."

"That only leaves about three per body," I said.

Theo agreed. The time for rationing was now. The time for *survival* was now. Let's live to die another day. The blunt words of my partner echoed around my head like bats. Quietly, I drew up both guns, bracing for the crimson tide.

Another volley of bullets whistled down the hall and splintered into the doorway. Sending wooden shrapnel flying into the room. With each bullet coming by, nearly missing either of us, adrenaline kept surging more and more through my veins. My vision narrowed. My breathing steadied. I didn't wait for them to stop shooting. Reaching both weapons into the hall, I squeezed both trigger fingers and fired back. Three bullets per body—I only needed one.

As I fired back, I heard Theo shooting from behind me. We mowed down the first wave of red ties. The two pudgy Asians got lit up and their faces were nearly ripped off. The thin one took two to the chest, a bullet from both of us. Blood from the slaughter sprayed back and hit the second wave of four men. Although they had numbers on their side, we had experience and the environment on ours. The narrow hall created a bottleneck effect that choked the men off from coming at us in full force.

The second group of red ties were armed with a bit more fire power. Semi-automatics and shotguns. They hurdled over their fallen comrades, who lay on the floor with blood pooling out around them. As they did, Theo and I opened fire on them as well. At this point, I no longer felt the recoil of either weapon as I fired back. My adrenaline was surging through every capillary of my body. I was high.

I was keeping count of how many bullets I was using up. When I was getting low, I motioned for Theo to cover me as I retreated back into the apartment. I could hear the empty casings hitting the ground behind me like deadly snowflakes. Inside the room, the bamboo blades continued to whirl around with astonishing indifference. Outside the building, the world went on.

When Theo was getting low, he too fell back into the room. Together, we flipped over the round table from earlier. Theo's unorthodox instruments of doom crashed to the ground. The snow-globe, again sprinkling snow over The Big Apple, rolled past me and stopped.

"I wonder how they knew we were up here," I said to Theo. He was in the midst of taking inventory of how much ammo he had left in his magazine.

"You heard the screams, good boy," he said, reloading his weapon. "Even hell heard them."

This was true. I thought back to Mr. Blanco. His inhuman shouting as Theo cut out his eye. He must have driven those tormented souls crazy down there, listening intently as a new soul was about to be admitted into their fiery realm of chaos and anguish.

In the midst of talking to Theo, I noticed that the shooting from the hallway had ceased. There was a lackluster pause as if the world itself had been put on hold. Outside the room, I could hear them talking amongst themselves. Their shadows danced around the hallway as the sun continued to plunge past the horizon. Now the room was but a purple sheet.

My heart began to beat again, and looking down, I noticed that my right hand was bleeding. During the chaos in the hall I probably took a splinter or two from the door. Tiny drops of fresh blood splashed against the floor, soaking it forever with my sins. My *bloody sins*. When push came to shove, my blood was no different than that of the dead men lying before us, their corpses twisted this way and that. I shuddered to think that my final burial ground would one day be on the floor of some unimportant apartment room. Forgotten in a world that continued to spin just as much as the fan overhead, clicking.

Clicking.

A loud noise came from the hallway. It was shouting. After quickly wrapping my bloodied hand with a piece of sleeve I had cut off from a nearby body, I checked my guns and braced for the next round. Theo was already waiting for them to come. He sat crouched on the other end of the small table, his tall frame just barely being concealed by the piece of furniture.

His face was fearless.

"Put down your weapons," someone yelled into the room.

Theo fired a single round into the hallway. "Fuck *you*," he said. "Come and take them."

There was murmuring in the hallway and more shuffling of feet. Two men lunged to the other side of the doorway. I caught a glimpse of what looked like an AK-47.

"I'll take the left side," Theo said. He then scrambled around me to the overturned couch to my left.

After Theo was in position, I nodded over to him. When he nodded back, I sought refuge in the position he had been in on the other side of the table. Now, both flanks were protected. Patiently, I aimed both guns at the doorway and waited.

Neither of us opened fire. Not at first anyway. I could hear more movement in the hall, their shadows giving up their positions for them. More talking. Then, all at once, four guns pointed into the room and opened fire.

It was by a stroke of luck that Theo had switched positions. Had he been where I was now, he would have taken a wave of piercing rounds. The bullets pelted into our makeshift barriers with unrelenting strength. The whizzing sounds as the deadly hornets streamed past our heads made me want to crawl into a ball. The bay window behind me exploded in a cloud of broken glass. The room was lit up, as if a bomb of daylight had been tossed in. Smoke from their guns moved in and filled every crevice of the apartment. Even after they stopped firing, it lingered like an unwanted guest.

Theo was trying to make himself as small as possible. The couch he was hiding behind was tattered and its ugly fabric was ripped beyond recognition. It was not going to last long. I took a deep breath, waiting for his command.

Something ahead of me stirred and Theo's gun went off. A man of lengthy features dropped to the ground. He had been shot in the throat, and as he fell to the floor, grabbing onto his neck, he bled out. His legs convulsed and then stopped.

This triggered the men outside the room to shoot back again. A crashing sound overhead announced that the bamboo fan had caught a stray bullet. Two of its large blades fell and made a dull thumping sound in the middle of the room. A few rounds ricocheted off the walls to my right and hit what was left of Mr. Blanco's body.

Theo grabbed my attention and motioned with his hand to look forward. The body Theo had just dropped was being dragged out by one of his partners. I reached around the table and squeezed off two rounds. The one hit the wall next to him, causing the man to shudder, but the second ripped half his face off. He slumped over the body he had been moving.

Both sides opened fire. The AK-47 rattled the air with arrogance. More gun smoke. It reminded me of one of those Wild West shootouts. The ones where the outlaws were in a gunfight with the sheriffs in some old saloon. The only difference was that in here, there was no clear distinction between which of us were the good guys and the bad guys. In the eyes of God, we were all bad men. Although not all of us were crazy enough to admit it.

The AK dry-fired. Before he could reload his weapon, I sprang to life and dropped my automatic weapon. Hurdling over the round table, I dashed across the room for him. Theo fired off a couple rounds to keep the other guy at bay. Just as he loaded in a new magazine, he looked up. His eyes quickly became saucers as I lunged into him. Grabbing his face, I pushed him against the wall of the hallway. As he moved to react, I shoved my pistol into his stomach and pulled the trigger two times. His body slid to the floor and I yelled. My lungs tightened as I released a blood-curdling scream.

The final man was kneeling to my left in the hallway. He had a semiautomatic, but his hands were trembling at the sound of my sudden wild cry—my renouncing of humanity. Before he could do anything a bullet tore through the side of his face and exited into the wall behind him. Thick blood spewed out with it. Theo was standing behind me with his gun drawn. He stared at me, but did not say anything.

I then looked around. In both the hallway and back in the apartment, I took note of all the dead bodies strewn across the floor. All the blood sprayed on the walls and floor. The acrid stench of fresh gun smoke. Something boiled deep within my throat and I yelled again. This was glorious. This was art.

A wide smile brimmed across Theo's face. "Your mother would be proud of you, Brendan."

CHAPTER FOURTEEN

He's coming, you know," Theo said. "The Chancellor will be meeting us here tomorrow."

After the bloody scene in Mr. Blanco's apartment, we had left through a fire escape on the side of the building and managed our way back to the safe house. It was late in the evening by the time we arrived, the sun well past the threshold of the night. Its dying flames reflecting peculiarly off thick clouds moving over the city found a gap near the horizon to give us a last hint of light that barely touched the sides of the safe house when we entered it. It had started to rain again, light specks of raindrops sloshed up against the basement's foggy windows. The heat remained, clinging to the air and making our clothes stick to our skin like gum.

"It's about my father, isn't it?" I was seated across a table from Theo. He had just made a fresh cup of coffee and we were both appreciating the treat of a stimulant. It had been a long day for everybody.

He took a sip from his cup and gently placed it down in front with both hands. It was still hot and the steam swirled, rising up from the cup, and dissipated into the darkness. A single light lit the basement. His face was pallid and unbarred.

"It's about what Mr. Blanco said today." Then, trying not to frown he added: "And yes, Brendan. It's also about your father."

I looked down at my cup of coffee, suddenly no longer interested.

"Were you able to find anything back there, during your search?"

Theo took a deep breath. I could sense his blue eyes were still on me. "That's enough questions for one day, good boy."

This was the same response he had given me back in the hospital room when I had asked him about who he was chasing—the man who turned out to be my father. Although he was being polite, then and now, I knew that what he really meant to say was, *I'm getting tired of your questions. Just let it be.*

After I heeded his request Theo got up. Before turning in for the night he thanked me for my 'courageous efforts today'. I said 'thank you.' He opened his mouth as if to say something else, but then, after a moment's hesitation, he pursed his lips and vanished into his room, leaving his coffee to get cold on the table.

When he was gone I sighed. Letting the silence of the basement seep into my skin, I sat there for an undetermined amount of time. Was it minutes? Hours? I did not know. Eventually I forced myself to take another sip of coffee. By then the black liquid was mild at best. I took another sip. Then another. Just letting things be.

When the coffee was all but gone, I withdrew into my own room, leaving both our cups to sit there idly on the table. The precipitation had since dissipated and only occasionally did I hear the gentle touch of rain caressing the window of my room. I lit the lamp by my bedside and for a while watched mindlessly as the shadows of the room bounced with the sway of the flame. Something had been on my mind.

One of the very last things that Theo had said to me back at the apartment was still stuck inside my head. Like the gum that refuses to let go of your shoe, his words were wedged tight to my mind. They haunted me just as much as seeing my mother die.

Let's live to die another day.

They were the sardonic lyrics of a true madman. And it wasn't merely just the *choice* of words that scared me so much as the way in which he expressed them. He had put on a display of absolute insanity today. Hearing him spew those words out of his mouth was like being forced to hear the decree of the crazed person just before he ran out in front of a moving train.

But still, it was hard to abandon such a beautiful creature as Theo. Even though my gun had been aimed at his head, my finger waiting for the call to make the ultimate strike, I still would not have been able to bring myself to do it. After all, how could I? I knew that deep down, Theo was in just as much pain as I was. He didn't have to say anything.

Like a bandage trying to cover a healing wound, his eyes revealed the heavy burden he wore on himself. I knew that, to him, it was like wearing a painful badge wherever he went. One that was transparent and hardly anyone could see or cared about, walking listlessly through this world. He and I were the same person. And to kill Theo meant killing myself.

At the far end of the room, the clock continued to click forward. *Tick tock. Tick tock.* With as much that had happened today inside the tiny realm of Mr. Blanco's apartment, I knew that despite it all, life would still continue to spin on its axis of apathy. What we had done today would eventually get torn out of the pages of history, crumpled up, and thrown into the fire. And still the world would go around and around. *Tick tock. Tick tock.*

Eventually drowsiness began seeping into my body. It was only when I finally swung my legs over the cot that I realized the full extent of my soreness. Physically as much as mentally. The coffee from earlier had done little to remedy this. My body ached from head to toe, and I was too tired to even undress myself. My clothes, dirty and bearing the stench of dried blood, would just have to wait until tomorrow. In the final twilight before drifting off completely, I watched with heavy eyes as the shadows of the night continued to dance against the bedroom walls. Somewhere beyond the shroud of darkness the clock kept ticking. And ticking.

When I woke up the next morning the room was still dark. The air was just as thick and cold. My stomach churned, only it wasn't from sickness. Being preoccupied the entire day with fighting and interrogations, I had forgotten all about the gun wound. But now the pain was back, rearing its ugly face and smiling up at me saying, *Hey, Brendan, I'm still here!*

The pain was pulsating like an automatic piston of knives driving into my abdomen. Sometimes it hurt really badly and sometimes it would be reduced to just low drawls. In a futile attempt to distract myself from the pain, I tried filling my head with other things. But that seemed to only make things worse.

After a while the pain slowly crept away—although I knew that sooner or later it would be back. Probably when I least expected it. For a long time I lay there on the cot. Sometimes my gaze would drift over to the painting of the small wooden vessel being pitched around in a violent sea; other times, it would move over to the foggy window over the clock—*Tick tock*—and I would mindlessly watch the particles of airborne dust floating in the glowing path of the morning sun.

For a while, I unleashed my mind and let it run around the yard, hoping that eventually, it would come back, scraping at the front door and barking to be let back inside. As the sun continued to rise I kept re-counting—more like *dwelling over*—yesterday's events; replaying them in my head like a broken record. A vinyl album that played only one song over and over again, with nobody in the room to change or stop it.

It was a lot to soak in, and I was hardly prepared to absorb it in its entirety. But letting my mind drift seemed to be the only thing that kept me from thinking about the pain in my gut and curbed the anxiety of thinking about what came next.

Every time I shut my eyes, I could still see Mr. Blanco's tormented face. The left eye gouged out and spurts of blood shooting out as the ocular muscles continued to twitch with the right eye. In the heat of the morning, it brought shivers down my spine and made my skin crawl. Thinking about it made my gut hurt more. In the end, it seemed that everything did.

Something else kept resurfacing in the back of my mind, bobbing up and down like a buoy in the water. The truth about my father. At one point I had thought—even *hoped*—that Theo was my dad. But given the twist in recent events, that idea quickly faded away.

All these years I had lived under the unquestionable fact that my father was dead. Knowing that he was still out there, this whole time, made me start to question a lot of things. It seemed as though I was living one lie after another. As if opening up one door only lead to smoky truths and more winding hallways of lies. It made me begin to question *everything*.

But with or without all the chaos of the past twenty-four hours, there was still a part of me that blamed him for everything. After all, it was *his* fault. Wasn't it? Whether my father was still alive or not, I hated him just the same. I hated him for bringing me into such a cruel life; for abandoning my mother and me when we needed him the most. He was like the fleshy scar on my right hand that never seemed to heal. Re-minding me that although he was gone, in some way, he was still there. The pain was still there. *He* was still there. I hated my father.

When Theo had told me he died in Algeria, I couldn't have felt more ecstatic. He was a disease to my family. To me. And he needed to be eradicated like one. If I had known it was him I was fighting in Berlin, I would not have let go of my hold around his neck. I would have crushed his throat and watched as the last bit of air left his body. Watched as the life left his eyes.

If given the opportunity again. I would kill Rafael. I would kill my father.

The sun's rays had washed over my cot and were reaching for the door by the time the pain in my abdomen was bearable enough to walk. The bustle of the streets above began their daily jig. Cars and other vehicles zipped and zapped. Banter of the foreign language of Taipei rose and fell in irregular strides. I smiled through the sun's golden shrouds. It really was nature's medicine and already I was feeling much better.

When I was sure the pain was low enough to move, I swung my legs around and pressed my feet, still wearing shoes, against the floor. After a few deep yawns, I stirred, realizing how hungry I suddenly was. In the midst of deep thought and trying to ignore the painful stabs of my stomach I had neglected to notice the raw hunger brewing within me. I got up, still smiling. Although my father was out of my life, the sun was not. It was the one thing that remained steadfast. Bidding me a good morning each day with the hopeful promise that, with each day, there was new hope.

The main room of the basement was dark and clammy. The windows lining the brick walls were too foggy to let in enough light and I was too tired to flick on the bulb hovering over the room. My stomach growled.

Theo was nowhere to be seen. The room was silent except for the occasional distant sound of the outside world reminding me that it was still there. There was a tiny kitchenette near the stairs. It was stocked with enough canned foods to feed a brigade. I made my way over to it.

In the low glow from the windows, I could just barely discern what I was grabbing for food: two cans of Campbell's beef and vegetables, a can of home-style baked beans, and what appeared to be a medley of pineapple chunks and cocktail cherries. After wasting a good forty-five seconds fumbling in the drawers for silverware, I gave up and took my food to the table where last night's cups of coffee remained idling. Sitting down, I tore into my food with savage interest. While my knife cut open the lids, my fingers did the rest. It never tasted so good.

Suddenly realizing that I was no longer alone in the room, I stopped eating and glanced up. The darkened, but unmistakable out-line of Theo's tall and slender frame came out from the depths of the basement gloom. Smiling as he went past me, he too began foraging the tiny kitchenette.

"How'd you sleep, good boy?" he asked. He turned on the light.

Letting my eyes adjust, I said, "Pretty well, thanks."

Behind me, I could hear him rummaging through the drawers. In a matter of seconds he had located the silverware. I thought I had checked well enough.

After finding his own array of canned foods, he rejoined me at the table. Theo saw my barbarism—I was in the midst of reaching for my second helping of pineapple and cocktail cherries with two dull fingers—and when I got up to accept a plastic fork from him, his eyes widened.

"What happened to *you*?" He exclaimed and pointed at my shirt.

"What do you mean?"

"Look down, boy," he replied. "Your clothes."

Doing as he had asked, I got up from the table and looked down. To my horror, a wide stain of something dark had spread across my dress shirt. Although my pants were black I could feel something sticky around my waistline. Both articles of clothing felt wet when I ran my hand across them.

Theo shoved me into the light. "Are you okay?" When I raised my hand into the light, revealing blood on my fingertips, his blue eyes al-most bulged.

"I—I don't know," I said, staring at my bloodied fingers. "I think so."

For a second, I hesitated to pull up my clothes, unwilling to do so and see what lay underneath. But at Theo's insistence, I unbuttoned my dress shirt and pulled up the undershirt. It became apparent fast why I had felt such piercing pain earlier that morning and I almost threw up the fruit medley I had just scarfed down. The scarring wound from the gunshot had reopened. Flaps of fresh skin and scar tissue were lying limp with blood.

"Mr. Blanco must have ripped it back open when he tackled me to the ground," I said. But if this were the case, I had slept through it last night. How did I not feel the blood then? Or the pain?

Although the bleeding appeared to have stopped, Theo didn't want to take any chances and beckoned for me to go lie back down.

"I'm fine, sir," I said when he opened the door to my room, usher-ing for me to go in with a wave of his hand.

He pointed at the bloodied shirt drooping over my pants. "That doesn't look fine to me."

I was beginning to get annoyed. I didn't need anybody looking out for me or telling me what to do.

"Theo, don't worry about me—"

"Why shouldn't I worry about you?"

"Because you're not my father!" I yelled.

The words flew out of my mouth like strands of silk and echoed through the empty basement. Just like that. I clenched my fists expecting a heated reaction. But Theo never stirred. Instead, he quietly moved back to the table, pulled out a chair, and sat down. His face staring blankly at the far wall.

"Theo, I'm sorry. I didn't mean to say that."

"But you're right," he replied, still facing the wall, "I'm not your father."

If there was any happiness at all left inside him, it was gone now. As he looked up at me, I could see that his eyes were just as hollow as the building upstairs. Three floors of nothing. The vague, empty shell of what used to be. Of what used to be a man who went by the name of *Theo*. This world was just as cruel to him as it was to me.

Grabbing a towel from the kitchenette, I pressed it up against my belly and sat down at the table. Looking down at the remaining cans of food, I found I was no longer hungry. Now, food was the last thing on my mind. Something else had surfaced instead.

"I saw the way you looked at me back in Beivrus," I said. "I suppose you were wondering why I never asked if you were my father."

I was careful to choose my words, cautious of stepping on a landmine that might blow up in my face. It was true, too. I saw the way he had looked at me back in the medical room. Staring at my likewise bewildered face, as I too wondered. Wondered if the tall Swedish man standing in front of me was indeed my father. The man who remained a dark phantom my whole life. Even though *I knew* that he could read my thoughts back then, as I lay there on the white bed, it never actually dawned on me to ask him outright. And truth be told, I never really wanted to know. The absence of my father was just another dismal part of my life. Besides, if I did know it was him, I may have tried to strangle him right then and there. With my father, all I saw was *red*.

Theo's head turned and his tall, slender body likewise did the same. I appeared to have captured his attention. Finally he spoke. And when he did, his voice sounded just as vapid as the dull basement air.

"I saw the look in your eyes," he said. "It was the same look a boy gives his dog that finally returned home after running away for a very long time."

Theo's words had struck a chord. I glanced down at the gray floor. The concrete was just as cold and gray as myself. As Theo. As all of us. What man built and constructed—large, stately structures that scratched the sky—they were all just intrinsic reflections of how he felt deep down; of what he imagined himself to *really* look like had Eve never tempted Adam to eat from the Forbidden Garden.

At length, I opened my mouth, now lined with dry spit that reminded me of the drying blood on my shirt. I could feel the words eddying at the bottom of my throat, waiting to be pushed up and out for the world to hear: *I wish you were my father, Theo.* It was as simple as opening a can of food with my knife. Yet, at the same time, it was impossible. My ability to speak had suddenly abandoned me. Even my own body had given up on me and left me to die alone.

But it was not me who had spoken then. It was Theo. "Brendan," he said. "I haven't been entirely honest with you." His eyes widened once more, as if he had surprised himself as much as me when he spoke.

I glanced up at him. It was all I could afford to do at the time. But no words needed to be said. He knew what I meant. He always did.

"Your father, Rafael. He didn't die in Algeria."

His doggish eyes weighed heavy as he stared back at me. This much I was certain. With hands still tipped in blood, I let go of the towel I had been holding, and gripped the end of my chair, bracing myself for what was to come next the same way I had gripped the bed sheets in Beivrus, thinking that The Chancellor was going to kill me. In some way, Theo *was* killing me; he was killing me with the truth about my father. How many times, I wondered, was I going to be killed before I actually died?

Theo, as if reading my mind, continued speaking. His words were light and floated around the room. "I know I told you that he was ambushed and killed. And I thought he had been. This much is true, Brendan."

Theo paused to wet his lips. In the mean time, I tried to say something—to say *anything*. But my throat was still on lock down, just as the city of Berlin had been after we blew up the IMF building. Thinking about that made me miss the company of the Englishman. Another reason why I wanted to kill my father.

The light bulb flickered. In front of Theo, his array of canned foods remained untouched on the table. Beyond that, his cup of coffee from last night—as cold and lifeless as the men we had slaughtered yesterday in the apartment building. I wondered how long it would be until they were found, and even then, who would find them first? The tenants, or the flies?

The sound of Theo's voice jerked me back to the present. "Rafael was in Algeria, but it wasn't to take a hit. It was to take another job offer. This I only found out later...*after* the funeral we had for him."

He shot a look of odd hysteria toward me. His wide blue eyes glistened under the light that continued to flicker occasionally. Perhaps he too was still trying to wrap everything around his head. The streets outside were growing in volume, swelling with the daily ritual of Taipei city traffic.

I sat deeper in my chair, staring back at him in return. Studying him. Although I had been very young at the time of the funeral, I still remember seeing the photographs; the Kodak pictures and media reels of an unnamed American tourist gunned down in Africa. The images of a pine-wood box covered in vibrant flowers being slowly lowered into the ground. My mother, dressed in a veil of black—almost as black as the heart of the man who had faked his own death. Yes, after all these years, the images were still burning in my head like an ugly cattle prod.

"My father was a Rogue," I said, finally finding my voice. The words were as clear as day. My father had been a Rogue, and I was the bastard son of one.

Theo tilted his head and his eyes narrowed. After a moment's hesitation he spoke. "I couldn't believe it either..." he tapered off. Looking back at the wall he added, "Until I saw for myself."

He then fumbled about on the chair and straightened up. Seeing that I had no response to give he went on. "Something changed in him. Something I had never seen in him before. Maybe it was all the years of killing that finally caught up to him. I cannot be sure. But not long after his *disappearance* in Algeria, a man of strikingly similar features to your father was reported to have been sabotaging hits taken on by The Program."

I glanced down at my food again, still not interested in eating it. "What would spur him to do such a thing?"

"He loved you, Brendan. There is no doubting that," Theo said. "But something sinister was growing inside his heart. Something malevolent and cancerous. Some men simply cannot help but allow their work to take over their lives. To consume them..." His voice trailed off again.

"Is that you, Theo?" I asked, remembering the sadistic look in his eyes as he tortured Mr. Blanco. Theo pursed his lips together and turned away. It seems I too had struck a chord.

The air was silent. It also had no remarks to make. As the outside world continued to stir, I couldn't help but think that sometime from now, after Theo and I were long dead and gone, the streets of Taipei would still be shuffling.

"I cannot take back the things I've done in the past," Theo said, his words cutting the air like a sharp sword. "All the killing. The atrocities." His hands flew up in the air as he spoke, as if surrendering. "Sometimes I even see myself turning into Rafael. I will not deny this. But what separates me from him is that I know when to flip the switch off. Otherwise, it would consume me too." His hands turned into fists that he then slammed against the table. The plastic silverware and empty cans bounced across the table. My half-eaten fruit cocktail spilled onto the floor.

Theo shrugged at the sight of this. I wondered if he really believed all that. Occasionally, a man lies to himself so much, convincing himself that the lies are truths, that he believes in his own lies. Who knows, maybe Theo is one of those men. Maybe this too would be my own fate someday. Killing monsters like Mr. Blanco, all the while turning into one. Sharks teeth are designed to replace one another, almost instantly. Perhaps monsters are made the same way. After all, you can't have good people without the bad ones. It's simply Yin and Yang. It's simply nature being nature.

My hands were white as snow as I continued to grip the wooden chair. It wasn't that I was still afraid of Theo. Far from it. I guess part of me just wanted to lose circulation—first in my hands, then in the rest of my body. Becoming just as numb as my feelings as I struggled to comprehend what Theo was telling me.

"It was about a year or so after the funeral," Theo continued, seeing no hint that I wanted to speak. "You were still very young. I had been commissioned with a job in France—Paris, to be exact. And after having to do the bloody reconnaissance myself I finally found the target. It was a Chechen nationalist, wanted for war crimes, hiding inside the city. The guy had sensitive files about Russian intel and was going to leverage that in return for French asylum. He was driving one of those gray compact cars, and I had been tailing him through the city when he finally parked and went inside some brick building. Parking close by, I waited a minute before going over and breaking into his car. The fucking fool had the Russian intel in a backpack. A bloody backpack!

"After taking the files, I then stuffed about two pounds of plastics into his trunk and got back into my own vehicle to wait for him to return to his car. About fifteen or so minutes later, the Chechen left the building and got into his car. As soon as he turned it on I squeezed the detonator and watched as his vehicle went up in flames." Theo waved his fingers in the air for emphasis. "I then tried to leave, but the car wouldn't start. I would have considered it just bad luck on my end, but given the circumstances…. So, grabbing the files, I got out and made my way down the sidewalk at a jogging pace. It was then that I was blindsided by somebody and knocked to the ground. At first, I thought it was the police. But as I tussled with the assailant, it soon became apparent who the man was." Looking up, Theo said, "Brendan, it was your father. His hair was long and he had facial hair, but I knew his face like the back of my hand. Rafael had gone Rogue."

The hairs on the back of my neck stood up. I felt my throat clotting up. Forcing up the words in a coughing jumble I said, "Why would he do such a thing?"

Theo shook his head. "He never said a word. Wouldn't even answer my questions when I realized it was him. It was as if he were someone entirely different." His blue eyes fixated on the wall again. "After about a minute or so into brawling, an actual French policeman had caught up to us. After hearing the sounds of the police cruiser, Rafael pulled a gun on the man and killed him. Then he opened fire on the cruiser. Fearing that he would turn on me next, I made a break for it and escaped. This was the last time I saw your father. It's been years since, but reports on hits being compromised or sabotaged by an unknown assailant kept filtering in. No one could ever find him. It's almost like he was a ghost."

A ghost I almost killed. I wondered how many jobs would get compromised until he was finally brought down. Punished not just for the sins he committed against others, but for those against me. His son. I dug my fingernails into the wooden arms of the chair.

Theo looked back at me. His eyes were still twinkling under the basement's scant light. His blond hair frayed, his face worn and tired. He shrugged again and proceeded to place his hands on top of the table, as if laying down a weapon and badge for the police chief.

"Brendan, my dear boy. There's something else you must know. It's about the car accident…."

A door at the far end of the room burst open. I looked to Theo for an answer, but his attention had since been diverted to the source of the noise. Within seconds the shape of two tall figures came out from the shadows. They were two men dressed in black and white suits.

Theo stood up. "We've been expecting you."

The man on the left produced a silvery smile that lasted only a few seconds before quickly fading away. His balding head glowed under the incandescent bulb. It was The Chancellor himself, and he was accompanied by his personal assistant.

Theo held out his hand and the two Frenchmen accepted it. I started to stand myself, but quickly sat back down, remembering the bloody mess below. The Chancellor then walked over to me, and I shook his hand as well.

"Theo, Brendan," he said, turning to both of us, "I'm glad to see you two are well."

The Chancellor's eyes went back and combed over me, giving the combined look of both scorn and concern at the same time. It was then that Theo moved across the table and pulled out two seats for the men.

He waved his hands, and like magic, the men sat down. After sitting back down himself, he said, "Thank you for coming out here, sir."

"I trust that everything is healing well," The Chancellor said to me. His voice was almost as intimidating as his stare and, for a second, I was back in the hospital bed, reeling with fear as he sat across me at the other end.

"Yes, sir," I said. "The scar just reopened a little while fighting yesterday—"

"And then some," his assistant chimed in. I followed his gaze to the bloody towel resting under the table.

Turning to The Chancellor I said, "Sir, I'm fine. I promise."

"We were able to interview Mr. Blanco," Theo said, interrupting. For that, I was thankful. For a second, I had dodged a bullet.

To my surprise the balding man chuckled. As he continued to laugh he threw up his fingers and made quotations in the air. "*Interview him.* I like that, Theo." Perhaps The Chancellor was human after all. Then, addressing his assistant he added: "Please show them the article, if you will."

I exchanged glances with Theo as the man nodded and produced a rolled-up newspaper. After taking off its rubber band he tossed it over to Theo. "Interpol is going crazy over this," he said, pointing at the title of the front-page article that read

AMERICAN FUGITIVE FOUND DEAD IN TAIWAN
APARTMENT.

Theo drew his chair up close to the table, seemingly untroubled by the gruesome photo of the dead Mr. Blanco on the first page. "Thank you, sir. I'll spare you the gory details, but we were able to find out who sold him that disk."

"Great work, Theo. Who was it?" The Chancellor asked.

Theo's blue-eyed gaze bounced over to me. I shrugged, not knowing what to say. He then looked down at the table and slid his index finger across it. At last he said, "It was Rafael, sir."

The assistant almost toppled over in his chair. "That's impossible!" Throwing a cautious stare my way he added: "Rafael's…gone."

"But he's not, sir," Theo shot back. "And I have proof."

The Chancellor pulled his seat up as well. Both he and Theo were only feet apart from each other. Twisting his face he said, "Are you sure of this?"

Theo nodded his head slowly. "Yes, sir. And I also have reason to believe that he's the one who's been disrupting our operations all these years." After he was done talking, he straightened up and broadened his shoulders so that he appeared even taller than he already was. His frayed hair, no longer in a ponytail, continued to cling to the back of his neck.

"What proof do you have then?" The other man asked accusingly.

Theo reached into his suit and pulled out what appeared to be a cell-phone and a piece of paper. He slid them both across the table toward The Chancellor and then stood up.

"And that's not all, sir," he said, watching as the bald man went for the items. "The boy here saw him face to face in Berlin."

The next hour or so was taken up primarily by me explaining, word-for-word, what had gone down. Starting in Berlin with the Englishman, stealing the disks, and then blowing up the IMF building. I told them about the man, Rafael, who had then killed everybody in the safe house and tried killing me in an attempt to steal the disks. I also told them about Mr. Blanco—the restaurant, the alley, and the *interrogation*. I told the two men everything, letting no detail left unsaid. No scene left unturned. The Chancellor then questioned me like a prisoner. I defended my claims. Theo sprinkled into the conversation when he saw things were getting too heated, taking up my side as well. It was a circus act to say the least—and I was the main attraction. In the end, I felt tired and sluggish, and my temples hurt.

After I was finished talking, I sat there quietly and tried to catch my breath. It stung along my abdomen, breathing so heavily, but I continued to clench the arms of the wooden chair and hid the pain. I had to.

The Chancellor's assistant had remained steadfast in trying to convince us all that what I had seen in Berlin, and heard in Mr. Blanco's apartment, wasn't true. He kept questioning me even more so than The Chancellor himself. But as mad as I got from his outlandish accusations, I could not blame him. Even though it seemed that nobody believed or *trusted* me, I couldn't blame them. Trust was a rare luxury barely afforded in my world. Besides, what would *you* think if somebody claimed to see a man who had been dead for over ten years? In the end, I tried to hold my own. It was all that was left in me.

"This doesn't prove anything," the assistant said. "It's the word of a delusional boy and an American psychopath who already conspired against us."

The Chancellor put down the phone he had been inspecting and folded his hands on the table. His gaze went from his assistant to me. So did Theo's. It felt like all the eyes of the world were now glaring down at me.

"I can't explain it, sir," I said, trying my best not to lose my shit. "But I *know* it was him."

Before either of the guests could offer a rebuttal, Theo broke in. "On top of that, how do you explain what the American was talking about? There was no hint of their connection, and yet Mr. Blanco kept talking about Rafael. On his own!"

Having said the last part, Theo sat back in his chair, blinking at the sudden frustration in his voice. The conversation had been spiraling out of control as wild and heated as the candle that sat flickering away nonchalantly between us on the table. It seemed to dance in convulsive mockery as the four of us continued to argue—civilized men dressed in business attire and arguing like primitive apes. The second main attraction of the circus.

While the older men continued to argue, I lost interest. I receded further and further back into the recesses of my mind, until I had finally found the subconscious. That little hiding spot we sometimes seek in moments of desperation or idle boredom. Either way, I had found it. In the background I could hear them talking, sounding muffled the way a voice becomes when you put a Styrofoam cup over your mouth and try to speak. Absentmindedly, I found myself staring at the Motorola phone Theo had discovered on Mr. Blanco and the slip of paper to the left of it. They appeared just as lonely and abandoned as I. Surely Theo and the others had not forgotten about the only true and tangible pieces of evidence that would prove my merit and set me free.

"Theo, what about the stuff you found in Mr. Blanco's pockets?" I asked, nodding toward the items on the table. By now they were screaming for attention.

This halted the argument completely and the faces of all three men turned, first to me, then down onto the table. Theo, who had since been standing, reached across and slid the piece of paper back over to himself.

"What's on it?" The Chancellor asked. His hands were still folded on the table. His assistant kept his mouth shut.

Theo unfolded the small square of notepaper and handed it off to The Chancellor.

"Read it, sir," he said, seating himself back in his chair.

The Chancellor's eyes narrowed as he read the paper. He flipped it over and then back again before handing it off to his assistant who did the same. When the suspense got too great I interrupted. "What's it say?" I asked. Then, remembering who I was seated at the table with, I quickly lowered my head.

The Chancellor paused and looked at his assistant. Then back to me, saying, "It's a number."

I found myself starting to ask *whose number*, but was smart enough to keep shut and wait. Besides, I already knew the answer to my question.

"It's Rafael's," The Chancellor said, taking back the piece of paper with the phone number on it. He folded it up neatly in its original display and slid it back across the table to Theo.

My gut twisted. The ghost was real after all.

"I checked out the phone earlier, too," Theo said, tucking the paper away in his pants. "It's blank. No contacts, no numbers. Even the call log is cleaned out."

The Chancellor, seemingly agitated, stared at Theo for a couple seconds. He then turned to consult with his assistant. This time I had neglected to watch my words and before I could stop myself, I spewed them out. "I wouldn't lie about something like this, sir." They came out in one large string of jumbled up words at lightning speed, and it would have been a surprise if anyone had understood me. Even I wasn't quite sure what I had just said. Feeling the eyes of the world bearing down on me again, I began fidgeting in my seat.

The light flickered once more. When The Chancellor spoke I saw myself shrinking into the wooden chair. His eyes glistened, but not in the good way. Not in the *kind* way. "Nobody's questioning your integrity, my boy."

But in a way you were. In a way, everybody was questioning my integrity.

Theo interrupted. For the second time that day, I was thankful for his presence. "Sir, what do you propose we do next?"

"What do *you* propose we do next?" The assistant asked sharply.

Theo pursed his lips. I knew that he was swallowing something he wanted to say. Instead, he kept still. The Chancellor tilted his head at him the way one does when studying a foreign object. For a second the room became silent. Only the dancing flame of the candle on the table showed any sign of life.

I was just about to say something when Theo finally spoke. "Well, sir, I *propose* calling the number on *that* paper with *that* phone," he said, pointing at each item in their respective order.

At length, I too found myself cocking my head to the side, studying Theo and wondering what was going on. This whole conversation seemed overly confusing, and I didn't understand why they couldn't just make the call already. Unfortunately, I was out of lifelines and didn't dare to add my two cents again.

"It's not as cut-and-dried, Theo," The Chancellor said. His voice had gone up an octave, but his hands remained oddly calm on the table. "I wish it were. But if we're dealing with a ghost, we must treat him like one."

Theo slouched back in his chair and stared into the center of the table. He then started drumming his fingers in a rhythmic pattern on the woody top. His blue eyes glistened in the candlelight as it continued to shine in fiery indifference to the conversation at hand. I supposed he too could feel the eyes of the world staring at him. Somewhere outside on the sidewalk, two men were arguing over something, I guessed.

"I got it!" Theo finally said as he straightened up. "I know what we'll do next."

And he *did* know. Theo was a genius despite his less-than candid behavior in the field. But there was no doubting that he was a mastermind of field ops. He was after all part of The Vice, and they didn't just hand out memberships like candy.

Theo divulged how we would get ahold of Rafael—setting up "a buy" at a disclosed time and location. But instead of meeting up with him, we would ambush the man instead. If Rafael indeed was a ghost, he would be treated like one. And ghosts were hard to spook.

The Chancellor was the first to respond to his plan. His face gave no emotions at first, the way a skeptical person looks at a shoddy car salesman. But then he let up and a slight grin appeared across the edge of his seasoned face, forming creases that were outlined by the dancing candle light. "I think it just may work. And given the immediate circumstances, this may be the *only thing* that will work."

His assistant was not as agreeable with the plan, but after some diplomatic coaxing from the boss, he retracted his opinion. Both men were on board it seemed. It looked as though Theo's strategy had the green light.

"That makes me happy to hear," Theo replied, "Because I already set up the buy." He looked away and I could see the highs of his cheekbones becoming red. The corners of his mouth had also curled up.

The Chancellor flicked his eyes at him and for a second he looked pissed. His hands had begun to bulge up. But after tightening his lips the way one does during careful consideration his posture shifted and his hands became flaccid once again.

Thinking back now, I do recall having heard a voice coming from Theo's bedroom. He must have made the call sometime in the night before I passed out. Theo, it seemed, was two steps ahead of us. Hopefully he would also be two steps ahead of Rafael, the *ghost*.

But the moment of cunningness was also one of brevity. The assistant was quick to chime back in, saying, "So who did you speak to? When is the deal going down?" Theo's grin vanished as he spun his head back to the table.

"I'm not sure *who*…but I can tell you that the deal is happening tomorrow, just before sundown."

The assistant's mouth flew open. The candle kept doing its jig, glowing off the steel cans like a dying sun. The table fell silent.

"It's not ideal," said Theo. "But it *did* give us a location, and will distract some of them while we scale the ship."

"*The ship!*" the assistant shouted. His face had become flushed.

Theo turned to The Chancellor and their eyes met. "Yes, sir, Rafael's situated on a nice little container ship in the Port of Kaohsiung— southwest of us."

"And you say the buy's tomorrow?" The Chancellor asked, rubbing the side of his face with a big palm.

Theo nodded his head like a child. His blond hair swayed a little, but for the most part it refused to unstick from the back of his head. Through the dusty windows the sun was reaching the threshold of noon.

"Well," The Chancellor said, looking from his assistant to Theo. "I'll be damned if you go in blind. Let me see what sort of reconnaissance we can drum up for you. Have you got the address of the port?"

Theo nodded again. He asked for a pen. The assistant handed him one and after jotting down the address on a piece of paper ripped off from the first piece, he gave it to The Chancellor. His pallid face had a look of benevolence that seemed to disarm even the old man as he took the slip of paper. "I'll see what I can do," he said. Then, after a long sigh he added: "For now, Theo, I suggest you wait in the shadows and try to get some rest. You and Clément have a long day ahead of you."

Theo's blue eyes became wide. "Actually, sir, I'd much prefer if the boy here tagged along with me instead."

The assistant was the first to argue. "Look at the kid. He's in no shape to do anything of the sort."

Theo started to get up but The Chancellor waved him down with a hand. "He's right. The boy needs to do some thorough healing and rest up as well."

"But I'm fine, sir—"

"And I was wrong to let you back so soon," he added, cutting me off harshly.

I started to see red again. Watching as my whole career—my whole *life* up to this point—began to crumble before my very eyes. There was only so much a man could take, so many blows before snapping. And this was it.

"I can do this! I *need* to do this!"

The room fell to complete silence again. Even the outside streets seemed to stop. The traffic, the people shuffling on the streets and sidewalks. It all seemed to stop. It was as though the whole world had heard my cry and stopped spinning on its axis, finally listening to the broken child of a broken system. In some way, it was all I could ask for. In fact, it was all I *ever* asked for. To be heard.

My own face was flushed with rage, and I felt my heart beating against my chest. Taking in a deep breath, I allowed myself to calm back down before continuing. The eyes of the world were still fixed on me, but instead of glaring, they were evaluating. Ears listened. I waited for the red to go away from my vision.

"Please, sir, I need to do this."

"This is about your father, isn't it?" The Chancellor asked. He pulled himself up to the table and folded his hands on it again.

I looked at Theo who simply gave me a warm smile in reply. "Yes, sir," I said. "This *is* about my father." I could feel my cheeks getting red again, but not from rage. It was from hope.

The Chancellor leaned over to his assistant and whispered something to him. There was a pause as this went on. When they were done, Clément looked over my way and nodded.

At last The Chancellor spoke. "No," he said. "I'm sorry, Brendan, but I just cannot allow it."

All at once the crimson hue returned in my eyes and I felt the wind being sucked out of my lungs. I suddenly stood up, no longer caring that everybody could see my blood-soaked clothes, or the fact that my wound started to bleed again as streaks of dark red trickled down my pants. I suddenly was not caring about anything at all. I blinked, but all I saw was *Red*.

"This is *bullshit!*" I cried out, not caring that my voice ran around the room before coming back. "I've done everything for you!" I was staring at three blank faces. Theo's mouth stuck open like a frog trying to catch flies. As I repeated myself I could hear the outside streets coming back to life again as the whole world resumed spinning on its axis of indifference. Everybody was done listening and my words had fallen on deaf ears.

In the midst of my yelling, I had toppled over my chair. I grabbed it in an attempt to smash it against the brick wall, but as I moved to do it, Theo quickly got up and wrapped his arms around me. The other two men continued to stare back as the events unfolded.

"I didn't choose this life!" I shouted. The more I struggled to break free of Theo, the tighter his grip got. Turning to The Chancellor I added: "Haven't I done everything you asked?" My eyes were welling up.

My strength was great, despite being injured, but Theo was stronger. It did not take him long to subdue me, and I reluctantly let go of the chair. It hit the floor and rolled on the side, and after staring at it longingly Theo spoke to me. "Please calm down, good boy. It's going to be okay, I promise."

But would it really?

Theo proceeded to escort me back to my room. Along the way he scooped up the bloodied towel and held it over my wound. My face was in tears and I didn't care who saw. He didn't say anything as he guided me into the room. Behind me, he shut the door and then locked it. Leaving me once more to my own accord, just as I have always been.

The room was small, and although it would have been nothing to press my ear up to the wall and listen to anything they were saying in the other room, I no longer found myself caring. The way I saw it, my career was over. I was over. After the stunt I pulled, there would be no chance at being let back into The Program. My only purpose on this earth was to serve others like a dog. And I was sure that I would now be put down like one.

Becoming the age of twenty was both a blessing and a curse for me. It was a double-edged sword. Turning to my cot I sat down and lay my head back, wondered where I'd be right now had I not left that hotel in Reggio; had I instead vanished, disappeared, melted away.

And I could have.

That is what ate at me the most. How easy it would have been for me to do such a blasphemous thing. And not just during the last ten years either. Holding up my right arm, I stared at the fleshy scar streaking across my palm. I caressed it. When I was six years old, I had been waiting inside my mother's Honda as she ran into the store for something. It had been raining and although it was in the early afternoon I could have opened the passenger's door and simply walked away. The crazy part is that I had thought about doing just that too. But just as I had decided to stay in that car until my mother returned, I decided to stay with The Program.

My Reason? I used to think that it was because it was my duty and that I had no other choice. But deep down I knew that reason was a lie I just kept feeding myself, spoonful after spoonful, day after day. No, the real reason that I stayed was because of hope.

I hoped that one day, after I had murdered enough people, after I had satiated the ever constant demands of The Chancellor, I would finally be set free. Free to taste just a tiny piece of the life that's been dangling in front of me this whole time. It was a new life that's been taunting me—consuming my dreams and stirring my thoughts—to one day be able to walk down that street, and just watch those waves breaking and the sea foam frothing over the pristine white beach. Feeling the sea breeze as it climbed over the sand and hugged me. The warmth of the sun pressing down with gentle embrace. For me, that was hope, and it's what kept me going all these filthy years. And now, as I sat here in the dingy basement, waiting for my death sentence to be drawn out by men who couldn't care less about me, I found myself regretting it all.

CHAPTER FIFTEEN

After moping around for God knows how long, I had fallen asleep. Something jerked me. When I woke up I saw that the room had become dim. Only scarce patches of orange sunlight made it through the foggy window. Even the sun, which had once brought me some measure of comfort, was leaving me. I felt like the man in that canvas painting above the cot; like the whole world was crashing down on me from all sides. No way out. I was drowning.

As the sun continued to make its communal lowering, the noises of Taipei were retiring as well. I could only hear the occasional murmur of people outside. The blood began to dry on my clothes and it stank up the room. On the far wall, the clock kept ticking away. Its black hands of time chipped away as my death sentence was surely being constructed. *Tick tock. Tick tock.*

Remembering the lantern below me, I fumbled for the matches nearby. My hands were still trembling from the ordeal in the other room and I dropped them. Although I could have just as easily found them, I saw no reason. Even fire couldn't take away the darkness that was my world. Lying back in the bed, I closed my eyes and drew in a deep breath. Beyond the room, I could still hear faint voices talking. Every now and again their tones would rise and fall. After a while I surrendered to idleness and let the tears run down my face.

Not long after falling asleep again, another noise woke me up. I tried shrugging it off and falling back to sleep, but a second sound brought me to full consciousness. The light was dying fast and it took me a while to adjust my eyes to the dark room.

I tuned my ears for the source of the loud disturbance and it was then that the door to my room unlocked and swung wide open. Theo was standing in the doorway. His face was brimming with that sly grin of his. His blue eyes were filled with concern. "Feel any better, good boy?"

My throat was stuck from all the crying I had done. Instead of answering, I just watched him, before rubbing my eyes.

His gaze moved from my face down to my bloody shirt. Pointing to it he asked, "How's the wound doing?"

Being stuck in such a dark hole of a room, I had failed to notice that the bleeding had stopped. Although the room stank of drying blood, no more streaks of it were trailing down my pants. Again, I just stared back at Theo, waiting for something to happen.

He moved into the room. His hair swayed as he bent down to pick up the lantern. Finding the overturned box of matches close by, he picked one up, caught it on the wall, and lit the lantern. "There we are," he said, placing it back on the ground. He then proceeded to take a seat at the edge of my cot.

"You know, Brendan," he said. "If my memory serves me right, I can remember a young boy who had once thrown a hell of a good fit because his mother refused to give him ice cream after dinner."

"I—I don't remember doing such a thing," I said, studying him. He had since taken a shower and his hair was drawn back again into a ponytail. The tie to his black and white suit shimmered dully from the other room's light.

He placed his hands on his lap and said, "That's because it wasn't you, good boy. It was me."

The air became still as if every particle had been suspended in time. Somewhere in the room the clock kept chipping away.

"You see, Brendan. The two of us are not all that different. You and I...we come from similar pasts. And I too was raised by my mum."

He became silent as he stared back at me. The lantern, coupled with the distant light from the other room cast his shadows on the floor in front. For a second I saw myself in him, making me wonder if Theo really was my future self.

"I don't know what came over me, Theo."

To this he smiled again. "Oh but you do, good boy. But you do."

I sat there in silence with my head cocked to the side, studying him some more; not knowing how to respond to such a comment.

"I see the way you move and the way you act," he said, looking me over. "And sometimes I wonder if it's either because you know so little, or if it's because you know so much."

The streets outside were quiet, and although I squinted, watching as the sun beyond turned a deep purple, I knew that I would get no help from them. I was beginning to apologize for what had happened when Theo put his hand up in the air and stopped me. My mouth stood open in mid-sentence as if he had waved an invisible wand that left me frozen for all the ages.

"Please don't," he said. "You don't ever have to apologize for your actions...or mine." He regarded the ground having said the last two words. I knew what he had meant.

"You once did the same thing."

Theo smiled at me again. Then, looking away he said, "Not exactly. But it was very similar."

"And they didn't toss you from The Program or try to . . ." My words trailed off. "What happened?"

His smile began to recede to the corners of his mouth. "That's old history, good boy. Another time ago. But yes, I'm still here."

"But did you try to pick up a chair and throw it?"

Theo chuckled and his face radiated. "Even worse," he laughed.

I glanced down at the floor, watching the shadows of our feet move. "What are they going to do with me, Theo?"

He put a hand on my knee consolingly. "Nothing at all."

"But I yelled back at The Chancellor. He thinks I've gone mad!"

Theo laughed again. "Do you think you're the first person who has gotten heated and screamed at him?" When he finished laughing he continued to speak. His voice was soft and understanding. "You know by now that this career—this *life*—isn't easy. It's not just some job where after work you can go home each day. Things get intense. *You* get intense. It's just part of the job description. You know that. I know that. And most importantly, The Chancellor knows that. Besides, you've got a personal vendetta to justify your actions. You only did what anybody else in your position would have. After all, you're still human, Brendan."

"Sometimes I forget I am," I said, staring up at him. When he didn't say anything, I added: "So I'm not getting the boot then?"

"Of course not." He then stood up, displaying the full height of his Scandinavian ancestry. "And I'll do you one better. You're coming with us tomorrow." Smiling, he held out his hand and helped me up. I couldn't be more grateful.

The remainder of the night was spent back in the center room. The Chancellor had left his personal assistant, Clément, who was to tag along and help with tomorrow's Op.

"I wanted to apologize to you, Brendan," Clément said.

The three of us were seated around the table again. A pot of coffee had been passed around. Its aromatic blend of Colombian joe filled the basement air. In the center of the table, the candle, now almost at the end of its wick, refused to die. The broken chair from earlier still idled next to the wall, reminding us of how heated things could easily get again.

Clément's smile was not as warm and inviting as Theo's, but it was still wholesome. And I accepted his truce all the same. He extended his hand and I reached across the table and took it. Theo's face brimmed at the sight of this.

While not as tall as The Chancellor, Clément still had a stately and robust physique. If it wasn't for the crows-feet hidden in the corners of his eyes, I would have assumed the man to be about Theo's age, if not younger. His hair was jet black and almost as thick as his French accent. In the flickering basement light, it shone like a freshly polished shoe. When he smiled, his brown eyes beamed, revealing a man of intense aura.

Leaving from Beivrus, I had brought along only one outfit. Theo had fetched me a new one, and although I was a little small for his size, I was still glad to have gotten rid of the bloodstained clothes. Never in my life was I so thankful to bathe, and then feel the touch of dry cotton against my skin.

"Thank you for changing your mind, Clément," Theo said when we were done exchanging pleasantries and had sat back down.

Turning to Theo he said, "Yes, well, you can be very persuasive at times."

This made me think back to the loud noise I had been woken up to earlier. "What's our next move?" I asked, staring at the phone on the table. It was still in its same position as earlier.

"We wait," both men said in unison. I twisted my face hearing this, and Theo refined his answer saying, "The Chancellor is going to see what recon he can find on tomorrow's location."

"Until then," Clément added, "I suggest you get some rest. Tomorrow's going to be a big day for all of us." He ended his sentence with a cryptic smile that didn't seem to alleviate my apprehension about him.

A thought occurred to me, and before I could catch my words, they flew out into the basement air. "Did you know my father?"

There was a pause. Theo leaned over the table, watching both of us.

"No, my friend," Clément said, shaking his head. "Not personally."

I slouched back in my chair. Enough digging was done for one day. Sometimes, if you dig too deep, you'll never be able to climb back out.

Theo pushed his chair away from the table and stood up. "Clément's right. You ought to get some rest." Looking around at both of us he added: "We all should."

Leaving the conversation at that, we vacated the room and retired to our bedrooms. It was quarter past ten by then, although it felt later.

Tomorrow would be a new day, and I had a hunch that we would need all the rest we could get.

That night, I hadn't slept much. Before turning in I had lit the lantern below my cot and sat down. At first, the stench of dried blood kicked me in the face after walking into the room, but within seconds it had dissipated. After seeing enough dead bodies, you get used to the smell, I guess.

But the dream I did have was so vividly real that it haunted me. I was back in Reggio again, but instead of starting off in the hotel or the street outside, I was on the beach. The air was warm and a gentle breeze had hugged me as I sat down. While I was wearing the same clothes, this time I had bare feet. I had dug them into the sand the way a child would. The way I had once did when my mother took me to the beach for the first time. For the longest while, as time was irrelevant, I stared off into the distance and marveled at the sea. It was an endless mural of blue-green, with the sun flushing over the horizon. Eventually, I caught the familiar glimpse out of the corner of my eye of a dark shape rising and falling with the uneven plain of the beach. It was again the girl from the hotel, and her athletic figure was flawless as she continued to jog up toward me. Her bronzed skin glistened under the sun. Her black hair bobbed up and down with her stride. When she was about ten or so feet from me she stopped, just as she always did. Only this time, instead of waving, she proceeded to walk up to me. And as she got closer, I began to feel the tips of my ears becoming hot and my face getting flushed. It was a sensation I had never known before. Everything just felt so real. The girl then smiled. Her bright green eyes stared into mine, seemingly piercing right through my chest and into my very soul. My breath was taken by her beauty, and for the first time in my life I felt completely vulnerable. But I did not care. I opened my mouth, but no words could be found.

After a brief moment she knelt down and smiled. By now my ears were hotter than the sun. Silently, I smiled back, staring at her elegance, staring at her innocence. She then raised her arms and placed her hands on either sides of my face so that her warm fingers covered my ears. Leaning into me, she kissed my forehead. I closed my eyes. Her lips were moist and soft. She kissed me again. Although my eyes were still shut, I could feel her face drawing into mine. Her breath was both sweet and warm as she whispered something into my ear. "Please don't lose hope, Brendan," I heard her say. But when I opened my eyes again, it wasn't the girl staring back at me. Instead, it was the inviting face of my mother. Her eyes, a deep amber, told a story of absolute peace.

It was then that I woke up with a jolt, gasping for air. What felt like sweat clung to my face. It was still dark and at first I didn't know where I was. As I began to dry myself off though, I quickly realized that it hadn't been sweat covering me. It was tears. The image of my mother's face came back into view. Everything from the dream came back to me all at once, and I broke down and cried once again.

Morning came soon enough. Although I was unable to fall back asleep the rest of the night, seeing the bright rays of daylight poking in through the cracks of the wall made me forget how tired I was.

After a while, I sat up and stretched. The smell of blood still clung to the air, but I paid no attention. Looking around, I noticed the bottom of my door was glowing with light from the other room. I rose, thinking that I was not the only one awake, and left the hollow tomb that was my bedroom.

The rest of the basement was empty, however. Somebody must have left the light on last night. The incandescent bulb kept flicking away as I continued toward the small kitchenette. I made a pot of coffee and soon the large room was filled with the aroma of Folger's, extra black. With nobody around to appreciate it with me, I drew up the first pot by myself and sat down at the table. The memory of last night's dream still resonated in my head like a flash of pictures on a movie screen.

It wasn't until I had already downed half the pot of coffee when the first of my two roommates came into the room and joined me.

"Smells great," Clément said in between yawns. His jet black hair was just as solid as yesterday.

Seeing him enter the room I stood up. "Help yourself, sir."

When he saw me go to grab him a cup of coffee he waved me down. "No, no. That's quite all right."

He got himself a cup and sat down at the table across from me. His cup sent a waft of steam floating up into the air before dissipating. After taking a sip he put the cup down. "How are you feeling today?"

His eyes were staring over at me, as if he could see right through the table and see my wound. Up until now, I had forgotten all about it and the excruciating pain from yesterday morning. Taking another sip of my own coffee I replied, "Much better, sir."

"Good," he said. "You're going to need your strength today." He ended his words with a wispy smile and resumed drinking his coffee.

"Can I ask you a question, sir?"

Clément took another sip. "Yes."

"Do you think we'll make it out of there alive?"

Clément nearly choked on his coffee. It was a question I had spent the remainder of the night dwelling over. Allowing the heavy words to ruminate in my mind like a bad decision. In some way, I knew it was.

Clément stared at me before finally opening his mouth. But before he could say anything, Theo walked into the room. "Good morning, gentlemen," he said, making his way to what remained of the coffee pot idling on the kitchenette counter.

As he passed by the table I noticed that his hair was frayed like a strand of old rope. His eyes were bloodshot and when he spoke his voice was strained. After fixing himself a cup of coffee he sat down at the table with us.

Watching him drink his coffee I said, "Did you sleep well?"

"Go to hell." He forced a grin.

"I'm already there," I said jokingly. Both men laughed.

It wasn't long before Theo was back to normal and his eyes had cleared up. Perhaps he too didn't get much sleep last night. Perhaps I was not the only one with nightmares keeping me up all night. Even the boogeyman was scared of something.

After downing another cup of coffee, Theo's voice was the standard Swedish one. Turning to Clément he asked, "Anything yet from the boss?"

Clément shook his head. The light continued to flicker above and its glowing aura shone against his black hair. "Nothing yet." It looked as though a thought occurred to him and he proceeded to pull out a silver phone from the depths of his trench coat. He placed it at the center of the wooden table where the candle from yesterday had been. Looking around at us he added, "He'll be calling us on this. And when he does, we need to be ready."

And with that, the three of us left the table and got ready for the day. We stole away to the armory room nestled into the brick wall, leaving our coffees to succumb to the effects of the chilly morning. For some reason I didn't think we'd be back for them.

The armory was much smaller than the one in the Berlin safe house. It was nothing but a tiny room with three long shelves skirting the far wall. On the shelves were films of dust, and the fluorescent light refused to turn on. The top two shelves were stocked with old automatic weapons and an array of handguns that hadn't been used in God knows how long. Clément, seemingly to know what he was doing, pushed away a crate labeled AMMUNITION under the first shelf. He then pulled out a large green case that had been behind the crate. It had Chinese characters written in yellow paint on the cover.

With the light not working, I had been holding open the armory door so that the basement light could splash into the room. Theo and Clément carried the large green case back into the main room of the basement. "What's in it?" I asked when they brushed past me.

Neither man paid attention to my question. After the case was carefully placed on the ground, Clément knelt down beside it. He played with the three latches, and then swung open the top. Inside were five MP5K submachine guns and about twenty black magazines of ammunition. Theo dove in first and pulled out one of the weapons.

"Compliments of the People's Republic," Clément sneered, watching as Theo loaded in one of the black magazines of ammo.

The MP5K was essentially the progeny of its German predecessor, the MP5. These guns were much more compact with folding stocks, and had a faster firing rate capable of bursting rounds in quick succession. I waited for Clément to pull out his before going for one myself.

"We're gonna need those too," Theo said. He pointed at the silencer attachments hidden beside the remaining ammunition magazines. The thin barrels shimmered under the basement light as I distributed three of them amongst us.

With the edition of the silencer attachments, the barrels of the guns grew an additional six inches. The black magazines were long too, each magazine holding thirty rounds and more than capable of dealing some heavy damage in mass quantity. Nevertheless, I knew how to conceal the lethal weapons under my clothes. Things like that came second nature to men like us.

I had seen a leather holster for handguns back in the armory. After taking that and dipping into my bedroom for my handgun and over-jacket, I joined my partners at the table in the other room. No sooner had I done so than the silver phone started vibrating on the wooden surface. Clément smiled sheepishly, and after waiting a few seconds he opened the phone. He put it on speaker and placed it back on the table.

"Hello, sir," Clément said. He then looked around the table. "We're all here."

I looked at Theo. He saw me and winked. Whispering, he asked, "Are you ready, good boy?"

Patting myself down, I nodded and sat down at the table. It was cold out this morning, despite us being in the Far East, and the thick over-jacket was a welcoming comfort. I felt the gun holstered against my hip and thought back to the hit when I was sixteen; how I had killed the target myself and carried my partner out as he bled out all over me. I just hoped the op we were about to embark on would not be like that.

The voice on the other end of the phone spoke. "Good to hear, Clément." It was The Chancellor.

"Any good news for us?" Theo asked. He began fidgeting in his chair and leaned in. His blond hair swayed over his face.

The other voice smirked. "Theo! It's good to hear you've calmed down a bit since our last discussion."

Theo blushed and kept silent

The voice coming from the phone spoke up again. "Yes," The Chancellor said. "I do have some information for you, gentlemen. But it may not be what you were expecting." There was a slight change in his voice while he said the last part.

This time we *all* were silent. The light bulb overhead kept flicking.

After a brief pause, The Chancellor continued. "Look, gentlemen. This may be bigger than just recovering those bloody disks, after all."

Theo raised an eye brow. "What do you mean, sir?"

"Brendan, are you there?" asked the voice on the phone.

Both men looked at me. "Yes, sir," I said, feeling the eyes of the world on me again. "I'm here."

There was a pause and a second of static filled the phone. At last The Chancellor said, "Brendan, you were right about your father. It *is* Rafael."

And there it was—*you were right*—said by none other than The Chancellor himself. The words were like sweet honey in the air. Theo slid over and patted me on the back with a wide smile. But I couldn't bring myself to return the smile. Butterflies were now in my stomach, but I knew it wasn't from excitement. They weren't the *good feeling* butterflies, they were the *be careful for what you wish for* butterflies. The ones with Black Death wings fluttering around inside you, red eyes as thick as arterial blood, and sharp fangs threatening to stab at any second. I suddenly felt queasy.

Clément scooted closer to the table. "What do you have for us?"

"Gentlemen," The voice on the phone said, "Please listen carefully. Clément, write this information down."

It started to rain outside. Pellets of water began spraying the sides of the building and the basement windows. I could sense the sun fighting for dominance against clouds. Today would be a cold one. And not just in the physical sense. Clément pulled out a pen and notepad.

"We're ready, boss," Theo said. His smiled had vanished.

There was another pause before The Chancellor spoke. "Rafael as you know is holed up in the Port of Kaohsiung. My sources were able to confirm this just an hour ago. He's aboard a container ship named *The Blue Horizon*. It's flying under a Liberian flag.

"The ship's docked at the Second Harbor Section, in the Zhongxing Terminal. It's the only ship at dock and there's not a lot of Port Authority activity going on…." The Chancellor's voice trailed off for a second. "Making me think that something is amiss. Rafael may have paid off the PA. There's another container ship docked at the next terminal, but it looks as though it's being fitted now and will have departed before the sun goes down. Isn't that what Rafael had said, Theo?"

Theo bobbed his head up and down. "Yes, sir, that's correct."

The rain picked up outside. Coupled with the wind, it nailed the sides and windows with more fury. Clément looked over at me but I jerked my eyes away.

"Very well then," The voice said. "But gentlemen, the red flag is what's *on* the container ship." The three of us stared at each other. The light went out completely for a few seconds before flicking back to life. "There appears to be a handful of armed men aboard…perhaps eight or nine, maybe more. All wielding automatics." I touched the aluminum stock of the MF5K that lay across my lap. "But what they're guarding on the hull of the ship is what disturbs me the most."

Clément kept silent. He twirled the pen around in his hand as he waited to write more.

Finally Theo spoke up. His voice had gone up a few octaves. "What's on that ship, sir?"

The voice on the other end of the phone sighed. "My sources spotted signs on the containers, designating explosive materials on board. We have reason to believe the cargo ship is carrying some ballistic missiles that were stolen from a Chinese Navy depot last week…." His voice trailed off once more. "I think Rafael is going to try and sell them. You must stop him at all costs and destroy those missiles."

The air in the room seemingly became colder. It felt as though ice had been poured down my spine. Clément was busy writing down what The Chancellor had said. His black hair continued to glow under the light like a freshly polished shoe.

"What of the disks?" Theo asked.

"You'll have to secure them as well," the voice said. "And Theo…"

"Yes, sir?"

Another brief pause. "I want you to capture Rafael and bring him in alive."

The words stung like razor-sharp needles. Hurting more than being shot. The butterflies in my stomach disappeared—or rather, were eaten by vultures—and in their stead a much heavier feeling dwelled. Be careful for what you wish for. The words rang inside my head again. How I hated karma.

"But what for?" Theo and I both asked loudly. Clément stopped writing and looked up at us. "For interrogation," he said, putting down his pen. His notepad was filled with a black inscription. When he saw the look in our eyes, he added: "Rafael knows too much—"

"Then we should kill him!" Theo shouted, jumping out of his chair. I would have said the same thing if it wasn't for the knot forming in the depths of my throat. The rain continued to slap against the foggy windows of the basement. It too seemed to agree with Theo.

At last The Chancellor spoke. "It's much more complicated than that. He has a lot of information stored up in that head. We need to get it all out."

Beyond the rain I could hear nothing more. No vehicles, no people, no hustle. Even the busy streets of Taipei needed a rest. We all did. But there ain't no rest for the wicked.

Theo started protesting, as if for himself as much for me. But between The Chancellor and Clément, they were eventually able to calm him down. He sank back into his chair with a heaving chest. For a split second I swore I saw the glisten of craziness return to his eyes. Maybe this time, I thought, that wouldn't be such a bad idea.

"How do you propose we handle this?" Theo asked. His voice was calm again. But I knew better than to judge a book by its cover.

Clément began to speak, but the voice on the phone cut him off abruptly. "I'm alerting the people we have now in Taiwan to be on standby. Clément, I want you to arrange the rendezvous."

"Yes, sir," Clément said. He proceeded to pick up the notepad, flipped over the page he had just written on, and began writing on a fresh sheet. His pen twinkled in the light.

"As for getting rid of the missiles," the voice went on, "use your imagination."

I thought the conversation was over. But as Clément reached to turn the phone off, the voice spoke again. This time it was airy. "Put Brendan on. I want to speak with him alone."

Both men looked at me. Clément hesitated before passing over the phone. He seemed puzzled. "You can use my room, good boy," said Theo.

After taking the phone from Clément I slipped into Theo's bedroom, leaving behind the smell of cold coffee that refused to go away without a fight. I wasn't sure what The Chancellor wanted, but I did have an idea—and I also had a hunch that I wasn't going to like it.

Theo's room was already dark, and after shutting the door, it became even darker. The room smelled of cheap candles and layers of sweat. After feeling around in the dark I found his cot and sat down. Somewhere in the room a window was being hammered by rain.

Holding the phone up to my ear, I said, "I'm here, sir."

"Good," The Chancellor said. "I wanted to talk to you in private before you left."

I started to apologize for yesterday, but then stopped, remembering what Theo had told me last night in my room about never needing to apologize for my actions. Even now, Theo's voice was as clear and robust as the rain outside. Instead I asked coyly, "What is it, sir?"

Another pause.

"I know that you know this is in regards to your fathe—"

"Rafael," I said, cutting him off without thinking. "He's not my father."

The Chancellor sighed on the other end before continuing. At last he said, "Very well. But I still need you to listen carefully all the same." I pressed the phone tight against my ear. "You have more allies than you think, Brendan. Don't take that for granted."

His voice was stern and I stood up, blocking out the sound of rain pelting the window from some depths of the murky room. "We need Rafael back here alive. If you don't think you are capable of doing this, you need to tell me now. You're in a very unique situation and, considering the *circumstances*, there's nothing wrong with tapping out this time."

Every time I heard Rafael's name it was like daggers to my side. Hearing The Chancellor's last sentence though made me wince even more. I was beginning to see red again, and despite how cold the room felt, my chest was now hot. The voice began to say something else but I moved my hand over the phone so that his words were muffled. Holding the phone as far away as possible I then shouted at the top of my lungs. Cursing the darkness. I shouted so loud that I thought my vocal chords would rip out of my mouth. The rain beat against the phantom window even louder, as if challenging me as I continued to scream with rage. If this wasn't Theo's bedroom, I probably would have destroyed it.

I let the rage pass. When I was done shouting I checked myself and to see if any of my partners had heard me—not that I really cared. Taking in a deep breath, I put the phone back up to my ear. My hand was shaking and I tried to settle it with the other. "I'll be all right, sir," I said, being careful not to let my voice spike.

The voice on the phone spoke. "That's good to hear," it said. "Because should you let me down, there's no going back. Do you understand me? There's no room for errors."

The Chancellor's voice was still echoing inside my head when I rejoined the others at the table. They were gathered around it with equipment, duffel bags, weapons, and ammo scattered across the top. Theo had cleaned himself up and his blond hair was pinned into his signature ponytail that raced down his back in a single robust stride. He was in the midst of oiling the submachine guns with Clément. When he saw me come into the room, he looked up.

"Everything okay?"

Without speaking I put on a smile and nodded. He resumed his gun cleaning and I joined them.

About two hours or so later, and after the last drop of gun oil had been used up, we were ready. By now it was going on four p.m. and the storm outside showed no sign of letting up. It was uncharacteristically cold despite the small electric heater Clément had dug up from the storage closet. Not only did the over-jacket I was wearing provide more warmth, it had extra room for storing and concealing things like magazines, my switchblade, the handgun holstered to my side, and of course, the big daddy MP5K—all greased up and ready to go.

Theo tossed me something as I patted myself down for the twentieth time. "Take this," he said.

I started to ask him what it was, but glancing down at the small device, I quickly realized what was in my hands. It was a trigger detonator for plastic explosives.

Clément was in the middle of packing something bulky into one of the two black duffel bags in front of him. When he caught me looking around he grinned. Theo too was beaming from ear to ear. "We were told to use our imagination," he said, looking like a young school boy who had just stolen something. Pointing up toward the ceiling he added: "This building's *filled* with imagination, if you catch my drift, good boy." He then gave me an unsettling wink. Clément laughed to himself as he zipped the bag closed.

The safe house was rigged with C4 explosives. And when I say rigged, I mean *rigged*. Aside from running the risk of exposing our cover, the main reason we never ventured upstairs was because it would be like walking on hot coals. Chinese-made hot coals that would do more than just singe the bottoms of your feet.

"Two bags-full?" I asked, peering into the one bag.

Theo chuckled. "Have you ever seen a ballistic missile, good boy?"

Needless to say, no. Handling weapons-grade ballistics was not on my résumé. After Clément had carefully filled the other bag with C4, we took one last check around the room to make sure we had everything. The bags were zipped. The table was cleared off. Strapped down with enough weapons for Armageddon, we headed for the back entrance that Clément and The Chancellor had come into the basement through. Something was telling me I would never set foot in this place again.

The sky was a pasty dark gray outside with thunderous rumbles hiding behind the scattered clouds. The storm was a steady and relentless agony of raindrops hitting our faces as we moved through the side alley toward the front of the building. Our feet sloshed through puddles of dirty water. In the cusp of the early evening, a chilling wind kissed our exposed faces. It felt ominous—wishing us the best of luck as we set out, while at the same time warning us of the impending doom that lay ahead.

Clément was walking ahead of us, while Theo and I trailed behind, burdened with carrying the heavy duffel bags that were filled with Chinese boom. He nodded ahead toward the sidewalk saying, "There's a vehicle waiting for us."

And there was. In no time, we had merged onto the sidewalk. A lengthy sedan was parked in front of the building—which I found odd.

The car was a rusty brown, with an exhaust pipe that flared dark smoke into the air as it idled. A van drove by and splashed water onto the other side of the sedan. Clément walked up to the front passenger's side and knocked on the door. Within seconds the driver rolled down the window, beaming a toothless smile at us.

Clément nodded his head and, after the driver rolled the window back up, we followed him over to the trunk. "Put the bags in here," he said, opening it. The space was tight and I had to push over a couple stacks of newspapers to fit the duffel bags in.

"Can we trust this man?" Theo asked.

"Yes," Clément said, closing the trunk. "He's someone we *can* trust here."

Tucking the weapons inside our jackets, the three of us poured into the vehicle. Despite its appalling look, it felt comforting to get out of the rain, and I didn't mind the heavy cigarette smoke that seemed to take up more space than us.

The rain continued to punish the already beat-up sedan as we traveled south toward the other end of the island. Looking out the windows revealed a countryside unlike any other. After leaving the densely populated city of Taipei the country seemed to unravel itself into a completely foreign place. It was something I had failed to notice when flying into Taiwan. Its hilly slopes, covered in dense green forests, dipped down at certain points, and then spiked back up into great mountains, scratching the dark sky with its snow-capped peaks. It was something an artist would have dreamed up in his studio.

It felt organic, but at the same time it felt surreal. It *all* felt surreal. And I expected at any moment to wake up in my bed, a child again, listening to my mother sing to herself as she cleaned the house. I closed my eyes tight and counted to five, thinking—no, *hoping*—that when I opened them again, it would all go away. That it was all just a dream. A very bad dream.

But I knew better. There was no room for naïve people in this world. I opened my eyes and saw the same men. In the same old car. In the same old world. This was *my* world. And you can't escape what's yours.

Nothing was said between us for the duration of the drive. Nothing needed to be said. We knew all there was to know about what we were doing. Even the driver, who continued to puff thick cigarette smoke into the cab, knew what he needed to know. It's what kept everything on an even keel. It was, after all, the cycle of the sea.

The sky had become much darker by the time we finally reached Kaohsiung. The dying sun was nowhere to be seen through the thickened clouds. The city itself, much smaller than Taipei, was still shuffling at full speed despite the dismal weather, and it took us some time to get across to the harbor. Once there, however, I could see right away what The Chancellor had been talking about.

Laid out exactly like a giant square grid, the port jutted out into the ocean. Inside the perimeter of the giant square port were stacks and stacks of ten-foot long containers with some stacks exceeding forty containers high. Three massive bulk-container ships were docked along the harbor. What surprised me, though, was the lack of activity going on within the port.

We parked as close as possible to the harbor without being spotted. The driver pointed his cigarette toward the ship at the far left, closest to us. Turning to Clément he said, "This *Blue Horizon.*" Then, forming a circle in the windshield with a finger, he added: "This *Zhongxing Terminal.*"

We then exited the vehicle and Clément handed the driver some money. Within seconds the car was off, leaving the three of us in the cold rain once more. I watched as the ugly brown sedan and its cab full of cigarette smoke drove off and out of sight. The vehicle's exhaust pipe kicking up black smoke in its wake.

"That was the easy part," Theo said. Drops of water were trickling down his ponytail. He smiled at me, but under the parka and black suit he was wearing, I knew that he was just as cold and miserable as the rest of us. That faux smile wasn't fooling anyone.

Clément raised his hand and pointed across the harbor. "Over there," he said, "There's a small boat with our name on it."

At first, it was hard to tell what Clément was pointing at. Visibility was extremely limited in the rain. But after holding up my hands to shield my eyes and squinting in just the right place, I could at last see a tiny rowboat about a hundred yards away from us. It was nestled up against the dock and being slapped against it with each passing wave.

Clément started for the rowboat. Picking up both duffel bags, I followed him and Theo at a jog. The wind was as unrelenting, throwing pellets of cold water into us as we maneuvered through the field of containers, being careful not to get noticed.

We started jogging faster. About halfway across my wound began to sting. A few times it made me wince and I bit my tongue to subdue the pain, but it wasn't enough to slow me down. Besides, at this point, there was no turning back. We were beyond the tipping point.

While Clément ran ahead of us, Theo was at a blissful stride in the middle. Looking back at me he said, "Almost there, good boy." By now, his long hair was soaked, as was mine and Clément's.

Clément was first to reach the rowboat. He wasted no time in prying at the rope tethering the boat to the dock. Theo and I weren't far behind. After catching up to him, we proceeded to lower our black bags into the boat before lowering ourselves. The rickety boat sloshed back and forth in the water as we took up positions. It kept knocking against the dock while Clément struggled with the rope.

At long last, Clément was able to free our boat from the dock. He threw the rope toward the harbor, and as he pushed us out, Theo began rowing. The wind was especially cruel to us out on the water, picking up force and threatening to blow us all overboard.

Whoever The Chancellors sources were, they had been right so far. The port was completely barren of any activity, and we had yet to see any harbor patrol cruising by in the water. The second ship he had mentioned, the one being fitted, was nowhere in sight. Aside from the other two container ships in the distant docks, *The Blue Horizon*, in all its gigantic glory, was alone at port.

The ship looked eerie in the storm. Like something created in a Stephen King novel. Its massive hull and bridge stood tall against the blackened skies. If it wasn't for the many lights decorating the ship and scattered across the dock—which kept getting smaller as we continued to row away from it—the three of us would have been in pitch blackness—Theo, rowing us into an abyss.

"Do you see anything?" Theo asked. He stopped rowing, but still held onto the wooden oars so that they didn't slip into the water and drift away. Clément shook his head.

Standing up, I tried to balance myself while at the same time straining to see beyond our tiny rowboat. It was a balancing act of sorts, but after a moment of teetering I was able to hold my sea legs firmly against the rocking vessel. I made a brief scan of the ship, and just as I was about to sit back down and abandon my efforts, I saw the vague semblance of three, maybe four people standing in front of the ship. They seemed to be dressed in black, but out here, everything looked black to some degree. However, I did see the unmistakable shine of guns, and I quickly sat back down.

"Yes," I said, wondering if they had spotted us. "There're men on the dock, standing by the ship. And they're armed."

Clément nodded his head in confirmation of my sighting. Theo, resuming his rowing, asked us to keep a lookout as we approached the side of the ship. The sea was becoming violent, and I was becoming nervous.

The sky rumbled as we neared our destination. Behind the clouds great flashes of bright white lit up the surface. Loud *cracks* of thunder followed the flashes. Just as I started to wonder how we were going to board the ship, a row of ladders came into view. The metallic frames extended down from a wall of the lower deck and disappeared into the murky water below.

Nobody seemed to be guarding the railings, probably being too occupied with waiting for Theo's "buy" on the other side. It looked like we had the element of surprise. Theo continued to row us up to the ship, but just as we came close enough to board it, a massive wave came roaring in. Before any of us could react the boat was tipped almost on its side. The three of us had just enough time to grab onto the wooden frame, clinging for dear life. Clément was screaming something, but it was impossible to tell what. Rain kept splattering down from above. The boat was pitched over at a strong enough angle that one of the bags was tossed overboard. It sank almost instantly. The other bag started slipping over as well, but Theo quickly grabbed it, with his other hand still grasping the side of the boat. After another series of violent pitches, the rowboat finally righted itself. All three of us hurried to bring the boat back to the ship. Theo rowed furiously as Clément and I paddled with our hands. The wind kept howling in our ears.

Eventually we came close enough so that the rowboat was within ten feet of the ship's belly. The dark figure of Clément stood and pointed up at something. "Look, gentleman, there's our entryway."

I followed the direction in which the Frenchman was pointing and at first couldn't comprehend what it was. Theo shook his head as well. However, as we inched closer so that our boat was parallel against the ship, the unmistakable outline of a rope ladder ascending toward the top deck became apparent.

"It's a starboard ladder used by the harbormaster," Clément shouted above the wind. "Consider it a back door to *The Blue Horizon*." Even in the torrential downpour his French accent was devilishly thick.

Theo was the first to get off the tiny rowboat. He jumped for the ladder, barely reaching its wooden steps, and turned around. "You're next, good boy!" Holding out a hand he added: "Take my hand, I won't let you fall."

I felt a set of hands press against my back. "I'll steady you," Clé-ment said from behind. The boat began teetering again under my feet, but it was with ease that I grabbed onto Theo's arm, jumped, and was hoisted onto the ladder almost face-to-face with him.

Before getting onto the ladder himself, Clément passed the one remaining duffel bag up to me. Theo had since climbed up the ladder a few feet so that there was enough room for all of us. He then called back down to me. "Here, give me the bag." And I was glad for it. Even the simple motion of jumping onto the rope ladder brought about a serious, nagging pain from my gut.

The Frenchman jumped off and landed effortlessly onto the ladder next to me. The boat itself started drifting off into the darkness.

"That was a little too close for comfort, my American friend," Clément said as he passed by me, following Theo who had continued moving up the ladder with the duffel bag.

With the wind at our backs and the rain pelting us from above, we continued up the ladder. After what seemed like an eternity of climbing I felt Clément's foot where I had meant to grab another step. I looked up to see that he had stopped moving. So had Theo.

Before I had a chance to ask what was going on Theo shouted down to us. "There appears to be a metal door above me with a ledge in front. It looks tight, but I think the three of us can squeeze onto it."

Clément nodded to Theo and within moments we were back to moving again. We were two-thirds up the side of the ship when I looked up to see that Theo had hoisted himself onto a small, metal ledge. Clément scrambled up what remained of the rope ladder and did the same. When it was my turn, they both helped me onto the ledge. Having my feet planted on relatively firm grounding never felt so good. Although I had a strong urge to look down past the ledge, I fought against it.

"Let's not do that again," I said in a joking manner. Needless to say, nobody had the will to laugh, nor dared to.

After catching our breath and patting ourselves down to see if any-thing had been lost, we tapped back in and continued with the mission. Looking up, I was an awe by the grandeur of the colossal ship. Between flashes of lightning, I could see that the giant vessel was splashed in white paint with a long line of red lining the underside that I had seen from the rowboat earlier.

The ship had to be at least a hundred feet high, but it was so dark that I was barely able to see the top deck above. The rain was thick, and

I could only faintly discern the green and red lights glowing on the bridge's tower.

Clément lead the charge again, pointing at the metal door Theo had mentioned jutting out from the wall ahead of us. I picked up the duffel bag and followed behind them. One hand clenching the bag of C4, while the other hand grasped the MP5K strapped around my shoulder under the coat.

When we were safely inside, Theo shut the bulky door behind us, leaving the wind and rain to howl, teasing us to come back out and play. None of us had a blueprint of the cargo ship and only Clément seemed to know where he was going. We were standing in a compartment full of life jackets and boating equipment. A halogen light above us flickered.

"Where are we?" Theo asked. He flipped his ponytail forward and wrung it out. An abundance of water splashed to the floor.

Clément pulled out a piece of paper. He scanned it, folded it back up, and replaced it back inside his trench coat. "Next to the crew's quarters," he said. His hair hadn't suffered the same fate as Theo's and it blended in well with the darkness.

After burning up a minute to look around the room, Clément found a hatch. Above the metal door were the words TO HULL. Repositioning the bag in my hand, I followed the men upstairs. To Hull we went.

Theo led the way this time, and I was glad, because no sooner had we emerged from below decks than we ran into our first guard. Or rather, he ran into us. And here I had just begun to suspect that the ship was empty—like it was a ghost ship.

As Theo reached the top stair and made for the door, it swung open. An Asian man stood there, stone-faced. After a moment's hesitation he reached for his gun. Theo stopped him. Clément and I watched from behind as Theo, who towered over his opponent, grabbed the man by his throat and pushed him up against the wall. With his free hand he then pulled out a knife and stabbed the man repeatedly in the belly. The Asian men let out a half-shriek and at first he struggled, his legs flailing wildly in the air. But it wasn't long before he stopped and his eyes closed. Blood was sprayed on the walls around us. Theo let go of his throat and his body slopped to the floor.

Clément knelt down and searched his body. "Good work, Theo." Finding nothing, he got back up and ushered us forward. Theo wiped his knife on the man's clothes and put it away. I followed behind as we continued through the door, doing my best not to step on the body.

We were again met with pounding rain fueled by the wind. Emerging onto the open deck, we took up position against a big red container. We had reached the hold of the ship and it was filled with containers. Most of them red, but some with blue or yellow. A few were even white, marked with bright words saying CLIMATE SENSITIVE that twinkled under the sky. The ship lurched to the side, making a low guttural noise as if it were greeting its new visitors.

Theo and Clément were on either side of me again. They stole away to the corners of the container we were hiding behind and peered around. Seeing nothing, they crawled back over to me. Both men had their submachine guns drawn.

"Where to next, Clément?" Theo wiped a film of water off his face.

Clément brought out his paper again. After teetering it at an angle for more light he said, "Toward the center of the hold." He folded the paper back up and glanced at Theo. "That's where the missiles are being stored. The boxes they're in should be painted black."

Allowing Theo to go first again, Clément and I lagged behind. The duffel bag and the stinging at my waist slowed me down some. The wind kept crying in my ears. Clément looked back at me but said nothing, urging me to keep up with a flick of his gun.

Moving across the giant ship was like running on top of a sky-scraper. The ship was so high up that the wind kept pushing against us on all sides as it changed directions every other minute. Each strong burst of air was threatening to knock us to the ground should we lose our footing on the slippery deck that skirted the hold. I guess this is how King Kong must have felt clinging to the needle of the Empire State Building.

At length, we stopped behind another container. This one was bright yellow. Theo smiled at me. "How are you feeling, good boy?"

I glanced down at my abdomen. It was throbbing from all the running and twisting. But I also felt queasy. The ship, the rain, the *reality*—it all made me nauseous and it would have been no great surprise if I threw up then and there. Forcing a smile, I took a deep breath. "I'm good. Let's get this job done."

The rain continued to slam against us at slanted angles. The clouds rumbled, mixed with flashes of bright white. The lightning stabbing into the ocean and harbor around us like giant, God-like swords. Clément informed us that we were close to the black containers.

We resumed jogging, skirting the outside of the hall on the right side to avoid detection. As we did so, I looked down over the railing of the ship. It was hard not to. It was nothing but utter darkness below. A black abyss that would suck a man into emptiness—into a void. Somehow it was like staring into my own soul. My stomach churned.

At a certain point, Theo and Clément, both leading the way, took a hard left onto a catwalk amid the thick field of containers. I followed behind, struggling to keep up. The temperature continued to drop and I could see my breath freezing in front of me. Suspending in the air for all of time. This made me think about the clock in my bedroom back at the safe house. Its black hands cutting out time. *Tick tock. Tick tock.*

The sound of Clément's hurried voice brought me back to the present. "Just up ahead," he said. Or at least that's what it sounded like. The wind was whistling violently through the many rows of containers. Demanding us to turn back now, before it was too late.

A couple minutes later, and after stealthily maneuvering through the sea of containers, we finally reached the heart of the cargo hold. All three of us took up shelter behind a red container. It stood horizontal to the ship and for the time being shielded us from the chaotic rain that sloshed up against the other side. Threatening at any moment to go the other way with the change in the wind. We really were just feathers drifting in the wind. At the mercy of nature.

Clément was crouched on the right side of the box, keeping guard with his gun drawn. Theo had knelt down on the left side. I scooted over to him, dropping the bag down between my feet so that it wouldn't slide across the floor.

"What do you see?" I asked.

He put his hand over his eyes like a salute and craned around the corner of the box. After mumbling something to himself he turned back to me. "I think I see black boxes," he said loud enough that we all could hear. "And there's something else."

Clément came over. He brought out a handkerchief and wiped his face off. Handing it off to Theo he asked, "What's that?"

Theo knelt down again and his knees popped. Taking the handkerchief and drying himself off he said, "It looks like there's two men guarding the containers."

Theo offered me the handkerchief but I shook my head. Instead, I slung the MP5K over my shoulder and cocked back the firing bolt. "How far away?"

The Swede crouched down even further so that his knees touched the ground. I heard him chuckle to himself after peering around the corner again. "I can't believe it."

I got closer to Theo, so our arms were brushing. "What?" I asked.

Clément also looked confused. After wiping his face down again, he slid the handkerchief back into the depths of his pants. The wind was starting to change course and I knew that it was only a matter of seconds before we would be back in the rain's crosshairs. A streak of lightning split the sky behind Clément.

"I just can't believe it," Theo repeated. Turning back to us he added: "There's like only two of them guarding these things. They're maybe twenty yards away."

I crept away to the other side of the red container. Clément had offered to keep tabs on the duffel bag filled with plastics. Drawing the MP5K up to eye-level, I waited for Theo's command. My finger slid over the trigger guard.

"*Now.*"

And with that, hell commenced. Theo's booming voice echoed across the ship as the two of us wrapped around either side of the red container. Our guns itching to kill. The rain splashing down on all sides. There were two men standing in front of the black box. We quickly closed in on them. By the time they saw us coming, it was too late. Theo was the first to open fire. Two rounds ripped through the air and blew the face off of one of the men. As the other man went for his gun, I too pulled the trigger. The back of his head spattered across the black box. Both bodies dropped to the ground as the wind continued to whistle.

We continued to press forward with our guns out. After clearing the perimeter, walking around the box, we gestured for Clément to come over. Seeing Theo's hand signal, he quickly jogged over with the duffel bag swaying in one hand.

Unlike all the other containers aboard the ship, this one was painted black on all sides. Against the sky it looked invisible. Had it not been for the many lights glowing on the ship, it would have been. Displayed on both doors of the box in giant white letters were the words **WARNING EXPLOSIVE MATERIALS**. Below the warning label was a skull. This was a pretty obvious clue if I ever saw one.

Theo jostled both doors. They appeared to be locked and bolted down. But that didn't matter. We had found what we were looking for. There were three more black boxes standing next to this one. All bearing the same warning label with a skull underneath.

Clément put the duffel bag on the ground. Wasting no time, we unzipped it and the three of us grabbed as many stacks of C4 as we

could carry. Each one of us moved to the four containers and planted the explosives. They were sealed in a weather-tight liquid that had
since congealed around the plastics. And for good reason. The darkened sky above showed no sign of letting up that night. It was as if all
the world's rain had concentrated over us. Diluting and then purging
our soaked bodies of the sins we were committing. And the ones we
were about to commit.

After all the C4 had been planted we rendezvoused back behind
the red container from earlier. This time the rain was pelting the
box from our side. Somewhere beyond us, the clouds grumbled and
growled. The sky gods were not amused.

Clément gave up trying to dry himself off. He threw his handkerchief into the wind and it floated away. Staring at both Theo and I he
asked, "Everything set, boys?"

The two of us nodded our heads. In unison we replied, "Yes, sir."
And with that we headed back toward the bridge. Toward Rafael. The
storm was fierce. But my willpower was fiercer.

Although there were no signs of others aboard the ship, we nevertheless continued to weave through the aisles of towering boxes to
avoid being seen. We moved lighter, no longer being burdened with
the bulky duffel bag. Pressed close to my heart was the only detonator
to the plastic explosives.

When we were about fifty or so yards away, the grandeur of the
giant bridge could be seen in all its entirety. You could tell that at one
point it had been painted white like the sides of the ship, but after years
of neglect and weathering it now told a different story. The glossy windows of the tower were like the bulging eyes of a maritime giant; perhaps Poseidon himself. Glowing lights of red and green and yellow
pulsated everywhere. The bridge looked the way an old woman with
make-up on her face does after the mascara and puffy white cheeks
began to fade and slowly trickle down—no longer displaying a woman
of intense beauty, but instead, revealing an aged fossil who refused to
succumb to the horrid ravishes of time. *Tick tock. Tick tock.*

A pile of yellow containers, running perpendicular to the rest with
a forklift truck abandoned at the base, lay ahead. Theo aimed his gun
forward and said, "Let's stop here."

We stopped behind the boxes and rested. Our breath formed tiny
crystals in the air. My stomach still felt uneasy and after all that running the pain was sharp. Biting my tongue even harder, I persevered.
We were almost done.

Theo watched as Clément brought out the piece of paper and scanned it. "What's our next move?" he asked. His blond strands of hair were draped over his chest.

Clément folded the paper back up and returned it to the depths of his pants pocket. "There's a hatch at the base of that tower," he said, pointing to the bridge in front of us. "If Rafael's still here, he'll most likely be inside."

Had he been watching us the whole time? I looked up at the bridge. Was this just one giant trap that we were walking into? My stomach flipped over at the thought.

Theo stood up. As he did a bullet whizzed by his face. He looked around in time for two more rounds to come flying dangerously close before tearing into the yellow containers behind him. One of the bullets ricocheted and bounced off into the darkness. I grabbed the bottom of Theo's parka and yanked him back down.

More bullets grazed by overhead, but we couldn't see from what direction they were coming. Theo shouted something in what I assumed to be Swedish before returning fire; shooting into the air.

After more firing, we finally saw the flash of the shooter's muzzle brake just beyond a container near the edge of the ship. But as we returned fire in that direction, another series of bullets came by from the other side. I looked around, but Clément was not there. Theo and I dove behind the forklift. More bullets ripped through the air and shattered the truck's glass. I held my arm over my face as the shards sprayed down on us. We were surrounded on all sides. The rain kept sloshing down.

A floodlight attached to the bridge had been shot out, making it next to impossible to see, save for the occasional flash of distant lightning fanning across the sky. Turning to my other senses, I strained to hear where the gunshots were now coming from. Theo, who was crouched down beside me, did the same. It soon became apparent that they were using semi-automatics; their weapons were subpar to what we were wielding. We both unloaded our empty magazines and put fresh ones in. Theo made for a large wooden crate positioned near the right side of the ship. When the coast was clear, I followed. It was our turn to play hide-and-go-seek.

Most of the gunfire had stopped. Here and there, a shot was popped off, but nowhere near us. Theo kept muttering to himself in his Swedish rhetoric. We moved past the crate and crept alongside the outermost row of crates, keeping our heads low lest a stray bullet pick our heads off.

The darkness was now on our side. In The Program, we had been trained for moments like these—when we would be forced to adapt and rely on our other senses. The outline of Theo's body stopped. Ahead, I could hear someone changing magazines. Theo turned around and tapped me on the shoulder, telling me to go. Pulling out my switchblade, I crept past him. I found the man kneeling about ten yards away, with his back to me. I came up behind him and jammed the knife into his skull, twisting the blade as it sunk in. Then, tossing his body overboard, I watched until it made a faint splashing sound and sank into the depths of the sea.

It was then that Theo stood up and shouted. He dipped back down and the shooting picked up again. Dim flashes lit up the darkness. A wave of lead peppered the railing and nearby containers as I dove back to Theo. When we didn't fire back the shooting stopped and the layer of darkness blanketed the ship once more.

There was silence.

I strained to listen. From the specks of lights still coming from the bridge, I could see Theo's outline, but Clément was still MIA. I wondered if he had been shot and lay propped up against a container somewhere with that jet-black hair of his. Bleeding out.

A gust of wind blew across my face and I pulled the collar of my over-jacket up against my neck. It's not like it made any difference though. My clothes and my body were past being soaked; they were beyond saturated. I looked up at Theo, but could not see his face or his bright blue eyes.

A violent gust of wind coming from the harbor rushed over the deck. Although the ship itself was steadfast and invincible to such elemental damage, the contents on-deck were not. That included us. Water that had been pooling somewhere on the deck sloshed into the side of the container we were hugging. Loose equipment stowed away nearby was pitched across the slippery deck toward the other side. After a few seconds flood lights streaming with a glowing red aura came to life on the front of the bridge. It was eerie. Seeing them reminded me of the casino job in Amsterdam; the red lights pulsating against the black mirrored walls. And like Amsterdam, I knew that I had to be the one to take charge and save the op. Only my Final Challenge was not at stake here. It was my life. All of our lives.

Taking a deep breath, I turned to Theo. "Yell again."

I could see the shape of his head nodding in understanding. He shouted, even louder this time. Within moments the fire squad resumed shooting. I put away the knife I still held, slung the submachine gun back in front, and ran toward the gunshots.

The wind whistled angrily in my ears as I surged forward. More shots were fired and I followed their source to two men crouching behind a stack of four blue containers marked AGRICULTURE. I held the weapon up to my left eye, steadied my aim, held my breath, and squeezed. The trigger was a bit touchy, but not loose. I squeezed it again. It was flawless. Both men slumped over with bullet holes in their temples. Behind me, I could hear Theo cheering me on.

Theo was still crouched where I had left him. His face gleamed at the sight of me. The shooting had stopped, but looking around, something was bothering me. Clément was still missing.

Theo patted me on the back. As he spoke his breath clung to the air. "Glad to see you're in one piece, good boy."

Looking him over head to toe I replied, "And you as well." A bullet had grazed his face and left a fleshy scratch on his cheek. But he seemed to be intact. Remembering our lost comrade I added: "Where's Clément?"

Theo looked down at the ground. He was shaking his head.

"Over here," called a familiar voice.

Theo and I both looked around.

"Over here," it said again.

The voice came from a pile of wooden pallets stacked neatly—having been tied down before the storm—against one of those bright white containers. We walked over to the source. Clément was sitting on the ground with his back against the box. He waved us over saying, "I'm not hurt." His slicked back hair had been ruffled up. Something I thought was impossible. Of course, being in the middle of what seemed like a typhoon could mess up anybody's hair.

"How many are left?" he asked.

Theo and I knelt down on either side of him. I looked him over just to be sure; he too seemed to be intact. "I didn't see any others," I said, shaking my head.

A gust of wind picked up and sent debris flying at me from a shattered crate nearby. I hunched over just in time for a piece of wood to slam into the container above me. It slid down and hit my head. Although it hurt, the real pain was coming from my stomach. The stabbing sensation had returned in full fury and biting my tongue no longer worked. I winced, dropped the MP5K, and grabbed my belly with both hands. It was all I could think to do.

I could sense both men staring at me. "How bad is it?" Clément asked, seeing me grimace.

The pain dulled and then returned, then dulled again. Each time it did, I dug my fingers into my jacket. I turned my head up toward the black sky, closing my eyes, and waited for the pain to pass. Drops of water being carried by the wind hit my face. But I did not care. After the stabbing pain was gone I opened my eyes. Turning to Clément I said, "I'll be fine."

Clément nodded. "Okay." He brought out the folded up paper and consulted it. After scanning it, he added: "Are you gentlemen ready?"

The wind whipped through the aisle of containers between us, as though it were pleading us to say *no*. Overhead the sky rumbled and roared with thunderous rage of the sky gods. I looked over to Theo for an answer, perhaps confirmation. He could only respond with an empty face, although his eyes revealed something else. I bobbed my head up and down. Speaking for the both of us I said, "Yes. We're ready."

Clément got up and the paper vanished within his pocket. "Excellent," he said. Then, addressing me, he added, "We're almost done, Brendan."

He proceeded to hold out his hand to me. I took it as he helped me back up. The quick movement sent a jolt of dagger-like pain back into my abdomen. Wincing again, I bit my tongue hard enough that I tasted blood. When I was able to stand on my own, Theo picked up my gun and handed it off to me. I slung it over my shoulder and told them I was okay.

"I'll lead," Theo said, shouldering his own gun.

Clément held up his hand in protest. "Not yet, Theo," he said. "Let me scout out ahead first. I don't want us walking into another trap."

Theo cocked his head to the side. His hair dangled over the shoulder. "Are you sure, Clément?"

Clément nodded. "I'll be fine." He glanced down at his watch and said, "Give me five minutes, okay?"

Theo knelt back down. "All right," he said.

And with that the Frenchman went ahead toward the bridge. He turned a corner and was swallowed up by the darkness. Leaving Theo and me at the mercy of the storm, uncertain of whether or not we would ever see him again. The wind continued to whine.

Theo slouched down further, taking up residence on the wet ground. He sighed. Too weak to do the same, I remained standing and kept watch, my weapon drawn.

I felt someone tugging at my jacket. It was Theo. Staring up at me he asked, "How's the wound, Brendan?"

Another crack of lightning. Theo's pallid face was lit up. Under his bright blue eyes the scratch on his cheek was bleeding.

I was about to respond, giving him the same answer I gave Clément when he had asked that question. But after seeing the concerned look held in his eyes I doubled back. At last I said with complete honesty, "I'm not sure. It seems to be getting worse."

Theo opened his mouth and I braced myself for the worst, already knowing what he was about to say. But after a brief pause he just smiled. "Don't worry, good boy," he said. "I'll see to it that you make it to the end of this. You have my word on that."

Another of his cunning smiles beamed across his face. It broke through my barrier. And despite the ice-cold rain beating down on us, I suddenly felt warm inside, like the heat had been turned back on. Without hesitation, I leapt down on Theo, ignoring the pain as I threw my arms around the great man and embraced him like a child.

At least that's what I saw myself doing. Although my muscles twitched as though I had, twitching is all it would be. In my world, emotions are like an Achilles Heel. A cancerous disease to the mind. I knew this, and even Theo knew this as he continued to stare up at me as if he identified what was going through my mind. In the end, I simply nodded my head and resumed standing guard as we waited for Clément to come back.

CHAPTER SIXTEEN

Very few people are afforded luxury in this life. And even fewer get to ever taste it. Instead, we're left to watch in silent, expressionless horror as the piquant flavor comes to us like a snowflake falling from the sky, melting on the tip of our tongue before disappearing completely. Luxuries such as hope and love are like a juicy steak being dangled in front of our faces. And the more we chase after it, the farther away it dangles, with the fat dropping off and sizzling onto the ground. If we're all pieces to the same puzzle, why can't we share in what that puzzle makes? Why can't we all enjoy the steak of life and happiness?

Time seemed to roll by slowly as Theo and I waited in earnest silence. It was painful, waiting and not knowing. Wondering when, or even *if*, Clément would ever come back. The rain continued to berate the ship, and the wind refused to tell us anything.

After a while, I checked my watch. But it had somehow been busted and the tiny glass face was shattered. Looking down at Theo, I asked, "You got the time?" Theo glanced at his bare wrist and shrugged.

"What should we do?" I feared the worst. Like a giant hourglass, time was quickly running out. The last particles of sand were spinning through the funnel. Something had to be down, *now*.

It was as though Theo and I shared the same brainwave. Before I even had a chance at suggesting we do something, he was already in the midst of replacing his spent magazine with a new one. Chambering a round in his weapon, he said, "Let's go find him." To this I smiled. Steadying my hand, I helped my partner up.

The bowels of the colossal ship lurched as we headed north, following the cold tracks of Clément. A loud boom, deeper than any battle drum, reverberated in the clouds overhead, announcing our assault. Our guns were drawn as we pushed forward. The blackened tips of our silencers glowed under the red flood lights of the bridge. My hands were steady.

Injury or no injury, I persevered through the sharp pain still nagging at my gut. More blood continued to seep into my mouth as I dug my teeth deeper into my tongue. Theo and I picked up our speed so that we were now running shoulder to shoulder with one another. My feet felt weightless as we glided past more rows of metal containers. Darkness at our backs. And darkness ahead of us.

"*Stop*," Theo whispered. We had just reached the left side of the bridge. He grabbed me by my coat and pitched me up against a nearby container. It was red and the rain slicked the long side of it. Theo also pinned himself up against it.

I looked around, struggling to see what made us stop. "What is it?"

Theo dropped to his knees. I followed his movement as best I could. Turning to me he asked, "Smell that?"

After wiping water away from my face, I began sniffing the air. My nose was turned up like a bloodhound. Within moments I found what Theo was talking about. Hiding between the rain and the incessant howling of the wind was the acrid but unmistakable odor of cigarette smoke. Theo then pointed toward the backside of the bridge. There were three dark shapes standing next to it at the base. Floating orange dots burned through the darkness as their cigarette smoke wafted up and dissipated into the rain.

My partner stood back up. Making hand gestures, he motioned for us to split off and flank the dark shapes. From trying to find Clément, we had circled around the backside of the bridge. The red box we stood against ran parallel to it. A row of smaller containers and two more forklifts, which had been bunkered down with rope, stood between us and the men standing idle next to the bridge. While Theo disappeared to the right side, I took up the left. Our guns were once again drawn up to eye-level as we quietly stalked the dark shapes.

As I crept closer, I could begin to discern what we were up against. All three of them had automatic weapons slung around their shoulders. The one in the middle leaned against the bridge's wall with his foot planted against it. The other two were talking to each other.

Getting low to the deck, I continued to watch them from the shadows. The wind blanketed my body as it kept howling. Something from the other side of the ship jerked away my attention. It was Theo. He was creeping up to them. But there was something behind him. My mouth went dry. The butt of a rifle was raised in the air. It glistened as it was brought back down on Theo's head. His body went limp. I yelled, in reaction to this, drawing the attention of the three men standing by the bridge. Stirring all at once, I shouldered my weapon and chambered a round. But before I could get a shot off, I felt searing pain as something struck me from behind. All at once my mind went blank.

My mother once told me that patience was the key to any locked door. She said that patience and serenity were the universal elixirs to all of mankind's troubles. But that man's inadequacy—his ultimate folly—would be from his inability to comprehend what was so comprehendible. To see through the trees as he searched for the forest. Because sometimes *patience* was hidden in plain sight.

My head was jarring when I finally came to. It felt like a carousel that was spinning on overdrive. At first, I couldn't see anything, but then I realized that it was because the lights were off. I was in a room. The pain in my stomach was bad, but the throbbing sensation coming from the back of my skull was worse. When I tried to feel it, I found that my hands were bound behind me. Off in the distance I could hear the guttural rumble of thunder saying, *I told you so.* And I could hear something else. Something, *familiar.*

The lights flashed on. Two Asian men dressed in all black walked in, carrying pistols at their sides. Their faces were grim and the one had a huge scar running across his cheek.

"What are you doing here?" the one asked.

The man with the scar pointed his gun at me. I glared back, picking myself off the ground.

"I said, what are you doing here?" he asked again. This time the man with the scar came over and kicked the back of my leg, so that I collapsed onto my knees. I winced, but kept glaring up at them.

While this went on I kept hearing the sound of heavy breathing. I looked over my shoulder. There was a body slumped over on the left side of the room near the wall. A long strand of blond hair was draped over his black parka.

"*Theo!*"

There was no response. Only his deep breathing as his chest moved up and down confirmed that he was still alive.

The man with the scar proceeded to kneel down in front of me. His ugly smile pissed me off even more and my eyes narrowed. He reeked of cigarette smoke.

His partner moved in, this time he whispered, "What are you doing here?"

I spat in the other man's face.

"You motherfucker!" He raised his arm and slugged me twice across the face with his gun. For a couple seconds, I blacked out again.

It's hard to understand what makes us who we are. What makes us *tick* like the black hand of time slowly chipping away at life with each indifferent stroke. It's an age-old question that's as old as the Great Pyramids themselves and the many men who had built them. Some people believe that it is our *purpose* in life. That when we were conceived, we were given a set of cryptic instructions laying down our entire life's journey. Information so enigmatic that it's entwined inside our very DNA. But then again, there are some people who don't believe in this at all. There are some of us with no destiny, who instead believe that we were never born at all. Some of us just *are.* And before we can understand what makes us tick, we must first understand *who* we are.

The second time I woke up, I was lying on the floor. I could feel warm blood on my face. It was mine. The two Asian men were hovered over Theo, searching his clothing. I could no longer hear my friend breathing.

"Leave him alone!" I yelled, struggling to get up.

Both men stopped what they were doing and turned around. The one brought out his pistol and threatened to shoot me if I didn't keep quiet. But I paid no attention. Shouting at the top of my lungs I screamed, "*I SAID, LEAVE HIM ALONE!*"

They both came at me. The one with the scar on his face pulled out a knife. As they got closer, I rolled over onto my back, staring up at the yellow ceiling of the mysterious room. Listening to the unapologetic wind outside.

In a flash of struggle, I felt the cold steel blade of the man's knife pressed up against my throat. His partner was holding down my feet. It was then that the door swung open. A man with jet-black hair walked in.

"You're alive!" I stammered, my Adam's apple being groped by the knife as I spoke. "We came looking for you."

Clément shut the door and glanced around the room. His dark eyes bounced from me to Theo, then back to me again. He opened his mouth. "Is he alive?"

I started to speak, but was swiftly cut off by the man holding down my legs. "I don't know," he said, turning to Clément. The other drew back his knife and let me go.

"Go check him," Clément said.

The man with the scar walked back to Theo's body. Stooping over, he checked his pulse. He nodded his head.

"Clément," I said, my throat sore from the ordeal with the knife, "What's going o—"

"Wake him up," Clément said.

Not knowing what was going on, I rested my head back on the floor, watching in utter shock as the situation unfolded. My skull kept spinning on a swivel.

The man with the scar slapped Theo across the face open-handed. After a few more times of this Theo came to and started choking. His blue eyes blinked wildly and he reached for the gun that was no longer at his side. Seeing this, the other man came over and bound his hands together.

In between coughs, Theo asked, "Where am I? What's going on?"

One of the Asian men kicked him in his side. When he cocked his foot back to do it again, Clément stopped him. "That's enough." The other two men silently took up positions along the side walls.

After coughing up a puddle of blood, Theo looked up at the Frenchman. His blue eyes were bulging. "What's going on, Clément? What is this?"

Clément smiled at him. "This is hell, my friend."

Theo's pallid face contorted into a mask. His mouth went agape. The wound on his cheek was dribbling blood. Clément came over to him. Grabbing him by the throat, he dragged the Swede over to where I was. Our eyes met.

"Are you okay, good boy?"

"I'm fine, Theo," I said, ignoring the swelling pain at the back of my skull. Remembering seeing his body slumped on the ground, I added, "I thought you were dead."

He shook his head, causing his ponytail to sway back and forth against the ground. "So tell me," he said, addressing Clément, "Was this your plan all along?"

Clément grinned again. "You're a smart man, Theo. Too bad you weren't smart enough."

It took me a second or two to figure out what was going on. But when it did, it hit me like a train. All at once, my head stopped spinning. All at once, it made sense to me. Clément hadn't scouted ahead to make sure we weren't walking into a trap. He had run ahead to draw us into one. I bit my tongue again. Somehow I had to get out of here—*we* had to get out of here. But how?

Theo sat up. "Does The Chancellor know how much of a dog you are?" he asked. His voice was calm. "Or is he in on it too?"

Clément smirked. The other two men held silent, watching from the sidelines with blank stares. "Do you really think that old man has any clue what happens behind his back?" Clément's voice went up a few octaves and his French accent became thicker. "The Chancellor doesn't run the show. *I DO!*"

"You don't run shit, you French pussy," Theo fired back, laughing.

This response seemed to anger Clément. Turning to the two Asian men he shouted, "Get them on their knees!"

Obeying his heated demand, the two men came back into play, forcing us to kneel on the cold deck. My head resumed aching as if two bullhorns had been let loose on both sides of my face, and the piercing sensation crept back into my abdominal area. It felt as though both injuries were fighting for dominance.

"If you're going to kill us, do it now," Theo said. While his voice remained unnervingly calm, I saw a flash of Mr. Hyde glisten in his blue eyes.

The man with the scar got behind me. I heard a gun behind cocked back. Clément waved his hand out in front. "Not yet."

This time Theo grinned. Looking up at Clément he said, "You never did have the balls to follow through."

"Tough words coming from the man who couldn't kill Rafael," Clément shot back.

To this Theo pursed his lips. A blanket of silence fell over the room. It sounded as though the storm outside hushed too; listening intently as an even bigger one brewed inside.

"Tell me," Clément went on. "What if Rafael were here right now?"

Theo cocked his head to the side. "What are you talking about?"

"I'm talking about putting a face behind the nightmare," Clément said, waving his gun in the air. Something stirred in the shadows, and for the first time I realized that someone else had been standing in the back of the room. Someone I dreaded to see again.

The man walked to the front of the room, carrying an air of cold death in his wake. His one leg limping slightly as he joined Clément. He whispered something to Clément and then turned to face Theo. My heart stopped. It was none other than my father. It was Rafael.

"It's been a long time, brother." He knelt down in front of Theo so that their eyes met.

Theo coughed again. "What are you doing here? Why are you doing this?"

Standing back up as he talked, Rafael asked, "Why am *I* doing this? Why are *you* doing this?"

What the fuck was going on? Both pains had seemingly combined forces and I felt a rush of pulsation throbbing up my torso. I bit my tongue even harder, forcing down the blood that flowed from it. My tongue bled so much by now that it was getting difficult to swallow.

"You don't have to do this," Theo said.

"Oh but I do, brother," Rafael said. "After all, it's in my blood. Isn't that right, son?" He turned to me as he said the last part. I felt the air leave my lungs.

For what felt like an eternity our eyes connected. His piercing eyes stabbed my heart, rendering me defenseless. It was like staring at the monster of all monsters. Clément was right. He had put a face behind the nightmare. And I wished, right then and there, that I could pinch myself and wake up from it. But my hands were tied. And besides, I knew that there was no way out. I wanted to speak but a knot had lodged itself deep inside my throat. *I'm not your son*, I wanted to say. It was that simple. Yet, so hard.

Rafael flashed a grin at me before turning his attention back to Theo, the man who was more of a father to me than my own flesh and blood. I felt lifeless. Like my soul had somehow been drained by those blackened eyes of his. The storm continued to fester like a bad disease.

"You leave me in a tough spot," Rafael said, looking down at Theo. Behind him, Clément had folded his arms. "I've given you countless chances."

"I'm never going to join you," Theo told Rafael. "You might as well kill me now."

Rafael gave him a sad smile and said, "Then suit yourself. As I see it, you're already dead." Having said that he walked back over to Clément and whispered something into his ear again.

While this went on Theo spat blood onto the floor. "There never was any backup coming, was there, Clément?"

Taking the bait, Clément walked up to him. He drew out the piece of paper he had used earlier, unfolded it, and held it in front of Theo's face. Letting it fall to the floor he said, "Precisely."

The paper fluttered to the wet floor between us. Theo glanced down at it and then jerked his head away. It was blank. There was no writing on it. The whole operation was empty and Clément had us running full-speed into an ambush set by none other than Rafael himself.

"You French coward," Theo said, still looking away. "You'll never get away with this. The Chancellor will—"

"*I OWN THE CHANCELLOR!*" Clément's voice boomed. Without warning he grabbed a gun from one of the men and shot Theo twice in the chest.

"*NO*," I cried.

Theo gasped for air. His blue eyes danced around the room as if for an answer. Clément knelt down in front of Theo. Whispering into his ear he said, "*I own him.*"

The two gunshots were loud in the room. But seeing Theo get shot was even louder. It took some time to register what had even happened. But when it did, my blood curdled and my body felt hot. I was seeing red.

Rafael started for the door. "Good bye, old friend," he said before vanishing with Clément, who added: "Search them for the detonator. It's on one of those fuckers." And with that, the door was shut.

Theo continued to gasp for air and was struggling to breathe. Blood from the two entry wounds dribbled down his chest. His eyes were now staring back at the closed door, and I could see that he was fighting to stay alive. If I was going to make a move, I had to do it soon.

The man who had been standing behind me came around. It was the one with the scar across his face. Turning to his partner, he said, "Clément wants us to find that detonator."

His accomplice shook his head. Pointing down at Theo he said, "I couldn't find it on this one."

All at once my voice came back to me. "That's because I have it." Before either men could respond, I bolted up and rammed my head into one of the men. There was a dull *crack* as the top of my skull connected with his forehead. He fell over, unconscious, and dropped his pistol. The man with the scar reacted. As he came at me, I rolled over on top of the pistol, feeling for it with my bound hands. When I had the gun, I flipped onto my stomach, closed my eyes, and pulled the trigger from behind. I heard the man drop. I then let go of the pistol and crawled over to Theo. When he saw me, he smiled.

"You're going to be okay," I assured him.

He twisted his body around so that his back was to me. "There's a knife in the back," he said in between gasping. Tiny rivulets of blood were forming at the corners of his mouth.

After locating the knife, I bit down on the handle with my mouth and pulled it out. Holding my hands up to it, I sawed the rope against the blade. When I was free, I proceeded to cut Theo loose. I then propped him up against the wall. "You're going to be all right," I said, pressing my hands over his chest wounds. I could feel his blood seeping out under my palms. "I'm going to get you out of here."

Theo looked up at me. I could see the shiny glimmer of life starting to fade out of his bright blue eyes. At length he placed his hands on my wrists and stopped me. "No, good boy. My time has come."

Our eyes locked as I stared back at him, my face felt warped and I was full of confusion. He smiled again, and I reluctantly let go, my hands caked in blood. "What am I supposed to do now, Theo?" I asked, trying to hold back tears. "I can't do this without you."

Theo's face lit up, and for a second I thought that everything would somehow be okay.

"Yes you can," he said, coughing up more blood. "Don't ever lose hope."

I lost it completely, no longer being able to hold back the flood of tears that began racing down my cheeks. "Theo, why are we in this life?"

The Swede chuckled and his smile grew so that it was brimming from ear to ear. "I don't know," he said, wiping blood from his mouth. "Perhaps it's just fate."

The rain outside resumed, pelting the roof of the room with unforgiving strength. The wind, however, kept listening. It had seemingly pressed its ghostly cheeks up against the windows running across the room. The smell of cigarette smoke clung to the air. Mixed in with the stench of fresh blood coming from the bodies of the two Asian men.

Theo held out his hand. Clenching it with both of mine, I closed my eyes. His skin was cold and clammy, and I knew his time was fleeting.

"Maybe you could tell me about my mother," I said, remembering our talk that first night together in the basement. Although my eyes were shut, I could sense him beaming at me.

"Of course, good boy."

He went on for the next couple of minutes, reminiscing of how beautiful my mother—Adeline—had been. Of how they would write secret letters to each other, expressing their eternal love for one another. He said he missed her every day—I could feel his hand trembling as he said this—and wished the two of them could have met in a different life. Theo then went on to describe her, closing his eyes as he did so, as if she were here right now. It made me sad. After a while, I could feel him getting weaker and his hand started to slide from mine. He felt cold.

When he was finished speaking he took a deep breath and sighed, coughing up more blood as he did. I threw my arms around his neck and hugged him. I couldn't remember the last time I had ever hugged anyone at all. But it still felt right. My muscle memory was still intact. Theo chuckled and embraced me as well. The tears were streaming out of my eyes. I squeezed him tighter. His chest stopped moving and I felt the air leave his body for the last time.

The great American author, Poe, once said that the boundaries which divide life and death are at best shadowy and vague. Adding to this statement, I believe that there is a translucent veil defining such boundaries, and that although one person may mentally step out to the other side, his spirit will always remain here on Earth.

I let go of Theo and watched him for a minute. I thought back to the last couple of days we had together. How I wished I could somehow reclaim the lost time. Although he was gone, I could still feel his presence radiating around me like the sun. It warmed me. It *empowered* me. I was going to see this through. I still had hope.

After saying goodbye to Theo for the last time, I stood up. I searched the other men's bodies and took what weapons and ammunition I could find on them, slitting the throat of the man who was still unconscious. Before leaving I turned back. Theo's blue eyes were shut, but under them was the unmistakable presence of a serene smile. Maybe now he was finally at peace. Smiling back, I made a promise to him and to my mother—I would never *lose hope.*

Even from within the safety of the harbor, the ship was being jostled ever so slightly. The storm was picking up in intensity. It felt as though gale-force winds were veering and careening all around me. My gut was telling me that this would be the storm of all storms. This would be the end.

Emerging on deck, I realized after a quick scan that I was at the other end of the ship's deck. The bridge was hard to see but the faint glow of its red floodlights persevered like devilish eyes in the darkness. The winds howled in all directions, but this time, they were urging me on. The storm had chosen sides, and I was its champion. Theo's face came into view—his charming smile rivaled only by those bright blue eyes. *Yes you can, Brendan,* I heard his voice say, carried on by the wind. *You can do this.* I started to run. Only this time I wasn't running away from what haunted me. This time, I was running *toward* it. In every man's lifetime he has but one chance to fight his demons head on. And this was it. This was my chance. Holding a pistol in either hand I ran toward the bridge. I ran toward destiny.

My face, at first flushed, soon became numb as I picked up momentum. The pain quickly evaporated like a bad memory. Before long I could feel nothing. Things started to blur away as I sprinted for the bridge, both guns glistening under the lightning that forked the sky behind me. The more I ran, the less I could hear of the rain. Even the thunder became muted. My eyes narrowed. My breathing steadied. I was one with the deck, the ship, and the sea. I was in harmony with all things nature. This was not my fate. This was my destiny, and I was finally alive.

The bridge got taller by the second as I neared it. Its fading white face stared at me. The many lights blinking in idle forgiveness. There was a group of four men standing by the hatch at its base. I had no fear as I raced toward them—both guns drawn. I didn't even shudder when they turned and shot at me, their bullets grazing past my body. It was if I could see the bullets. Those tiny particles of death. But tonight *I* was death. On this long night, *I* was the reaper.

With even more speed I ran forward and fired back. Unloading a fury of hell. The thunder roared at my side, beating the deep battle drums. Announcing my war.

In times of war, dead or alive, on the front line or seas away, all men suffered casualties. No man was immune to the atrocities of strife and conflict. In some form or another, we all die. Even miles away the sound of gunshot reverberates back home, affecting those we love most and hold dearest to our hearts. Because in the end, we're all dead men.

The wall the men had been standing next to was quickly sprayed with blood. Every bullet I fired had found its mark. The bodies of the four men clumped on the ground. I reloaded my guns and moved toward the hatch. Leaving behind a trail of death. Their blood would streak across the ship's floor, where streams become rivers, and rivers become seas. Tonight the seas were crimson. I watched the blood flow, knowing I had spilled it. I was beyond Death. I was one with the blood.

I took a deep breath and said, "I am blood. I am crimson."

I pried the hatch open. There was a metal stairwell past the hatch door leading up to the bridge. The space leading up to it was confined, but I climbed it nonetheless. Having reached the control room, I stopped and looked around. It was quiet. The wide room was dark. The only illumination came from the distant flashes of thunder seen through the room's giant windows overlooking the bow of the ship. Here and there a yellow bulb on the many control panels lit up. Finding the room empty, I walked over to the windows. The sea beyond the ship was dark and listless.

But I was not alone for long. No sooner had I made it to the other side of the room than I heard multiple sets of footsteps coming up the stairs where I had just ascended. A surge shot through my body and my reflexes took control. I spun around, guns held at the ready. There were three men in total standing next to each other. I shot two of them just as they began raising their own weapons. The third man just stared at me. It was Clément. His face had gone white.

"I guess I shouldn't be surprised," he said. There was no trace of inflection in his voice.

The Frenchman took a step toward me, ignoring the two guns I still held by my side. His menacing posture said *leave now*, but the skewed look on his face screamed *come and get me*. For the time being though, I held my ground. Behind me, rain was sloshing up against the giant windows of the control tower.

We both stood there in silence. No one spoke, because nothing more needed to be said. Our ties were severed off. This was it.

A streak of lightning split the sky around us, lighting up our faces. Clément reached behind and drew out a gun; the same one he had used to shoot Theo with. But I was quicker at the draw. As he went to shoot, I fired first. Both guns let loose in a blaze of hellfire, filling the dark room with a series of flashes. When it was over, Clément slumped down to the ground. Blood began seeping out through a series of bullet holes torn across his chest. Theo would have been proud.

But there was no time for celebration. Time was still against me. *Tick tock.* There was one more monster that needed to be destroyed. As I made my way past Clément he grabbed my ankle. I glanced over my shoulder to see him staring up at me, dribbles of blood already running down his opened mouth.

"I suppose you know your mother's death was no accident." Although Clément tried to say more, he began to cough up blood.

There was no use talking to a dead man about something I knew in my heart to be truth. Theo had tried to tell me, but I knew, even if I had hid it from myself, that The Program had killed my mother. I freed my leg from his grasp and continued down the stairs, every cell—every molecule—of my body knowing what else had to be done. My spine tingled.

At the mercy of the storm outside, the ship moaned like a tired beast. Below decks was a labyrinth of confined corridors and shrunken rooms. My footsteps echoed through the halls, amid more moaning by the ship. Each corner was like a maze of infinite wrong-turns. Nothing but floodlights suspended from the ceilings guided me as I pushed on.

Sound traveled eerily far down here. My shoes clanging against the metal floor made it seem like I was being followed. Even gently closing the metal hatches of the rooms I searched sent a heavy clanking noise that went on forever through the many lengthy halls. Keeping quiet was proving to be a difficult task.

CHAPTER SEVENTEEN

*S*hould *we go to the store today, honey?* My mother had asked. *I'd rather if we went another time.*

But mommy, I want to go today!

To this day I still blame myself for what happened; ruminating on how it had been *my* fault that she died. And it was because of me that I was plucked out of my first life and tossed into this one like a bad factory product. The image of her face on the steering wheel, as blood poured out of her nose and mouth, haunts me. Twisting and tormenting me like an insect in the hands of a child. I know that I can never forget the horrific ordeal. Like a bad scar refusing to heal, rubbing itself back open from time to time and letting in the air so that it can burn up once again, I am forever stuck with that shame.

Up ahead, the hallway broke off into two directions like a *T*, and I could hear sounds coming from around the corner. With guns still drawn, and my hands fiercely glued to them, I slowed up and stopped just around the bend.

I could hear two men whispering in their own native Asiatic tongue, the one voice breaking out in laughter at something the other must have said. Taking a deep breath, I curved around the corner to the left.

They looked familiar. Men I had seen before in Mr. Blanco's restaurant. Wearing black suits and red ties. The man who had been laughing stopped abruptly as I raised both guns up to eye-level. Their faces became grim altogether. One of them yelled at me, but his voice was quickly cut off with the force of a bullet tearing through his face. The other started running down the hallway in the other direction, his breathing frantic. Before he could disappear behind another bend in that hallway, I squeezed the trigger twice, ripping two holes down his backside. He fell forward and did not get back up.

The sound of more voices coming from up the hall stirred me and I turned around just in time to see four more red ties racing down toward me. They started firing, automatic weapons mixed in with handguns, and I did my best to sprint down the hall away from them as bullets whizzed by and bounced off the metal walls in dull flashes. At the end of the hall was a doorway with something written in Chinese above it. Bolting for the hatch, I continued to shoot back, firing in all directions to slow down my attackers.

After crawling in through the small metal hatch, I found myself inside a large gray room. A series of dim halogen bulbs lined its tall ceiling. But even then, the room was very dark. I sought shelter behind a machine that kept rattling in the darkness. The air itself smelled musty, and a low humming sound filled the void. It was a boiler room.

With guns pointed back the way I had come, I waited patiently as the voices in the hall grew louder and closer. The small door created a bottleneck effect that I would use to my advantage. My aim steadied. All at once, the voices stopped and there was a pause. Seconds later, the floodgates were opened.

The first red tie ran through the opening haphazardly and I quickly picked him off. The blowback from his head spewed across the wall. The next man was more cautious and I had to duck when he reached his weapon into the room and started spraying. The automatic rifle hit everything, sounding like large nails being thrown against a metal surface. Only these nails ripped holes into everything they touched.

When he stopped to reload, it was my turn to start shooting back. But when I looked up, I saw that he had sneaked into the room and was hiding behind an overturned crate. Another man was just entering, and I momentarily shifted my attention toward him. Aiming at his torso, I put two rounds into his chest cavity. The fourth guy in the hallway tried dragging his partner out, but exposing his head, I took advantage and picked him off.

The familiar sound of a magazine being inserted into a gun caught my attention and the last red tie opened fire again. This time nearly ripping my head off as the bullets peppered the wall behind me, leaving holes a quarter-inch in diameter. Intermittently, I returned fire, shooting off a couple rounds here and there to hold him off should the man get bold.

The low humming sound grew louder and the room came to life as some of the bigger machines started to steam, filling the area with smoke. It was indeed a boiler room, and as the machines turned on, the temperature started to rise. My skin began to perspire. I had to do something, and it had to be fast.

Dropping the empty ammo magazines, I quickly put new ones in, and waiting for a pause, I shuffled over to another machine that was off to the right. This one wasn't steaming, but it still gave off a menacing growl as its little lights flashed on and off. The steam continued to rise and the air was getting thicker.

Off in the distance, I heard the sound of another door being opened.

"Put down your weapons, Crimson," said a familiar voice that echoed throughout the industrious room.

Crimson? Suddenly, the air was cold, and it felt like ice cubes had been poured down my back. My spine tingled again. That name, heard in my childhood. Me?

"You're trapped," the voice continued. "There's nowhere else to hide."

I strained to see where the voice was coming from, but the room was dark. The storm had done a great job in killing most of the electricity in the ship. Behind me, I heard the red tie moving again. This time getting closer. He resumed shooting and I did my best to not get hit.

There's an old adage that states, *people will say anything*. They will claim to be anything their mind can think up. But it's being under pressure that reveals who they really are. When the heart shows their true side and their soul comes out, exposed.

The room was choking with steam, and I had difficulty seeing exactly where everybody was. I shot toward where red tie had gone to, but each time he shot back his bullets were getting more accurate and more deadly.

"Come on, Crimson," said the voice again. Me? Crimson? I heard the hammer of a gun being pulled back, but still no face. This man really was a ghost.

Red tie opened fire again, and from somewhere in the gray fog, Rafael had started shooting as well. I abruptly found myself in the middle of a cross-fire. In the middle of hell. Each bullet from either side was becoming deadly close. Inching closer by the second. I was stuck. I was trapped.

As a child, I was afraid of many things. Snakes. Spiders. Even dogs. But I was chiefly afraid of lightning and thunderstorms. I don't know why, I just was. And on one particular night during an intense storm that sweltered over our house for hours, I decided to lock myself in my bedroom and hide. Trembling under a blanket, I started to cry. Not long after, there was a knock at the door followed by my mother's soothing voice from behind it. *Don't be afraid Brendan*, she said. *Storms are just temporary. They will come and go, but I will always be here for you.*

Crouching to the ground I made myself as small as possible. Not out of fear, but out of composure. I closed my eyes and blocked out everything. The humming. The machines. The gunfire. Everything. I just let myself go and listened to what the world had to say. We may have surpassed all others in the animal kingdom. Forming speech. Wearing clothes. Driving cars. But we are still a part of nature, and if we just stopped for a second and listened, we could hear what it had to say.

Listening, I could hear the intricate sounds of the ship, coming to life as a great beast. I could feel the hard floor coming up through my shoes. The air, as it wrapped through the room, whispered secrets in its own language that only the air knew about. Everything came to life, and I was suddenly in sync with it.

Picking myself up, I sprinted for the corner, cutting through the smoke like a sharp knife. The man in the black suit, kneeling over a fallen shelf, looked up as I came toward him. His face was in complete shock and his eyes bulged out of their sockets. I lunged over the shelf and knocked him over.

He tried to grab his gun, but I held it down with my knee. I pressed both of my guns up to either side of his neck, and he stared up at me with vacant eyes. This was it. I let out a blood-curdling scream, renouncing my humanity. Even the humming from the machines stopped as my sadistic voice filled the room. I pulled both triggers and watched as blood flew back into my face. This time I was the lightning. I was the storm. I was Crimson.

But the victory was finite. A loud bang echoed through the steamy room. Starting for the source of the noise, I forgot my triumph and sprinted across the room. Picking up speed, running faster. Everything looked still and time itself seemed to slow down, in retrospect. Even the dense smoke appeared congealed and stationary; like it was held in suspension through the air.

At the other end of the room, I caught up to the ghost. I saw my father. He shot at me again, but I ducked behind a piece of equipment. No longer was I afraid of him, and I could face my nightmare head-on.

"That scream you made," he said. "Did Theo teach you that?"

Wrapping an arm around my face, I tried not to inhale the thick smoke as it continued to billow out of a grate I was standing over.

"He always seemed to be short of a few screws in that head of his." The voice said. I could hear him reloading his weapon somewhere just beyond the edge of darkness.

I was no longer afraid of my father, and the knot in my throat was miles away. "Why did you do it?" I yelled back. "Why did you leave us?"

This was the question I had waited many years to ask. My whole life, actually. Not knowing who to direct it toward. It's a frightful thing, going through life—going through the motions day to day—not knowing the answers. Holding onto questions that may never get answered. It's like being attached to a bomb and not knowing when, or even *if*, it will ever go off. This was my weakness. This was my vice.

"Oh come on now," he said. "Don't make me feel bad. You know as well as I do what this life is like."

My father's words split through the air and flew around the room like bats in the night. Latching onto everything before being absorbed into the walls and machines and floor. His words were acid.

"But why my mother?" I yelled. "Why *me*?"

He spoke again. This time I could sense that he was getting annoyed. "Sometimes bad things happen to good people. It's just the way this world spins, son." Rafael shot back, and I returned fire, the bullets ricocheting off the machinery in all directions like heated pinballs.

This went on for a good minute or so as each of us moved around in a circle, trying to gain the better vantage spot over the other. We were both shrouded in our own veil of steam and blackness. In the end though, it was hopeless, and we soon found ourselves at a standoff once more.

"Did you ever love us?" I asked.

Through feeding fresh magazines into my two guns, I realized that I was down to one extra magazine.

There was a pause in the conversation, and I could hear the wind outside becoming quiet as it pressed its translucent cheeks up against the windows and listened in. It too wanted to hear answers. Off in the distance, the waves continued to slap up against the hull of the massive ship.

At long last there was a sigh in the room. "There was a time, yes," he said. "But in the end, my boy, like crimson blood spilled, love betrays us all. It was only a matter of time."

My heart split and the pain in my stomach returned, forcing itself back into my crummy reality. The air felt light, and glancing down I could see myself from above. As if my soul had parted ways from my body. It looked unhuman and otherworldly.

The sound of Rafael's laughter filled the room. "Don't tell me all of this is over the absence of a father in your life. As if killing me will somehow fill the void in your heart."

"I—"

"Because it won't!" he shouted, cutting me off sharply. "No matter what you do, child, there will always be a hole there. Remaining as empty and transparent as this world. But it will also make you stronger, my son."

As he talked, I was inching my way around him, using the thick smoke as a protective guise. The air continued to pour through the room as I silently crept over, not daring to give up my position. With both guns drawn I pushed myself forward. Each step, becoming heavier than the last.

His voice was growing louder as I kept getting closer, and I could begin to see his face in what light remained in the room.

"Your mother's death, as I'm sure you know by now, was no accident. She was a necessary casualty of a predetermined outcome. As was Johnny, the one you knew as The Englishman, Mr. Blanco, and of course, Theo."

Hearing his name out loud, from *that* mouth, felt strange. It felt bizarre knowing that Theo was no longer with us, with *me*. The effects were just kicking in. What he had told me just before dying was still fresh. *Don't ever give up hope.* My heart was pounding.

Again, Rafael's voice spliced through the large room. "Yes, I've heard you two have grown attached as of late. This is what I mean, son. You get used to people—familiar with them—and then, when they leave, you get hurt. At least with me, that hurt, that *pain* was never there!"

I could see his brown eyes and his wicked lips as they moved. The smoke was perfect. It was all perfect. This was my chance.

"Theo only showed you misery. Theo only showed—"

Leaping into the air like a wild animal, I lunged for his face. "Theo showed me life!"

Time stood still again and it felt as though I was momentarily gliding through the air in slow motion. A pocket of gray fog dissipated as I broke through it. My prey was in front of me. I was about to confront my nightmare.

And then all at once I saw hell again—another careless error. Time sped back up, this time increasing two-fold. Rafael turned his head toward me, his wicked smile stretched from ear to ear. In his left hand, a revolver was out and ready to greet me. It happened so fast. I didn't even hear the blast as a bullet was tearing through my chest. Then another one. Both bullets ripped through my body and I could feel them exiting my back like two hot worms eating through me.

I fell on top of him and for a fraction of a second our eyes met. It seemed inevitable. It seemed destined. Looking into his face, I could feel that same sense of familiarity; that eerie sagacity of déjà vu, like we were sharing the same aura. My mouth opened, but instead of words, I let out the most horrific sound imaginable. Pain was crawling all over me.

Seeing my agony, Rafael threw me off of him, abruptly ending that aura. Hitting the floor, I landed hard on my stomach. The pain multiplied exponentially, and I uttered more shrieks involuntarily. At this point, I was barely in control of my body. It was a mutiny of the worst pain imaginable, and I wanted to quit. I wanted to wave my white flag and surrender.

"It didn't have to be this way," Rafael said. I could hear him getting back up.

Biting my tongue, I clenched my fists and started dragging myself across the floor. It was all I could do. With each movement, I felt a heated knife being thrust even deeper into my chest. I could also feel my clothing getting warmer as I began to bleed out onto them. Soaking up my misery, my *horror*.

I could also hear Rafael walking toward me. My head was ringing and each footstep sounded like a loud *GONG*.

"In fact," he said. "I almost wish it wasn't. In time, you could have joined us. You could have joined *me*."

Taking in as much air as my lungs afforded me, I held my breath as his footsteps got closer and the ringing got louder.

"Just imagine," he continued. "Father and son, reunited. It has a certain wholesome feel to it. Wouldn't you agree?"

Stopping in front of a wall, I shut down. My body was tired and what felt like the last drop of air left my lungs. Pain fanned out over my body like poison, and I was bleeding out. But at this point, I was too exhausted, too jaded to care. The ringing was so loud that I could barely hear my own thoughts, or anything else for that matter. The white flag was up. Catching a stroke of wind, it flapped back and forth in the air. I was so close, yet still so far. I closed my eyes.

At a certain point, in times of ultimate desperation, when you finally realize that there is no more rope to hold onto, the truth comes out. It's not obvious though, and you most likely will trip over it. Falling hard onto your knees as you panic convulsively. Like a caged bird finally being granted its long-desired freedom, the truth hesitates to come out. Looking back, it reconsiders, momentarily refusing to let go of a familiar life, filled with lies and deception. But then, at the very last second, just as the steel door begins to close again, it flies out. Stretching its tender wings for the first time, the bird flies, not daring to look back again. Flying higher and higher, its unused wings first start to drag, and for a second it appears as though the bird will fall to its death. But then something kicks in. Not quite memory, but something else. Its *instinct* takes the wheel and drives it higher. Pushing it further. As the bird gains more altitude it can feel the sun, those heated rays blanketing the bird with a comfort it has never known before and only dreamed of. This is what awaits you when you're at the end of the rope. This is the truth. This is freedom.

All at once, the loud *gonging* sound vanished, and the footsteps ceased. Instead, a new sound took up its vacancy. Directly over me, I heard the sound of a revolver being cocked back. My heart raced and my skin started to crawl. I didn't want it to end like this. I didn't want to die. A small metal device pressed up against my skin told me I didn't have to. Not yet, anyway.

"Say hi to your mother for me," he said. "I'll see you in the afterlife, son."

I rolled myself over onto my back. Out of the faint glow of the lights, I could see the gun aimed down at me, and the face of the man holding it. "I'm not your *son*."

I am Crimson.

Holding the detonator in both hands, I squeezed its trigger, clenching down on it with a strength I have never known before. Releasing a monster capable of destroying even nightmares.

The sound, or rather the absence of sound, is what hit first, like the volume on a television suddenly being muted. Although I could see everything, watching the room light up and seeing Rafael's shocked face, my ears failed me. It was as though we were sucked into Limbo, halfway dead, but still halfway living. A low-pitch whistling followed soon after, and it quickly picked up momentum as the volume on the television resumed. Growing louder, the whistling noise filled the room. It got so loud I thought my head was going to pop, and plugging my hands over my ears did little to help.

What came next was just as bad. Even though the C4 explosives were fitted up on deck, as fate would have it, we were directly below it—below its epicenter. The blast above sent a horrific shockwave all the way down, dispersing into every hole and corner. The ship lurched and Rafael was tossed to the side. I was pushed even farther toward the wall. My head slammed into it, and I was knocked out cold.

When I woke up, the whistling was all but gone, remaining just as a low drone in my ears. At first I could not feel my arms or my legs. I thought I was dead. But within minutes I could sense the blood spreading back into my extremities. But being able to feel again came with a price. My chest hurt in ways for which there are no words to describe. It even overpowered the sharp sensation I felt in my abdomen as I struggled to sit back up. My pants were soaked, and at first I thought it was blood, but upon further inspection, it was revealed to be water. All around me on the floor was water—about an inch deep and increasing with each passing second.

Water was everywhere. I sloshed around trying to stand up, struggling like an infant learning to walk for the first time. After taking two nasty falls, I finally succeeded in getting up with the help of the wall. The boiler room was covered in a flood of dark water that seemed to race outside the room and into the hallway beyond. How much was actually there, I was unsure of.

"What the hell did you do?" boomed out a voice from close by.

At first I could not find him. But as I started to move around, peering through the darkness, I found Rafael on the floor about ten feet away. He was on his back.

"What the *FUCK* did you do?" he repeated, splashing his fists into the water as he spoke.

The thunder outside continued to rumble and a cold breeze coming in revealed that the windows had been shattered. As I moved over to Rafael, I felt dribbles of water hitting me. Small rivulets of seawater were pouring down from the exposed floors above us, revealing the source of the flood. Streams become rivers, and rivers become seas.

Coming closer to Rafael, I noticed that he was hurt. Struggling like a wounded dog, he tried to move. It seemed as though the tide had turned on him. Funny how the world spins.

"I am not your son," I said again. "And this is not your victory."

Rafael gasped for air as he started to get back up.

"This is your fate, Rafael. This is where you die," I continued, using the support of the wall as I got closer to him.

His gasping became laughter as he fumbled around on the ground.

"Don't you see, *boy*?" he shouted. "I'M ALREADY DEAD!" He laughed again and fell flat on his face.

His booming voice echoed through the room before disappearing into the walls, and I was no longer afraid of him. Like a small child seeing his nightmare for what it really was, I smiled and my eyes gleamed.

I saw the revolver lying on the floor, submerged in the water. Picking it up, I checked to see how many bullets were left—there were three. I only needed one.

A stroke of lightning flashed and lit up the room. The water around me was dark and discolored as I continued to bleed out. The pain was getting worse and I started to feel weak. My head was spinning on a swivel. How much longer I could go before bleeding out completely, I wasn't sure of. The only thing I was sure about was that this man in front of me—my father—deserved to die. Yet...in some strange paradox, so did I. We all did.

"What do you plan on doing now, boy?" he asked.

My smile vanished, being overtaken by a more sinister face.

Rafael looked up at me. "Are you going to shoot me? Are you going to shoot your own father?"

A couple more streaks of lightning lit up the room, exposing his face. He looked desperate. Like a man just barely clinging on to life, who already knew his fate was sealed.

My knees popped as I got down in front of him. Staring back, I kissed him on the head. "Yes," I said. A rush of blood left me while I stood back up. "Get on your knees."

"Wa…WAIT!" he stammered, holding out his hands in front. "You don't have to do this, son. It doesn't have to end this way!"

"Yes, it does," I said. "And I'm not your son."

Rafael's mouth closed for what would be the last time and his eyes grew to the size of saucers. We both knew it had to be this way. Aiming the gun at his face, I looked away. This was one set of eyes I could not bring myself to watch.

It happened so fast and I didn't even hear the gun go off. When I looked back there was a pool of blood circling Rafael's body. I felt a rush of warmth come over me. It felt like an anvil had been lifted off my chest. But it was only temporary—like all good things in life—and the pain of reality pushed its way back in.

Falling over, I collapsed with a splash onto the floor next to Rafael. Lying there for a minute I soaked in what little satisfaction was still there. Like feeling the last rays of heat before the sun finally disappeared behind the clouds forever.

I had just enough energy left to make my way over to the wall and prop up against it. More blood was leaking out of me and soon the room was filled with dark water as it spread out. Water kept gushing down from above and my legs were fully submerged as I sat there. Each breath I took was more difficult than the last as the heated knife continued its way through my chest cavity. This was it.

Closing my eyes, I could see my mother—her youthful face smiling back at me—something I had all-but forgotten through the years. How I missed her. I wondered what it was going to be like to die. I wondered if I would finally see her again—mother and child reunited after all these years. Now that had a ring to it. I chuckled to myself.

The air continued to parade through the room, and the thunder kept booming, announcing the Shakespearean tragedy. It certainly was a tragedy. But all things in life are.

I went through my pockets, searching for a phone to call back to Beivrus and let them know what happened. If it was going to be anyone to tell The Chancellor what had happened, I wanted it to be me. It only seemed right after all. I would use what air was left in my lungs to tell him everything. Now *that's* poetic.

Fumbling through my pants however, yielded nothing but empty magazines. I frantically searched but could not find the phone. What I did find, however, was my wallet, with my *Crimson* pendant and a small white envelope tucked inside. It was the letter given to me back in Reggio. For some reason, I had never tossed it.

With just enough light coming from outside, I put the pendant around my neck, and then delicately opened the envelope. Inside was a letter, and tiny blobs of wet blood dotted its surface as I read it. This was more gold than my pendant or any phone. It was a short message addressed to me, and although it was written in English, I knew who it was from. A wave of warmth swept over my body as I read it, and read it again. It said, *Dear mystery man from the restaurant, why don't you smile more often? I run on the beach every morning. Why don't you stop by and say hi sometime?*

My face melted and my ears became hot. As I closed my eyes I could see the beach. I could smell the ocean and taste the salty air. I could hear the distant slapping of water against the pier. I could see her bright green eyes as she smiled back at me.

I was finally at peace.

Then, the familiar rush of coldness swept over my body and the air left my lungs for the last time. My hands went limp and the letter fell into the water. It was the cycle of the sea, after all. It was nature, being nature.

B. D. Valle is the author of all things crime and all things dark. But he does it with a twist. He's interested in character development as much as he is in shootouts; particularly stories about second-chances given to otherwise faulty characters. After all, it's how these characters behave in the story that makes it enjoyable to read. Although intense, adrenaline-soaked action scenes are cool, too.

B. D. lives alongside his two ball pythons, whose solid, expressionless stares sometimes scare him more than his writing does. It's the author's experiences in life that fuel his ideas and keep his passion for the craft of writing going. He advocates writing for the sake of writing, and believes that everybody has a story to tell.